Can I Get an Amen

Can I Get an Amen

JANICE SIMS

KIM LOUISE

NATALIE DUNBAR

NATHASHA BROOKS-HARRIS

BET Publications, LLC
http://www.bet.com
http://www.arabesquebooks.com

Contents

A LOVE SUPREME   1
by Janice Sims

LOVE AND HAPPINESS   109
by Kim Louise

A LOVE LIKE THAT   211
by Natalie Dunbar

LOVE UNDER NEW MANAGEMENT   297
by Nathasha Brooks-Harris

A Love Supreme

Janice Sims

Dedication

This story is dedicated to the memory of J.Z. Sims, Isaac Hammond, Frank Long, and James Jones, all of my father figures whom I miss every day.

Acknowledgments

My sincerest thanks, and big hugs, to Leslie Esdaile and Nathasha Brooks-Harris who e-mailed me in December of 2003 and offered me an early Christmas gift, the chance to write a story for this anthology. Thanks also to my editor, Demetria Lucas, for signing me on. I've enjoyed working with you very much!

You awakened desires that
had lain dormant too long

Made my heart sing
a whole new song

It became clear that, for you,
I'd go to any extreme

God had granted us
a love supreme.

The Book of Counted Joys

One

Jared Kyles opened the sliding-glass door and stepped onto the patio of his new home in Red Oaks, Georgia. It was a beautiful May morning, and the sweet smell of wild jasmine was in the air. The temperature was cool. The dogwood trees were in full bloom. Fallen pink and white petals covered the ground around them.

He inhaled the heady fragrance of good, clean, fresh air as he stood there wondering which of the six burly black men presently removing huge squares of old sod from the lawn was Alex Cartwright. A big hand brought the coffee cup to his lips. He frowned as he sipped thoughtfully. The man *was* here, wasn't he?

He lowered his gaze to his watch. It was nine o'clock, and Cartwright, whom he'd hired over the phone, sight unseen, hadn't come up and introduced himself yet. Cartwright's secretary had promised he would show him the blueprints that had been drawn up for the final layout of the yard before the work progressed too far. Jared didn't like to be kept waiting. Time was money.

This was the last time he would hire someone based solely on the opinions of others. When he'd sent out feelers to various colleagues in the construction business in Macon, they'd all concurred: Alex Cartwright was the best to use when it came to landscaping, a consummate professional.

Looking at the vigor with which Cartwright's men performed their duties, Jared had to admit one thing: Cartwright knew how to pick dependable workers.

He placed his cup on the only piece of furniture on the patio: a deep green, molded plastic chair which could be bought at any discount store. He made a mental note to buy patio furniture, and then he turned and walked up to the man closest to him.

"Excuse me, would you tell me which of these fellas is Alex Cartwright?"

The guy, who was at least six-four, over two-hundred pounds, with skin so dark it gleamed, ran a hand over his bald head before saying, "Good morning!" His grin was wide and white. The first image that flashed into Jared's mind was that of a black Mr. Clean. All the guy needed was a single gold hoop earring in his left earlobe.

"Good morning," Jared said, smiling back. People in small towns rarely forgot their manners. His mother would be disappointed that he'd forgotten his.

"Alex ain't here yet," the bald man told him. "She went to pick up her brother, Sam, at the airport. He plays basketball for the University of Florida."

She? Jared thought but didn't voice his surprise.

The guy saw it on his face. "Don't worry, man," he said with a short laugh. "She does the work of *two* men."

Jared laughed too, but it irked him that Alex Cartwright had misrepresented herself to him. Or had she? None of the men who'd recommended her had thought to mention her sex. They must be having a good laugh at his expense right about now! Then again, perhaps her gender had not mattered to them, just the fact that she was good at what she did for a living. He put his sexist tendencies in check and offered his hand to the guy. "Jared Kyles."

"Ruben Jackson," the black Mr. Clean said, with a firm handshake. "I'm the foreman. Alex told us to get started on removing the old sod, and by the time that was done, she'd be here to supervise the landscaping."

Jared nodded. "All right, Mr. Jackson, you fellas seem to have everything under control. Tell Ms. Cartwright she can knock on the patio door when she arrives."

"Will do," Ruben said, and promptly returned to his work.

~

Alexandra Cartwright was in her element, speeding down I-75 with a Shemekia Copeland CD on low and her kid brother by her side, complaining. She'd missed this. There was a smile on her face and a happy light in her dark brown eyes.

"All of my friends are either in Daytona Beach or Atlanta gettin' their freak on!" Sam said. He was nineteen and the spitting image of their father: tall, dark-skinned, and rangy, with light brown eyes. Alex had been the only one of them to inherit their mother's dark brown eyes.

"How often do we get to see each other, Sam?" Alex asked reasonably. "I haven't seen you in nine months, and it's been longer for Vicky. She'll be here tomorrow afternoon, and we'll all be together for the first time in over a year. You know Momma and Daddy would have wanted us to stay close."

Sam sighed. He turned his head to look at his older sister. "You're gonna get me with the guilt trip now, huh?" His thick brows arched as he smiled at her.

"I'll use every trick in the book, little brother. You know I'm right," Alex said, her full lips curving in a winning smile.

"Yeah, I know you're right," Sam conceded. "But that doesn't mean I'm gonna stop giving you a hard time. You'd think something was wrong with me if I didn't."

Alex laughed. She pushed a lock of wavy, shoulder-length black hair behind one ear and briefly peered at him. Eyes back on the road, she said, "You know, I think you've grown an inch since I saw you last. When are you going to stop growing?"

"I guess when you stop treating me like a child," Sam countered.

"Never, then," Alex returned, still grinning.

Sam groaned. "I could be in Hotlanta right now with a sepia honey all over me."

"Sepia?"

"I've been paying attention in English class. I'm broadening my vocabulary."

"I'm sure the honeys are impressed."

"Well, you know, what can I say? I'm all that!"

"Oh, now, hold up. Don't go gettin' cocky on me. I changed your diapers!"

"See? That's why I'm never gonna bring a sweet thing home with me for Thanksgiving. I don't want to be embarrassed by comments like that," Sam said.

"I have no doubt that one day you *will* bring a 'sweet thing' home with you. But do me a favor, make sure she's good people before you get all up in her business."

"All up in her business?" Sam asked, shocked that his sister had suggested she knew anything about sex. Didn't she know it was taboo to talk to her brother about such things? No, he could answer that question himself. Since their parents' deaths, Alex had assumed the role of the parent. She thought she had the right to say anything!

"Don't you think it's a little too late for that talk?" Sam asked, sounding calmer than he really felt. He was a man, after all. A man who knew the score. He'd been sexually active since he was sixteen. Three years now. Not that his sister knew that. She didn't have to know *everything!*

"It's never too late for that talk," Alex said. "Oh, don't go looking all puffed up like Daddy used to when Momma would say something to upset him. I just want you to stay safe, Samuel Edison Cartwright. Choose your partners with care. Never, and I mean never, have sex without using a condom. Use two if you need them."

Tight-lipped, Sam turned on the seat so that he could see her face. "You're so interested in my love life, what about yours? Do you use a condom every time, big sister?"

"Honey, it's been so long since I did anything, I qualify for sainthood. But, yes, little brother, I most certainly did always use a condom."

If it were possible, Sam's face would have turned a bright red hue. "Good God! I thought you were a virgin!"

"At twenty-seven?" Alex asked with a short snort. "I'm not exactly a femme fatale, but no, Sam, I'm not a virgin."

"Who?" Sam asked, his curiosity piqued. He knew she'd dated Rick Washington, a local attorney, about two years ago. She'd never mentioned why they'd broken up.

"A lady never tells, just like a gentleman never tells," Alex said lightly.

"All right," Sam agreed. "But you know this conversation is creeping me out, right? Now I'm going to be looking at every man in town who's around your age and wondering, could he be one of Alex's ex-lovers?"

"There have been only two, so you can put your mind at ease."

"Oh, so the number of ex-lovers you'll reveal, but not their names."

"Their names are of no significance," Alex said. "I'm not still involved with them, and it's highly unlikely we'll ever interact with them socially. I only told you I'm not a virgin so that you wouldn't think me a prude for giving you advice about your sex life."

"Fair enough," Sam said, reaching over to turn up volume on the CD player. "Now, can we let Shemekia serenade us the rest of the way home? I'm afraid you're going to bring up something else embarrassing."

"Like that big bag of dirty laundry you brought with you?" Alex asked.

"I was hoping you wouldn't notice," Sam said, chagrined. "I just didn't have time to do it before I left. I'll do it as soon as I get home." He lowered the volume.

"I know you will," Alex said. "You and the washing machine have been on good terms since you were ten years old. I hope you aren't letting some 'sweet thing' do your laundry for you while you're at school."

"Well, if they ask, who am I to refuse?" Sam said, smiling roguishly.

"If I didn't need both hands to drive, I'd knock you upside your head! You don't use women like that, Sam. Do your own funky laundry!"

"It's not as if I don't do them favors," Sam defended himself. "It's the barter system. I fix their cars for 'em or something, and they do my laundry. It ain't nothin' negative."

Alex eyed him briefly. "Are you telling the truth?"

"Cross my heart," Sam said. When they were kids, that had been the sign that absolute truth was being spoken. You *had* to believe whatever was being said.

"All right," Alex said. "It's just important that you respect women. We work hard for it, and we deserve it. Daddy never disrespected Momma, no matter how much they argued."

"They argued?"

"You were only seven when Daddy died. I guess you don't remember much. Yes, they argued like any other couple. But I always knew they loved each other, so I never worried that they were going to get divorced. They were so close. You could feel the love coming off of them just by being in the same room with them. That's how much they loved each other." Her eyes grew misty at the memory.

"I can't believe it's been ten years since Momma got killed," Sam said, his voice low and wonder-filled. "All I remember about her was that she always hugged me before I went to school, and she always kissed me on the forehead before I went to bed at night. She never forgot to do that."

"No, she didn't," Alex said softly. She wiped a tear from the corner of her eye with her index finger. "Now, tell me about your studies. Quickly, so I can get my mind off of sad things."

~

The Kyles residence was located in The Heights, a section of town where homes started in the two-hundred-grand price range, and went up to a million dollars or more. Alex had several clients in the neighborhood, but she had no friends who lived there. Her friends were middle-class people like herself, working jobs that paid the bills but allowed for few luxuries.

When the SUV rolled to a stop in front of the two-story Tudor-style home,

Alex got out and strode confidently across the torn-up yard, her work boots making deep imprints in the soft soil. She noticed, with satisfaction, that the old sod had been removed. Her men were now using a forklift to take the new squares of St. Augustine grass off the back of a flatbed truck.

She waved to Ruben, and he gave her a crisp salute. "Hey, boss, Mr. Kyles said to knock on the patio door."

"Thanks, Ruben! You all did a great job. I'll join you in a few minutes!"

She continued around the back of the house, the muscles in her long legs flexing with each step. As she had done the first time she had seen the Kyles property, she paused to look at the twin dogwood trees in the backyard. She was glad no one had cut them down. Some people had no respect for trees. She could tell by the size of them, both over twenty feet tall, that they were old. But they were still healthy. What would the South be without its old oak and dogwood trees? They lent an air of serenity to the landscape. She could picture a white-painted bench underneath one of those trees and her sitting on it sipping iced tea or lemonade.

She was momentarily lost in her daydream.

"You must be *Mr.* Cartwright," a deep masculine voice said with a hint of humor.

Alex looked up to find Jared Kyles smiling at her. She smiled back. He was standing on the patio, wearing jeans, a Morehouse College T-shirt, and white athletic shoes. He was moving a silver dollar between his fingers. She watched, totally charmed.

"It's something I learned as a kid when I was laid up with a broken leg for months," he explained. He tossed the silver dollar in the air, caught it and pocketed it. Their gazes held as she closed the space between them. He was a leg man, and noticed at once how long and shapely hers were. He guessed her height at five-ten, give or take an inch. She wore a short-sleeved khaki shirt and a pair of mid-thigh shorts.

His eyes moved downward. She had on tan work boots with a pair of rolled socks. Her calves were as conditioned as a long distance runner's. All that masculine garb, but there was no mistaking her feminine curves. Full breasts, small waist, full hips, and those gorgeous legs. When she got closer, she reached up and took off the sunglasses. Her eyes were a deep shade of brown, almost black. They were sable-colored, dark brown with black centers. He could get lost in those eyes. It was her mouth, however, that made his own fall slightly open and a soft sigh of longing escape from between his lips. It was heart-shaped, full-lipped, and had such sensual contours that all he could think about was what it would feel like to kiss her. *Damn*, he thought, *I was complaining about the fact that the fellas might have gotten one over on me by not telling me she was a woman. Hell, they did me a favor!*

Alex removed her black cap before offering him her hand to shake. Her hair fell down to her shoulders in a single braid. "Mr. Kyles, it's a pleasure to meet you."

As she was approaching, she'd been sizing him up, too, as she did with everybody she met. Jared Kyles's height was around six-three, his weight was a bit over two hundred pounds. He was solid: muscular and in great shape. And, from the expression in his light brown eyes, he was surprised by her appearance. To be truthful, his appearance was upsetting her equilibrium, too. For one thing, she loved dark-skinned brothers. His was like bittersweet chocolate at room temperature. With skin that color, she'd expected brown eyes. But no, his were the color of golden wheat. Darker striations ran through the irises. She had to consciously will herself to stop staring at him. And he wore his dark brown, partly nappy, partly wavy hair in a natural style, like actor Michael Ealy's.

They allowed their hands to fall to their sides. It was then that she recalled his first words to her: He'd called her *Mr. Cartwright*.

She laughed shortly. "I guess it's safe to assume that Marcy didn't tell you I'm a woman." Marcy, her secretary-cum-accountant and everything else she needed to be in the office, was a mother hen. She was always telling her that she'd get more business if she didn't advertise that Alex was short for

Alexand*r*a instead of Alexand*er*, which was her father's name. She still used the business cards her father had used. Everybody had called him Alex, too.

"No, she left out that bit of information," Jared said. "Not that it matters." *How magnanimous of you*, he silently chided himself.

"Great," Alex said. She withdrew the large sheaf of rolled up papers she carried under her right arm. "These are the blueprints for the layout of your yard." Turning, she looked for someplace where she could spread out the plans. She wound up squatting on the patio and quickly showed him where the flowerbeds would be planted with impatiens, marigolds, azaleas, roses, and sunflowers. Her work was neat and precise, showing exactly how she'd envisioned his yard.

When she'd finished, they rose and regarded each other rather shyly. The close proximity they'd shared for the past few minutes had left both of them aware of one thing: They were strongly attracted to each other. How to proceed?

Their eyes met and held.

"Excellent plans," Jared said with a smile. "I can't wait to see the end results."

"All right, then," Alex said, reluctant to draw her eyes away from his face. "It'll probably be nearly sundown before we're done. I'll knock on your patio door before I leave to consult with you again."

Jared offered her his hand. They shook on it. It was just an excuse to touch her once more. His big hand engulfed her smaller one. He imagined he could feel the strength and energy coursing through her luscious frame. Alex, too, felt something akin to electricity emanating from him. A wave of warmth swept over her. Her heart raced. She had a sneaking suspicion she was smiling like an idiot.

She cleared her throat. "Well, I'd better get to work."

He let go of her and she hurried away, self-consciously adjusting the cell phone on her utility belt as she did so. She felt his eyes on her. *Felt them!*

Nervous energy crawled up her neck, making her ears burn with embarrassment. Had it been that long since a man had looked at her like that? As if all he wanted to do was grab her and kiss her senseless? There had been no mistaking Jared Kyles's intentions. She hoped that her own thoughts hadn't been so easily read. She took a deep breath as she quickly walked across the large yard to join her men. If her reaction to Jared Kyles was an indication of her state of loneliness, she was one sad sister!

Two

"Mornin' gentlemen, did everyone remember to use sun block?" Alex looked at the six men standing around getting their breath after unloading the flat bed truck. There was Ruben Jackson, her foreman, twenty-seven, who had gone to school with her. Then there was Joe Wallace who was in his fifties and, still, one of her better workers. He'd been a teacher before his nervous breakdown and forced retirement. These days, he preferred physical labor over intellectual pursuits, saying the physical gave him instant gratification, whereas the intellectual caused him stress. Everybody called him Mr. Wallace. Even though *he* wanted to forget he'd been a teacher, *they* could not.

The other four men were Ed Hall, nineteen, on the team for a year, he said, to save money for college; Pete Green, twenty-nine, an ex-cocaine addict who was working his way toward becoming permanently drug-free. Like Mr. Wallace, he felt physical labor helped clear his mind and put things in perspective; Mike Lennard, twenty-five, an ex-Georgia State prisoner who'd served five years for car theft; and Tyrell Anderson, seventeen, a high school senior who only worked Saturdays.

"Yes, Mother," Ruben answered for all of them.

Alex smiled at him as she pulled on her work gloves. She and Ruben had been friends since they were first graders. He was married to her best friend, Gayle. The couple had been on the fast track in Atlanta three years ago. Ruben had joined a prestigious law firm, and Gayle worked for a popular record label.

Then, one rainy night, Ruben had gone headfirst through the windshield of his BMW when a drunk driver hit him from behind. Six months later, after he awoke from the coma, they discovered he had minor brain damage and would probably never be able to work as an attorney again. He and Gayle decided to come home to the people who loved them, and whom they loved. Gayle went to work with her mother at the family bakery. Ruben expressed an interest in learning the landscaping business, and that's all it took for Alex to offer him a job with her company. She adored Ruben.

"What'd you think of the boss man?" Ruben asked, his eyes alight with pent-up laughter. He took every opportunity to rib Alex.

"He's tall," Alex said, as if that was all she'd observed about Jared Kyles.

"That he is," Ruben agreed. "Sorta stuck up, too."

"Oh, I wouldn't say that," Alex said hurriedly.

Ruben smiled triumphantly. "So, you noticed he was more than tall, huh?"

The other men laughed.

Alex smiled again, and narrowed her eyes at him. "Really, Ruben, you'd give Chris Rock a run for his money, you're so hilarious. Shall we get to work? We can gossip while we're stuffing our faces at lunch."

The men laughed even harder, but between guffaws they set to work planting the new St. Augustine grass in the yard.

Inside, Jared had gone directly to the phone to place a call to his best friend and brother-in-law, Fletcher Henderson, in Macon. It was only ten-thirty in the morning and he knew Fletcher slept late on Saturday, but he didn't care.

His sister, Carena, answered. "Hullo," she said in a drowsy voice.

"Hey, sis, how you doin'? Put Fletch on the phone, please."

"Hi, Jared. He's snoring. Can't you hear him?" Carena asked, laughing.

"Wake him up. I'm about to cuss him out."

"What did he do now?"

"Carena . . . ," Jared said a tad impatiently.

"Oh, okay . . ."

About thirty seconds later, Fletcher said, "Damn, Kyles, can't you phone at a decent hour?"

"It *is* a decent hour. It's nearly eleven o'clock."

"At night?"

"You must have your curtains drawn. No, in the morning!" Jared said, laughing.

"We aren't playing basketball this morning, are we? I was still gettin' some z's."

"I'm not calling about basketball. I couldn't wait any longer to tell you I got your joke, chump! Alex Cartwright is a woman," Jared informed him.

"And a good-looking one, too," Fletcher said, sounding more awake now.

"Who's a good-looking one?" Jared heard Carena ask.

"Nobody, baby," Fletcher said, soothingly.

"You were talking about a woman!" Carena accused him.

"See what you started?" Fletcher asked Jared. He sighed heavily. "Baby, there ain't no woman on earth as fine as you are! It's a woman I wanted your confirmed bachelor brother to meet."

"Oh," Carena said, somewhat mollified.

Fletcher spoke into the receiver. "Tell her, Jared!"

He handed Carena the receiver and she spoke into it. "Jared?"

"It's true, sis. Take it easy on him."

"Okay, I will this time," Carena said. "Do you need to speak back with Fletcher?"

"No, just tell him thanks. Alex Cartwright is interesting. Very interesting."

"Looking to add her to those notches on your bedpost?"

"Ah, you're too cynical to be so young," Jared told his sister.

"And you need to stop fooling around and get serious about somebody. You'll be thirty-three on your next birthday."

"Don't remind me."

"*Somebody* needs to remind you!"

"Mother does a good enough job of that. I don't need both of you riding me to get married."

"Personally, I don't care if you never get married, Jared. Hey, that rhymes . . ."

Jared laughed. "Go back to bed, sis. Goodbye."

"Bye, sweetie. Love you."

"I love you, too."

Jared replaced the receiver, a grin on his face. Carena was four years younger than he was, and she'd been married to Fletcher for five years. She was beginning to sound more like their mother, Emma, every day. That's why he avoided marriage. It changed you. Turned you into your father, and the last person he wanted to become was James Kyles. His father had cheated on his mother for years. He tried to conceal his philandering ways but it was obvious, especially toward the end when he figured that because he was dying, he deserved what little happiness life offered.

Instead of keeping his affair with his longtime mistress a secret, he began taking her with him to social functions. To be honest, Jared, his mother, and his sister had known for years that James Kyles didn't care about convention. He'd transformed a small construction company into a multimillion-dollar concern, and success had made him haughty and insensitive to the needs of those close to him. He asked Emma for a divorce, and when she refused, saying it was against her religion, he took that as a go-ahead to do as he pleased. Jared had run interference for his father many times, simply because he didn't want his mother to suffer any public humiliation.

James drank heavily, and when he found out he had inoperable liver cancer, he began drinking in earnest. It was as if he were trying to speed up his death. The last few months, he moved in with his mistress who, it seemed to Jared, genuinely loved him. Jared had nothing but pity for her. Undoubtedly, his father had promised her he'd divorce his wife and marry her. She was faithful to the very end. Hers was the last face his father saw the day he died in the hospital.

Living through his father's infidelities, Jared felt that perhaps he, too, had the cheating gene in his make-up. So he kept his relationships light. Not promising anything except a good time. He didn't want to hurt anyone. Why would he marry a woman only to break her heart somewhere down the line? No, it was best to stay single. The single life suited him just fine.

Besides, he had never known a woman who could make him rethink his convictions.

It was dusk, the sky purpling and the breezes becoming cool, before Jared heard the men starting their vehicles and pulling away from the house. He walked outside to the patio, remembering that Alexandra Cartwright had promised to consult with him before leaving. Plus there was the matter of the bill. He'd already made out a check for the amount they'd agreed upon.

He found her walking the yard, double-checking their work. *Conscientious,* he thought. No wonder she has a good reputation.

Alex looked up and smiled at him. He felt his heartbeat picking up its pace as she approached. A nervous flutter began in the pit of his stomach. Really, it was akin to nausea. He hadn't felt like this since he was a teenager when he'd been hot for Sherry Townsend, a senior, and the head cheerleader at his Macon, Georgia, high school and *he*, a pimply-faced sophomore with about as much chance of getting with her as a snowball's chance of remaining frozen in hell.

"Well, we're done," Alex announced once she was standing within five feet of him. *She stands back on her legs like a country woman,* he noted with pleasure. Maybe it was her wholesomeness that made her so attractive to him. Lately, he'd been on a steady diet of cosmopolitan women who would probably cry "slavery" if you asked them to get their hands dirty doing yard work.

"St. Augustine grass is ideal for this climate, which gets more warm days than cool days. We fertilized it. All you need to do is water it on days when there is no rain. Same thing for the flowers surrounding the dogwoods and in the borders ringing the lawn. But don't over-water them. A lot of people make that mistake."

"Gotcha," Jared said.

Alex was glad that the fading light concealed how flustered she was standing there under his scrutiny. The last thing she needed was to be called out on the fact that she was succumbing to the magnetism of a perfect stranger's smile. Lord, but he had the sweetest smile. Dimples in both cheeks. Gorgeous teeth. She appreciated that in a man she was anticipating kissing. And she *did* want to kiss him. Thank God this job was over and done with! There was no telling what she would do if she didn't put some distance between the two of them soon.

"Hey, why don't you let me take you out to dinner to thank you for doing such a wonderful job on the yard?" Jared asked, interrupting her spiraling thoughts.

She thought she was imagining things. "Huh?"

"I just asked you out to dinner."

She cocked her head to the side, her mouth hanging slightly open in shock. Then she came to herself, and said, "I never mix business with pleasure."

"Actually, our business is concluded."

He promptly handed her the check.

She took it and continued to look up at him with a simple expression on her face. "Thank you."

Jared smiled warmly. "My pleasure. My brother-in-law was right, your company does excellent work. He recommended you, but he didn't tell me how beautiful you were."

She seemed not to have heard the compliment.

"And your brother-in-law is who?" she asked, her brows slightly raised.

"Fletcher Henderson."

"Ah, yeah, Fletch. We landscaped a new bank in Macon for his company about four months ago. Beautiful building."

"Fletch married my sister, Carena."

"I think I saw her once when she came to the site. Pretty girl with short, curly hair. Kind of petite?"

"That's her. She inherited Mom's height."

"Then your father is tall?"

"Was. He died two years ago."

"I'm sorry," Alex said softly. "I hope I didn't bring up sad memories."

"No, you didn't," Jared said, although his tone had turned solemn. He smiled at her. "Are you ever going to answer my question?"

"Go out with you?"

"Yes!"

"I'm sorry, but my brother is home from college and I promised I'd spend the evening with him."

"How about lunch tomorrow? I have to be back in Macon by Monday morning, so I'm leaving tomorrow evening."

Alex reluctantly shook her head. "I have church tomorrow."

Jared sighed. "I see. Isn't there any way we can get together this week-end? I'd like the chance to get to know you better."

"You're welcome to meet me at my church."

This time it was Jared's turn to raise his brows in surprise. *Church*? He hadn't been to church since Easter of 1999. His mother had tried to get him inside their family church on numerous occasions, with no success whatso-ever! What made this tall country girl think she could get him in the Lord's house?

"Listen," she said—a little breathlessly, he thought. It was apparent she was not immune to his charms. She just chose to try to hide it. "You're new in town, right? Church is the perfect place to meet people. And I'm truly not trying to put you off. I'd like to get to know you better, too. It's just that I can't make time to go out with you right now. Not only am I busy with church functions in the morning, but my sister, Vicky, is getting home from college tomorrow afternoon. And I have to be there to welcome her. We, the three of us, my brother, sister and I, haven't seen each other in nearly a year."

Jared understood perfectly. "Which church is it?"

"Red Oaks Christian Fellowship. It's—"

"I know where it is," he said with a smile. "I pass it every time I come into town, *and* when I leave."

"That's the place," Alex said cheerfully. "Like Mother Maybelle says, we get 'em goin' and comin'."

Jared laughed shortly as he stepped a little closer to her. "What time does the service begin?"

"Eleven o'clock."

"I'll be there."

Alex regarded him skeptically. "Are you sure? Because if you aren't, it's okay. I understand that church isn't everybody's cup of tea."

"Do I look like a heathen to you?" Jared joked. "I'll have you know our mother, Emma, raised us in the church."

Alex smiled more confidently. "It's a date then," she said, and immediately regretted her slip of the tongue. "I'd better go. Sam's going to wonder where I am. Good night."

"Sam?" Jared called to her retreating back.

"My kid brother," Alex tossed over her shoulder as she made a hasty departure. Her face was burning with embarrassment. She didn't have to appear so eager to spend time with him, did she?

"Good night," Jared said.

"Night!" She climbed into her SUV, started the engine, and pulled away from the curb.

Jared stood there until he saw the SUV's red taillights receding in the distance. He loved the fact that he made her just as nervous as she made him. Sweet, that's what she was. Sweet and unsophisticated. What was a man like him going to do with a woman like her? He would enjoy finding out.

As for Alex, by the time she was pulling into her driveway she'd convinced herself she'd never see Jared Kyles again. He'd looked kind of panicked when she'd suggested meeting her at church.

~

The Red Oaks Christian Fellowship Church sat on seventy-five acres of prime Georgia land which Mother Maybelle, that venerable lady who is mother, auntie, sister, and friend to every single soul who worshiped there, donated following a generous inheritance from her fifth, and final, husband, Dr. Mackenzie Carmichael. Mac, who was a beloved obstetrician/surgeon, had the regrettable habit of taking care of everybody except himself. Subsequently, he dropped dead of a heart attack, leaving poor Maybelle, a woman who'd never wanted anything from a man except his love, even richer than any of her previous four husbands had.

The church was a magnificent round edifice made of stone and glass. Georgia workmen had spent two years constructing it, and it had been Alex's pleasure to design and execute the landscaping with the help of her men and scores of volunteers.

The church was dedicated in 2000, the year when some folks feared the world was getting ready to change for the worse. The congregation of Red Oaks Christian Fellowship Church begged to differ. They put their faith in God and built a house for Him that would hold more than two thousand worshipers, a tweak to the year, in direct defiance of the doomsayers. They had been going strong ever since.

This Sunday morning in May, for the first time in her life, Alex felt apprehensive pulling into the big parking lot and alighting from the SUV with Sam at her side. They began walking toward the church's entrance. She didn't want to think too much about Jared Kyles. It wouldn't do to place her hopes in him actually showing up.

She'd dressed with care anyway, wearing a linen cream-colored skirt suit with a silk bronze shell underneath. The bronze tones accentuated the golden hue of her skin. On her feet were strappy bronze sandals with three-inch heels. She wore hose with them, because her mother had always said that a lady wasn't fully dressed for church unless she wore stockings. Her black, wavy hair was combed away from her face and fell to her shoulders in a glorious cascade.

"If it's possible, you're even more beautiful in your Sunday best," a baritone voice said from behind her.

Alex spun on her heels and a smile automatically came to her lips. Jared looked so handsome in his dark blue summer suit, replete with a white silk shirt, gold cuff links, and a silk, striped navy blue tie. His black wingtips were shined to a high gloss. She thought he'd been sexy in his blue jeans yesterday, but the man cleaned up *very* nicely!

"Sam," she said to her brother, who was watching his sister's reaction to this guy who was obviously trying to make time with her. "Meet Jared Kyles."

The two men shook hands, but Jared could not take his eyes off of Alex.

"I'm over here," Sam joked.

Jared smiled at him. "I guess I'm a little distracted."

"No, man, you're a *lot* distracted," Sam corrected him, totally delighted by the turn of events.

When he and Jared finished shaking hands, he took a step backwards and said, "Uh, Alex, I see some fellas I need to get with before services begin. I'll catch up with you inside." He trotted off in the direction of a group of boys his age.

Alex and Jared gazed into each other's eyes as folks walked around them.

"I just knew I'd seen the last of you," Alex admitted.

"I would have whupped the devil's butt to see you again, Alexandra," Jared told her, a twinkle in his eyes. "Going to church should be a cakewalk."

He gently placed his hand beneath her elbow, and they entered the vestibule.

Three

"Alex, there you are!" an exasperated Gayle Jackson said as she thrust her six-month-old son, Tyler, into Alex's arms. "The twins are missing in action, as usual. Would you take care of Tyler while I go hunt them down?"

Alex happily agreed, holding the chubby baby close to her chest and breathing in the sweet scent of him. "This boy sure is getting big. What are you feeding him? Collard greens and fatback?"

Gayle laughed. "Now you know Ruben would be feeding him just that if I'd let him!" She placed Tyler's baby bag onto Alex's right shoulder.

"Before you take off, meet a newcomer to Red Oaks, Jared Kyles. Jared, this is my best friend, Gayle Jackson. You met her husband, Ruben, yesterday."

Gayle, a petite redhead with warm, golden brown skin and rich, dark brown eyes, smiled up at Jared. "A pleasure," she said. "Ruben told me about meeting you. Welcome to Red Oaks. I hope you like it here."

Jared returned her smile. "Thanks, Mrs. Jackson. I already like it here."

Gayle really grinned then. "Mrs. Jackson? That's my mother-in-law. Just call me Gayle. And I'm gonna call you Jared, whether you want me to or not. That's how we do things around here." She laughed again before turning to go in search of her four-year-olds and her husband, an even bigger kid. "I'll be right back."

Alone with Jared, and with Tyler held firmly in her arms, Alex looked around for a place to sit. The stadium-style seats were already filling up.

From the looks of things, there would be a nearly full house today. Although the church could seat two thousand, it was a very rare occasion when all of the seats were taken.

"She won't be right back, I assure you," Alex said with a short laugh. "The twins always keep her busy on Sunday morning."

They were walking down the aisle as they talked. The buzz of human voices was all around them, soothing violin music was being played over the sound system, and every few steps some friend of Alex's would call her name, and she'd stop and chat for a minute or two after introducing Jared.

"The twins?" Jared asked when he could get a word in without interruption from a parishioner who was happy to see Alex.

"Oh, her oldest is Ruben, Junior. Everybody started calling Ruben, Junior and Ruben 'The Twins' because Ruben, Junior is the spitting image of his daddy."

Alex spotted three consecutive seats in the fifth row. They sat beside each other, and Alex saved a place for Sam by putting her purse and Tyler's baby bag in the extra seat on her right. She settled Tyler onto her lap. He smiled up at her. He had the sweetest temperament, and, since his parents had been bringing him to church since birth, the many sounds tended to soothe him.

Jared watched her with the baby. This was one weird date, if you could call it a date. Not only was he in church, but the woman he'd come to see was cuddling a handsome male, and it wasn't him!

She looked perfectly content to do so, too.

"He seems to like you," he commented.

"Oh, he's a charmer all right," Alex said. "He's had me wrapped around his little finger since I first laid eyes on him." She raised her gaze to Jared's. "Sort of like you."

Jared smiled, dimples showing in both cheeks. "That's good to know. I thought the little diaper-wearer was beating my time."

Alex laughed softly, her eyes still on his face. "No. You had me when you actually showed up today."

"Why is that? You've invited other men to church and they never showed up?"

"Yes, and yes again. They ran for the hills."

"Satan's spawn!" Jared joked.

"No, they just thought I was playing mind games with them. You see, some men believe that a woman thinks if she can get a man to come to church with her, then his intentions must be honorable."

"It's not as if a dishonorable man is going to burst into flames like a vampire upon entering a church," Jared said. If it *were* so, he'd be burning right now.

"I've met some men who I wished would burst into flame. But, no, I suppose there's no risk of that happening."

"You naughty girl, you actually admit to evil thoughts in God's house?"

"God knew what I was going to say before I said it."

"You sound like you have no doubts whatsoever that God exists," Jared said.

Tyler started wiggling impatiently, and Alex stood him on her lap. He grinned happily as he bounced up and down. "No, I have no doubts now," Alex answered.

"What do you mean by 'now'?"

Alex smiled at him. "Our Dad died from cancer when I was fourteen, and our Mom was killed by a drunk driver when I was seventeen. Things like that can test a person's faith."

Jared was quiet. He hadn't expected a revelation of this sort. To tell the truth, he was only looking for a good time here with Alex. Perhaps some rousing spirituals sung by what was sure to be a great choir, a generic sermon from the pastor, and some firm handshaking from congregation members at the end, when he'd undoubtedly be the subject of some curiosity. Then, one day next week, he would have phoned her and asked her out on a real date. A date that didn't include a baby and hundreds of other people.

He must have been silent for too long, because Alex said, "Sorry. That's not a good topic of conversation for a first date, is it?"

Jared smiled gently at her. "No, I'm the one who's sorry. You told me something very personal and I sat here like a bump on a log without responding. The fact is, I didn't know what to say." His autumn sunrise–colored eyes had a contemplative expression in them. "I would have been a total mess if I'd lost my parents that young."

"You would have survived," Alex said quietly.

"What happened to you and your brother and sister after your mother was killed?" Jared asked. Alex had put Tyler back in the crook of her arm, and he'd closed his eyes. Jared watched Alex's reaction to the little charmer. She fairly glowed, and a lovely smile curved her full, red lips. She looked up at Jared.

He blushed because she'd caught him watching her so intently.

Alex's smile never wavered. "We perpetrated a fraud on the state of Georgia."

Jared's eyebrows rose with interest. "How?"

"Since we were minors and had no relatives, the state had the right to put us in foster homes. I was in my senior year in high school. Sam was nine, and Vicky was twelve. After Mom's funeral, Sam, Vicky and I sat down and had a discussion. We knew the house was paid for. It seemed to us that if we could earn enough money to pay for food, electricity, and certain other incidentals, there should be no reason why we couldn't stay in the house."

Jared shook his head. He knew instinctively what she was going to say: After their mother's death, she'd taken on the responsibility of raising her brother and sister alone.

"It was just a matter of avoiding the social workers who came knocking on the door," Alex confirmed. "That went on for four years. After I graduated, I started up the family lawn business again. All three of us worked on weekends, but during the week, it was just me out there digging, and planting, and mowing."

Jared couldn't believe his ears. His respect for her grew tenfold. "That must have been hard on you."

"I was young and fit and motivated. It was fun! Sticking it to the establishment while keeping our family together. When I turned twenty-one, I became Sam and Vicky's legal guardian."

Jared shook his head at the wonder of this woman. He wished he were worthy of a woman who showed that kind of courage. But he knew he was not. No matter how much he wanted to get to know her better, today would have to be the last time he saw her. He might be incapable of being faithful to one woman, but he wasn't a *complete* dog.

The notion of never tasting her lips or holding her in his arms was a mighty big incentive to ignore his higher morals. However, adding to the pain she'd already experienced in life was an ugly prospect. He couldn't bring himself to hurt her. Not even to satisfy his curiosity about how her lips would feel under the onslaught of his.

By the time Sam joined them and the service began, he resolved to have a good time in the present and get out of there as soon as the closing prayer was said.

During the opening prayer, while everybody's heads were bowed, Jared glanced over at Tyler, lying so comfortably in Alex's arms. The baby smiled at him, and he smiled back. He'd never given much thought to having children since he'd decided never to marry, but this little fellow made him entertain thoughts of fatherhood. What would it be like to raise a child, and would he be a better father to his children than his father had been to him and his sister?

The one hundred-plus member choir sang three rousing gospel songs that, he had to admit, made him want to get up and shout. Some of the parishioners were not as reticent as he was. They were dancing in the aisles with abandon. He expected someone to do a back flip before they were done. One young sista in a killer dress got "caught up by the spirit" and fainted dead away. A muscle-bound usher easily lifted her in his arms and carried her from the room. Jared supposed, as huge as the church was, they had a nurse on the premises to help the afflicted at times like these.

The rest of the congregation went on praising God as if succumbing to the spirit was a common occurrence. He felt like a visitor in a foreign country. A place where he was unfamiliar with the language and the customs of the natives.

Shortly after the choir sang their third selection, a deacon went to the pulpit and began making the announcements for the week. He informed them who was ill or hospitalized and needed prayers and visits from their brothers and sisters. He reminded them of the upcoming Mother's Day program. There were still plenty of spots left for children who wanted to recite a poem or an uplifting story about their mothers.

"We call it Hat Day," Alex whispered to Jared.

"Why is that?" he whispered back.

"Because every female from great-granny to infant wears a hat."

He smiled at her. "Of course."

After the announcements, the youth choir took the stage and did a spirited rendition of a Kirk Franklin song. The gangly boy who led them strutted up and down the stage, just like his role model. Jared had always considered Kirk Franklin the James Brown of gospel music. The two men even moved alike when the spirit hit them, doing splits and wild gyrations which left their audiences shouting for more.

Finally, the pastor, Reverend Terrance Paul Avery, went to the pulpit and cleared his throat. He was a tall caramel-colored gent with broad shoulders, a completely bald head, a bushy black mustache, and dark penetrating eyes. Jared put his age at around forty, but he knew from experience that it was difficult to tell the age of a bald black man. Black skin aged slower, and, without the hair, which could be completely white for all he knew, there were few other indicators to go by.

"Good morning, brothers and sisters," Reverend Avery said in a deep bass voice.

"Good morning, Brother Avery!" the church said in unison.

Quiet descended on the gathering. A sense of expectancy could be felt.

Jared felt it, too. He looked around at some of the faces of those closest to him. Joy. Peace. Complete confidence in their pastor. *These people are brainwashed*, he thought acerbically.

Then Reverend Avery began to speak: "Beloved, I want to give to you today a *gift*. A gift that our Lord and Savior, Jesus Christ, gave you *all* over two thousand years ago. It's a recycled gift, but still valuable. It's the gift of life. You see, loved ones, nobody forced Him to offer His life as a propitiatory sacrifice for you. God didn't tell him. 'Son, you do this or I'll punish you.' As a matter of fact, He was His Father's firstborn heavenly Son, and His favorite. Yet He said, "I'll go! Send me!"

"Amen!" an attractive senior citizen with silver curls sitting two rows ahead of them passionately shouted. She threw both hands in the air as if to emphasize her support. Then she closed her eyes, shook her head, lowered her arms, and fell silent.

"That's Mother Maybelle," Alex whispered.

Jared remembered she'd mentioned the lady yesterday.

"We're going to talk about sacrifice today, brothers and sisters, beginning with Jesus' sacrifice of His life for you. We're beginning with a heavenly being, but we're going to end with an earthly being, His mother, Mary. Now, not much is said about Mary after she gave birth to our Lord and Savior. But I'm going to give you scripture and verse about how she continued to love and support her Son all the way to His death on the cross. I ask you, how many mothers would have followed her son's lead to that ignoble end? I dare say, not many!"

Hooked. That's how Jared felt. Not only was Reverend Avery presenting him with a challenging theory, that Mary had had a bigger role in Jesus' life than just giving birth to him, but it was a theory he'd never been taught in Sunday school. All he'd been taught was that God had impregnated a virgin called Mary. She'd been engaged to a guy named Joseph, and, after being convinced that her pregnancy was really miraculous in nature and she hadn't been tipping out on him, Joseph married her. That was his father's version. James Kyles had had a way of reducing anything to its lowest denominator. He hadn't been much of a churchgoer.

Something struck Jared as he was sitting there listening to Reverend Avery: Could it be that he was letting his father's behavior dictate his own actions? His father hadn't gone to church, except on very special occasions; therefore, he didn't, either. His father had been a womanizer; therefore, he was one, too. Wasn't it possible to break the cycle of negative behavior?

He looked at Alex's profile. Fine hair grew on the side of her face. It only made her more beautiful in his eyes. He wanted to kiss her there, and linger, inhaling her sweet essence. What was wrong with him? Thinking carnal thoughts while sitting in the Lord's house?

He'd gotten more than he'd bargained for when he'd accepted her invitation. Now here he was thinking about fatherhood and overhauling his character! There was nothing wrong with his character, thank you! He was a good guy. He just didn't want to get married. *Ever*! He continued to look at Alex. And no pretty country woman was going to change his mind.

He lowered his gaze to Tyler. Wouldn't you know it, the kid smiled at him again. Lord save him from pretty women and charming babies!

~

Mother Maybelle Carmichael couldn't get past those in her row fast enough to run interference for Alex. Freda Hodges was making a beeline for that handsome man who'd come with her this morning. No sooner had Alex given Tyler back to his mother, and Sam departed, than Freda zeroed in on the new guy and pointed her bosom in his direction. How many scarves and shawls must she give her before she got the hint? *Hint* was the operative word. Mother Maybelle would never dream of telling Freda she was showing way too much cleavage in a place of worship. For one thing, she knew Freda only did it to make her husband, George, jealous. George, God bless his thick-headed soul, paid no attention to the woman. She was literally starving for it. So she got it vicariously through the admiring glances of other ogling males.

Mother Maybelle smiled as she walked toward the threesome. To his credit, Alex's gentleman friend's gaze did not lower one smidgen to the ravishing Freda's chest area.

". . . Construction business. I would never have guessed," Freda gushed in a low, husky voice. "What with those broad shoulders and . . . ," she boldly encircled his upper arm with both hands, ". . . rock-hard biceps!"

Mother Maybelle had come in on the tail end of Freda's statement. She went straight to Alex and hugged her. "Hello, sugar!"

Alex squeezed her and kissed her cheek. Smiling down at her, for she was a couple inches taller than Mother Maybelle, she said, "Mother Maybelle, how do you do it? You get more lovely every day. You look marvelous!"

Indeed, for a woman in her seventies, Mother Maybelle still made a striking figure. She was invariably dressed to the nines, from the top of her beautifully styled head to her expensively shod feet. She always said that she might live in a small town in Georgia, but there was no reason why she shouldn't look like she was from "Gay Paree!"

"You oughta quit, child," she said now, her warm brown eyes sparkling in her pecan-tan face. She rubbed her cheek against Alex's and released her. "I have no illusions about beauty, Alex. My time is past, whereas you are in the full bloom of your attractiveness. Isn't that right, young fella?" She put this last query to Jared, who beamed at her, grateful for the interruption and the chance to pry Freda's hands from his arm. Jared looked at Alex appreciatively. "I most definitely agree."

Freda let go of his arm and stood aside. She forced a smile as she listened.

Alex happily made the introductions. There was no one she was prouder to know than Mother Maybelle. When she was done, it was Mother Maybelle who had hold of Jared. "Well, now," she said, smiling up at him. "I hear you're in construction. What a coincidence! We're looking for someone to volunteer for the home-repair ministry. Alex and a couple of others have been taking care of it, but they could always use more help." She held his big hand between her two.

Alex laughed softly. "Mother Maybelle, this is Jared's first visit. Let him come again before we put him to work."

"Nonsense," Mother Maybelle said, smiling up at Jared. "Strike while the iron is hot. If Jared's new in town, there's no better way to get to know his neighbors than to go to church with them and volunteer to help them in some way. Besides, God will bless him, and, as an added bonus, Alex, he gets to spend more time with you, since you're in charge of the ministry."

Alex knew Mother Maybelle meant well whenever she interfered in the personal lives of various members of the congregation, but Jared didn't, and she feared he might be offended. After all, there was nothing written in stone that said he would ever want to see her again after today, let alone want to see her on a regular basis.

Jared, however, only smiled at Mother Maybelle. She reminded him of Momma Sook, his maternal grandmother. If God had created a pushier woman, he'd never met her! Momma Sook thought that by virtue of her advanced age, she could say or do anything she pleased. Apparently, so did Mother Maybelle.

He glanced at Alex. From the mortified expression on her face, she'd been surprised by the good lady's comments. "Sure, I'd love to work with Alex on the project," he said, to which Alex smiled.

Jared felt that smile was worth whatever hassles he'd invited upon himself.

Four

"Thanks for inviting me, I had a good time," Jared said, as he, Alex, and Sam walked down the front steps of the church after the services had ended.

"What's the rush?" Sam asked. He and Jared were about the same height, but Sam had the long, lanky build of a basketball player. Whereas Jared was built like a linebacker on a football team. "It's still early. Why don't you two go to lunch somewhere?"

"Sam!" Alex protested. She smiled at Jared. "Forgive him. I'm afraid the thought of getting rid of me for the afternoon so he can hang out with his friends was too much to resist." She regarded Sam. "Vicky's coming today, or have you forgotten?"

Sam shrugged. "Well, Vicky isn't going to get here until late. Four or five, at the earliest. You know she had to work this morning. Then she'll probably take her sweet time driving, the slowpoke."

Alex knew that was probably true. Vicky, twenty-two, was a very cautious driver. However, she and Jared hadn't made plans beyond attending church together and she wasn't about to force herself on him. Although Macon was only fifty miles away, he could have very important business to attend to once he got there.

She looked up at Jared. Every time she looked at him, she felt a tumult in her stomach. A pleasant, expectant twinge that made her smile inside, even when she was able to control her facial muscles. If she smiled every time she felt like smiling around him he'd probably think she was an idiot. "I'll walk you to your car," she said.

Jared was, frankly, lost in her eyes. He reached down and clasped her hand in his. "If you don't need to get home right away, I'd love to take you to lunch. That *is* what I originally wanted us to do, remember?"

"Then it's settled," Sam said, holding his hand out for Alex's car keys. "I'll drive the SUV home and put it in the garage, and Jared can bring you home after lunch."

Alex reluctantly surrendered her car keys. She knew Sam wasn't going straight home. He'd only said it to appease her. She looked her little brother in the eyes. "Don't write a check your behind can't cash, now," she warned with a grin.

"I'll be careful," he assured her, smiling roguishly. He wasted no time leaving.

Jared laughed. "That's one happy kid."

"He always is when he's got plans to have some fun."

She and Jared continued down the steps. At the bottom, he put his hand beneath her elbow and directed her toward his black Acura. Once they were within a few feet of the car, he pointed his key ring at it and pressed a button. The car's doors automatically unlocked. He helped Alex in, then jogged around and got behind the wheel.

He smiled at her before turning the key in the ignition. "Alone, finally!"

Alex laughed softly. "Too many people for you, huh?"

"The last time I was in a room with that many people, I was at a conference in Atlanta."

"You're more of a solitary man?"

"I do like my solitude, yes." He turned the key and low strains of John Coltrane's "A Love Supreme" filled the air.

He reached over to eject the CD.

Alex placed her hand over his. "Don't. I like John Coltrane."

Jared raised his gaze to hers. A woman who liked John Coltrane? Could this be another sign that he should not get any more involved with her? The longer he was around her, the more he liked her. One minute, he was convinced that he should simply be honest with her, tell her she wasn't his type and say good-bye forever, and the next he was making plans to join her home-repair team. Why was he being so indecisive? She was just a woman. A woman he didn't know very well at all. It should be easy to say good-bye to her and get on with his life.

"Buckle up," he said, as he put the car in reverse and backed out of the parking space. He didn't want to express surprise that she enjoyed improvisational jazz. That conversation would probably lead to something else they had in common, and he didn't want to find out that she also, for example, loved Kung Fu movies and got a kick out of watching football on Sunday afternoon.

He frowned. In the close confines of the car, she smelled wonderful. Her cologne was a soft flowery fragrance with a spicy oriental after-note and was very provocative. He breathed deeply. Nervous tension worked its way up his spine.

"What's wrong?" Alex asked.

Jared had been so lost in his thoughts, he hadn't noticed she'd been observing him the whole time. "You've got me questioning my ethics," he said simply.

"Why?"

Jared thought for a moment as he drove the Acura slowly through the crowded parking lot, looking for an opportunity to get on the main road. "I'm not the marrying kind, Alexandra."

Alex turned in her seat to stare at him. "We've just met, Jared. And you're already talking about marriage? Believe me, I don't want to marry you, either."

"Not yet, but the point is, you will eventually want to get married one day and have children. I *don't*. Therefore, we're probably wasting each other's time."

Alex laughed. "Couldn't you tell me this before I got in the car with you? I could have gone home with Sam."

"No, I don't think I could have," Jared told her. He looked at her with such longing that Alex felt compelled to remove her seatbelt, lean close to him and kiss him on the mouth. She was grateful for the tinted windows, because if the other parishioners had seen her lay one on him like she was doing, they would have been scandalized.

Jared pressed down on the brake pedal and put his arms around her. The first kiss was tentative at best. She was testing whether or not he would kiss her back. He was caught off guard by her decision to go in for the kill. But the second time their mouths came together, there was no holding back. Tongue tasted tongue, and liked the flavor. Her mouth was as sweet as he'd imagined it would be. His was, too. She moaned with pleasure. He cursed the day he'd met her.

When they parted, they looked into each other's eyes for a solid minute. A car horn blared behind them.

"I guess we're holding up traffic," Jared said hoarsely.

Alex calmly moved over and refastened her seatbelt. She was quivering on the inside. What had possessed her to kiss him? She really didn't care. Maybe she'd kissed him out of curiosity, or perhaps desperation, because she feared this might be her last opportunity to do so. It didn't matter. He was right. They weren't suited for each other. She was an independent woman, but she did eventually want to get married and have children. If he didn't, there was no future for them.

As Jared inched the Acura forward, she said, "What makes you think you're not the marrying kind?"

Jared glanced at her before returning his attention to his driving. "From the time I was fifteen, I knew my father was cheating on my mother. I would try to help him hide it from her. Not because I condoned what he was doing, but because I didn't want to witness my mother's pain if she found out. As I grew older and started dating, I found myself behaving just like my father. Something always goes wrong in my relationships, Alexandra."

"Something?" Alex asked skeptically. "Can't you identify what always goes wrong in your relationships?"

"In the past, I would always find a reason to break it off before it got too serious. Then I started being honest with the women from the beginning. I told them I wasn't interested in a serious relationship, just a good time. Some agreed to that, even though there was still drama whenever I'd break up with them. Others chose to walk away before anything could get started."

"Which is what you're hoping I'll do?" Alex guessed.

"I'm being honest with you, Alexandra. I'm drawn to you. I don't know why. Sure, you're a beautiful woman, but I've known lots of beautiful women I had no trouble resisting. I wanted to kiss *you* the moment our eyes met."

Alex watched him as he spoke. Was she being played? She'd heard of playboys who put the burden of the relationship on the woman so that they wouldn't have to take responsibility for any part of it. If the woman got hurt, then so be it! It wasn't his fault. He'd been up front with her from the get-go.

Jared appeared sincere to her. But wasn't that the hallmark of a good con man, his sincerity? Well, she was going to call his bluff!

"Then it's up to me? Is that what you're saying? I can choose to see you with the knowledge that getting serious is out of the question, or I can tell you good-bye right now?"

"I'm hoping you'll decide to see me."

"I'm tempted, Jared. I'm very attracted to you, too. As you could tell from that kiss. But you're right about me: I do want a husband and a family one day. So I think you should take me straight home, please."

〜

A few minutes later, Jared pulled the Acura into the driveway of Alex's Southern-style home with its wrap-around porch. Alex turned to him. "Then I suppose your promise to Mother Maybelle about the home-repair ministry is null and void?"

"No, I never lie to women like Mother Maybelle. I don't want her to put a hex on me or something." He was trying to keep it light, but he certainly didn't feel like laughing. He felt saddened at the prospect of never tasting Alex's lips again or holding her voluptuous body in his arms. Their eyes met and held. He respected her decision, though.

Alex went into her purse and produced one of her business cards. "We meet at the church, at noon, every third Saturday of the month. From the church, we go to the home that needs repairs. There will be six of us. Gayle and Ruben, two other gentlemen and myself, and now, you." She forced a smile. "Call me if you forget what I've just said."

Taking the card, Jared said, "May I kiss you goodbye?" His eyes caressed her face. He wanted to commit every inch of it to memory. Silly of him, really. He was going to see her again on the third Saturday of May. That wasn't so far away.

Alex lowered her gaze to his sensually curved mouth. She wanted to kiss him again. But why get used to something when you were to be denied it from then on? It was better to go cold turkey.

"Sorry, Jared," she said softly. She quickly got out of the car and closed the door behind her. "So long."

She didn't look back as she strode away.

～

Vicky arrived at around four that afternoon. Alex and Sam were in the kitchen preparing Sunday dinner when they heard her old Toyota pull into the driveway. There was no mistaking the chug-chug of the motor nor the ever-present backfire of the exhaust pipe once she turned the engine off.

Alex put down the tomato she'd been slicing and looked over at Sam, who was putting a pan of homemade dinner rolls, his specialty, into the oven.

"That's our girl," she said, a broad smile on her face. She hastily wiped her hands on a dish towel, hung it on the peg next to the stove, and hurried out the back door, with Sam close behind.

Sam knew to stand back if he didn't want his ears assaulted by shrill screams of delight or to be caught up in a group hug. He didn't mind the hugs so much, but his sisters' screams sometimes left his ears ringing.

Sure enough, the moment Vicky and Alex saw one another, Vicky let out a yell that could probably be heard all over the neighborhood, and Alex let out one of equal volume. Sam just stood back and shook his head.

Then they were hugging and jumping up and down simultaneously.

At five-seven, Vicky was not quite as tall as her big sister, but she was shaped similarly, with long legs and a curvaceous figure. She had a head full of hair, too, but she cut it so often you could never know for certain how long it would be from month to month. Apparently she was letting it grow out, because it was nearly to her shoulders and colored a rich auburn. Her natural hair color was black.

"Girl, you look *good!*"

"No, *you* look good!"

"We *both* look good!"

"You're both nuts!" This from Sam, who had come forward to join in the group hug. After the embrace, Vicky stood back and gave him the once-over. "Boy, when are you going to gain some weight? Ain't they feeding you at UF?"

"You look like you're eating enough for both of us," Sam said, looking down at Vicky's ample hips. She wasn't fat. She was just well-endowed when it came to her gluteus maximus.

"This here is a Georgia butt," she joked. "Fed on grits and catfish." To which her brother and sister burst out laughing.

"And undoubtedly anything else you can get your hands on," Sam quipped.

He and Vicky were always ragging on one another.

Later, as they sat around the table in the dining room, Sam confided to Vicky, "Our big sister met a man."

Sam hadn't been at home when Jared had dropped Alex off, so he didn't know her lunch date with Jared had never gotten off the ground.

Vicky's light brown eyes sparkled with excitement. "Really? Tell me all about him, Alex."

Alex smiled. "There's really nothing to tell, Vicky. We've just met."

"He owns a construction company," Sam volunteered. "He's new in town, and Alex landscaped his yard. That's how they met. And they look at each other like no one else exists."

Alex's eyes stretched at Sam's revelation. If Sam had noticed, no doubt others had, too. She wished she'd been more circumspect about her attraction to Jared. She'd apparently worn her heart on her sleeve for everyone to see. "Now, Sam," she said gently. "Don't exaggerate."

"If I'm lyin', I'm flyin'," Sam said emphatically.

"And you ain't flyin'," Vicky said. She regarded Alex with clear eyes. "Is it true, Dearest?" She and Alex shared a fondness for the Emma Thompson film, *Sense and Sensibility*. They identified closely with the sisters in the film, who often referred to each other by the endearment "Dearest."

Alex met her sister's eyes across the table. "I'm afraid so."

Vicky screamed her pleasure and stood up to go around the table and hug her sister. "Thank the Lord! At least one woman in this family is on the right track when it comes to the male sex. I'm so happy for you, sis."

"There's just one problem," Alex said when her sister let go of her.

Vicky's smile faded. "What is it?"

"Jared told me that he's a confirmed bachelor, and, well, I told him I didn't want to see him again."

Vicky pursed her lips, thinking. After a moment or two, she said, "Is that all? A confirmed bachelor, huh? That was before he met *you*. And it's a woman's prerogative to change her mind. Give him a second chance!"

~

That night, just before she turned in, Alex walked past Vicky's bedroom door and heard sniffling on the other side. She grabbed the doorknob, was about to open it without knocking, thought better of it, and knocked.

"Just a minute!" Vicky called.

Alex could hear her walking in the room and closing a dresser drawer. Then Vicky swung the door open. Her eyes were red-rimmed, and she held a wadded up tissue in her palm. She smiled wanly as her eyes met Alex's.

"Kenneth broke up with me," she said softly.

Alex hurried inside and pulled her sister into her arms, rocking her gently. All evening Vicky had wanted to catch up on Alex's life, and Sam's. Whenever they'd suggested she tell them what had been going on in her life, she'd changed the subject. Now Alex knew why. Kenneth Bowman had been the love of Vicky's life. They'd met in their freshman year. Both were destined for pre-med. Kenneth wanted to become a pediatric surgeon, and Vicky wanted to become an obstetrician/gynecologist.

Alex held her at arm's length so she could look her in the face. "I knew something was wrong when you made that comment during dinner. Now, tell me, what happened?"

Fresh tears came to Vicky's eyes. "He's getting ready to do his internship at a hospital in California. He said a long-distance relationship wouldn't work."

They went and sat on the bed and turned to face each other. Alex shook her head. "I don't buy that, do you?" She felt Vicky was holding something back.

Vicky paused to blow her nose before replying. "No, I didn't believe that for a second. That's why I pressed him. He finally admitted that he'd been seeing Cecile Wells on the side for months."

"That girl you brought home with you for Christmas one year?" Alex was truly puzzled.

Vicky nodded in the affirmative. "It seems that Cecile fits in his social circle. He comes from old money, you know. So does Cecile. Both their fathers are doctors. He told me he loved me, would always love me, but he had to think of his future. He said when it comes time for him to marry, Cecile would make a better match."

"That pig!" Alex said vehemently. "What did you tell him?"

"I told him to go straight to hell, no detours, just straight there, and never to bother me again because I didn't have time for trifling males who didn't know their own minds. Love me? He didn't love me, because if he *had* loved me, he never would have cheated on me with Cecile of the bony posterior!"

Alex was glad to see the fire back in Vicky's eyes. She laughed shortly and hugged her. "That's my warrior-woman! You want me to go to Athens and kick his behind? Because you know I'll do it."

Vicky breathed in deeply, and exhaled. Her eyes were clearer now, as was, it seemed, her perspective on her break-up with Kenneth. "No, I don't want his legs broken. I want him to be in the best of health when he sees how well I'm going to do without him. The best revenge is living well. I'm not going to rant and rave and hope that one day he'll learn the difference between true love and the pursuit of wealth and power because that would be a waste of my energies. Some people never learn the difference."

"Amen," Alex wholeheartedly agreed. She hugged Vicky one last time and got to her feet. "I have the whole day off tomorrow. Let's go to a day spa and get the works. My treat!"

Vicky grinned. "I could use a massage."

~

Cartwright Lawn and Garden Service's work week began on Tuesday and ended on Saturday. Alex had established that schedule long ago because most of her residential clients preferred their yards to be done on the weekend so they'd be at home while the work was being done. The bulk of the commercial contracts were handled from Tuesday to Friday. Oftentimes work took them out of town, as the job she'd done for Jared's brother-in-law, Fletcher Henderson, had done.

Mondays usually found Alex doing housework, maintaining her own yard, or shopping, which she loathed. Nothing was more monotonous and boring to her than walking down the aisle of a supermarket, filling her cart, and then having to empty it again onto the counter for checkout. This Monday found her doing just that, although after she and Vicky had spent the day getting rubbed down, being given manicures, pedicures, and fresh hairdos. Vicky had volunteered to get dinner started. There were steaks in the freezer, but Alex needed to get the salad makings, fresh corn on the cob, and something for dessert. When she had looked at Sam, hoping he'd accompany her to the grocery store, he'd feigned total absorption in a hockey game on ESPN. "Right," she said, unconvinced. "You love hockey, just like I love shopping!"

He'd only grunted and concentrated even harder on the screen.

"Okay," she said. "Don't expect me to bring back that ice cream you like."

"Aw, sis," he'd moaned pitifully.

"Oh, you heard that, didn't you?" She laughed and left him to his game.

She was bending over, picking up Sam's favorite flavor of ice cream from the bin, when Jared walked up behind her. He took time to peruse the shapely curves of her hips in the well-worn jeans she had on before saying, "Going to spend the evening curled up on the couch with a big bowl of ice cream?"

Alex smiled as she straightened to her full height. By the time she'd turned around to face him, though, she'd managed to mask her delight at seeing him again behind a bland expression of mild interest. "Hello, Jared." She glanced at the basket in his hand. *Just like a confirmed bachelor*, she thought. *Your basics: eggs, milk, cheese, and bread. Oh, and imported beer.*

Jared hoped he'd been able to school his facial muscles before she'd turned around. Excitement had seized him once he'd recognized her exquisite form a few feet away. He had not been able to get her off his mind for the past twenty-four hours. She'd been with him throughout the drive to Macon, while he prepared for bed, this morning in a business meeting, this afternoon as he consulted with his partner about the new project in Macon, and on his drive back to Red Oaks. He'd gotten back in town twenty minutes ago and had stopped by the first supermarket he'd spotted to pick up some breakfast things.

They fell into step beside one another, Alex pushing her cart and Jared carrying his basket. "Did you do something different to your hair?" he asked.

Alex smiled lazily. "Vicky thought I needed some color, so I got streaks in it. Does it make me look awful?"

Jared abruptly laughed. "If you only knew what I was thinking the moment I saw you, you wouldn't have asked me that."

Alex was glad they were alone in the frozen food section. "What *were* you thinking?"

She paused in the aisle and observed him. He was wearing dark suit pants, black dress shoes, and a white long-sleeved shirt. He'd probably doffed the tie some time ago. The shirt was open at the collar, and she noticed for the first time that curly, dark brown hair grew on his broad chest. That glimpse enticed her, made her want to walk up to him and slowly finish unbuttoning his shirt, then run her hands, with slow deliberation, over his chest.

She was so deep in her daydream that she almost thought she'd misheard him when he said, "I was thinking that you are the most beautiful sight I've seen all day."

Alex smiled warmly at him. "How sweet," she said softly. She continued down the aisle with him right beside her.

"How sweet?" Jared said, disappointed by her unemotional reaction to his compliment. "I say you're the most beautiful thing I've seen all day, and you say, 'how sweet'?"

"Jared, after our conversation yesterday, you really shouldn't be giving me compliments anyway. We agreed that we're acquaintances only, didn't we? We're going to work on the home-repair ministry together, and that's all. Isn't that what you wanted?"

She stopped again to await his response.

A frown drew Jared's brows together. "I slept on it and decided I was too hasty in my decision not to convince you to give us a try."

"I slept on it, too, and I've decided I made the right decision," Alex told him. "It'll save us both a lot of heartache." She held his gaze like a magnet. He could no more look away from her than stop breathing. Alex went to stand directly in front of him. When they were a mere foot apart, she said, her voice low and sultry, "We have to do the sensible thing and resist each other, Jared."

Resist her? Jared wanted to kiss her right in the frozen food section. Her luscious lips were moving, but he could barely hear her for the pounding in his ears.

"So whenever we see each other, let's remember that, shall we?" she continued. With that, she turned her back on him, collected her cart and left him standing there.

Jared didn't move for a minute or two. He had to wait for the tightening in his groin to subside.

Five

A lex and her crew spent the week in Red Oaks doing regularly scheduled lawn maintenance for their commercial accounts at banks,
restaurants, schools, government offices, private businesses, and churches.
Sam joined the six-man crew to earn extra spending money. His big sister offered to give him the two hundred dollars he wanted, but he insisted on
working for it. It was gratifying to Alex that Sam had remembered the work
ethic their parents had instilled in them. She accepted his offer and worked
him as hard as she worked anyone else, including herself.

When she and Sam got home in the evenings, Vicky had a hearty meal on
the table. They would engage in lively conversation throughout dinner.
Afterwards, Sam would excuse himself to go hang with the boys, and he'd
be out the door. Then Alex and Vicky would clean the kitchen, chatting the
entire time. Later, while Vicky swept the kitchen floor, Alex would go outside to water the flowers and plants in the yard, then she'd go into the
greenhouse. It was only a transparent plastic 16'x16' enclosure with a wood
frame, but it was sufficient for the potted plants and flowers that needed
protection from the elements. A couple of years ago, she'd had lights and an
automatic watering system installed.

She was in the greenhouse on Saturday evening at a later time than usual
because it had slipped her mind to go do her normal inspection after dinner.
Now she was in her pale blue short nightgown and its matching robe, slip-
pers on her feet, with her hair piled high on her head the way she'd arranged
it just before she got in the tub. A few minutes ago, she'd been soaking in a

fragrant bath when it had struck her that the only flowers that weren't automatically watered in the greenhouse were the orchids, due to their delicate nature. They were more trouble than any other plant she'd ever grown. But she loved them so much that they were worth the effort.

So she'd trudged outside in the dark for the love of her orchids.

Inside the house, the doorbell rang. Vicky was sitting on the sofa in the den with the phone to her ear. "Hold on, Clarisse, somebody's at the door."

She slipped her feet into the leather slides underneath the coffee table and rose. Smoothing her T-shirt over her blue jeans, she hurried through the living room to the front door.

She squinted through the peephole at the tall, good-looking, dark-skinned man she was certain she'd never seen before. "Who's there?"

"Jared Kyles," Jared said. "I hope I'm not calling too late. Is . . ."

Vicky opened the door before he could finish his sentence. She wanted to get a good gander at the man who had her sister in a quandary. Alex had worried all week that her behavior in the grocery store had completely turned him off. Vicky smiled at Jared as she asked him in. He was here, so obviously his ardor hadn't cooled off yet!

". . . Alexandra at home?"

"Yes, she's here," Vicky said, extending her hand.

Jared shook her hand. "You must be Vicky."

Vicky appreciated how fine he looked in jeans, a black T-shirt, and white athletic shoes. Smelled good, too. Like he'd just showered and shaved. "That's me, Vicky. Middle child, younger sister, and closest friend in the world to Alexandra, who, I might add, is *not* expecting you." She raised her eyebrows as if awaiting an explanation.

Jared smiled. Yeah, she was Alex's sister, all right. Same "take-no-prisoners" attitude.

Jared produced a dozen long-stemmed deep red roses from behind his back. "I know. It was a spur of the moment decision. I just need to see her to explain why I acted like such a fool."

"Stop!" Vicky cried. "Any man who wants to admit to being a fool is all right with me." She began walking toward the kitchen. She looked back at him. "Are you coming?"

Jared put on some speed.

He admired the warm family feel of the house as he hurried through it. Hardwood floors, large airy rooms, solid well-made furniture. It looked like one of those traditional Southern homes his mother loved to *ooh* and *ah* over in decorating magazines. As an architect, he knew a well-built home when he saw one. Whoever had built this house had known what he was doing. He paused a moment. They didn't make molding like that anymore, solid pine and shaped with such precision it was as if the artisan had left his signature upon it.

"She's in the greenhouse," Vicky was saying when they got to the back porch. She stood in the doorway and pointed outside. "Go down the steps and follow the cobblestone path. You can't miss it."

In the greenhouse, Alex was pruning the roses. After making sure the soil of the orchids was moist enough, she'd checked the roses and found that some of them needed to be pruned in order to encourage fuller growth.

She hummed as she worked on a Peace rosebush. She stopped, recalling that her mother used to do the same thing. Smiling as her mother's face appeared in her mind's eye, she continued.

A couple of minutes later, she stopped and looked in the direction of the entrance to the greenhouse. It was such a small space that she couldn't help hearing everything that went on inside of it. She put down the pruning shears and turned to face Jared. In the space of those few seconds, she realized how much she had missed him and how afraid she'd been that her reaction to his attempt to apologize in the frozen food section of the supermarket a few days ago had alienated him. Relief flooded her. Still, she could not afford to run into his arms and declare her feelings for him. If there was ever a time to protect her heart, it was now. She'd decided that even if he continued to be against marriage, she wanted to see him.

Jared felt foolish offering her roses when it was obvious that she already had all of the roses she'd ever need. There were roses of every conceivable shade surrounding them. He smiled at her. "I guess I should have brought wild flowers."

Alex stepped forward and accepted the roses, which were fresh from the florist's shop and wrapped in green paper. She inhaled their heady scent. Then she looked up at Jared. "Thank you. Roses are my favorites. But why are you giving them to me? What are you doing here?"

"Basically, I'm here because I lost an argument with my mother," Jared said. Seeing the puzzled expression on Alex's face, he explained. "Last night, at dinner, I told her I was very interested in you, but because of my tendency toward infidelity, and yours toward a faithful relationship, that we weren't compatible. She asked me why I thought I couldn't be faithful to one woman, and I told her."

"That spiel about your father's proclivities, and your belief that you in-herited them?" Alex asked.

He nodded. "Yeah. After she'd stopped laughing, she told me I had a fifty-fifty chance of being faithful to one mate. While my Dad obviously failed the test, she'd passed it with flying colors. She never cheated on him. I do, after all, have fifty-percent of her DNA floating around in my body."

"Your mother's a wise woman."

"Very wise," Jared agreed. He held his arms open to her.

Alex placed her roses on the table where she'd been pruning the Peace rosebush and walked into Jared's arms. They simply held each other for a while, relishing the feel of their entwined bodies. "You smell good," he said softly.

"I put lavender in my bath water."

He nuzzled the side of her neck. "I missed you so much."

"I missed you, too. I was almost certain that my comments to you the other day had made you give up on me."

"They made me crazy. There's no denying that. We should try to resist each other? Girl, you already had me at that point. All I wanted to do was kiss you as you stood there telling me to practice self-control."

"*You?*" Alex said, tilting her chin upward, presenting him with her mouth. "I could barely keep my hands off of you."

"Then you didn't mean a word of it?" He gently kissed the tip of her nose.

"I had my pride, you know. You rejected me without even knowing me. Because I invited you to church, you automatically assumed you would be wasting your time with a woman like me. That hurt. You don't know how much I was looking forward to being alone with you, and then you laid that whole 'I'm chronically unfaithful' bit on me. As if you were protecting my honor." She looked deeply into his eyes. "I'm a woman, Jared. I'm not an innocent who can't hold her own in a relationship."

"You mean you're not a virgin?"

Alex laughed softly. "I can't claim a lot of experience. But, no, I'm not."

"But I thought single women who went to church were celibate."

"Women who go to church come from all kinds of backgrounds. Some of us *are* celibate. I haven't been with a man in over two years. That's because I prefer to be *in* love when I *make* love. The last man I dated couldn't handle that, so he stopped calling. I don't do booty calls. I've never slept around, and I have to know that a man cherishes me before I can give myself to him. But I'm in no way a prude. I like sex. I like everything that leads up to sex. I'm a healthy woman with healthy appetites. Does that answer your questions about me?"

Jared bent his head and kissed her full on the lips. Alex clasped her hands behind his neck and held on. She had to stand on her toes to accommodate his height. When his big hands moved down to caress her hips, she moaned deep in her throat and pressed closer to him. Jared was hard. Where she was concerned, he had no control over that particular physical response which his body manifested whenever he was near her. She had to feel it through her thin robe because he could feel her answering response to his nearness; her nipples were erect and pressing against his chest.

When they parted, they were both slightly breathless.

Alex gazed up at him. "Does this mean we're officially dating?"

"Definitely," Jared concurred with a devastating smile and kissed her again.

~

The next morning was Mother's Day. Jared had gone to bed late after leaving Alex's place sometime around midnight. They had wound up sitting in the gazebo in her backyard for more than two hours, just talking about anything and everything. They had laughed so much his cheeks were still sore this morning.

He rolled over in bed and glanced at the clock on the nightstand. It was half past nine. If he got up now, he'd have plenty of time to get ready for church. Alex had invited him, but he'd told her he wasn't certain he could make it. Actually, the thought of attending Hat Day appealed to him. He wanted to see how the good folks at Red Oaks Christian Fellowship honored the women among them. If he'd thought of it, he would have invited his mother down from Macon to join him. Emma Kyles would've been in her element. Jared wouldn't lie to God, though, even in his thoughts: the *real* reason he was getting out of his comfortable bed was to see Miss Alexandra Cartwright again. He sat up and swung his long, muscular legs off the bed. He couldn't wait to see what kind of hat she would be wearing, probably something chic and sassy.

~

Alex stood at the bottom of the steps of the church in the midst of an animated exchange between Vicky, Gayle and herself. All of them were wearing sleeveless dresses in varying shades of yellow, this year's color. Each year they chose a certain color and then shopped separately so that their dresses would not be unveiled until Mother's Day. Their "crowns," or hats, were all hand-me-downs. They had been wearing their mothers' vintage hats to the Mother's Day service for years. It was a tradition. Alex and Vicky's late mother, Lutece, had owned a closet full of fashionable hats which her daughters proudly wore in remembrance of her. Lutece had worn a hat to church every Sunday.

Gayle's mother, Henrietta, who was still with them, allowed her only daughter to raid her closet with one proviso: *She* got first pick on Mother's Day.

"No, he didn't!" Gayle said as she handed around wintergreen LifeSavers. Vicky had just told her about Jared's visit. Alex tried not to appear too pleased by the turn of events but it was obvious she *was* by the dreamy expression in her dark eyes.

Her solid medium-yellow dress was made of a cool linen material, with a scooped neck and a scalloped hem. Her hat, purse, and sandals were all cream colored. The hat had been one of her mother's favorites: a wide-brimmed cloth creation with two roses on the left side. It framed her face beautifully. She wore one-carat diamond studs in her earlobes and a simple gold bracelet on her right wrist.

"Oh, yes, he did!" Vicky exclaimed. She'd opted for color in her yellow this year, and tiny lavender lilacs danced across her scooped-neck dress with a ruffled hem. Her shoes, hat, and purse were all lavender. Her purse and sandals were leather, and the hat she'd lovingly taken out of its hatbox this morning was made of straw and had a big floppy brim made of a sheer material that was practically transparent. She wore plain gold studs in her earlobes and no other jewelry.

By contrast, Gayle looked like a twenties flapper. Her dress was pale yellow and had big white gardenias on it. It had spaghetti straps, a V-neck, and she wore a long strand of bright yellow pearls with it. Her purse, sandals, and hat were in a light shade of red. The hat was a cloche. The brim almost covered her eyes, and it gave her a mysterious look. She didn't have on any jewelry except the necklace and her wedding rings.

"I don't know, Alex," Gayle joked. "It's been so long since you had a man, do you still remember what to do with one?"

Alex laughed. "I think it's all coming back to me."

"If you need a refresher course, you know where I am," Gayle countered.

Vicky suddenly poked Alex on the arm and cried, "Look who's coming this way!"

Alex followed her sister's line of sight and almost swallowed her LifeSaver.

"Now that's a good-lookin' brother!" Gayle said. "Why didn't you tell us he was coming?"

"I didn't know!" Alex told her as she excused herself to go meet Jared.

Even from ten feet away, Jared could tell he was the topic of conversation. Women had a way of cocking their heads and pursing their lips that gave them away every time. Gayle and Vicky were both going through those motions. Alex, however, was his main concern and she was exhibiting the one emotion he'd hoped she would: pleasure at seeing him again.

"You're a sly one," she accused lightly as he approached. He caught her checking out his dark blue summer-weight suit. He had his suits made by a tailor in Macon so they all hung beautifully on his frame. Her gaze settled on his striped yellow tie.

She smiled, and he figured she was wondering how he'd known she'd be wearing yellow today. Fact was, he hadn't; it was purely coincidental.

She walked right up to him and touched his tie. "Nice."

Jared wanted to embrace her and kiss her right there in front of everybody, but he settled for grasping the hand she'd touched the tie with and gently squeezing it.

Their eyes met. "You look beautiful in that hat."

Alex's cheeks grew hot with embarrassment. Not because of the compliment, but because of the state her body was in due to his nearness. In less than a minute after seeing him, she was tingling all over. It didn't help that vivid images of the passionate kisses they'd shared last night in the green-house and the gazebo were going through her mind.

"This old thing?" she asked, lightly touching the brim of her hat.

"I wish I had a picture of you in it," he told her. He fairly devoured her with his eyes. Alex, unused to such intimate perusal by a man, felt she might turn into a puddle right there on the sidewalk. She took him by the hand. "Come on, let's go inside before I forget we're on church grounds and kiss you!"

Jared laughed softly and let her lead him back to where Gayle and Vicky were waiting.

The service that day was a mixture of the traditional and the contemporary. The mass choir sang several emotion-filled spirituals which reminded them all of the sacrifices mothers make for their families. Then the children got up and gave their Mother's Day speeches. The really young ones, such as Madison Avery, age four, the reverend's youngest daughter, and Ruben, Junior also four, were performing in front of the congregation for the first time. They fidgeted, forgot their lines, and finally dissolved into tears, which made them even more precious to their audience, who gave them standing ovations. Some of the older children were seasoned pros who gave impassioned recitations and evoked tears of joy from a grateful congregation.

After the children presented their offerings, the youth choir got up and sang two Sam Cooke and the Soul Stirrers songs, "Were You There?" and "Must Jesus Bear This Cross Alone?" The boy who sang lead was a tenor, and his young voice was so lilting and sweet that nobody was unmoved by his performance. Both songs were about the death and resurrection of the Lord and made several parishioners cry out, "Amen, amen!" in recognition of the passion the sentiments provoked within them.

Finally, Reverend Avery went to the pulpit and began his sermon: "Good morning, beloved!"

"Good morning, Brother Avery!"

"Church, as I look out amongst you in all of your finery on this beautiful morning the Lord has given us, I'm reminded of how blessed we all are. Yes, blessed to be able to come together as a family under the Lord. But, lest we forget, allow me to remind you why we're really here. To show appreciation for the Lord's blessings? Yes, that's why you got out of bed this morning and came here. But you could have thanked Him at home. No, the reason you're here is because Christ personally asked you to keep gathering together in His name until He came back, and, as we know, He hasn't come back yet. He also gave us step-by-step instructions on what kind of observance He required of us. He said, 'This bread is my flesh,' and 'This wine is my blood, keep eating it and drinking it in remembrance of me.' Therefore, brothers and sisters being passed among you now are the sacraments of His body. The body that suffered so much on the cross, the body that was raised on the third day and was transformed into something that was more than physical: a spiritual body."

A small army of attendants lined the aisles, carrying trays with tiny glasses of red wine on them, and other trays with unleavened bread on them. The trays were passed down the rows by the parishioners as they partook.

When it was over, the reverend said a prayer of thanksgiving, and the mass choir rose and sang "This World Is Not My Home," whereupon the reverend got happy and joined them, his big bass voice rising to the rafters. There was a running joke among the flock that whenever his wife, Cheryl, wanted to see him show off, she would always ask the choir director to add that particular song to his line-up.

The reverend, who was usually rather understated in his delivery, would be touched by the spirit, which in turn infused the church, and everyone ended up getting out of their seats and singing along.

By the time the song ended, Reverend Avery was washed in sweat, and Cheryl went up to the pulpit and presented him with a pristine handkerchief.

Cheryl sat back down, and the reverend smiled at his wife. He was on to her ruse after all these years. But nothing pleased him more than making her smile.

"We'll have closing comments from Reverend Hunter Danforth." Terrance turned to smile at the assistant minister. Hunter was a tall, rugged, good-looking and sophisticated single brother in his mid-thirties. Many of the unattached sisters in the congregation made it more than clear to him that they would love to be the future Mrs. Reverend Danforth, but, so far, he wasn't biting. "Reverend Danforth . . ."

Terrance went to sit in one of the tall chairs behind the pulpit while Hunter closed the service.

"You *are* coming to the house for dinner, aren't you?" Ruben asked Jared after the service ended. He was holding Tyler in one strong arm and had hold of Ruben, Junior, with his other hand. Ruben, Junior, wiggled mightily. "I wanna go play with Madison!" He was at that stage where he wasn't averse to making a scene to get his way. Ruben looked at Jared. "Would you mind?"

He placed Tyler in Jared's arms and snatched up Ruben, Junior. He stopped short of shaking him. He never got physical with him because he thought striking a child only convinced him that striking someone else got you what you wanted in life. He held Ruben, Junior, at eye level and said, "Listen, boy, I know you're cranky from having to sit for so long, but if you don't behave, there will be no Nintendo for you for the rest of your natural life, *comprende?*"

Ruben, Junior's eyes stretched wide with fear. "Okay, Daddy," he said in a tiny voice.

Ruben set him back down and patted his head. "Okay, Daddy won't be much longer, then I'll take you to Mickey D's for a burger."

Ruben, Junior, immediately brightened.

In the meantime, Jared was bonding with baby Tyler. He couldn't believe the kid hadn't started bawling the moment his father had placed him in his arms. But he hadn't. He'd given Jared a crooked grin instead and commenced passing gas. Being male, Jared understood that fully and whispered, "Better out than in, huh, buddy?"

Ruben had sniffed the air and reached for his son with a grin. "I should take him. He's getting ready to load his diaper."

Jared didn't have to be told twice.

Ruben cradled Tyler in his muscular arms. "Alex and Vicky are coming to our house for dinner. We do it every year on Mother's Day. You're invited."

"I'd hate to intrude on such short notice," Jared began.

Ruben gave him a stern look. "Are you, or are you not, dating Alex?"

"I am," Jared said with a smile.

"Then from now on you have an open invitation. Don't be a stranger."

Jared could say nothing to that except, "Thanks, man. I appreciate it."

"Alex is my girl. We—she, Gayle and I—have been friends since we were in the second grade together. Alex has impeccable taste in friends. So I suspect you're good people, too. Bring your appetite. We always cook too much."

Standing across the room, watching Jared and Ruben, Alex's attention drifted away from her own conversation with Gayle, Vicky, and Mother Maybelle. Mother Maybelle promptly got it back, with: "She told me to mind my own business. Yes, she did, and I've loved her ever since."

Alex laughed because she'd heard that story numerous times. It was about her encounter with Mother Maybelle at age seventeen, when Mother Maybelle came snooping around to check on her and her siblings after their mother's death. Mother Maybelle had insisted on seeing the adult who was living with them. Alex had dragged her inside because she didn't want any of the neighbors to overhear what she had to say to her, then she'd confessed to what they'd been doing: hiding from Social Services, even when they should have been collecting their parents' Social Security payments.

After patiently listening to Alex's reasons for not getting in contact with the proper authorities, Mother Maybelle had surprised her by not turning them in. Instead, she'd insisted that they rely on her in case of emergencies, come to church every Sunday except in case of illness, and have Sunday dinner with her so she could see for herself, every week, that they were fine. Even though she was a Christian woman, she'd helped them pull the wool over the government's eyes. "Sometimes," she said now, "a person has to listen to a higher power." Meaning God's rules were more important than man's.

It was Mother Maybelle who'd facilitated Alex becoming Vicky and Sam's guardian at twenty-one. She'd also made sure that they collected back Social Security payments for all of the months they'd missed getting the monthly checks. That lump sum of money had been enough to shore up the business and put some aside for Sam's and Vicky's college tuition. As it turned out, Sam received a basketball scholarship at the University of Florida, and Vicky received a full academic scholarship from the University of Georgia. Alex had set up bank accounts for them for incidentals that their scholarships didn't cover. She didn't want them to have to get part-time jobs which could interfere with their studies. In spite of her well-meaning efforts, both of them wound up getting jobs anyway. As it turned out, they were as industrious as their big sister. Therefore, the accounts that Alex had set up as checking accounts became savings accounts. When they graduated they would each have nice nest eggs.

"Mother Maybelle," Alex said now. "Every time you tell that story, I feel like kicking myself for being so disrespectful to you that day, when all you wanted to do was help us."

"Child, you didn't know that," Mother Maybelle said sagely. "You helped me to recognize what some of our children have to go through to survive. You were a blessin' to my soul."

"And you were a blessing to mine," Alex said and gave the shorter woman, by two inches, a warm hug.

Mother Maybelle moved away from her after a while and smiled. "Don't you have someone waiting for you over there?"

She didn't miss a thing. Indeed, Jared was standing next to Ruben and his sons, but he was looking at Alex. "It seems I do," Alex said to Mother Maybelle.

"Well, what're you waitin' on? God helps those who help themselves, and if you've got the sense you were born with, you'll help yourself to that man. Humph, he reminds me of my dear husband, Mac. He had big shoulders and narrow hips like that, too, and that was a whole lotta man!"

"Mother Maybelle!" Vicky said, pretending to be aghast.

"Darlin', God put woman here for man, and man here for woman. That's the way it was from the beginning, and if it ain't broke, don't fix it! And don't nothin' look broke on that man. He's mighty fine. Go on, Alex, you lucky girl."

Shaking her head at Mother Maybelle's wit, Alex went to claim her man.

Six

Jared saw Alex's SUV the moment he pulled up to the address in one of Red Oak's older neighborhoods. He was reporting for duty for the home-repair ministry's newest project: a porch for elderly Sister Wilhelmena Kendall.

He got out and began walking toward the house. At seven-thirty in the morning, there were four cars in Sister Kendall's yard, and several people standing around the sagging porch. Alex saw him and waved him over. Jared's heart did a somersault at the sight of her. She looked beautiful, in a pair of well-worn jeans, a white tank top tucked into the waist, and a pair of tan work boots. Jared smiled. They'd worn the same colors today. He was wearing blue jeans and a white T-shirt, as well. His work boots were black, though.

"Hey," Alex said, smiling. They hugged briefly before joining the others.

Jared greeted Ruben and Gayle, the only two other people in the group that he knew.

"Glad to have a real builder join us," Ruben said.

"Yeah," Gayle agreed. "The rest of us are well-intentioned but only know the basics, like how to hammer a nail."

Everybody laughed.

"Jared Kyles," Alex said, introducing him to the other two men. "Wallace Bradley."

Wallace was a tall, broad-shouldered black gentleman in his sixties. He had an intense stare and fairly bristled with nervous energy.

"Mr. Wallace," Jared said politely.

Wallace pumped his hand. "C-call me Wally," he stammered. "E-every-body does."

"Wally, it is," Jared said with a smile.

"And this is Patrick Wilson," Alex said next, smiling at a stocky young man of medium height with dreadlocks down to his waist. "Patrick, Jared Kyles."

Patrick nodded his hello. "Good to meet you, man." He narrowed his light brown eyes at Jared. Puzzled by his attitude, Jared assumed it was simply a touch of xenophonia, or wariness of strangers, on the younger man's part. Then Patrick's gaze fell on Alex, and Jared knew that Patrick had a crush on her.

He didn't have time to dwell on the revelation because as soon as Alex had finished introducing him around, she addressed the group. "Mrs. Kendall's going to spend the night with Mother Maybelle. She's not feeling her best and construction noises make her nervous." She glanced at her watch. "It's seven-forty now. The materials were delivered earlier this morning. Jared was nice enough to draw up the plans after coming last week to check out the old porch, and I estimate that we should be able to do the job in under eight hours, with a break for lunch from twelve-thirty to one. Okay! Let's get the fun part out of the way."

Jared took the lead in tearing the old porch down due to the experience needed to pry old nails out of the house without causing damage to the siding. After he had detached the porch from the house, the rest of them made short work of dismantling the footings, posts, and floor boards that comprised the porch.

They worked well together, everyone pulling his or her weight, and no one displaying ego when it came to taking directions from Jared, who was slinging commands at a fast pace. By noon, they'd all broken a nice sweat, and the frame for the large porch was up and resting on proper supports.

Alex and Jared were working next to each other. As she hammered a nail into a post, he said, "You swing that hammer so well, you could be part of my crew."

Alex briefly looked up at him. The sunshine rendered his eyes the color of a copper penny. His skin glistened with perspiration, and the muscles in his chest and arms were nicely delineated beneath his T-shirt. She could have spent the day just admiring him in that shirt. "I don't think working for you would be a good idea."

"Oh? Why?"

"I've been on lots of construction sites, and the crews are never shy about expressing their appreciation for the female form. Could you handle your men gawking at me all day long?"

"I don't have a jealous bone in my body," Jared professed.

Alex laughed softly. "So you say!"

Jared looked serious. "You can't possibly mean that if I offered you a lucrative landscaping job on one of my sites, you'd turn it down. Think of your company. Think of the extra money your men would earn."

"Yeah, think of us!" Ruben put in. He couldn't help overhearing their conversation because he was working less than five feet away from them.

Alex laughed even harder. "Listen, you two, keep your minds on the job. We'll cross that bridge if we ever get to it."

"I'm offering you a job now," Jared challenged her. "The company's building at least fifty new homes in a subdivision outside of town."

"I'll think about it and give you my answer later," Alex said noncommittally. She looked pointedly at the hammer in his hand as if to tell him to stop dawdling.

Jared smiled and continued working.

By four o'clock that afternoon, the porch was finished. The floorboards of pressure-treated pine had been stained, and all that was left to do was allow it to dry before putting Sister Kendall's swing and rocking chairs back where they belonged. Wally and Patrick volunteered to come back in the morning to do that, leaving everyone else free to collect their tools, say their good-byes, climb into their respective vehicles, and drive away.

Alex's cell phone rang as she was driving. She carefully flipped it open and answered it. "Hello, handsome." She'd seen Jared's number on the cell phone's screen.

"About our date tonight. Can you be ready by six?"

"Yes."

"Do you like seafood?"

"Yes."

"Would you come to my place right now so that we can make love the rest of the afternoon?"

"No."

Jared laughed. "I was on a roll."

"Yes, you were," Alex said, laughing softly. "Where are we going tonight?"

"It's a secret."

"Give me a hint."

"Do you like black-eyed peas?"

"Yes, of course I do. Is that the hint?" Alex asked, sounding disappointed. "Is that all I get?"

"Be patient, church girl. I'm gonna show you a real good time. Wear something funky. See you in a couple of hours."

He hung up before Alex could ask another question.

As soon as Alex got home, she went to her bedroom to check her messages. She sat on the edge of the bed and pressed the play button, hoping Sam or Vicky had phoned while she was out. Sam was spending the summer in Florida working as a counselor at a basketball camp for high school students. Vicky was interning at an Atlanta hospital and had precious little time for anything other than work. Alex missed them desperately.

She laughed out loud when she heard Vicky's excited voice. "Girl, you're not going to believe who came to see me last night. I was coming off a tough shift, and so darned tired I could barely get the key into the lock, when I heard a voice from behind me in the hallway. *Kenneth!* Looking like he hadn't slept in days. Fool that I am, I invited him in and for the next hour he told me what a mistake he'd made when he walked out on me. Alex, I sincerely don't know what to make of him! But I told him I'd think about taking him back. *Think about it*, nothing certain. He really hurt me." She sighed deeply. "Well, Dearest, I'm not the basket case you would imagine I would be due to this surprising turn of events. I'm okay. Just wanted to fill you in. Love you much!"

Turning away, Alex smiled contentedly. Her baby sister definitely had her head on straight. She would phone her in the morning when they would both be rested. Vicky usually had Sundays off.

～

"Look in the glove compartment. There's a black scarf in there. I want you to blindfold yourself before I make the next turn," Jared told her as he was driving down the highway a couple of hours later.

Alex thought his request was peculiar but went along with it. Jared was being very secretive tonight. After she'd complied, he said, "We're almost there now. You won't have to be blindfolded for much longer."

"Good, because I hate being in the dark about anything," Alex told him.

Jared smiled in her direction. She looked like a gypsy in her sexy multi-colored silk skirt that swirled around her long legs when she moved, and a fly midriff top in deep purple. The shirt was sleeveless and had a modest neckline but afforded a nice glimpse of her toned stomach. Her golden brown skin was fairly flawless as far as he could see. He couldn't help wondering if it was the same all over.

"No one's going to jump out at me and yell in my ears when I remove this?"

Jared laughed shortly. "No."

Momentarily, he stopped and parked the car. "Don't move. I'm coming around to get you."

Alex waited patiently, although her stomach muscles were twitching nervously.

Jared opened her door and helped her out. When her feet touched the ground, her first thought was that they were standing on asphalt.

She heard another male voice say, "Good evening, Mr. Kyles. We have beautiful flying conditions."

Alex's heart leaped with excitement. *Flying?*

Then she felt Jared's hand on the blindfold. "Okay, you can take it off now," he said.

When she could see again, a mid-sized Cessna and a tall gentleman she'd never seen before were in front of her.

"Captain Deweese, this is Miss Alexandra Cartwright."

The captain bowed from the waist, his green eyes twinkling with humor. "A pleasure, Miss Cartwright."

Alex couldn't help staring in amazement at the Cessna. "It's gorgeous!"

She shook the captain's hand. He grinned down at her. He was in his mid-fifties with thick, wavy iron-gray hair, an angular face and a solid build. He was dressed in a pair of navy blue dress slacks, a pale blue short sleeved shirt, tie, and a pair of black wingtips. She supposed he was a private pilot and that was his uniform of choice.

"Thank you, ma'am," Captain Deweese said, smiling. "I keep her in great shape." He turned to Jared. "Shall we get underway?"

Jared nodded. He was beaming at Alex. When the captain walked away to do his final check of the plane before taking off, Alex spontaneously leaped into Jared's arms and kissed him repeatedly on the cheek. Laughing, Jared hugged her tightly. "Come on, now, darlin', the evening's just getting started. Save some of the good stuff for later."

Alex gave him one last kiss for good measure. "You've already impressed me. Whatever comes later is just icing on the cake."

Jared grinned, grasped her by the arm, and helped her up the steps of the plane. "My goal tonight, sweetness, is to woo you to the full extent of my abilities. And be forewarned, I will do anything to meet my goal. Next stop, Atlanta."

~

An hour and a half later they were seated at Jared's favorite soul food restaurant in Atlanta, *Hoppin' John's*. Alex was charmed by the restaurant's down-home atmosphere, replete with red-and-white checkered table cloths and glass pitchers of ice water on every table so that patrons could serve themselves.

"Hoppin' John," Alex said as she perused the menu. "That's the black-eyed peas part of your question."

"My question?" Jared feigned ignorance of where she was headed.

"You asked me if I liked seafood and black-eyed peas." She raised her gaze to his. "This isn't a seafood restaurant."

"Fried catfish is on the menu," Jared said, a smile crinkling the corners of his golden-hued eyes.

"Okay," Alex said, letting it go for now. She would get to the bottom of the mystery before long, though. "I think I'll try their Hoppin' John with that fried catfish you mentioned."

Jared inclined his head in agreement and beckoned the waiter to their table.

A few minutes later, as both of them were finishing their meals, Jared kept glancing at his watch. Alex refrained from asking him why he was doing that for as long as she could tolerate his odd behavior, then blurted out, "Why do you keep looking at your watch? Do you have somewhere else to be?"

Jared smiled wickedly at her. "No, we have more than enough time to linger over our meals. I'm sure Seal won't start the concert without us."

Alex stood straight up, pushing her chair back with her legs. Hands on her hips, she stared down at him with a peevish expression on her face. "Jared Kyles, do you mean to tell me you have tickets to the sold-out Seal concert, and I couldn't get tickets to save my life?"

Jared went into his inside coat pocket and produced the aforementioned tickets. "Third row, center," he said proudly.

Alex snatched the tickets from him, kissed his lips briefly, then sat back down, not wanting to make a spectacle of herself. "You are a prince!" she cried, keeping her voice low. Their eyes met and held across the table. "But how did you know I'm a Seal fan?"

"Ruben and I had a chance to talk while you and Gayle were getting coffee after dinner on Mother's Day. He says you have all of Seal's CDs, and you have a huge crush on him."

"A crush?" Alex denied. "Not really, I just think he's super talented, that's all."

"Oh, I don't mind if you have a jones for him, Alexandra, as long as I'm the one you go home with."

At the concert, they held hands and cuddled while Seal entertained them with a selection of old and new songs. Alex kept stealing glances at Jared. He'd taken the the time to plan a perfect evening for her, even going as far as asking her best friend about her likes and dislikes. He was a special man, and she was glad he was in her life. More than glad, delighted!

When Seal launched into an "unplugged" version of "Love's Divine," accompanying himself on an acoustic guitar, Alex leaned over and whispered, "This is my favorite."

Jared kissed her forehead, and she rested her head on his shoulder as they listened. The lights were dimmed, and there were more than two thousand other music lovers in the auditorium, all enraptured with Seal's mesmerizing voice.

After the song ended, Alex and Jared gazed into each other's eyes. Then they kissed without saying a word. It was as if the melodious tones and heartfelt words of the song had infused them with the need to come together in as passionate an embrace as they could, given the fact that they were in a public place. Around them, other couples were likewise engaged.

"I've never said this to another woman before," Jared said once they parted.

Alex looked up at him expectantly. "What?"

Jared sighed. "I want to take you to meet my Mom."

Laughing softly, Alex threw her arms around his neck. "I'd love to."

Seven

"Alex, would you please drop by the trailer before you leave this afternoon?"

Alex and her crew were having lunch in the shade of a tree at one of the houses in the fifty-home subdivision. She looked up from eating a sandwich, and acknowledged Jared. "Sure," she said. *Boss man*, she tacked on silently and acrimoniously.

"Gentlemen," Jared said politely as he turned to leave.

"What's got his goat?" Ruben asked after Jared had gone.

Alex squinted up at the clear blue July sky before saying, "I don't know. We're ahead of schedule, so I don't see what he's got to complain about." She was certain he had a complaint though. She and her people had been working for Jared's company for more than two months now, and it had been an eye-opening experience for her.

At the end of the first two weeks, Jared had called her into his trailer, which served as his office on the site, and told her that some of his men were distracted by the shorts she was wearing. She suspected that the only male on the site who had a problem with her shorts was him, but she didn't say anything. She switched to slacks.

The next time he asked her to meet him in his trailer, he'd asked if it was really necessary for her to be on the site supervising her men when she had a perfectly good foreman who could do that. She'd told him that it most certainly was. She did a full day's work, every day. It was her way, and she didn't see any reason why she should change it.

Alex was prepared to give him a piece of her mind today, if he had another complaint about either her apparel or the way she ran her business.

She bit savagely into the sandwich and looked at Jared's retreating back. Men! They couldn't come right out and tell you what was on their minds. They had to make you work for it!

Ruben smiled at the fierce expression on her face. "You know what the problem is, don't you?"

She met his eyes. "What?"

"He can't stand the fact that his men ogle you like you're somethin' good to eat."

Alex laughed. Ruben was very perceptive, always had been. The accident hadn't robbed him of that ability. "Yes, I know, but he's not ready to admit it. He's just going to take it out on me until he blows like a stick of dynamite, and then I'm going to get mad at him and tell him where to go."

"Be gentle," Ruben said. "After all, he's just a man."

Alex smiled at him. "Your momma raised you right."

"Sho' did," said Ruben with an infectious grin.

She could have told him that the other reason why Jared was so tense was because they hadn't made love yet. But that was an entirely too personal conversation to have with her crew around.

"I'll be gentle," she promised him. "That is, if he doesn't set me off!"

Alex purposely waited until everyone else had left the site that evening before venturing over to the trailer. When she opened the door, a current of cold air washed over her. After being in the July heat all day, the air-conditioned trailer felt like a freezer to her.

Jared heard her entering and got up from behind his desk. The trailer was a single-wide model and had few amenities. It was just a place to conduct business while on a construction site. The carpet was a murky brown, and thinning, and there was standard office furniture: a desk with a swivel chair, two straight back chairs, and plenty of filing cabinets.

Jared motioned for Alex to take one of the chairs in front of the desk.

She sat without saying a word. Her eyes were on his face.

He stood with his arms akimbo. "Alexandra," he began. He paused for so long, his gaze on something in the back of the room, that Alex started to think something really *was* wrong. He frowned and refocused on her. "I was going to ask you if you could cut down the number of days you work with your men on the site or if you could wear baggier pants, but that wouldn't solve my problem."

Alex coolly crossed her legs, her gaze never leaving his face. "Which is?"

"I can't handle what my men say when you walk past. I can't stand the way that they look at you. It burns me up!" Jared cried, his eyes narrowed and his nostrils flared with pent-up anger. "How can you stand it? I know you hear their wolf calls. I know you notice how they leer at you."

"I wouldn't be so successful at what I do if I let a few wolf whistles and salacious stares upset me," Alex told him. "Sure, I notice, but just like my crew learned to stop looking at me like a sex object, your men will eventually learn, too. That is, if I ever work for you again!"

"What do you mean by that?" Jared asked sharply.

Alex stood up and faced him. "This hasn't exactly been a wonderful experience for me. I've never had anyone treat me the way that you do on a job. And it's all because we're dating. You're territorial, Jared. If any other male comes near me, a male who isn't a member of my crew, your back goes up! You need to snap out of it once and for all, or we can't work together in the future. I only took this job because I'm not the type of owner who hogs all of the profits, and my crew's mouths watered at the notion of extra income."

Jared looked surprised by her admission. "You didn't want to work for me?"

Alex smiled at him. "No, because I figured this would happen."

"Because I'm territorial," Jared said as he began walking toward her.

Alex took a couple steps backward. "Yes."

"What if the situation were reversed, and I came to work for you, and *your* company consisted of nothing but women?" "I'd probably have kittens," Alex said at once.

Jared laughed. "Do you always tell the truth?"

"No, but I don't want you to have to guess about me. I'm the jealous type. Not insanely jealous, but when you look at someone with lust in your eyes, I want that someone to be me, not some other woman."

"Like I'm looking at you now?" Jared said, his golden brown eyes raking over her with slow, deliberate longing.

Alex had backed into the chair she'd previously been sitting in. He walked up to her, pulled her none-too-gently into his arms, and tilted her head back with his thumb. "Do you know how much I want you?"

Alex felt his erection on her thigh. Yes, she had some indication.

She smiled seductively and pressed her lower body against his hard member. "About as much as I want you," she told him.

Jared licked the side of her neck. Her skin was salty due to perspiration, but she tasted good to him. Alex shivered, and her knees went slightly weak. He softly kissed her mouth and raised his head to smile at her. "But I'm going to be a good boy right now because I know you'd feel awkward tonight, meeting my Mom for the first time, after we'd made love in this shabby trailer. So get out of here before I change my mind."

Alex looked panic-stricken. It had slipped her mind that they were going to a dinner party tonight. It was his mother's birthday, and she'd asked Jared to bring Alex. She'd specifically asked for no gifts; she already had everything she needed.

Alex quickly shrugged out of his arms. "Oh, Lord, I'm meeting your mother tonight! I have to go. I've got a lot to do before seven-thirty."

Jared calmly glanced at his watch. "It's already half past five."

Alex sprinted for the door. "Why didn't you remind me earlier!"

She could hear Jared's laughter all the way to her truck.

~

"That's not a house, it's a castle," Alex said upon seeing the Kyles's home later that evening. "It's something out of a King Arthur fantasy."

Jared laughed as he slowed the Acura and turned onto the circular driveway. "You're right, it's James Kyles's castle. Emma, however, would prefer something smaller. It's for sale."

Alex stared at the three-story gray stone house that had turrets on each corner. She sided with Emma Kyles. No doubt it was a luxurious home, and people passing by probably gaped in awe at it, but it didn't belong in the Georgia countryside.

"Your father didn't let your mother have much say in its construction, huh?"

"If he had, it would have turned out something like your house."

Alex turned in her seat to get a glimpse of his face so she could discern whether or not he was pulling her leg. He didn't appear to be. "Did you grow up in that house?"

"No, he built it in 1997. Carena and I grew up in a normal place." He stopped the car in front of the house, and, in a matter of seconds, a valet came bounding down the steps to retrieve his car keys.

Jared jogged around the car and helped Alex out. "I'll give you a tour," he said. "It has hidden rooms and walls that move. My father was a very eccentric man."

They walked up the ten steps leading to the double brass front doors. The pulls on the doors were lions with their mouths open. Jared had to put his hand inside one of the lions' mouths in order to open the door. He pushed it wider and gestured for Alex to precede him. Alex stepped inside a vast foyer with a black-and-white checkerboard floor. The sound of her heels resounded on it as she stepped down the two steps. A petite, middle-aged black woman with a salt-and-pepper Afro welcomed them.

Her dark brown eyes narrowed accusingly at Jared. "Mr. Jared, you're late."

Alex smiled as Jared kissed the woman's proffered cheek. "Alexandra, meet Miss Sadie Canton, my mother's personal assistant."

"Tell it like it is, child," Miss Sadie said. "I'm the head housekeeper, the cook, and the chief bottle washer."

"And she puts Florence of *The Jeffersons* to shame with her sassiness. Momma should have fired her years ago."

"Who do you suppose would put up with that woman, except me?" asked Sadie with a mischievous grin.

"Any number of loyal, discreet servants," said a haughty feminine voice from behind them. Alex tensed as she turned to face the petite woman of indeterminate age who had Jared's skin color and eye color. Emma Kyles's long black hair was pulled back in a perfect chignon. She was wearing a flowing emerald silk kimono over a simple black shell and black slacks. Low-heeled emerald sandals adorned her small feet. Trim and vibrant, her face mirrored her pleasure at seeing her only son.

"Don't let us frighten you with our banter," she said to Alex, as she grasped both of her hands in hers. "Sadie and I bicker all the time. I'd think she was sick if she wasn't complaining about something. And she'd think I'd lost my mind if I didn't give her tit for tat."

"Then there will be no fistfights here tonight?" Alex joked.

"Not unless *she* starts one," Sadie said before disappearing.

"She always has to have the last word," Emma said peevishly. Then she yelled at Sadie's retreating back, "I'd mop up the floor with you!"

"That would be the only time you ever mopped a floor!" Sadie tossed back.

"See what I mean?" Emma asked with a laugh. "The last word. Come on, let me introduce you to everybody."

Emma looked back at her son as she led Alex to the library, where the rest of the dinner party guests were enjoying drinks and hors d'oeuvres. "What kept you?"

"It's Alex's fault, she couldn't decide what to wear," Jared said, unashamed.

Alex glared at him. "Now, you *know* you're lying! We're late because . . ."

She stopped abruptly. They were late due to a rather heavy petting session which had almost ended up in the bedroom. Humor flashed in Jared's devilish eyes.

Alex would have slugged him if his mother weren't still holding onto one of her hands. "Darlin'," Emma said to Alex. "I could always tell when my son is lying to me. I know you aren't late because of your indecisiveness. By the way, you look beautiful tonight. I always wanted legs like yours, but I stopped growing at five-two."

"Mrs. Kyles, I'd trade my long legs for your sophistication and self-assurance any day."

Emma laughed delightedly. "Fooled you, didn't I? I was born in a tar-paper shack, fifty-four years ago, in Normal, Alabama. We were so poor I didn't know what plumbing was until I was seven years old. But I thank you for the compliment, because I worked hard to become the person you see today. Which is why I'm so happy to finally meet you. Jared tells me you're a self-made woman, too."

Alex felt at ease enough to say, "I'm still a work in progress."

"Aren't we all?" Emma replied.

Jared walked behind them, aware of the fact that his mother and the woman he loved were forging a strong bond. They were alike in a number of ways. He knew they would have fun finding that out.

I love Alex.

He was momentarily stunned by his own thoughts as he arrived at the entrance to the library. That he desired her with every fiber of his being he had no doubt. But love? That had taken him by surprise.

In the library, everyone looked up when Emma and Alex walked in.

Alex felt a little jittery with all eyes trained on her, but she had survived worse and knew she'd make it through tonight's goings on unscathed.

"Everybody, this is Alexandra Cartwright, Jared's girlfriend," Emma announced.

Alex smiled bravely as Emma gestured to a young couple sitting near the fireplace. "That's my daughter, Carena, and her husband, Fletcher Henderson."

"Hello, Carena," Alex said.

Carena, petite like her mother, had smooth caramel-colored skin and jet-black hair that she wore slick and straight, nearly to her waist. Her light brown eyes were almond-shaped and lent her a somewhat Asian aspect. She smiled warmly. "It's a pleasure, Alexandra."

Fletcher was on his feet, coming across the room to shake Alex's hand. "Of course, we've already met. How are you, Alex?"

Tall, dark-skinned, and in splendid shape, Fletcher dwarfed his wife. He wore his natural black hair cut close to his scalp, and his eyes were dark, almost black, and deep set. Both he and Carena were dressed casually, Carena in a pale green lightweight twin set and a pair of moss green slacks, and Fletcher in an even paler green polo shirt and a pair of jeans. Alex was glad she'd decided on slacks tonight, too.

"I'm fine, thanks. Good to see you again."

"Where's Jared?" Carena asked.

Everyone looked toward the door. Jared sauntered in, grinning.

"Did you get lost?" Fletcher asked.

"Sort of," said Jared, his gaze on Alex's inquisitive face. "But I finally found my way."

"Does anyone know what the heck he's talking about?" Emma inquired. However, the manner in which her son was looking at Alex made her so ecstatic that she didn't care that he wasn't making any sense. "Come on in, sweetie, and finish introducing Alex around. If I were Alex, I would never go anywhere else with you, the way you've been behaving tonight. First you try to blame her for being late, and then you hang around in the hallway when you should have been in here being the doting boyfriend."

"Well then, Mom, I'm glad you're not Alex," Jared told her.

Everyone laughed, including Emma.

Jared introduced Alex to the other four couples in the room.

Emma purposefully did not sit Alex and Jared together at the dinner table. She sat Alex on her right and fairly monopolized her all night. She regaled Alex with stories of Jared's misspent youth. He continuously shot warning looks at his mother, but Emma ignored them. She was having too much fun. Jared had never brought a woman home before, and Emma wasn't about to miss her chance to relate thirty-two years of stored-up Jared stories to an appreciative audience.

When he heard his mother say the word "bounced," he knew she was telling Alex about the most embarrassing episode of his high school years.

"Mother, don't!" he demanded from across the table. His eyes narrowed ominously.

Emma smiled sweetly. "Baby, it wasn't your fault that the ball bounced off of your big head and went into the other team's basket."

"It *was* his fault that he had such a hard head," Carena put in with a snicker.

"It was the Afro he used to wear," Fletcher said. He'd been playing on the same team that fateful night. "It served as a springboard for the basketball. And, of course, coach had to wipe off the Afro Sheen before the game could resume."

Alex was laughing so hard that tears came to her eyes.

"I bet you were adorable," she said. "How old were you?"

"Seventeen," Emma provided. "It was his last year in high school."

"Thank God," Jared said ruefully.

Later, as they said farewell at the door, Emma warmly embraced Alex and softly said, "Welcome to the family, Alexandra. I'm looking forward to getting to know you better. Make him bring you again. Real soon."

Alex whispered back, "No, next time you're going to come to my house for dinner."

Emma smiled up at her. "I'd love to!"

Jared, having heard only his mother's comment, asked what she was talking about.

"Going to Alexandra's house for dinner," his mother replied.

"Good," said Jared. "Wait until you see her house. You're gonna want to buy it."

He bent to kiss his mother's fragrant cheek. Now he *knew* he wasn't going to get away from her without their customary hug. She grabbed him and got her hug. Then she stood on the bottom step and waved good-bye to them.

They were the last of the guests to leave. Sadie was waiting for her in the foyer when she closed the front door.

"Well, what did you think of her?" Sadie asked.

"I always wanted another daughter," Emma said with a smile. "I thought she was fabulous!"

"Me, too," said Sadie. "Did you hear the way she called him on it when he tried to pin being late on her? She's got what it takes to tame a man like that big ol' hardheaded boy of yours."

Emma began walking back to the kitchen. She wanted a seltzer. Something Sadie had cooked hadn't agreed with her, but she wasn't about to tell Sadie and get into an argument with her tonight. She was tired.

However, she couldn't resist saying, "*My* hardheaded boy? You spoiled him more than I did!"

After which an argument ensued.

In Jared's car on the way back to Red Oaks, Alex relaxed against the leather seat and closed her eyes. It had been a wonderful, though stressful, evening.

"She likes you," Jared said, breaking the silence. He reached over and lowered the volume on the CD of Andre Watts as guest pianist with the New York Philharmonic.

Alex turned in her seat to smile at him. "I know. Your mother doesn't have a false bone in her body. What you see is what you get. I liked her, too."

Jared was quiet for a moment. Then he cleared his throat. "I was thinking that if you could get next Saturday off we could go somewhere for the weekend. Carena and Fletcher stayed at a bed and breakfast in Savannah a few months ago, and they said it was a very romantic place. The Ballastone, I think it's called."

"I've heard of it, but I've never been there," Alex said, trying to conceal her excitement. This was the first time Jared had mentioned going away for the weekend. Did this mean he was finally going to proposition her? For three months he had been wearing her lips out with hot, passionate kisses, but something always happened to interrupt them when she felt he was about to go further. Like today, when he'd reminded her that they were going to his mother's for dinner. There was something else he'd said in the trailer today, she recalled. That he didn't want her feeling awkward about having *made love* to him just before going to his mother's birthday dinner. Therefore, he was going to be a good boy and stop tempting her with kisses.

"Will you make love to me when we get there?" she asked suddenly.

Jared laughed shortly. "You shouldn't say things like that while I'm driving."

"On the contrary, that's the best time to say something like that. You have to keep your hands on the wheel and your eyes on the road. I can say anything to you, and, unless you pull over, all you can do is listen."

Jared turned off the music. "Let's get something straight, Alexandra. I've wanted to make love to you since you walked onto my back lawn three months ago, because you are a dangerously sexy woman. And men are drawn to women who have it going on. But in the past few months, I've come to appreciate a lot more about you, and I know that no matter when we make love for the first time, it'll be worth the wait."

When Alex spoke, she sounded like she was on the verge of tears. "I have a confession to make."

"I'm pulling over." Jared looked for a suitable place. When he saw a well-lit park, he slowed and turned into it. He parked and let the car idle.

After unfastening his seatbelt he reached over and undid hers. He pulled Alex into his arms. She clung to him. "What's wrong, baby?" he asked softly. "Why're you upset?"

Alex sniffled. "Tonight, when your mom was telling me about that time the basketball bounced off your head, and you begged her not to tell me, it suddenly occurred to me that I love you. Isn't that ridiculous? That I should come to that realization at that moment? Not during a romantic moment, but when we're surrounded by other people? I looked over at you and my heart did this little flip-flop thing and I just *knew*."

She raised her head to look him in the eyes. Jared was smiling at her. "I beat you to the punch."

"What do you mean?"

"I knew that I loved you a good half hour before you knew you loved me. It hit me when we were outside of the library. That's why I didn't enter with you and Mom. I was floored by it. I had to regain my equilibrium. I was thinking that you and Mom have a lot in common, and I was glad because I knew that I loved you, and more than anything I wanted you to get along since you're the two most important women in my life."

Alex remembered his odd behavior. "That's what you were talking about when you said you'd been lost? You gave me such a strange look!"

"I was stunned," Jared said. "How else is a self-proclaimed player supposed to react when he's hit right between the eyes by love?"

Alex sniffed some more, and her cheeks were moist with tears. "You don't think it's too soon? What if it's lust we're feeling?"

"I've never been in love before, Alex. I think I can tell the difference between love and lust. You, on the other hand, might want to take some time to think about what you really feel for me because I'm telling you now: If you make love to me and then decide you don't love me, I'm going to be pissed!"

Alex laughed through her tears. "Would you really?"

"Highly. I don't want to be used by you. I have my reputation to think of. A player getting played by a little church girl? I'm not having it!"

Alex could hear the humor in his voice, but deep down she knew he was serious. Jared Kyles had his heart to think of. He had probably broken a lot of hearts in his day, but he would be devastated if the tables were turned. She could understand that.

She sighed in his embrace. Jared held her more closely. They stayed that way for a few minutes, then Alex raised her mouth to his and kissed him. Jared moved over, so that he was no longer sitting under the steering wheel and gently pulled her onto his lap. She straddled him. They were now crotch to crotch.

His big hands grabbed hold of her hips and pressed her firmly to his erect penis. Alex moaned with pleasure. She raised her head to look up at him. "Do you have any condoms?"

"Not on me, no," was his regretful response. He pulled her down for another quick kiss, and then set her on the seat next to him while he slid back under the wheel. "We're not going to make love in a car." He gave her a pleading look. "Work with me here. Behave yourself. We've got nearly fifty miles to go before we'll be home. Until then, don't talk about making love to me. It turns me on."

"We could spend the night in a hotel."

"Alexandra!" His tone didn't brook any disobedience.

Alex laughed and fastened her seatbelt. "Okay, I'll behave."

Once they were on the road again, Jared said, "What would Mother Maybelle think if she knew I took you to a hotel?"

"She'd probably pull a shotgun on you and make you marry me."

Jared laughed. "You know, she probably would. And my Mom would be there encouraging her."

"Okay," Alex said as she sat back on the seat. "What's a safe topic for discussion?"

"You can tell me about your most embarrassing high school moment, since Mom has already blabbed about mine."

"All right," Alex said. "I told you I was a cheerleader in the eleventh grade? I had no time for extracurricular activities my senior year. Anyway, we used to wear these little sweaters that bared the midriff. On homecoming night, when we were cheering the football team on, my bra strap broke, and the next time I went for a midair split and raised my pompoms high, the doggone sweater rode up and one of my breasts was exposed. Unfortunately, the yearbook photographer was there and snapped a picture of me at that very instant."

"They couldn't put that in the yearbook," Jared pointed out, trying not to laugh.

"No, but the little creep made sure the picture got passed around to practically every kid in the school!"

Eight

It was an overcast night, and the stars were hidden. A slightly cool breeze danced on the muggy air. The breeze, coupled with the smell of ozone in the air, told Alex that it would probably rain before dawn. She ran up the steps to the front door with Jared close behind. Her hand trembled as she slipped the key into the lock. Jared noticed and placed his hand over hers. "If you'd rather wait until next weekend, I'll understand. I want time to make everything perfect for you, baby." He bent his head, kissed the side of her neck, and inhaled her essence. "I want to take you someplace special where we won't be disturbed. I want to wine you, and dine you, and then take you back to our suite and slowly undress you."

Alex closed her eyes and sighed. The sound of Jared's husky voice in her ear and the feel of his warm mouth on her skin sent her libido spiraling out of control.

She turned to meet his eyes. "You must have a will of steel, Jared Kyles, because I want you *tonight*. What if I take my fill of you now? By next week, I'll be ready for another helping. Does that work for you?"

Jared pulled her close to him, just to show her how mistaken she was. "You're wrong, I'm only human. I'm trying to be a gentleman."

Feeling his aroused state, Alex smiled and kissed his chin. "Don't try so hard. At any rate, you *are* a gentleman. We've had countless meals and gone to church together. We've done all the things couples do when they're dating, and every night you walked me to my door and kissed me good-bye. We're going to have a problem if you're going to insist on treating me with kid gloves. This is your first time dating a woman who goes to church on a regular basis, and maybe that's throwing you off. But, like I've already told you, I can take care of myself. So give me the unadulterated Jared Kyles, or get to stepping!"

"What?!" Jared's lips curled in a sensual grin. Was he actually being called on the mat by this girl who was still wet behind the ears when it came to sexual matters? *Two lovers*. That's all she'd had in twenty-seven years. Okay, what if she were sexually active by the time she was twenty-one? That meant in six years, she'd gone to bed with two men. She hadn't really been made love to! He'd have to show her how it was done.

He grabbed her and kissed her with such skill and intensity that Alex's legs were weak when he let her come up for air. She searched his eyes. They were determined and held a dangerous aspect in them that made her tremble. He kissed her again, laving her tongue with his, inciting wanton thoughts that crowded her mind and left little room for logic.

She still hadn't unlocked the door.

She made an attempt to do so again, but ended up dropping the keys onto the porch.

Jared bent and picked them up. His hands were steady as he put the key in the lock and turned it. He pushed the door open with one splayed hand, and gently pushed her inside. Closing the door, he maneuvered her against it and made her raise her arms so he could pull her shirt over her head. Alex wore a lacy beige bra underneath. Her firm, full breasts heaved. Jared stared. He'd never seen her without a shirt before. Damn, if he didn't feel like a kid seeing his first girly magazine, wholly fascinated by the female form. He snapped out of it and pulled her against his chest so that he could reach behind her and unhook the bra. He wondered if she would try to cover herself once he removed the offending article of clothing. She didn't.

Her breasts were perfect as far as he was concerned. Naturally heavy with a gentle dip. They were honey-brown, with milk chocolate areolas and dark chocolate nipples. His mouth watered.

"You're staring," Alex said softly as she moved closer to him and allowed him to put his arms around her.

His callused hands caressed her back. "I know. I lost my mind for a minute there. You're beautiful, Alexandra."

"I'm glad you think so. You've got a whole other half to see."

She placed his hand on her hip to encourage him to explore further.

Jared bent his head and trailed kisses from her clavicle to the space between her breasts. Her warm skin smelled like fresh melons. He guessed it was the lotion she'd rubbed on after her bath. Alex flinched when his mouth found one of her nipples, and his lips teased it before he started licking it with idolatrous abandon. The other one got the same treatment. Alex's toes curled, and she kicked off her shoes.

Jared got on one knee and undid the button on her slacks. Carefully, he rolled the zipper down until he could slip the slacks off her hips. Alex stepped out of them, wearing only a pair of bikini briefs whose waistband didn't reach her belly button. Jared kissed her stomach and rose. All the while, he devoured her with his eyes.

He coaxed his athletic shoes off with a little foot action, then said, "Your turn."

Alex smiled at the invitation to undress him. "Mmm," she said as she pressed her chest against his. Jared grabbed her bottom with both hands. She slowly unbuttoned his denim shirt and ran her hand over his hairy chest. "Are you hairy everywhere?"

"You're in charge. Find out for yourself."

Alex pulled his shirt down and Jared shrugged it off. She ran her hands over his rock-hard arm and chest muscles. The hair on his chest was soft and curly. She ran her fingers through it. Smiling indulgently, she said, "You're a gorgeous man, Jared Kyles." Jared kissed her for that, and Alex returned it with such fervor that it was a while before it ended. Then Alex reached languidly for the waistband of his jeans.

She took great care as she lowered the zipper. Jared lent her a hand by stepping out of his pants. He stood before her in a pair of gray briefs. She gulped inaudibly at the size of the bulge in them. When she raised her eyes to his, he gave her a knowing smile. "I'm a big man in more ways than one. Don't worry, I'll be gentle with you, my little church girl." He bent and planted a chaste kiss on her forehead.

Alex gave him a saucy smile. "I'm not worried, sweetie. I know I'm woman enough for you."

Jared put her hand on his manhood just to prove her wrong. Big mistake. He wanted her so intensely that her touch nearly made him climax prematurely.

Noticing his enhanced stiffness and shortness of breath, Alex removed her hand.

"I think we've had enough foreplay, don't you?" she asked with a smug smile.

She took one of his big hands in hers and began leading him to her bedroom.

When they walked past the den, where the stereo system was, Alex suggested, "Why don't you put on a CD while I get things ready in the bedroom?"

Jared didn't know what she needed to get ready in the bedroom, but at this stage of seduction you didn't question a woman, you simply gave in to her. He got an eyeful of her shapely bottom as she turned the corner heading into the hallway, then went over to peruse her CD collection.

He was so eager to join her that he decided he'd put on the first CD his hand touched, but when he looked at the cover it was a rap CD. He might be old-fashioned, but he certainly didn't think rap was the appropriate music to set a romantic mood. One mention of the word so many rappers insisted on calling females, and Alex would take issue.

Several CDs later, his hand fell on Brian McKnight's latest recording. Now that was a CD to make love to your lady to. He smiled when he put it in the CD player. Then he danced down the hallway, looking like a body-builder auditioning for a spot in *The Full Monty*. Being in love made you do silly things.

In the bedroom, Alex was in her closet tossing through sexy lingerie. At last she found it: a baby-doll negligee whose hem fell just below her crotch. It was red, had long sleeves with frills around the cuffs and was completely see-through. A red silk thong went with it.

She quickly changed from her bikini underwear to the thong and put on the top. Prior to the dinner party, she'd luxuriated in a bath so she didn't need to freshen up, or did she? She sniffed under her arms and stopped short of sniffing her bikini panties. Oh, the things you went through when you were about to make love. She'd forgotten how stressful it could be. A quick freshening up couldn't hurt. She ran into the adjacent bathroom.

Jared danced into the bedroom. He'd seen it once when Alex had given him a tour of the house. He was glad she didn't have one of those ultra-feminine beds that looked like something out of a French bordello, adorned with a flowery bedspread and thousands of frilly pillows. Alex's queen-size brass bed looked firm and comfortable. Maybe it was a tad opulent, he allowed, what with the hot pink and lime green bedding.

"What kept you?"

Alex stood framed in the doorway. Jared went mute, because he definitely couldn't find his voice at the moment. That negligee was obscene! It was worse than being naked. She was a feast for the eyes. Voluptuous breasts, small waist, curvy hips. What was that V-shaped thing barely covering her sex? He didn't know and didn't care. Her long legs, and what lay between them, called to him.

Alex walked slowly toward him. She reached back and pulled her long, wavy hair from beneath the negligee top and shook it out with a toss of her head. Jared's heart beat triple-time as he watched her innocent actions. She didn't know that she was setting off a riot of reactions in his body.

He had to remind himself to breathe.

Alex felt tender. It seemed as if her nerve endings were on alert. Her nipples were erect, and her female center was in the throes of a meltdown whose ignition had been fired when Jared had begun undressing her in the foyer. Now it was just a matter of control. Would she be able to delay the climax that she felt was so close to the surface that all Jared had to do was touch her or say something provocative to set it off? Climaxing at his touch would definitely label her as the inexperienced lover that she was.

Oh, girl, quit psychoanalyzing and go get your man!

"I wanted to pick just the right music." Jared answered her question after finding that if he spoke, something still came out. He went and pulled her into his arms.

"Brian," Alex said approvingly. The music could be heard in every room of the house.

They slow-danced with their arms wrapped around each other, swaying to the music and to the intoxicating feel of their bodies in sync. Jared had known that she would fit wonderfully in his arms. If this was a dream, he didn't want to wake up anytime soon.

They danced over to the bed, and when Alex backed into it, she sat down. Jared bent and kissed her ripe lips and, as Alex lay back, he got on top of her, deepening the kiss. Alex scooted back on the bed until her entire body was on it, and Jared's entire body was atop hers. He made sure his full weight wasn't on her by holding himself up with his strong arms. Alex quivered with anticipation. Her hands didn't know where they wanted to settle: on the hard muscles in the backs of his arms, or his back, or his taut butt? He had all of her senses engaged. She loved the taste of his mouth, the feel of his breath on her skin, and the crazy way he had of nuzzling her neck with his nose, as if he were trying to save her unique smell in his memory bank.

Licking the side of her neck, Jared said, "Alex, please tell me you have condoms somewhere in this bedroom."

"Nightstand drawer," Alex said breathlessly. "I bought them last week, just in case."

"Good girl," Jared said, and lowered his head to tongue her nipples. Alex closed her eyes and sighed with obvious pleasure. Jared circled her areolas with his tongue, suckled, and gently bit down on her nipples. Alex squirmed impatiently, wanting to extend the magnificent state of arousal that was building within her, but anxious to have him inside of her, too.

Jared was enjoying watching her wiggle under him. She would moisten her kiss-plumped lips every now and then, and the movement of her tongue over her lips made his manhood pulse. This wasn't like him. He was a seasoned lover who had mastered control in the bedroom. He wasn't some young pup who would get so excited by the sight of a woman's naked body that he'd ejaculate before he even entered her.

Was he some kind of a satyr? A man who got off by seducing innocents? Could that be the reason why he was so turned on by Alex? She was a woman who did not give herself to a man easily, and, in fact, hadn't had a lover in over two years. Was the prospect of being the one to get into her panties so enticing to him that he'd deluded himself into believing he loved her? He wouldn't be the first man to covet a conquest like her.

She ran her hand on the inside of his briefs, grabbing his bare behind. "Jared," she said softly. He looked down into her golden brown eyes. They were smoky with desire. She had spread her legs and his groin was pressed against her moist mound.

He had to get up and get the condom now, before he took her unsheathed.

Pushing up on his arms, he said, "Hold on, baby."

Alex raised up on her elbows to watch him. After rummaging in the nightstand drawer for only a few seconds, he found the unopened box of latex condoms and wasted no time getting one out and rolling it onto his engorged penis. Alex got up so that Jared could more easily remove her thong. Jared did so gently, mindful of where the back strip was positioned. Alex took one leg out of it, then the other.

Jared looked deeply into her eyes. "No regrets in the morning, church girl?"

"None." She clasped her hands together behind his neck and drew him down for a slow, wet kiss. Jared moaned. He'd never been kissed like this before. Most women waited to be kissed, as if the man had to always initiate it. Alex was more aggressive. She took what she wanted. He liked that in her.

She fell backward onto the bed, Jared on top of her. Again, she scooted back and he followed her lead, walking on his knees, his heavy member on her flat belly.

The head of his penis found the opening in her feminine center. He'd meant to go slowly, penetrating in degrees, but when she raised her hips his hard shaft drove all the way home. She was warm, slick, and tight. He cried out. She sighed alluringly. Jared knew then that she'd been right, she *was* woman enough for him. They were a perfect fit. Their rhythm increased. He grew harder. Alex met each thrust with aplomb. There was something to be said for hard work in the Georgia sun. It had fine-tuned her muscles, made her impervious to strenuous labor, and this was sweetly strenuous labor. Jared's muscles rippled with every movement. She placed her hands on his butt, spread her legs wider, and totally surrendered.

After several minutes, she had to admit that Jared's stamina matched her own. It was after this that the first orgasm claimed her. She quivered inside. Jared felt her come and slowed his rhythm because he didn't want to climax yet. He wanted to make love to her all night long. He bent and kissed her. She breathed shallowly into his mouth. A thin layer of perspiration moistened her forehead. She clung to him, her arms and legs wrapped around him. He stopped thrusting and waited until he felt her muscles relax.

At last, she let out a little sigh and opened her eyes to meet his steady gaze.

"I think you enjoyed that," he teased.

She smiled slowly. "Very much so. Got anymore?"

"My, my, you're the greedy one."

"Not greedy, just hungry for you. I've wanted you since we met, too. But a woman has to wait a certain amount of time before giving in to her desires."

"Especially a church girl like you."

Alex laughed. "Will you stop calling me that? You make me feel like I'm being a bad girl with you or something!"

"Aren't you being a bad girl?"

"Only if you're being a bad boy."

"I'm trying my best," he told her with a wicked grin.

Alex laughed again. He was still inside of her and he was still hard. She thrust upward and instantly felt his penis throb. She tightened her vaginal muscles around it and licked her lips with an excruciatingly slow, sensual premeditation. Jared couldn't take his eyes off her. "How can this be bad, when it feels so good?" she asked, her voice breathless and rife with passion. Jared came. She smiled with satisfaction.

~

Alex was awakened by the sound of rain against the windowpane. She and Jared were spooning in bed. After their first session of lovemaking, they had gotten up, showered, and made love again.

Jared slept with his arm thrown across her hip, and his lower half flush with hers.

Alex lay there, content, remembering the delicious sensations of the past few hours. She was so glad that she and Jared had realized that although on the surface they didn't appear to be suited for each other, deep down they were.

Jared opened his eyes. Alex's back was to him, but he assumed by the sound of her breathing that she was awake. "Marry me, Alexandra."

Alex turned around in bed to face him. "What?" she asked, astonished.

"You know," he said. "A wedding in a church. You and I would go on a honeymoon and then spend the rest of our lives together. That's a marriage. It's quite common and generally thought of as a very positive thing."

"But three months ago you were determined to never marry."

"Don't hold that against me. I was an idiot."

Alex kissed his chin. "You were not an idiot. Don't get upset with me, but I'm going to have to decline."

"What?" Jared cried, clearly hurt and confused by her stance.

"Let me finish," Alex implored. "I just think that you shouldn't ask something that important after making love for the first time. I don't know about you, but I'm high right now. Ask me again when you've had time to think about what you're saying."

"You're the only woman I've ever asked to marry me, and you're turning me down?" Jared asked, incredulous. He sat up in bed and looked back at her. The lamp on the nightstand on his side of the bed was turned low so he could see her beautiful face clearly. He could tell she was sincerely regretful about her decision to say no to his proposal. That knowledge didn't salve his male ego, though. She was supposed to say yes, no matter when the proposal came. Even though, logically, he knew he should not be hurt by her rejection, he was.

Being this in love with someone was new to him. He'd let down his guard, allowed his usually hidden emotions to come to the surface, and risked getting skewered by her. Now here it was, the big hurt. This was why he'd been a player for so many years. Players didn't get their feelings stomped on.

He got up and began gathering his clothing, a trail that led him to the living room. Alex slid off the bed and grabbed her robe, which she'd put on after her shower. Getting into it and tying the sash as she followed him to the living room, she said, "Jared, there's nothing to get upset about. Come on, I'm not rejecting you outright. I'm only asking you to give it some thought, that's all."

Jared rounded on her, his jaws clenched in anger. "Why don't you try a little honesty? You said you're not holding the fact that I was dead set against marriage before I met you against me, but, in fact, you are! You're afraid to say yes because you don't think I can be faithful to you. Tell the truth and shame the devil!"

Oh, Lord, where had that saying come from? Frowning, Jared realized that he'd heard his mother say those exact words to her father when they were arguing about his coming in late after a night of carousing.

He experienced a moment of clarity: Maybe he *hadn't* gotten over his conviction that he was just like his father. Alex was probably right to refuse him.

"You're wrong!" Alex exclaimed hotly. "I do believe in you."

They were in the living room, and Jared was picking up his jeans from the floor. He'd put on his underwear in the bedroom, and now he pulled on his jeans and retrieved his denim shirt. He met Alex's eyes from across the room. Tears sat in her eyes, and he knew he was probably going to cause her even more heartache with his next words, but he had to say them. "Maybe the problem is I don't believe in myself."

He stepped into his shoes and bent to tie the laces. Straightening, he smiled ruefully. "You deserve better than I have to give you."

"I'm not going to beg you to stay," Alex said quietly. "You're angry now, and maybe you need to be alone. But listen to me, Jared. You are not your father. You're upset because I didn't jump at your proposal, and that's understandable. I don't get how you came to the conclusion that I don't have faith in you. I love you. I have the utmost faith in you and I'm not giving up on us. And I ask *you* not to give up on us, either."

Jared looked back at her after he opened the door to leave. "Good-bye, Alexandra."

Alex fought the urge to run to him, fling herself into his arms, and beg him to stay. That wouldn't accomplish anything except postpone his leaving. He had to dispel his own demons. "Good night," she said. Not good-bye.

Nine

Jared's phone rang at ten the next morning. He rolled over in bed and grabbed the receiver. It seemed as if the moment he'd gotten to sleep, the phone had rung. "Hello!" he said gruffly.

"You break my Saturday routine of staying in bed by making me feel guilty because I don't get enough exercise, and I catch you snoozing when you should be here on the basketball court? I don't think so, buddy. If I have to be here, so do you!"

Fletcher. Jared had forgotten their standing appointment to play one-on-one. Fletcher and Carena lived a thirty-minute drive away. Jared didn't think he was up to it this morning. "I'm sorry, Fletch, but I had a bad night."

"What kind of bad night?" Fletcher asked. Jared could hear traffic sounds in the background, so he knew Fletcher was probably standing on the basketball court in his neighborhood park. The park was extremely busy on Saturdays. It was where the area teens gathered to play some hoops, meet the opposite sex, and shoot the breeze.

"None of your business," Jared said. "I don't want you going back and telling Carena. If you tell her, she'll tell Mom, and the next thing you know, Mom will be on my doorstep calling me all kinds of fools."

"This sounds bad," Fletcher said, concerned. "Is it about you and Alexandra?"

Jared sat up in bed and swung his long legs over the side. He obviously wasn't going to get rid of Fletcher easily. "Listen to me, Fletch. If you tell Carena, I'll never confide in you again."

"All right, all right," Fletcher agreed. "I won't talk, not even if she puts lit matches under my toenails."

Jared sighed tiredly. "I asked Alexandra to marry me, and she turned me down."

"Man!" cried Fletcher. "I have to say I'm surprised. I know she loves you. Carena and I have been talking about nothing else for the past month, how well you and Alexandra have been getting along. And after last night, we just knew you two were in love."

"We are," Jared said. "I mean we *were*. I don't know what I mean! Apparently, she doesn't think I'm marriage material."

"What makes you think that?"

Jared explained his theory about his earlier gaffe. He thought that if he'd never told Alex that he was a confirmed bachelor, she wouldn't have had that image of him burned in her memory, and then, when he'd asked her to marry him, she would have accepted. But because of his past, she'd been reluctant.

Fletcher was silent for a couple of minutes after listening to Jared's woes. "Tell me something," he said suddenly. "Where did you propose?"

This time it was Jared who fell quiet on his end. "We were in bed," he finally admitted. "We made love for the first time last night."

Fletcher laughed uproariously.

Jared was appalled by his best friend's lack of sympathy. "I knew I shouldn't have told you anything."

Fletcher got control of himself and said, "What do I have to do, take you by the hand and lead you through this relationship? I tricked you into meeting her, and my sneakiness paid off. Now you've gone and ruined it!"

"I don't get you, man," Jared said.

"Of course you don't. You've been single too long. But there is one thing a married man knows that a single man has yet to learn: Women might say they want to be swept off their feet by some stud, but they really prefer security.

What you did last night did not make Alexandra feel secure. You proposed to her after making love. Sex, Jared. Now, you know men aren't thinking straight after gettin' some. What was she supposed to do, accept and then risk you taking it back the next day after you'd sobered up?"

"That's exactly what *she* said!"

"But did you listen to her? Or did you go off and lick your wounds?"

"I left, saying something stupid like she's better off without me."

"She probably is," Fletcher said. "But are you better of without her?"

"You sure know how to kick a brother when he's down," Jared told him, but he managed a short laugh. "I did everything wrong last night, huh?"

"Well, not everything," Fletcher said. "Hopefully the sex was good."

"The best ever," Jared said without hesitation. Now they were two buds talking about their favorite subject: women. He felt calmer. He knew what he had to do. The problem was, would Alex give him a chance to apologize?

"I know I have to apologize," he said. "But how? She told me that she loved me before I left last night and asked me not to give up on us. But I know I hurt her. How do I make it up to her?"

"That's simple," Fletcher said. "You've got to propose to her in such a way that she would never doubt your sincerity. And Jared, buy her a really nice ring! You can afford it."

Jared laughed. "Of course I'm going to get her a nice ring. What do you think I am, a cheapskate?"

"No, just an idiot in love," Fletcher joked. "Talk to you later. I can't wait to tell Carena about this."

"Fletcher!"

"Just kidding."

After Jared hung up, he rose and went to shower. He had a busy day ahead of him, what with trying to come up with the appropriate ring for Alex and dreaming up an idea of how to propose to her properly.

~

"Alex, what are you doing here?" Mother Maybelle asked when she opened her door to find Alex on the other side. Maybelle was dressed casually in a royal blue silk caftan and a pair of white slacks. Her feet were bare, and she'd apparently just had a pedicure because her nails were neatly trimmed and had soft pink polish on them. Alex had noticed, a long time ago, that Mother Maybelle always took excellent care of her person, making certain that all the feminine touches were given attention.

It was Saturday night, and Mother Maybelle's girls' poker night was in full swing. Before Alex had started dating Jared, she'd been a semi-regular. Mother Maybelle reminded them that nowhere in the Bible was drinking forbidden, only drunkenness. After all, Jesus' first miracle had been turning water into wine. She joked that their gathering was simply an activity to keep bored women out of trouble on a Saturday night. Of course, they should be prepared to lose a few bucks (they played for pennies), and partake of her famous frozen daiquiris. Virgin daiquiris if they were driving.

Alex stepped inside, talking as she did so. "I apologize for interrupting your game, Mother Maybelle, but I phoned Gayle's and Ruben told me she was over here. I thought to myself, good, because there's no one better to offer me advice on a man than Mother Maybelle."

"Sho' you right!" said Mother Maybelle with a gorgeous smile. She took Alex's arm and together they walked back to the game room in her spacious home. The game room had a big-screen TV, a pool table, a bar complete with a semicircular counter behind which were bottles with all the potent potables needed to make any drink you could think of, and a genuine poker table. Not a folding card table.

Three women sat around the table nursing drinks and talking all at once, sounding like a room full of women instead of just three. There were Gayle and Sarah Jackson, Ruben's mother and Mother Maybelle's best friend, and

Cheryl Avery, the reverend's wife, who was presently winning. They ranged in age from twenty-something to over seventy.

"We've got a fifth!" Mother Maybelle announced as she and Alex entered the room. Everyone called hello to Alex. Then, of course, Gayle had to say, "Why aren't you out somewhere with Jared like any respectable newly-in-loves would be?"

Alex sat down on the empty chair at the table. Mother Maybelle put both hands on her shoulders comfortingly. "Take your time, sugar. Mother Maybelle's got banana and strawberry daiquiris tonight. Which do you prefer? And do you want leaded or unleaded?"

Alex smiled back at her. "Banana, please. Unleaded." Which meant no rum.

Mother Maybelle hurried over to the bar, moving with the alacrity of a woman half her age. Alex looked around the table. "Jared and I had our first big argument last night, and I need reassurance that I made the right decision when I did what I did."

Mother Maybelle was behind the bar pouring the already prepared banana daiquiri mixture into a large round glass with a long stem on it. "Honey, you're getting ahead of yourself. Start from the beginning."

Alex paused a moment. She definitely wasn't going to tell them that she and Jared had made love last night, but she could give them the gist of what went on without revealing too much. "We went to Jared's mother's birthday dinner last night. After we got back, we, uhm, spent some time at my place together, and during the course of the evening, he asked me to marry him."

Mother Maybelle was crossing the room with Alex's daiquiri balanced on a tray. She nearly tripped on her own feet when she heard Alex's statement. She arrived at the table without spilling the drink and set it before Alex. Everyone else was in the midst of expressing delight at the news. But Mother Maybelle said, "There must be trouble in paradise if you're here tonight instead of with him. You didn't accept his proposal, did you, Alexandra?" She looked Alex straight in the eyes. "That's it, isn't it?"

Alex lowered her gaze. "Yes, ma'am."

The other ladies exchanged curious glances.

"She probably had a perfectly good reason not to," said Sarah Jackson, frowning. She was a tall, stout woman with dark brown skin, like her son's, a head full of wavy silver hair that she wore in a bun, and the most lovely pair of brown eyes. "Didn't you, sweetheart?"

"I don't know," Alex said with a sob. "I think I did, but now I'm not so sure."

Gayle got up and hugged Alex. "Don't hold back, Alex. Nothing you say will leave this room!" She peered around the table. Mother Maybelle had pulled up an extra chair, and now she nodded her agreement. "That's right. Word, ladies?"

"You've got my word," Sarah said.

"Mine, too," Cheryl put in. "Not even the Reverend will get it out of me." Everyone laughed at that.

"Well," Alex began. "As most young people do, we, uhm, got closer last night."

"You made love," said Mother Maybelle.

"Did the horizontal mambo," Sarah said, offering elucidation where none was needed.

"Expressed your love for one another," Cheryl said, staying within spiritual parameters.

"You got *down?*" Gayle said, excited for her.

"Yes, to all of the above," Alex said with a smile. She should have known these ladies wouldn't be shocked by her revelation. Collectively they'd had much more experience with men than she had.

"Why in heaven's name did you turn him down?" Mother Maybelle asked. "If you two are that close, the next logical step is marriage."

"I would have said yes," Alex said. "I wanted to say yes, but I didn't think he was serious. But when I told him I thought he should wait and propose at another time, not right after we'd made love, he got upset and left."

"You wounded his pride," Sarah said. "Men wear their pride like a bantam rooster, all puffed up. But it's so easily deflated."

"Is there something else you're not telling us?" Cheryl astutely deduced. "It seems to me that most women would have said yes, even after making love. Some men let down their guard at that particular moment and it's the perfect time to pounce!"

"Cheryl!" cried Mother Maybelle. "I didn't know you had a mercenary bone in your body."

"I was a single female once," Cheryl joked.

"You're right, Cheryl," Alex conceded. "Early in the relationship Jared admitted to me that he thought he'd taken after his father where women were concerned. His father was a ladies' man."

"Ran around?" asked Sarah.

"Yes, ma'am," Alex answered. "Anyway, Jared seemed to believe that he couldn't be faithful to one woman either, so he put it out there right from the start. Wanted me to be forewarned!"

"I see what you're saying," said Gayle. "You turned him down because you wanted him to be really sure of what he was asking you, and not under the influence of some good lovin'."

"Exactly!" Alex said. "I've known too many brides who were left at the altar by grooms who suddenly got cold feet. But when I tried to explain my position, he accused me of not having faith in him."

"Which you didn't!" Mother Maybelle accused her.

Alex stared at Mother Maybelle. "I didn't?"

"You just said that early in the relationship he'd told you he'd never been faithful to one woman. You had the same expectations of him, child. That's why you hesitated."

"Oh, my God," Alex said softly, the truth hitting her full force.

"As someone who's been married five times, I have to tell you, the worst thing a woman can do is not have faith in her man. It makes him doubt himself. I've been unlucky in love. I lost every last one of my husbands to death,

God rest their souls. I miss each and every one of them. Now you, Alex, are just getting started. That's why I'm encouraging you to rethink what you did and give love a fighting chance. If you love him, you should give him the benefit of the doubt. Next time you see *him*, ask him to marry *you!*"

"Amen!" Gayle said happily as she hugged Alex again. When they parted, she said, "Honey, get used to arguing. Ruben and I do it all the time. Making up afterwards is sweet though, very sweet."

"Now those are some precious memories," Mother Maybelle said with a wistful smile. "Making up after an argument. Some of the best loving you'll ever get."

"Who're you tryin' to fool?" Sarah asked, looking at Mother Maybelle with a smirk. "Everybody knows about your gentleman caller. Precious memories, indeed. I'd wager you're still in the making-memories mode."

"Girl, hush!" said Mother Maybelle, laughing good-naturedly.

~

The church is alive with energy this morning. Alex felt it when she stepped foot in the vestibule. She needed the energy today. She needed all the strength she could get, because after the service she was going over to Jared's house to propose to him. For now, though, she needed to be lifted by the spirit.

Looking around, she spotted Gayle and Ruben with the kids in the middle section. Gayle waved her over. She'd saved her a seat. As she got closer, she noticed a tall man sitting next to Ruben on the outside. His back was turned, but there was no mistaking his carriage. It was Jared.

Her legs went weak. She wasn't prepared to see him so soon. Why was he here? *Selfish*, she chided herself. *He has the right to come to church like anyone else.*

When she began moving down the row toward them, she saw Ruben get up and vacate the seat next to Jared's. It was clearly a conspiracy. Had he and Jared gotten together and planned this?

She kept moving. What else was she going to do, bring attention to herself by turning and running in the other direction? She was resigned to sitting next to Jared during the service. A little embarrassment never killed anybody.

"Good morning," she said to everyone when she finally arrived and sat down.

"Good morning," said Gayle cheerfully.

"Mornin', boss lady," Ruben said. "Good to see you didn't actually work yourself to death like I thought you were tryin' to do yesterday."

Alex had still been upset about how things had ended between her and Jared Friday night and had tried to work off her frustrations. All she'd gotten for her efforts were sore muscles.

When Alex turned her head to gaze at Jared, he smiled at her and said, in barely a whisper, "Good morning, Alexandra." His intonation was really saying, "I love you."

She stared at him as if she'd never seen his unique juxtaposition of dark skin, nappy-wavy hair, honey-brown eyes, and sensually contoured lips before. Nor how he filled out his Sunday-go-to-meeting suit. Or how *big* his hands were. "Good morning," she said, her voice cracking. She cleared her throat.

For his part, Jared's heart had not stopped hammering since he'd laid eyes on her. He willed himself to calm down, but it wasn't easy. The next few minutes had to go smoothly. He reached into his inside coat pocket and retrieved a small envelope. He handed it to her. "This is for you. Please read it, now."

Alex accepted the envelope, opened it, reached in and pulled out the vellum card.

On it was written in Jared's careful cursive, "First Corinthians 7:9. 'But if they do not have self-control, let them marry, for it is better to marry than to be inflamed with passion.'"

Alex's pulse raced. It had suddenly gotten very warm in there. She raised her gaze to his. Tears gathered in her eyes and spilled over onto her cheeks.

"Where you're concerned," Jared whispered. "I have no self-control. I love you with all my heart, Alexandra Cartwright. And if you let me, I'll spend the rest of my life proving it. Will you marry me?"

He reached for her hand. Alex gave it to him. He slipped a beautiful five-carat white-diamond solitaire onto her finger.

Alex hadn't taken her eyes off of him. "I love you, too, Jared. And my faith in you will forever be as strong as my love for you. Yes, I *will* marry you!"

They shared a chaste kiss.

Gayle had been listening closely to their conversation, and when she heard Alex say "Yes," she got up and signaled Cheryl in the front of the church, who, in turn, signaled the choir director, who then rose and began leading the choir in an energetic rendition of "Oh, Happy Day!"

For it was, indeed, a happy day.

Love and Happiness

Kim Louise

Dedication

For my grandmother, Goldie Mae Bratton Downing, who took me to church every Sunday.

Acknowledgments

I thank God for everything I have been given. Through ups and downs, my life has been a miracle. I thank Salem Baptist Church in Omaha for their warm welcome during my visit. Lisa Jackson, thank you for your continued friendship and for setting the example of Christian womanhood. Bless you and your family. Maurice Gray, thank you for being a writer-friend for all these years—we knew each other when.

Thank you, Sister Lasley—you did it again!

One

The woman standing in Renata Connor's office looked like she'd just walked straight out of the Amen Corner. Rich, camel-colored suit—matched perfectly with hat, earrings, gloves, and shoes—she stood flagpole straight. She held a Bible in her right hand and had eyes that looked straight down into Renata's soul. The only thing that kept Renata from shouting, "Glory be to God!" was the pound cake in the woman's left hand that smelled freshly baked and made her mouth water.

"May I help you?" Renata asked, recognizing more than the woman's countenance.

"I hope you can help me eat this cake," the woman said, setting the delicious-looking dessert on the desk between them and taking a seat.

Renata smiled, and for the moment forgot about the past-due utility bill for her agency, Success Unlimited. "I think I can help you with that," she responded, against her better judgment. She chastised herself in her mind. She didn't know this woman from Eve. She could be a crazy cook who put cough medicine in the cake mix and had no idea where she was right now.

"I'm Mother Maybelle. I attend Red Oaks Christian Fellowship Church, and I was at the Farmer's Market yesterday."

Now it came back to her. Renata had been pouring her heart out to her assistant, Gidget, while shopping for fresh vegetables at one of the town's most popular attractions.

Renata's business was failing. She didn't know how much longer she would be able to provide "world of work" assistance to at-risk young men.

The economy was taking a toll. Just last week she'd had a meeting with one of her most ardent business supporters. But even B and B Telemarketing, one of the largest employers in Red Oaks, Georgia, couldn't contribute in the way that they had in the past.

Renata had noticed Mother Maybelle. The older woman had been searching through bushels of greens like a woman on a mission. She just stood out from the crowd. She was impeccably dressed for an afternoon of shopping for collards in an open-air market.

But soon the impressive image of the woman was overshadowed by her own concern over the dire straits of her agency. The woman must have heard Renata's tales of woe and was here trying to cheer her up.

"I remember you," Renata said. "Those greens looked awfully good."

"And they *will* be, sugar. As soon as I cook 'em!" Mother Maybelle chuckled. "If you come by the church tomorrow for our Saturday evening potluck, you can have you some."

Renata searched her brain, hoping to find an appointment. The last place she wanted to be was in anybody's church.

"Thanks for the invitation. I'll probably be trying to drum up some support for my business," she said.

Mother Maybelle sat forward, and Renata's eyes darted over to the pound cake, looking utterly delectable in the cellophane. She knew that at any moment her stomach would growl like a wild animal.

"That's why I'm here," Mother Maybelle said, breaking Renata from her hunger. "I heard you talking about your business like it had one foot in the grave. So, I came to see if I could help."

Hope rushed inside Renata as if she'd just been handed a check for a million dollars. But what could this little old lady do to help her, she wondered. *Maybe she's rich and is about to hand over a check along with her cake.*

"How?" Renata asked eagerly. "How can you help?"

"Well, not me *personally*, but my church."

Renata's hopes fell like the stock market on a really bad day. Her mind flooded with images of bake sales, fish fries, and, worst of all, prayer circles.

"Now what you lookin' so down in the mouth for? A church on a mission is one of the most powerful forces on Earth. Against that, no evil can prosper. Now, we have an outreach ministry at Red Oaks that may be able to sponsor one or two of those boys you're trying to help."

Mother Maybelle sat back in the chair and folded her arms, letting her words settle into Renata's mind. Renata liked the sound of her proposal.

"That would be wonderful," she said, knowing that if even *one* young man could be sponsored, that was one less financial drain on her dwindling budget. It might just keep the agency going for a while.

She glanced at that past-due bill, along with all the others piling up on her desk. "That's . . . that's . . . I mean . . . I don't know what to say or how to thank you."

"Well, chile, it's still up to the members of the ministry as to whether to take you on. But I don't see why they wouldn't."

Renata was celebrating early and thinking about Malcolm Goodwin. He was the next youth on her growing list of young men who needed job training. Already she was restructuring her week in her mind, hoping to meet with a representative from the church as soon as possible. She was imagining talking about her agency and conveying all the wonderful aspects of it with warmth and enthusiasm—enough enthusiasm to make any person jump at the chance to work with her organization.

Mother Maybelle strummed her arthritic fingers against a Bible that looked like it had seen decades of use. "Well, I can see the wheels are already turnin' inside that cute little head of yours."

Mother Maybelle rose, tucked her Bible under her arm, and offered her hand. Renata shook it with full appreciation.

"Someone from the outreach ministry will be by to see you. *Next week.*"

"I'll be ready, Mother Maybelle," Renata said, sounding and feeling happier than she had in days. "I'll be ready."

~

Devin McKenna sat ramrod straight in the pew. Reverend Terrance Paul Avery was delivering his usual "take all sinners" sermon, the kind no unsaved soul could resist. Devin believed that Pastor Avery probably had the highest conversion rate in the entire South. Over the years, he'd learned that if one entered the Red Oaks Christian Fellowship Church as a sinner, chances were that they wouldn't leave that way. By the time the call to a church home came at the end of the sermon, God found his way into all unholy souls and turned them to his face.

By the shouts, testimonies, and body praises of the parishioners, Pastor Avery's talk was especially moving.

Too bad Devin couldn't feel it.

He hadn't felt it, the spirit that is, for some time now. And it wasn't the fact that his wife had divorced him and joined another church. It was as if he'd lost the taste for good sermons, along with a thousand other things which involved leaving his house and being social.

Devin grunted and stood for the doxology along with several others who'd chosen that particular moment to show the youth choir just how much their rendition of "The Sweet Name of Jesus" was appreciated. He wanted to encourage them. Keep them moving in the footsteps of the Lord.

Even though he tried to make it clear with every action that he was enthusiastic about what was happening, underneath lay a different reality. Devin's life had become too monotonous. Too tedious. Too routine. Since he and Helen had divorced, he'd stopped pushing himself in new directions, stopped growing, both personally and professionally. He'd just settled for the same ol' same ol' and thought he would be comfortable with it.

He was wrong.

The change he'd planned was drastic. He looked around, settled back down on the pew, and pushed out a breath. He would miss this church, but a clean break would do him good. His writing held the only excitement in his life right now. He'd written freelance magazine articles for eight years, and he could do that anywhere—not just Red Oaks, GA.

His goal was clear. He would turn in his resignations from the outreach ministry and the entrepreneurial ministry in a few days. Devin was determined to start over. He had been a decent ministry member and steady church-goer. He anticipated that there may be some—especially Mother Maybelle—who might try to persuade him to stay. But his mind was made up. And nothing was going to change it.

⌒⁻'

Devin recognized her march and tried, unsuccessfully, to thread his way through the throng of parishioners funneling out the church doors. That march, and the determined gaze of the eyes that came with it, told him one scary thing: Mother Maybelle was on a mission. And, although he was having difficulty just keeping up with the flow of people who were headed in his same direction, Mother Maybelle was having no trouble at all.

Damn it, he thought. Then cursed himself for cursing in church. Whenever Mother Maybelle came after someone in the church like that, it meant that she had a job for them to do. And, more than likely, she believed that job was requested by God and it was his Christian duty to fulfill it.

He had to make a decision. Either he made a quick-step to the door and tried to out walk the old lady, or he let her do what she was bound and determined to do, which could delay the much needed changes in his life.

As she approached and a sense of inevitability fell upon him, he decided that Mother Maybelle wasn't changing his plans to leave the church. Just postponing them.

"Brother McKenna," she said, placing a wrinkled but surprisingly firm hand on his shoulder.

"I know," he said, feeling a smile lift his spirits. "You're on a mission from God."

Two

R enata moaned in her sleep. She knew she was sleeping. And she knew she had a meeting in less than half an hour. But being pumped up about the prospects of finding a job for Malcolm hadn't kept her from dozing.

But right now she was preoccupied with the man in her arms. She'd been fantasizing about him for weeks now. The first time he'd come to her, she'd been shocked that for once she wasn't dreaming about someone she knew. And glad that it wasn't a nightmare about her brother. No, this gentle stranger had come to her nightly, held her close, and, for the first time in many years, quieted her terrible dreams. So this afternoon, during her catnap, she'd decided that to repay the favor, she would hold *him*. And she did, right up until the time Gidget Lawless came into the multipurpose room and woke her up.

"Renata wake up *now*," she said, voice lowered. "There is a man in the conference room and he is too gorgeous to be believed."

Renata sat up and stretched, knowing that the man waiting for her in the conference room couldn't possibly be as good-looking as the man in her dreams.

"Is it Mr. McKenna from the church?"

"Yes," Gidget said, still whispering. She put on her best I'm-a-fine-black-woman stroll and walked toward the door. Before stepping out, she stuck out her chest like Lil' Kim. "Just remember . . . I saw him first," she drawled.

Renata did a quick retouch on her makeup so that she wouldn't appear as though she'd just awakened, grabbed the stack of papers off of her desk, and headed to meet the man she hoped would be Success Unlimited's new benefactor.

When she stepped into the conference room—dossier, annual report, and client list in hand—she realized that Gidget was wrong. She hadn't seen Mr. McKenna first. Renata had. In her dreams.

The papers made a swooshing sound as they fell from her hands and onto the floor.

"Let me help you," he said, with a voice that couldn't have rendered her any more shocked than if it had whipped around the room and smacked her on the butt. He knelt before her. She knelt, too. And their eyes never left each other's as they gathered the papers and then stood. Renata smiled. Then he smiled, just like in her dream.

"Sweet Jesus keep me near the cross," Renata breathed, fingering her necklace.

"I beg your pardon?"

"I just wasn't expecting . . . you."

"Oh? I have a 2:30 appointment."

She cleared her throat. "No. That's not what I meant. You just don't look like a church guy to me."

He came closer. "Really? What do church guys look like?"

Not like you, she thought. *You look like you belong on a stage in a coffee shop somewhere, reciting spoken-word poetry next to a man playing a stand-up bass.*

She didn't say that, though. She just stared at his cinnamon-brown hair, honey-brown skin, topaz-colored eyes, and said, "You know, leisure suit, leather shoes, Bible super-glued to his palm."

He shook his head and smiled. "I can tell you haven't been in a church for a while. I'm Devin," he said, extending a hand.

"I'm Renata," she offered, and wanted to add, "and you're right. It's been a long time since my behind has been in pew." Instead, she shook his hand

and enjoyed the strong, firm grip of a man who looked like he was used to getting what he wanted.

She motioned to the conference table. "Please, have a seat."

Tall, dark, and handsome began to describe him, but there was so, so much more—strong forehead, thick eyebrows, narrow sultry eyes, sharp cheekbones, and lips that whispered *kiss me for a long time*. And instead of a suit she expected, he came in jeans and a knit shirt which fit snugly enough to show off more muscles than she could count. *Where did you come from, Devin? The church of neo soul?*

His hair was a walk on the wild side. Thick two-inch twists of brown hair just this side of dreads. *What kind of church does this brother go to?* she wondered.

Her closet of a conference room was barely large enough to accommodate herself and a man of Devin McKenna's size and stature. She'd had to furnish the room on a tight budget, which meant the furniture was not only cheap, but also considerably smaller than a better-quality brand. With Devin in the room, it looked more like a conference room in a Barbie dream house than a real place to meet.

They'd only just sat down when Gidget poked her head, and her breasts, into the room. "Do you guys need anything? We've got coffee, bottled water—"

"Mr. McKenna?" Renata asked.

"I'm fine, thanks."

There was no mistaking her assistant's muffled reply of "You got that right." And the smile on Devin's face confirmed it.

"I'll take some coffee, Gidget."

Gidget rolled her eyes, and Renata knew that meant "Get it yourself, cow!" Renata was surprised when less than a minute later, Gidget returned with a steaming cup of coffee just the way she liked it: black.

"Thanks, Gidget," she said, sincerely grateful for something to hold in her hand besides her pen. She'd been tapping it ever since she sat down at the table, and she *knew* the reason wasn't her nerves.

By the time Gidget left them alone for good, Renata had already given Devin the Success Unlimited spiel. The Spiel, as she called it, was the standard speech she gave potential sponsoring organizations. It contained all the exciting facts about her agency and the success stories of the young men she'd placed. She'd been giving that speech for so long, she didn't need to think about it at all. It just came rolling off her tongue so naturally it was effortless.

She watched for Devin's impressed reaction. After The Spiel, company reps usually asked technical questions, like how soon can someone start, how long will the appointment last, and what happens if things don't work out?

Why did his silence sound so loud? It was as if he were waiting for something else, something more.

"Tell me about the outreach ministry," she said, eager to fill the silence. She felt as though she were being scrutinized. And she wanted to let him know he wasn't the only one with an analytical mind.

He sat back in the chair as if he'd been waiting for that question all day. "We've had the outreach ministry for six years now. Every year we choose a nonprofit organization to partner with and give our parishioners the opportunity to give back to the community . . . and hopefully save some souls in the process."

Renata winced. Saving souls. She hated that kind of church talk. But she supposed that her agency and the church were in the same business.

"Something wrong, Mrs. Connor? Or is it Miss?"

"It's Ms. And no, there's nothing wrong."

Oh, damn, here we go. She'd had reservations about hooking up with a church as a sponsor. The last thing she wanted was some Jesus freak, quoting scripture and telling her she had two choices: Go to church or go to hell. She hoped, for the sake of her agency—and the sake of her libido—that Devin wasn't *that* kind of Christian.

Instead of the dreaded, "Do you know my Jesus?" speech, he simply nodded and continued. "To date, Red Oaks has partnered with the Red Cross, the Salvation Army, the United Way, the Girls and Boys Clubs, the Urban League, and the NAACP."

Renata's hopes sank. They weren't going to help Malcolm. Malcolm and her youth agency were small potatoes to such a big-time church. She was out of her league.

"So, is this a satellite location?" he asked, casting a thorough glance around her humble surroundings.

"No, this is the whole enchilada."

The look of shock on his face convinced her even more. He probably felt as though he were wasting his time. And if he was wasting his time, then he was wasting hers as well. She couldn't afford to spend another minute interviewing an organization that had no intention of helping her.

"Look, brother McKenna, it's obvious that . . ."

"Actually, it's not obvious. You've told me a lot of perfunctory information about your agency. I'll bet you say that stuff to all the guys."

Suddenly, he didn't seem so Christ-like. No, the devil had definitely crept into that comment.

"Tell me about your heart," he said, leaning forward.

Renata warmed.

"Tell me about the heart of Success Unlimited. What's your agency's vision, mission, and values? What's the driving force behind what you do?"

Renata debated telling him the whole sad story of her tragic life. How close she'd been to her brother, René. She debated telling him about how brilliant René was—genius almost—and how bored with the world he'd become because most people didn't see things the way he did. She considered telling him how René found solace in the company of people who weren't what you'd call reputable. And she wondered what he would think if she told him that her brother had died senselessly after joyriding with some friends, and that since then, she'd decided to spend the rest of her life trying to prevent other African-American male youths from ending up like René.

Just when she'd decided that she could not share anything so personal and close to her heart with a total stranger, she told him every unfortunate, unhappy, tragic event of those years with her brother. And all the while, as Devin sat and listened, his eyes grew serious with concern and then liquid with sadness. She realized that she couldn't stop herself from telling this man—who looked like an angel on earth—everything that had been simmering in her gut for years.

At the same time, she didn't want to risk ruining a relationship with potential investor. So she skipped the potent parts of her past. The uneasy parts which threatened to spring from the tip of her tongue, like the fact that when her brother was taken from her, her relationship with God was broken. God had forsaken her brother, and, if God couldn't be counted on for help, then she would step in and do as much as she could with her agency. And *that* was why she created Success Unlimited. No, she kept that troubled part of her past to herself.

"So?" she asked, eager to change the subject. "I've given you the whole sordid history of my past . . . I mean, the origin of my agency. Tell me about Red Oaks Church."

"Well," he began. He hadn't thought much about how he came to be a member of the church for a long while. "Red Oaks is the largest church in the city. We have over two thousand parishioners. Reverend Terrance Paul Avery is really interested in taking Red Oaks, and the ministry of Christ, into the next millennium. So, we have several ministries." *Many of which I founded*, he thought. "Including the radio ministry, the television ministry, the DVD ministry, the Internet ministry. We also have the traditional ministries, like the women's ministry, the youth ministry, the men's ministry, the singles' ministry." Why did he look up involuntarily at her when he said that? It was as if his mind snapped to attention and fixed on the one thing in the room that would correlate to the single life . . . Renata.

"Our outreach ministry has been active for five years. We usually choose an organization and work with them for a year doing volunteer work, fundraisers, and even Bible study if they request it."

"So, this is sort of an interview for both of us."

She said that, and the way her eyes flashed made him realize that he was going to take a cold shower tonight and say a long prayer.

"Yes," he said, wondering if she'd meant that comment the way it sounded.

He told her a few more things about the church, but nothing about the agreement he had with Mother Maybelle and her mission from God. After a while, it seemed they'd both run out of questions. But it was obvious that neither wanted to end their time together. It was as if the silence was allowing them to gather their thoughts and come up with more things to talk about, or just savor the experience of being near, of sitting near someone that so quickly had become . . .

"Well, Devin, I don't want to take up all of your time. Besides, I've promised that I would call Malcolm and let him know how the meeting went."

"Malcolm?"

Renata smiled. "Yes. Malcolm Goodwin. He's seventeen and did me a big favor once. I was unlocking the front door to the agency, and some kids ran past me and took my purse with them. Before I could call the police, Malcolm—who I didn't know at the time—ran after them.

"I thought he was with them at first, but when he came back with my purse, I realized that he wasn't. He's a kid who was busted for shoplifting a few months ago and was recently placed in a foster home. I've been trying to get him a sponsor ever since."

Shoplifting, Devin thought, turning his mind back to the purpose of his visit. *Sounds like trouble.* "I should probably meet him . . . Malcolm. Can you arrange that?"

"Yes."

"How soon?"

"This evening if you like." She didn't dare tell him that Malcolm was living in The Bottoms, the poorest part of town, with the Smith family. The Smiths were an elderly couple with a big house and warm hearts. They had a reputation in the community for taking on the worst foster kids—the kids that no one else wanted or could handle. Sometimes the Smiths could help the kids; sometimes they couldn't.

Renata believed that Malcolm didn't belong there. No, the boys who stole her purse belonged there. They could use a good straightening out by the Smiths. Malcolm just needed a supportive place to live.

"My schedule is full tonight," Devin said, needing to break the spell which seemed to catch them both up like deer in headlights. "How about tomorrow?"

"Sure," Renata replied, mentally rearranging her day so that she would have time to get the two newest men in her life together. "What time?"

"How about seven? We could have dinner at Manna's if you like Italian."

Wow, a man that knew her intuitively! "I love Italian!" *Damn, Renata. Don't sound so eager.* She checked his reaction. He actually seemed pleased by her exuberance.

"What about Malcolm? Does he like Italian?"

In his position, he'd probably be glad to get any meal that he didn't have to hustle for. "I think he would appreciate going out to eat."

Devin rose. "All right. Seven it is."

She rose, too. But not to his six-foot-something height. Only to her five-five-in-heels stature.

Her heart triple-pounding in her chest made her remind herself that she was not on a date. Nothing of the kind. She was having a meeting. And now the meeting was over. Over.

She extended her hand. They exchanged handshakes and business cards. It was still up to her to sell her business and services to Devin. To entice him as a representative of Red Oaks Church and convince them to become a sponsor for Malcolm.

Their eyes locked again and they both smiled.

"See you tomorrow, Renata," he said and left the conference room.

Renata took the warmth from his handshake and touched the side of her face. *Not tomorrow, tonight.*

She cleared the conference room thinking, *See you in my dreams.*

Three

She must know I'm making a date with her. Devin McKenna sat in front of his computer reviewing his latest article on men's health. He'd gotten a lot of mileage out of that topic recently, taking the premise of a piece on stress and cholesterol he'd written over six months ago and putting a unique twist on it for four different publications. His latest was a three thousand word feature for, what else? *Men's Health* magazine.

Although he'd finished his article, he'd been sitting in front of his computer, tweaking and word-smithing it like he was an editor instead of the writer. But the truth was, he'd been pleasantly captivated by Ms. Renata Connor. Of course, she was beautiful, there was that. But he was drawn to something else, something vulnerable and simmering. Something that, though hidden, functioned as her adrenaline. Like a blast of energy surrounding her—an aura that he could *feel*.

There was something there he wanted to touch.

"Psss," he mumbled, and clicked the print button on his keyboard. His laser printer hummed to life, and page after page slid out of the feeder tray.

He got up to stretch, realizing that he'd thought himself into a corner. Ms. Renata probably had a man, or—devil's dream—she was married, with a husband and maybe some kids.

I can't believe this, he thought. *I just met the woman and already I'm staking her out.*

He picked up the pages of his article as they slid out of the printer. They were hot in his palms. He intended to read through the piece one more time, taking a red pen to it to correct any last-minute typos. Then he would get his mind in the right place for dinner tonight with Renata.

He checked the clock on the wall—the simple, round metal clock that matched his simple decor. Helen had been the decorator. When he gave her the house, he hadn't thought twice about his lack of decorations. Plain brown furniture was all he needed. Bare walls, no rugs, nothing frilly, frou-frou, or metrosexual. Simple surroundings for a simple, uncomplicated life. *Only that*, he thought to himself, *has become complicated*.

Two-thirty. He had just enough time to finish the edits, e-mail them to the magazine editor, and go to Bible study before dinner. He hadn't been to Bible study in a long time. He needed something to get his mind right. He figured the word of God was always good for that. But with all of the thoughts he'd had about Renata today, he wondered if the devil would be working over-time.

~

The devil is working overtime, Renata thought. She looked sinfully good, even though she'd toned down her evening attire out of respect for spending time with a Christian man. Cobalt accents in her eye makeup, her favorite blue dress, and a pair of low-heeled mules completed out outfit.

She licked her lips over the stay-on lipstick she wore and headed out the door. She was surprised to find Malcolm already sitting on the porch waiting for her.

"Malcolm, why didn't you let me know you were here?"

"I don't know," he answered. He was dressed in different clothing than what he'd had on yesterday. Either the Smiths had given him some of the clothes left behind by another foster child, or they had gone out that morning and bought him a new outfit. Knowing the Smiths, it was the latter.

"You look good," she said. She couldn't tell FUBU from Phat Farm, but he was sporting something like that.

Malcolm stood, stuck a toe into the ground, then slowly looked up. "Thanks."

They walked to her relatively new Elantra. Malcolm seemed to be impressed when he got in.

"Nice whip," he commented.

"Thanks," Renata replied, trying not to think about the car payment that she'd missed last month and the possibility of her car being repossessed. But she couldn't afford to pay herself her usual salary and keep her agency in business. So she'd cut her pay and used the money to keep her office insured for a few more months.

As they drove to the restaurant, Renata noticed how quiet her passenger was.

"Why so quiet? Usually, you're Mr. Chatty."

Malcolm kept his eyes toward the road. He didn't glance her way. Instead, he paid more attention to the streets.

"I'm just thinking about how you don't know me from Suge Knight, but you hooked me up like we're family or something."

Renata smiled. If that was all this young brother had on his mind, she could allay his fears quickly.

"First of all, I've heard of Suge Knight and you are nothing like him. Second, I *do* know you . . . in a way. I mean, when you trace it back, we're all related, right? And like they say, the children are the future. So you're my future. I just want to make sure that the future is positive."

It didn't take long to make the trip to the waterfront, the trendy part of town where Manna's Restaurant was located. Renata put the car in the parking space right in front of the place. Malcolm reached for the door, but Renata held him back.

"Uh, Malcolm . . . I just want to say that when we get inside . . . Mr. McKenna, I mean, he's still deciding whether to recommend Success Unlimited as a sponsorship candidate for the Red Oaks outreach ministry. So you should probably be on your best behavior if you are really serious about getting a job."

He sighed and leaned back against her leather seat. "I'm serious. I just don't know about working in a church."

Well, for that, she couldn't offer any words of consolation. She hadn't set foot in a church for . . . well, for a long time. And if she had her way, any meeting she had with any member of the Red Oaks outreach ministry would take place anywhere but inside the sanctuary.

They got out and walked toward the door, when Malcolm swung his head around slowly and said, "So, you like him, huh?"

"What?" she asked, tripping over nothing in the sidewalk.

"Ol' boy. You've got that look."

Oh God, if there is one, she thought. If even a teenage boy could see her attraction, maybe a grown man could see it too. She would have to be more careful.

~

When Renata stepped into the restaurant, Devin licked his lips and said another prayer. Unfortunately, the ones he'd said earlier either hadn't worked or were wearing off. He was feeling a definite pull. Like a yoke around his neck with Renata holding the reins. *Shake it off, Brother McKenna. Shake it off.*

But it was too late. The body in the blue dress Renata wore would remain etched in his mind for a long, long time. He watched her walk and thought of St. Augustine's prayer for God to remove his lust. He smiled despite himself, just thinking of what a boring existence that would be.

"Hey, Devin," she said, extending her pretty, soft hand. He took it gladly, held it just a bit too long.

"This is Malcolm Goodwin."

He exchanged a handshake with the young man.

"Pleased to meet you," Malcolm offered, and the hairs on the back of Devin's neck flared as if they'd been set ablaze. Something uncomfortably familiar about Malcolm rubbed Devin the wrong way.

Rather than acknowledge his unease, he said, "Good to meet you, Malcolm."

"Me, too," the young man said.

They all sat at the table Devin had chosen for them. It was the best spot in the restaurant, at the junction of the wall-window and a collage of paintings of flowers so vibrant that anyone would swear the aroma of lilacs and roses hung in the air.

"Nice restaurant," Renata remarked.

Malcolm nodded. "I think I'd like to come here again one day . . . when I can pay for myself."

At that one comment, a stone of sadness fell in Devin's stomach. So often kids like Malcolm grew up to be adults who could never afford to eat in a place like this. He wondered about Malcolm's fate.

When the waitress came, they ordered. Lasagna for Devin. Spaghetti and meatballs with extra meatballs for Malcolm. When Renata ordered a dish called "hot and naked pasta," with olive oil and spices," Devin felt as though he'd been pleasantly violated.

Before Devin was saved, that kind of thought would have turned him on, and quite possibly turned him out. His instinct would have been to ditch the kid. To say anything and everything that Renata wanted to hear in order to get into her pants, or in this case her little blue dress, and to have sex with her until he'd had his fill. But as it stood now, all he wanted to do was handle the evening professionally, come to a decision about working with Malcolm, and keep his composure around the most beautiful woman he'd ever seen.

The problem was, he'd taken one look at the kid and become immediately suspicious. *I don't like him*, Devin thought. His reaction was acute and exacting. Part of it he understood as his own bias, but part of it was unrecognizable. He wondered himself why his reaction was so strong.

He imagined that everyone had an experience with people who just rubbed them the wrong way. Often, you're not sure why. The cause was elusive, like a word on the tip of your tongue. His response to Malcolm would trouble him, he knew. And the reason why would come to him later, like a name he was trying to remember or a song he'd forgotten. It would hit him when he least expected it, and then he would either be vindicated or apologetic. Until then, he would keep his guard up.

In her description, Renata had spoken of the young man in respectable tones, had almost hummed his phrases like a sweet song. The only cloying endearment she hadn't called him was "lad." Looking at the youth before him—one part DMX, one part 50 Cent, and the rest Tupac Shakur—he could have orchestrated the theft of her purse himself, as a gag or a ploy to get in her good graces. Devin had heard about thugs like that. Scam artists. Grifters. They all had games, ways they twisted the truth to gain trust. They manipulated their victims until they had them just where they wanted them and then, *poof*! There goes your life savings. There goes your check book, credit cards, social security number, your identity.

Fortunately, this rap academy drop-out looked like he didn't have the finesse to pull off identity theft. But burglary, robbery, petty thievery: this kid not only looked capable, but Devin was sure he was guilty of all three, plus who knows what else.

Devin reasoned that, as far as Malcolm was concerned, Renata was a mark. Someone to get close to and then break. He'd seen it before. Hell, when he was a teenager and living in the world, he'd done it before.

Devin swallowed hard. Some folks need prayer. Some folks need redemption, forgiveness, grace. The rest need to be on lockdown, straight up. Don't just throw away the key, destroy it. He knew from personal experience.

He'd been the best booster in three counties. He'd found out early that the best way to steal was not the snatch and grab, but the let-me-help-you-across-the-street, let-me-help-you-with-your-bags, let-me-help-you-up-the-stairs kind. With snatch and grab, some women would scream bloody murder—or worse, chase after you. But if you gain their trust and *then* betray it, they are so stunned and surprised and hurt that they don't do anything for the first few minutes except stand and stare. That gives you just enough time to get a—

"Devin?"

Malcolm must have sensed Devin's ill feelings. Rather abruptly and awkwardly, he excused himself and headed for the restroom.

"Devin, why are you staring at him like he stole something?"

"Because I'm sure he has. And if we leave this room for four seconds, I'm sure he will again."

"You're judging him and you don't even know him!"

"Please. He looks like he gets his clothes from Thugs'R'Us."

"The Smiths would not buy him thug wear! Those are just clothes. It's a style called hip-hop. All the kids wear it. It doesn't mean he's not a decent kid."

"Sure it does. Decent kids don't wear clothes like that. Wait a minute . . . did you say the Smiths?"

Renata lifted her chin. "Yes."

That explains it, Devin thought. That's where the reaction came from. Everyone in town knew that the unsavable kids went to the Smiths. Kids with violent tempers, drug addictions, or disorders like pyromania. He would not put the church at risk.

"What do you know about *decent* kids?" Renata asked.

"What?" Devin responded, roused out of his thoughts.

"I said what do you know about decent kids? Do you interact with kids on a regular basis? Do you spend time with them in their world? Do you talk to them? Do you even *know* any teenagers?"

Devin thought about the teenagers that attended Red Oaks Christian Church regularly. He was about to answer when Renata interrupted his thought.

"Any teenagers that don't go to your church?"

His stomach hardened. The only teenager he knew was Mallory, his ex-wife's daughter. Well, actually, Mallory was his ex-wife's step-daughter, and he didn't really *know* her. He just knew of her. But she seemed like a good kid, and knowing his ex, Helen would never let her leave her bedroom dressed in anything close to what this kid was wearing.

"That's what I thought." Renata leaned back in her seat and let out an exasperated breath. "Look, Devin. Brother McKenna," she amended. "Maybe there's someone at your church who is more amenable toward kids. It's obvious to me that you have a problem with them."

"I don't . . . ," he began, and then stopped himself. What was he going to say? He didn't just have a problem with kids. He had a *big* problem with kids. He didn't like them and they didn't like him. And he had a special dislike for kids like Malcolm who probably had no respect for themselves or others. Kids today weren't raised right. They didn't know their place. They didn't do anything their parents told them to do. They were disrespectful, combative, argumentative, and just plain obnoxious. He could count on one hand the number of kids who would sit down, be still, and shut up, if they were instructed to do so by their parents. Even the children at Red Oaks seemed to have more devil than savior in their hearts sometimes.

And kids took up so much time and so much money. Devin had too many goals to accomplish in his life to become one of the tired and broken down parents who had given up their dreams only to raise children who didn't appreciate the sacrifices they'd made. Devin had been dead set against splitting the prime years of his life between a struggling career and an unruly child.

It had been the downfall of his marriage. When his ex-wife figured out that instead of postponing having children, he'd had no intention of having them at all, she'd filed for divorce so quickly Devin hadn't known what hit him.

He was probably the only adult in the church who hadn't at some point taught Sunday School, led the Youth Ministry, or helped coordinate the yearly holiday specials.

Devin's participation in the Outreach Ministry had come at a time when he was working hard on his spiritual walk. He'd started the ministry with five other members of Red Oaks Christian Fellowship Church knowing full well that it would force him at least once to face his most challenging demon—kids—or rather his distaste for kids.

No. Devin did not like kids. His—if he'd had any—or anyone else's.

"Well, Brother McKenna. You've obviously not interested. Come on, Malcolm," she said when the young man returned. "I'll find you another sponsor."

Devin watched Renata and Malcolm leave. The dinner disaster saddened him. He wished things could have worked out differently.

He might be in for a stern tongue lashing and a bible beating from Mother Maybelle, but if Malcolm Goodwin was an example of the types of youth Renata Connor was trying to help, then Devin couldn't in good conscience recommend that Red Oaks Church become a Success Unlimited sponsor.

Mother Maybelle would just have to understand.

Four

"Well?"

Mother Maybelle was in rare form, dressed to the nines, as usual. Devin stared at her, amazed at how each Sunday she was able to color-coordinate her outfits as if she were being dressed by the finest designers in the country. This Sunday, she'd sat in seat number one in row number two like an orange flare—beautiful, powerful, and not to be toyed with. Against his better judgment, Devin had attended the early service, knowing full well that Mother Maybelle would accost him at the first chance she got.

And he'd been right.

"Good morning, Mother Maybelle. How are you this fine Sunday?"

"You can see with your own eyes, sugar. I'm doin' a lot better than some-a these young folks here today. But that's neither here nor there. Tell me about the outreach ministry."

"Yes," he answered, rocking on his heels. He'd gotten up from his seat and managed to get halfway to the door. Patrons filed out of the sanctuary around them. Many stopped to pay what might as well be considered homage to Mother Maybelle. "The outreach ministry is going slowly. We had a candidate . . . Success Unlimited . . . the referral you gave me, but . . ."

"But nothin'!" Her mouth crimped with annoyance. "I sent you over there for a reason. Now what you *need* to do is get that boy in here and bring that gal to church. And while you're at it, study up on Reverend Avery's last sermon on judging folks."

Devin glanced at the woman standing in front of him. She was a spitfire.

She looked like a wrinkled brown reed, refusing to bend in any wind. Devin admired Mother Maybelle. She had gall. He respected that.

If she'd been a man, a right cross to his chin would have come so fast he probably wouldn't have seen it. If she'd been any other woman, he would have walked away after her stern admonishment to never approach her again. But Mother Maybelle was a different story. He didn't dare do anything except what she asked. Or else . . . his soul would probably be damned to hell.

For better or for worse, he'd be at Success Unlimited tomorrow morning. He wondered what Renata's reaction would be.

"You're going to get your smooth talkin' behind back there first thing Monday," Mother Maybelle demanded. "Not only are you going back, but you're going back with your tail between your legs, and you're going to apologize for whatever it was you did. After that, I want you to speak with Brother Mack and arrange a tour of the sanctuary."

"Mother—"

She held up her hand. That was it, the first sign of Mother's Bible beatings. They were legendary. She would quote the exact verse of scripture she needed to make you see the error of your actions. Each one more powerful than the first, until you felt broken by the power of truth in the Word. Broken and strengthened at the same time. So much so, that whatever it was that you'd done wrong, you wanted to rush out and rectify it immediately. He looked into Mother's eyes. His beating was only seconds away.

"Let me tell you something, Brother McKenna. The first time I saw you, you were on your way to juvy for yankin' old lady's purses. You had *good for nothin'* written all over your face. But you straightened up, and the Lord touched your heart. And look at you now. You've still got a ways to go, like the rest of us, but you've already come a mighty long way. God's grace didn't stop with you, Brother McKenna. And he's not the only one capable of grace either."

When she stopped talking, Devin looked up. He couldn't believe how easy he'd gotten off. This little talking-to he could take.

"Yes, Mother Maybelle," he said, grateful for the break. He started out the front doors of the church when she stopped him once again.

"Walk me home while I tell you about a few scriptures."

"Yes, ma'am," he said, smiling inside.

~

"Devin! Devin!" Renata mumbled in that sweet place between being awake and asleep. "Devin!" she called once again. He was . . . doing things to her. Things she liked.

Bored and frustrated at her desk, she'd given in to her fantasies about Devin McKenna despite their abbreviated dinner the other night. Now, in her mind, all hostilities were forgiven, since they were well into a second round of carnal pleasure.

"What's my name?"

"Renata," he answered loud and clear.

Damn, this fantasy is good. That sounded real.

Just then, her body temperature went up at least five degrees as her imaginary man kissed her on the neck.

"Please . . . say it again."

"Renata," his voice said. Louder this time.

Her eyes snapped open and the heat of her embarrassment matched the heat of her libido. Devin McKenna had stepped out of her dreams once more.

Her immediate reaction was one of gratefulness. Then the reality and horror of the other night made her angry all over again. She crossed her arms in front of herself, making no apologies for her sensual outbursts. "What do you want?"

A small smile appeared on his lips. "Apparently, you."

"Do you believe in knocking?" she asked, maintaining her indignation, but just barely. "You scared me half to death."

His smile grew. "You didn't sound frightened in the least when I entered, and your assistant wasn't at her desk. When I heard someone calling my name, I came on in. Besides, you should lock your door when you are alone."

Seeing Devin again knocked all the fight out of her. "You're right. I sent Gidget to the office supply store to get envelopes. Got to mail out sponsor letters," she said with a sigh. "Please have a seat."

Despite herself, Renata drank in the sight of the man with the woolly hair and sensuous features as he took a seat opposite her. She'd never been one to hide her feelings. So she was sure that her I-think-you're-quite-attractive look was front and center on her face. And she knew something else . . . she didn't want to hide it.

Devin licked his lips and took a deep breath. "I apologize for the other night. I shouldn't have said those things about Malcolm without getting to know him first. If you would still like to take Red Oaks Church as a client, the outreach ministry would be glad to partner with you." He waited for any disapproval in her eyes. He didn't see any and decided it was safe to continue. "He'd be working for us in the church actually. In maintenance. It's not a glamorous job by any means, but he'd get solid work experience."

His words were too clean. Too rehearsed. Someone had put him up to it. And she knew without a doubt who it was. Mother Maybelle. "I'm not sure if Malcolm will want to work with you," she admitted, as another memory forced itself to the surface. The morning after their disastrous dinner, Malcolm had been waiting for her when she came into the agency. She'd asked him to come in.

The expression on Malcolm's face had burned a hard knot of anger in the pit of Renata's stomach. He had been disappointed and hurt. It never ceased to surprise her how soft, fragile, and vulnerable even the most hardened teens could become when something they wanted strongly was taken away from them. Even in the midst of anger, which was the reaction for some, she could see how just the slightest drop in confidence dulled the sparkle in their eyes.

She knew Devin would have made an impression on Malcolm. Some boys just need a male who was about something positive to be in their presence for them to begin to imagine their own potential. She could tell which ones would be impressed and impacted and want to emulate what they saw and do the kind of things to make the male figure proud. Malcolm was like that.

She'd first thought that Devin was worth respecting . . . looking up to even. He carried himself so well, like a man whose pride in himself made him seem even taller than he actually was. He was well-spoken, intelligent, and to call him handsome would be a grand understatement.

He and Malcolm had something in common, she'd thought. Just from the brief time she'd known both of them, she'd known that something about them felt the same to her. She imagined that it was the way they both spoke so directly and seemed to scrutinize everything. But it was probably the way she'd been strangely drawn to them both. As though they'd both come into her life at this moment in time for a reason.

Oh well, she had thought when she'd walked toward the young man, standing dejected in her office hallway. Maybe a hug would do them both some good. Then she would get on with the task of finding another sponsor for Malcolm's success program.

When she'd approached him, he'd pulled back slightly. When she moved her arms to give him a hug, he surprised her when he'd flinched and stepped back quickly.

"Don't," he'd said. "I'm not cool with hugs."

Renata released a breath slowly. "Okay," she'd said. "Do you want to hang out here for a while?" Renata thought if she could keep him there, give him something to do, paperwork, filing, sweeping up, anything, maybe she could keep him out of trouble just one more day.

"Nah," he'd said, already headed out. "I gotta go."

She got up, chased after him, her heart rising in her chest. "You'll be back tomorrow, right?"

"Yeah," he'd said, not looking back.

Before she could say anything else, he was down the sidewalk and around the corner. She knew he had no intention of coming back.

She hadn't seen him since.

"Renata?"

Devin's voice broke into her thoughts, but she was already imagining the drive to the Smiths' house. She couldn't wait to see Malcolm and tell him about his sponsor.

"When do you want him at the church?"

"How about tomorrow?"

Five

Malcolm was nervous. Renata could see it in his eyes. They darted from side to side, person to person, as if he were watching Venus and Serena in a doubles tournament at Wimbledon. If she didn't know any better, she'd think it was his first time in a church. Or, if it wasn't, he was such a bad seed that he was afraid he would be touched by holy water or that he might spontaneously combust by being inside the sanctuary. If he were any more nervous and fidgety, she thought he'd pass out or throw up.

They hadn't gotten through the doorway and Renata could feel the nerves stirring inside him. She couldn't believe that the wild cocky kid, daring enough to run after thugs and get her stolen purse back now looked like the one who needed rescuing.

"Calm down, Malcolm," Renata admonished. "If there was ever a time when you could be completely relaxed about anything and anyone, it's now. These people are harmless."

"Me?" he responded. "Look at you!"

Renata blew out a breath. Malcolm was right. Renata had a strong urge to run out of the church before something . . . happened. She just wasn't quite sure what.

"Don't worry," she whispered, trying to divert the attention from her own unease. "If you get too uncomfortable, all you have to do is say a few 'praise Gods' and 'amens.' They'll think you're one of them."

No sooner had she said those words than she saw Devin standing in an adjacent hallway. There wasn't a need to wonder if he'd overheard. The expression on his face told her all she needed to know.

So much for her booty-call fantasy.

"Devin—"

He held up a hand and turned a more buoyant expression to Malcolm. "Are you ready to meet some people?"

Malcolm glanced at Renata before answering, "I guess."

"You guess?" Devin repeated. "That's not an answer." He placed his arm around the young man. "You better be sure, because you'll spend a great deal of your waking life working for a living. So if you're not sure, you shouldn't do it, son."

Malcolm blinked and shook his head in understanding.

"So," Devin continued, looking sexy in a silk fitted shirt and cocoa linen slacks. Renata wondered where he was going after this brief meeting at the church. "Let me ask you again. "Are you ready?"

A sweet smile curled across Malcolm's lips. With it, his nervousness and fidgeting diminished significantly. He looked up. "Most def!" he said.

Devin chuckled. "Where'd you get this kid?" he asked.

Where did the church get you, Renata wondered, noting the complete change in Devin's demeanor. She followed them into the corridor of the sanctuary and into the back storage room thinking about how sincere he looked and sounded.

Even though Devin hadn't asked, Renata was ready. She had her clipboard, pen, checklist, and work agreement. She had a process that she followed for every first day on the job. Above and beyond the paperwork, she was there to assess whether her client's work style and the sponsor's work expectations meshed or clashed. If they clashed, she would use her skills as a facilitator to work through the issues. If they meshed, she would note all of the basic information on the forms and put them into a "recommend for continuance" file.

She had no doubt in her mind that Malcolm, once he calmed down, would do wonderfully well. Something about the way they were all getting along right now made her believe that his experience at Red Oaks Christian Church would be, to coin a phrase, a blessing. And thinking of blessings, she'd need one if she didn't get out of this house of worship soon. Something about it was making her feel very, very . . .

"Oh!" Renata said, seeing a woman come out of the shadows. She'd walked straight into her without realizing she was there.

"Watch where you're going!" the woman said, her face snarling into a frown.

"Renata," Devin said, stepping gently to her side. Pulling her arm, he brought her close to him. After he saw that she and the other woman were not harmed, his face softened with concern.

"Sister Edna, we didn't know you were here."

"Yeah well, I don't see why not. You see me standing here don't you?" The woman in front of Renata looked like her name could have been Old Mother Hubbard. She couldn't imagine the woman going home to anything other than bare cupboards, cobwebs, and rat traps. Sister Edna looked like little more than a rat trap herself. Small, dark, bird-like eyes; tall, thin frame; hook nose; and clothes that although they were probably size three, hung off of her skeletal frame. Renata had to fight the urge to buy her a double Big Mac with extra cheese.

"Pleased to meet you," Renata offered. She was surprised to find that the woman's grip was not as fragile as she'd imagined.

"Who are you?" the thin whisper of a woman asked.

"Sister Edna," Devin said, a knowing smile growing on his face. "This is Renata Connor and Malcolm Goodwin."

She smelled like powder. Baby powder to be exact. And she was dressed in what was only a short step above a robe. Nothing short of a miracle from the Son of God would do that woman any good.

Devin pulled Renata even closer. The nearness of him canceled out any comment of shock she may have uttered.

"We're sorry, Sister Edna. We'll be more careful in the future."

"You'd better," she said, spitting out the words like a bad taste in her mouth.

Renata folded her arms, wondering if she should put the woman in her place. Devin must have sensed her thought process. He hurried with her and Malcolm until they were out of sight of the bird-like woman.

"I know this is a church, but I was ready to tell the ol' girl thing or two up in here."

Malcolm laughed first, then Renata joined in. She could tell that Devin was fighting it. But even in that, there was a small victory.

"Sister Edna has a kind of dementia."

The laughter stopped.

"The next time you see her, she'll probably be so nice to you that you won't believe that you saw the same person today."

"What's dementia?" Malcolm asked.

"That's when your brain doesn't function correctly and sometimes it believes things that aren't true."

The definition did something to Malcolm. Not like knocking the wind out of his sails, but more like squeezing the air out of a tire. His nod came slowly this time as his comprehension grew.

She wondered what things kids with lives like the one he'd led make up in their minds.

"Why don't you have a seat in the security office, I'll take Malcolm back to see Brother Mack."

Renata didn't feel like being alone in the church. There were too many memories her mind could find to dwell on. "That's all right. I'll come with you. I'd like to see what he'll being doing."

The expression on Malcolm's face told her she was being more like a mother than a mentor.

"Damn," Malcolm said under his breath, but nothing got past Devin. His quick glare caught the young man's attention and he shrugged his shoulders as if to say, "Well?"

Renata sighed and maneuvered herself down the hallway like a twig off to find a pot to plant herself in. "I'll be fine out here, I guess," she said, looking around and hoping they would be quick.

Their words and footfalls, even though on carpet, sounded loud in the large open sanctuary. Renata took a seat in a pew as if waiting for service to begin. She could pull the memories from her childhood as if they'd only happened moments ago. Her parents were fanatical about two things, their children and their God. Days and days, and evenings upon evenings they'd devoted to church. Her family spent more time in church than they did in their own home. At first, church life was all she knew. Greater Faith Church of Christ. If someone had asked her what her address was, she would have pointed in the direction of the church.

As she got older, she resented the time she spent there, wearing dresses, and watching people fall out as if some maniacal puppeteer had suddenly picked up their strings and started them dancing.

She knew where the squeaky floor boards were in the back of the church. She knew how frayed the velvet altar drape was; she had counted the number of mosaic tiles in the abstract painting of Jesus in the vestibule. She even remembered that the choir closet room was once the pastor's office, until there was enough money in the building fund to actually build a larger office for the head of the church.

No, her home-town church—gas station turned house of worship—was not the structure surrounding her. This building was grand in every sense of the world. More than large enough for the two thousand members Devin told her they had. The massive stained-glass windows—six windows in all—humbled any other church she'd been in. They seemed large enough to drive a diesel truck through. She hadn't picked up a Bible in years, yet she could identify the scripture depicted on each window.

She sighed again and rubbed the sides of her arms. Her anxiety about being inside a church had come back. Devin and Malcolm couldn't return soon enough.

Six

Renata had been thinking about Devin and Malcolm all week. Things were working out well with the church. She'd already received Red Oaks's sponsorship application in the mail, taken pride in Malcolm's achievements, and had grown even fonder of Devin. She'd spent time with him to get Malcolm acclimated to his duties, and Devin had been wonderful to work with. He was open and supportive of all the monitoring she would have to do as part of her agency. They'd seemed to grow closer by the minute. Soon they were speaking to each other like old friends.

Happily, she turned away from her list of appointments and things to do, picked up the phone, and dialed Devin's number.

He answered on the first ring, as if he'd been expecting her call.

"Hello?" his deep voice said, full of expectancy and knowing.

"It's me," she said, already breathy from the mere sound of his words.

"Hello, me," he responded. She could hear him smiling. He was pleased that she'd called. And she was pleased that he was pleased.

"I want to see you," she said, wasting no time with formalities.

"I want to see you, too. Today," he added.

She pushed her appointment book aside as if it were an insignificant thing. "I don't have much to do this afternoon. I'll be off work early."

"Good," he responded. "The Red Oaks entrepreneurial ministry is meeting tonight. I'm speaking on how to run a one-person business. Even though there are two people at your agency, I'd love to see you attend."

For a moment—no, for several moments—Renata couldn't move her lips. They were sealed shut by the thought of attending any kind of church *service*, even one in which Devin McKenna was presenting.

"Renata?"

"Devin . . ."

"I want to see you," he said. "As soon as possible, I want to see you. But I'm on deadline now, and I have to e-mail an article by three p.m. But if we hook up this evening for the meeting, we could go to a coffee shop afterward, or go for a walk."

Immediately, a vision of the two of them holding hands, walking leisurely in a green park, played like a letterbox movie in her mind. She could smell him, feel his heat, she could . . .

"Renata?"

"Yes, Devin. I'll come to the service with you, and a walk sounds nice."

"Being with you sounds nice, Renata. I'll see you tonight. Should I pick you up?"

"No, I'll meet you there."

"You won't change your mind, will you?"

"No, I won't change my mind."

"All right. Oh and Renata, don't let Sister Edna seat you in the corner. She has a habit of putting new people in a corner. We don't know why she does that. She's harmless."

"Okay."

When Renata hung up the phone, she knew that she would fly through her duties today. And that the evening walk with Devin couldn't come fast enough.

It was that part about the service that she was worried about.

～

Devin couldn't remember the last time he was nervous about anything. He wouldn't classify what he was feeling as nerves, more like a deep concern that Renata first of all show up; second, gain something from the experience; and third, have a good time with him afterward.

He glanced around the sanctuary with pride, remembering how many souls had been saved there even in the time that he'd become a member. He knew it was much too soon for Renata to accept the spirit of God and to have a "revelation," but he was hopeful that God would open a window in her soul, even a small one. He'd prayed for it, and his heart told him he was doing the right thing, and that God, and Mother Maybelle, were leading him in the direction of this woman's life to make a difference. And for final validation, the slight nod from Mother Maybelle let him know that he was on the right track.

"Mother Maybelle," he said, getting her attention. She sauntered over like a woman half her age.

"Brother McKenna, she said greeting him. "Praise God."

"I've invited Renata Connor to attend the meeting tonight," he told her. "She should be here any minute."

Mother Maybelle took his hand, patted the back of it, and smiled broadly. "Bless you, sugar. Woo . . . I'm tired today. I hope you speak fast and pass a quick plate. My dogs have been in service all day, and the Lord will understand when I finally sit down."

"I'm sure he will, Mother. I'm sure he will."

The sanctuary was starting to fill. The entrepreneurial ministry didn't usually pull in a full house, but a good number of people had showed up that night. Devin's eyes searched the crowd for a woman with wavy brown hair, sparkling brown eyes, and the cutest walk he'd ever seen.

His heart strummed slowly in his chest, trying to distract him from the fact that Renata was nowhere in sight. He clenched his teeth against the discomfort rising in his stomach like a ball of frustration. He rubbed his palms together and got ready for his presentation. He made his way down an aisle and took one last look at the entrance.

She was there. And she was stunning. Better yet, she looked as though she'd been a member of the congregation for years. He could tell she was looking for him the same way he'd been looking for her. He stood fast, straightened his height even taller than his six-plus feet. Her eyes darted from person to person until she found him. And when she did, her stare caught him up, like a hot thread holding him. He smiled, liking the feeling of her gaze, wanting it on a more regular basis. It seemed his list of things to pray for was growing by leaps and bounds.

Just having Renata present in the sanctuary doubled his confidence. Something about her made him feel invincible.

∼

Her first inclination was to sit in the back. To sneak in like a good heathen and take a seat where she wouldn't be noticed. But when she saw Devin front and center, a rush of adrenaline moved through her like a whirling dervish. At that moment she knew there was no way she could sit so far away from him. She didn't think it was God, but Devin's good looks which had moved through her soul, and she had to be near him.

Only a few moments after she arrived, Mother Maybelle came up to her and placed an arm around her shoulder.

"How you doin', Sister Connor?"

"I'm fine, Mother Maybelle. You?"

"I'm doing well. Now, that boy's got a lot to say about business. And he's come a long way since he joined the entrepreneurial ministry. His testimony tonight is sure to help someone turn their business around."

"Testimony?"

"Praise, God. When Brother McKenna decided he wanted to be a writer, he did everything wrong. Sister McKenna, that was his wife back then, was about frettin' all the time, wondering if they would lose their house."

Mother Maybelle smiled as if the whole scene was playing in front of her on a screen. "I don't know if it was the money, the marketing, or the mortgage, but something got that boy in gear, and right before the collectors bounced them out of their home, he turned the whole thing around. And he hasn't looked back since."

Mother Maybelle leveled her gaze at Renata. Renata felt like her mother had just flown in from Boston and was about to give her a good talking to.

"Brother McKenna always speaks from the heart. You'll see that if you pay attention." And then she was off, smiling as if she'd done her good deed for the day.

With curious eyes spying her from every pew, she strolled toward the pulpit and took a seat as close to Devin as possible without being obvious. He looked so good, he could preach about fire, brimstone, and against all-night sex. She was ready for the message. She straightened in her seat, crossed her legs, and smiled.

Devin nodded. She knew the nod meant "thank you for coming." She wanted so much to read into it, *I'm feelin' you. As soon as this is over, I'm going to take you back to my place and . . .*

"Welcome saints, brothers and sisters. Thank you for coming to the Wednesday night meeting of the entrepreneurial ministry. I know you would probably rather hear Brother King, but since he's out of town, he asked me to step in, so thank you for coming anyway."

The members laughed.

Renata realized that wild horses couldn't have kept her away from seeing Devin like this. She ordered her earlier apprehension away and told herself that nothing and no one was out to get her. Although the unease of being inside a church rose inside her, she managed to focus on Devin.

He was absolutely stunning. As if he belonged in front of people, teaching them, leading them. Preaching.

She hadn't felt this way about a man in a long time. Moved down deep. Riveted. She listened, even though she ran a nonprofit business, and everything he said made sense to her. And the individuals attending the meeting seemed to think so, too.

He spoke so well, she soon forgot that she disliked churches, couldn't stand to be in a place where people's lives consisted of tent revivals and come-to-Jesus meetings, and patrons wore the concept of a church home like a badge of honor. But she wouldn't think twice about coming back on a Wednesday night to hear what new, riveting pieces of business information Devin would impart to her eager ears.

The parishioners broke into her thoughts with their resounding amens and platitudes of agreement.

Although Renata sat quietly in the house of the Lord, her mind was racing. Devin looked hotter than Paco Pickles. He wore a brown knit shirt that didn't leave room for so much as air between the fabric and his skin. And the black trousers he wore hugged him about the hips, then set him free on the lower part of his legs. It was definitely the attire of a man who knew the power of his own allure and wasn't ashamed of accentuating it. Without hesitation, she reached for the Red Oaks Church fan in the seatback in front of her and fanned ever so discreetly.

"Lord forgive me," she mumbled under hear breath.

A woman sitting in an adjacent pew chanced a glance in her direction, then turned her attention back to the man speaking so eloquently near the altar.

Renata settled into Devin's message, enjoying the sound of his voice and the way she felt like warm honey just listening to him.

But as she watched and listened, Renata knew that it was much more than seeing him and hearing him speak. It was the mere idea and experience of being in his presence. It made her feel like her soul was unfolding, relaxing, and calming. Until that moment, she hadn't realized how keyed up she'd been recently—maybe always was.

She sighed, sank back in the pew, and smiled inside, feeling like someone had just rubbed her feet.

There is nothing more attractive than a man confident in his mission. Renata glanced round. All eyes were on Devin, and rightly so. He captivated an audience like Tony Robbins, Les Brown, Zig Ziglar, and any other motivational speaker she'd ever heard.

I could listen to Devin talk for hours and hours, she thought.

Damn, she knew she was cheesing up a storm. She knew that the grin on her face was about as wide as the Grand Canyon. She also knew that she couldn't help herself.

And then, in a second, she lost her happiness. All the good feeling deflated upon one single question: Why would a man like this come into her life? She could tell by his dedication to Christ that Devin was the kind of churchman who would never hook up with a woman who wasn't "in God" or walking with the Lord. But she wasn't about to fake having a civil relationship with God just to get a man. That didn't, however, stop her from thinking that maybe she could persuade Devin to come over to her side . . . just a little.

She made up her mind there in Red Oaks Church that if he ever showed any interest in her, she would not dissuade him from pursuing her romantically.

He started the second half of his talk, and Renata placed the fan back in its slot. She hoped that after the session they could go out for coffee. Her smile returned again just thinking about it.

"That's where most business owners go wrong. They either don't have the expertise to run a business, don't have the enthusiasm to see their dream to fruition, or just flat out mismanage the business," Devin said, pacing before his audience.

"In today's market, business owners either know what they're doing or they don't. There is no room in this economy for anything else. There is no such thing as *kinda* making it."

Renata realized she had come empty-handed. She should have brought pencil and paper. Devin spoke of budget planning as if he was the CEO of a large company instead of a freelance writer. But it all made sense. As he talked, Renata took mental notes of all the important points of his presentation.

She was glad she'd come.

Seven

"Thank you for inviting me," Renata said to Devin as they set out for their walk. "That was a very good message. I never thought about looking at my business as if it were a living entity."

"When I quit my job at the *Macon Telegraph* newspaper and started working for myself, I didn't do so well at first. I didn't have a clear vision of my business or what I wanted to accomplish. When it started taking on a life of its own, I realized that my business really *did* have life, or it could if I started treating it like something that had a purpose and could grow with the right care and attention.

"The first year I had to file my taxes didn't go well, either. That's when I started to think of money and other resources as the fuel and nutrition my business needed to survive. When you think of it that way, suddenly you want to put your business on a diet or at least create a well-balanced meal—the kind that will provide the correct portions of energy and sustenance to keep it running."

The night cooled Renata's skin. They walked past rows of trees full and green from a perfect spring. It was almost eight-thirty in the evening. Their footsteps were the only sounds in the air as if the entire town was getting ready for bed.

Renata thought back to Devin's presentation. He'd used phrases like *trim the fat*, *portion control*, and *healthy choices* when he'd spoken of ways to get a handle on runaway budgets. Considering what her agency was going through right now, his message made perfect sense. She would use some of his ideas immediately.

"What's that?" he asked.

"What's what?" she asked back.

"That thing on your face," he responded, faking a frown. "It looks like a smile."

Renata held back the laugh as long as she could. Then it burst freely from her as if she were being tickled.

"Ah, you've done it," Devin continued. "Now, that I know you can smile and laugh, I'll expect to see more of that, and I'll be doing stupid things from time to time to see if I can get you to do either one, or both."

The smile on Renata's face felt broad and, if she wasn't careful, permanent.

How quickly he'd figured her out. She didn't smile or laugh much. She didn't have time with everything that had to be done with the agency. And the hard lump of sadness which had lived in her stomach since her brother died was also to blame.

"Don't lose that smile," Devin said. "It looks good on you."

Truth be told, Devin thought anything would look good on Renata Connor—faded jeans and holey T-shirts, a burlap bag, nothing at all. Doggone. That was the third time he'd mentally undressed her that evening. He'd better keep his attention on her smile. And, since it was a beautiful smile, that wouldn't be hard.

"So, where is this coffee shop?" Renata asked with the sweet haunting taste of anticipation in her mouth.

"Just a few blocks ahead."

Renata nodded.

"Well, actually it's more than a few blocks ahead. It's more like half a mile. And it's not really a coffee shop, it's a restaurant that serves coffee along with everything else on their menu."

Renata smiled again. Devin liked it. Could get used to it.

"So," she said, running her hand across the leaves of a begonia bush. "You got me here on false pretenses. Whatever happened to 'Thou shalt not lie'?"

Now she was really smiling. In the evening light, her face couldn't look anymore radiant than if the sun had decided to follow her wherever she went. And if Devin wasn't careful, it wouldn't be the sun following her around, it would be him. The spirit of the woman walking next to him was so compelling, he wanted to find out more about it—about her.

"I didn't lie. I was simply a little vague about where we were going."

No smile this time. He wondered why. "What's wrong?"

"Nothing," she replied.

Devin bit down on his tongue. He didn't want to risk offending Renata by saying something she would consider inappropriate. But confrontation was his nature. If there was a rat on the table, he believed that the best thing to do was to say, "Hey, there's a rat on the table!" and do whatever was necessary to get it off. Not everyone agreed with his philosophy. Some people preferred to ignore the dirty little problems they had and allow them to eat at their souls until the problems became huge monsters. That kind of thinking had ended his marriage. Since then, Devin had made it a habit of learning from his mistakes.

"There's nothing wrong with being happy," he said. "It's okay to feel good sometimes."

She was silent for a while. In the distance, the music of a child's laughter broke in the air. Devin knew he'd overstepped his boundaries. But then she said, "What if you don't feel happy?"

"First, you have to give yourself permission to. We all deserve to be content."

She stopped walking then, the smile gone from her face. Not even a hint of it remained. "Then why is there so much unhappiness? I mean—" She did a half turn. "It's all around us."

Devin took both her hands in his. She seemed so lost in the moment that he couldn't help himself. "First you have to work on finding your *own* joy. When you do that, you see more joy in the world and, ultimately, it helps you to see how your gifts can bring joy to others."

"Damn," Renata said, then shook her head. "I'm sorry."

"Not a problem," Devin said, smiling himself.

"You make a lot of sense, Mr. McKenna," she said, taking her hands back.

They resumed their walk, and Devin was amazed at how empty his hands felt without Renata's to hold. Cool air flowed over the places on his palms where Renata's hands had been. He much preferred the sensation of her warmth.

Like part of an unspoken agreement, they both picked up the pace and headed to the restaurant. The summer evening temperature dropped rapidly. Neither of them had dressed for a cool night.

Their walk took them to the Hedgefield Inn. The inn was named after one of the town's founding families. For years, the inn, which was originally an antebellum mansion, had been closed and in disrepair. Renata remembered hearing that someone had purchased the mansion and recently opened the downstairs as a restaurant and gift shop. She'd wanted to go for weeks, but she'd—to use a McKenna term—put her agency and herself on a financial diet.

They were ushered to seats in a room that looked as though it had come straight out of a Civil War movie. Only this was the real thing. Brass and crystal chandeliers, floor-to-ceiling windows covered with drapes too heavy to lift, and wood furniture so sturdy and heavy it would take five men to move each piece. As they studied menus, Renata's stomach grumbled at the aroma of smoked ham, grilled onions, and fresh baked biscuits. She hadn't been hungry during their walk to the inn, but now . . . she couldn't wait to order.

They continued their conversation by discussing the remaining details of the agreement between Red Oaks and Success Unlimited. Renata kept all the figures in her head. Red Oaks would pay the three thousand-dollar sponsorship fee. In exchange, Malcolm would work for the church for three months. Renata would continue to monitor and evaluate his progress weekly. Malcolm would receive a stipend from both the church and the agency. At the end of the three months, Malcolm's performance would be evaluated in hopes of a permanent position at the church.

Over an appetizer of hot wings, they agreed to all the standard terms of the agency contract. It happened so quickly, Renata wondered what they would talk about for the rest of the time they were there.

She glanced around the inn. There weren't a lot of folks eating at this hour. Probably most had come and gone with the dinner rush. What seemed to be left were couples who wanted an intimate and romantic setting in which to spend time with someone special. Then she glanced at Devin. He was definitely special. And after his presentation tonight, she knew he was even more special, attractive, and intelligent than she had originally imagined. Almost enough to bring her backsliding butt back to church.

Almost.

Along with the aroma of the food surrounding them and the wings on their table was Devin's aftershave. She'd been trying to ignore it but wasn't being too successful. It made her wonder if he'd splashed it anywhere else on his body besides his cheeks and neck. It smelled so good she became lost in the fragrance for a moment and believed for a hot second that she and Devin were on a date and not in a restaurant discussing business.

"There it is again," Devin said, then polished off the last of the wings.

Before he asked her to explain the smile spreading on her lips, their meals came.

Renata had ordered the veggie plate. She wasn't a vegetarian, but she couldn't resist the selection of greens, cabbage, and fried okra. Devin had ordered barbequed ribs with baked beans and cornbread.

"You really should do that more often," he said. Then they dug into their food.

Devin was playing it cool, but inside he really couldn't understand his feelings. His emotions were rushing inside him, and he barely even knew Renata.

What's wrong with me? he asked himself. But it wasn't what was wrong that concerned him. It was what was right, which seemed to be everything since a few days ago when he'd met Renata. She'd been on his mind since then, and not in a small way.

"You make me laugh," she said, wielding the beautiful smile of hers like a weapon. And it worked. It did make him a little weak.

If women only knew what goes on in men's minds, he thought. *They'd be surprised to find that we're not as shallow as they sometimes think. It's just that we compartmentalize things.* Like right now, Devin's faith was fighting a strong battle with his hormones. Which was why the business portion of their dinner went so quickly. He had agreed to everything she asked because he couldn't stop looking at her mouth and believing that anything that came out of it must be good.

And her eyes . . . they were so accepting and so inviting. One look into them and it was all over with.

For the remainder of their time at the inn, Devin successfully pushed away his feelings of attraction and concentrated on the fact that he'd just met Renata, and that it would be a good idea to get to know her before considering the possibility that he might like her. Truly, *deeply* like her.

~

On the way home, Renata thought about how grateful she was for a night out. She hadn't had one in longer than she could remember, and being out with a man like Devin McKenna was a refreshing change from hanging around teenage boys and an oversexed administrative assistant.

And Devin had seemed as though he'd been on a subtle mission to keep her smiling all evening.

He'd done it in so many ways. His comments, his facial expressions to *her* comments. Even the way he ate his food was funny. Devin ate everything on his plate except the ribs. He'd saved those for last.

Renata chuckled. She missed smiling and laughing so freely.

It felt good.

The best part of the evening came at the end, though. It was cold when they came out of the inn. Her short sleeves had been no protection for the wind.

"I'd offer you my jacket, if I had one," he'd said.

Renata hugged herself in an effort to get warm. It didn't help much. And then out of the blue . . .

"Here," Devin had said, and put his arm around her shoulders. He pulled her closer—but not too close—and the two of them walked together like that the rest of the way back to Red Oaks Church.

They didn't say much. It was as if they'd been afraid of what might come out of their mouths if they had—something crazy like, *I don't know you from a can of paint, but I don't want this night to end . . . ever.*

Renata sighed and steered her Elantra into her driveway.

I'm projecting, she thought, having no way of know if Devin shared her feelings. She turned off the ignition, knowing that her strong attraction to Devin would make working with the outreach ministry difficult.

A Christian! Why did he have to be a Christian?

Eight

The next day, Devin felt good. Walking and talking with Renata had inspired him. Made him want to be creative—sit down and write until his fingers were tired.

He opened an electronic file on his computer and wrote a pitch for an article on the benefits of male/female friendships. He was in the zone, and the words poured from his hands like water.

He stopped there, knowing that he would have to fill in the blanks he'd left with a specific editor's name and address. He stretched his fingers, cracked his knuckles, and smiled. The query was only two pages long, but that was the fastest letter he'd ever written. And he had Renata to thank for it. Seeing her, being with her, had put the idea in his head. Only he realized something: He already thought of Renata as more than a friend.

He turned around at the knock on his apartment door. Curious, he rose and walked toward it. He wasn't expecting company. Some of his friends had a habit of popping over anytime they were in the neighborhood. He'd worked the day away and couldn't imagine what his friends might want that late in the evening. *Darn.* Sometimes he wished they would call first.

When Devin opened the door, he blew out a breath of relief so thick, it should have been visible.

Renata, his mind whispered, then unleashed a whirlwind of thoughts.

Promise, responsibility, duty . . . requirement. All words he would have used to describe his involvement with Renata Connor—until today. Today there was another reason.

He wanted her.

The more she seemed to be exactly the kind of woman who was all wrong for him, the more he wanted to be near her. To watch her. To talk to her. To watch her some more.

He'd awakened wanting it. Her presence. Looked forward to it all day. His obligation to Mother Maybelle was secondary now, or maybe not even a factor at all.

Humph.

He rocked back on his heels. Squared his shoulders, sucked in a deep breath, released it, and took a good look at the woman who'd diverted his thoughts, detoured his ideas, and shanghaied his focus. He kind of liked it actually. Liked the prospect of having something other than his writing, his ex-wife, or his stagnated life preoccupying his time and thoughts. His life had been on pause, or on hiatus. The same life that hadn't moved forward an inch for so long he was thinking of packing up all of his things and moving, just to start fresh and rejuvenate.

But this spitfire of a woman was enough excitement for a while. For a *long* while. He realized that maybe it wasn't just this morning that his thoughts had changed and become engaged and reawakened. She'd been creeping in, like a light behind a cracked door swinging slowly open. He was caught. Paralyzed. He couldn't wait to see what she would do next—what brightness she might bring to his life.

"May I come in?" she asked.

Slowly he remembered that he couldn't just lean against the doorway and watch like he wanted to. He had to talk, speak, interact, ruin his fantasy.

Had he been fantasizing?

"Yes," he responded.

"Why are you looking at me so hard?" she asked, walking in. "You'll make me think you're interested in me and at last that Christian-Baptist persona you have has gone bye-bye."

The smile he wanted to suppress made its way to his lips and ultimately his whole face. He liked her sarcasm.

"You fascinate me, Renata, that's all. And as for the Christian-Baptist thing I got goin', no chance of me lettin' that go. As a matter of fact," he said leaning forward, peeling himself off the wall, "you should try it sometime."

Her hard frown shocked him. He hadn't imagined her reaction would be so strong.

"I thought we had an agreement. I won't try to get you in bed, overtly that is, and you won't try to convert me."

"When did we ever agree to that?" he asked, motioning for her to take a seat. She remained standing.

"Who are you kidding, Devin? We've had that unspoken understanding since the moment we met."

He grunted, stood across from her. She was right. It was no secret she was attracted to him. He'd seen the admiration in her eyes and in her demeanor. At first, he thought she was going to turn out like so many other women he'd met—and even a few of the women in his church—making it known in no uncertain terms that they were available, very, very available.

But where others had fallen short, Renata had remained respectable, and far from desperate.

"What were you thinking just then?" she asked.

"I was thinking that you aren't as obvious or as obnoxious as some women."

"Gee, thanks!" she said, slapping her hand against her thigh.

"Sorry, that didn't sound right. What I meant is I know there's an attraction between us. I know you're attracted to me." She struck a pose that would make any ghetto-fabulous woman on *Soul Train* proud. He guessed he'd better try again. "I know that we are attracted to *each other.*"

The smile that softened the pose was worth waiting a lifetime for.

"So," she said, approaching him. "What are we going to do about it?"

Oh, what to do, he thought. Hadn't he been imagining that very thing for several days now?

She was approaching him. Pretty much the same way he'd imagined once. Only in his mind, he'd stopped her from getting too close, told her that a physical relationship was not only too soon, but out of the question, and had mumbled something about being born again.

But reality, as is often the case, was quite different from imagination. When she was less than three feet away, he reached for her, pulled her in fast, breathed hard.

Her fragrance closed his eyes. From afar, she'd always smiled, sultry and alluring. But up close, she smelled like a raging fire, wild, hot, untamable. He pulled her into his body. She molded perfectly, and before she could say one more thing, he took her mouth.

Their moan was synchronous. The sound of their mutual pleasure excited him further, made him drive deeper into her mouth. He sought the slick soft muscle of her tongue and ravaged it. Was selfish with it. And the way she gave it, freely, made him feel like he owned it. He pulled her closer, frustrated by the space separating them, and let the fire between them build.

Their hands traveled slowly over each other's bodies; then their exchange became more urgent, more driving, more frantic. Needy. How long had they each been waiting for this? Too long, as they groped each other for more feeling, more intensity, and a deeper connection.

He wished he could have imagined the sensations raging through his body. But not even a fantasy could have prepared him for the realities of Renata's mouth.

It was sweeter than the sweetest dream he'd ever had. And just when he was about to pull her closer, pull her all the way into him, and, goodness help him, take valiantly whatever came next, Renata pulled back.

"Woman, you are habanero hot and have no qualms about seducing a Christian man. How do you sleep at night?"

His words were serious, but his tone was playful. For that she was grateful, and decided to play right back.

"I'm just testing your word."

His arm circled her waist easily, warmly, strongly. He pulled her back into him. Her body brooked no argument. Just slid into the hard contours of his chest.

"You'll get enough about testing my word."

"Never," she whispered, nearly out of breath, but certainly out of patience. She'd waited so long to feel his strength. Imagined this moment too many times and could not wait another second to take in his heat.

"What I want to do to you is . . ."

"Primitive" he finished.

Both their chests heaved as they tried to stop touching each other.

"We wouldn't have to get buck wild," Renata offered. "I mean, really . . . can you imagine . . . us? . . ."

Devin breathed deeply. "Yes, I can."

"Me, too," she added.

They kissed again, more tentatively this time. Then, better sense seemed to halt their sensuous attack.

Renata felt tingly. "For a minute, I was having some crazy thoughts."

"You can say that again. Crazy, crazy thoughts."

"I mean there's no way we could . . . is there?" she asked.

Devin pursed his lips. "Absolutely not. I take my faith very seriously."

"Yes you do. I mean, I admire you for that. Seriously."

"Of course, that was a serious kiss we shared. I don't want you to think I'm making light of what happened."

A smile tickled the corners of Renata's mouth. "No, no. I wouldn't think that."

"Good," Devin murmured.

Renata assessed the situation and felt guilty about putting Devin in a position to betray his faith. "Well, I'd better be going. I just stopped by to . . . um . . . uh . . . I don't even remember why now."

He nodded and took half a step backward. "You're sure you have to go?"

"Woo, yes . . . I'm sure."

She turned to leave. The warmth of his hand caressing her back stopped her in her tracks.

He turned her toward him. "Don't go," he said. "I want you near me right now."

And just then, a phrase came out of him that he never thought he'd hear himself say, "And I promise not to try to recruit you into God's good service."

Renata threw her hands into the sky, "Thank ya, Jesus!" Then her hand few across her mouth in apology. "Sorry," she said, but he was already laughing.

"It's okay. I'm getting used to you and your—your heathen ways."

"So," she said, "Is there anything else around here you're getting used to?"

He didn't want to smile at her remark or acknowledge in any way that he had given in. That his defenses had crumbled the moment he'd happened upon her fantasizing at her desk, and that all he'd been doing since then was put up a bold front.

But his move toward her belied his intentions. And the broad smile warming his face was a dead giveaway. And for sure, his fingers brushing back strands of hair from the front of her face was a definite tell. *But the sure-fire bet,* he thought as he leaned toward her, breathed the smoky fire-heat of her, was this kiss he was about to press softly against her lips.

Only, she wouldn't let him . . . go slowly. He stepped closer, pressed deeper, as her heat rose, flared in intensity, summoned to him, and—God bless it—he was ready to go.

The inside of his body felt combustible. He reveled in rediscovering what it meant to need desperately, urgently, to remember passion, and what it meant to yearn for another. When Renata pulled away, his soul cried out for more.

"Renata," he whispered, stepping back from her once more, determined not to go too far with her.

She smiled. "What time is it?" she asked, eyes drunk with passion.

"Eight," he said, without looking. His internal clock was pretty good. He was usually only off by five or so minutes. "Why?"

"Because," she said, snuggling closer. "I was just thinking that maybe we could hang out tonight, visit Malcolm working at the church . . . stay out of trouble."

He twisted the cross at the end of his necklace between his thumb and forefinger. A pang of guilt surfaced and retreated. Devin took a deep breath.

"I think that's a good idea," he said.

Malcolm watched Miss Connor and Mr. McKenna and shook his head. They hadn't forgotten about him, but they were so into each other that, unless he injured himself seriously, they probably wouldn't look his way any time soon. He wanted to laugh and often had. They didn't know they were in love, but over the weeks that had passed. He'd bet that everyone else did.

They said they had both come to check on him, to see how he was doing. And in a way, that was Miss Connor's job. But he'd been working at the church for several weeks now. And he'd gotten the sweeping, mopping, and taking out the trash thing down. He'd also tried his hand at moving furniture and fixing a few things. Brother Mack had shown him how to replace warped tile, spackle a wall, and rewire a light switch. It wasn't the greatest job, but it was kinda fun sometimes.

The best thing of all was that he was getting paid tomorrow. He couldn't wait to show his paycheck to Mr. and Mrs. Smith. He knew they would be

proud of him. And he also knew that he would treat Mr. Smith to that barbeque dinner he was always talking about. Even if he couldn't chew it. If his
dentures didn't work, he would buy a meat grinder and grind up the pork.

He couldn't wait!

He emptied the big trash can and took one more look at the two grown
ups who acted more like children than some of the kids he hung around
with. At least the kids he knew admitted that they liked each other and went
for what they wanted.

But the two adults just kept trippin' like they had all the time in the world
to get to the point.

Malcolm let himself laugh anyway. He calculated his six-fifty-an-hour income in his head.

Maybe he would buy them something, too.

As soon as Mr. McKenna and Miss Connor left, he released a deep breath
of frustration. The eyes were on him again. Malcolm kept propelling the
sweeper in front of him. Kept his head down. He was starting to like manual
labor. It was quiet, he could use his muscles, and no one bothered him. Well,
at least it had begun that way. He'd started out this job quiet and by himself.
But a few of the old folks had something against him. They were always staring at him, and now they had taken to making sure that someone *just* happened to be around every time he cleaned up. Malcolm ignored it. He'd been
told to respect his elders, even when it seemed like they were disrespecting
him. He had, however, mentioned it to Miss Connor. When they had their
last weekly meeting, she'd asked him how things were going and he'd been
honest.

"It could be better," he'd said, hoping he didn't sound ungrateful.

"Better how?" she asked.

"It's the people, man. I mean, they are on me."

"Explain 'on me.'"

"I mean, I can't move. I can't even wipe my own a—uh, behind—without somebody checkin' for me. If they don't want me at the church, they should just tell me."

"Malcolm, I'm sure they are happy to have you at the church."

"Then can't you tell them somethin'?"

He would have thought that the best place for a sinner was in a church. He glanced quickly at the old man straightening Bibles in the pocket of the pew across from him and realized that in some cases that wasn't true.

Nine

When the phone rang, Devin was in the middle of a long dream. He and Renata had been on a picnic. At first, they were surrounded by the members of the congregation, but after a while, their audience disappeared and it was just them. They had been laughing, talking, and running like children all afternoon in the dream.

And then the phone rang.

"Yeah," he said, barely awake and refusing to open his eyes under protest.

"Brother McKenna, you better come down to the sanctuary. We've got some trouble."

He sat up, eyes wide with concern. "Why? What's wrong?" And then his blood ran cold. "Has something happened to Malcolm?"

"Yes. You'd better get down here." And before he could ask more questions, Sister Patterson hung up.

Devin bounded off of the bed and headed for the closet. He yanked on his clothing, wondering if he should call an ambulance. But if it was life-threatening, or if the boy had been injured, certainly one of the members would have called the paramedics.

As he headed out the door, he wondered two things. What could be so urgent that they would call him to the sanctuary, and, second, why apprehension shot through his veins so acutely for a young man he'd harbored reservations about in the past?

Devin jumped into his SUV and sped down the street, hoping the answers to his questions were only minutes away.

"Praise God," Sister Patterson said as he entered the church. The sanctuary was dark and quiet. "I convinced them not to call the police until you could get here."

"Police?" Devin asked. Now dread replaced his apprehension. He followed Sister Patterson into the pastor's study and scanned the room. Brother Banks and Sister Courtney stood, looking like they'd just eaten rotten eggs. Malcolm, on the other hand, looked as though he could kill someone with his eyes. Right now, his assassin's glare was blaring in Devin's direction.

"What's happened?" Devin asked, hoping to defuse the bomb of tension in the room before it went off.

"They set me up!" Malcolm blurted.

"Satan is a liar!" shouted Sister Patterson.

Sister Courtney folded her arms in front of her. "Yes, he's a thief *and* a liar!"

"Thief!" Devin said, the word sinking in his stomach like a stone.

"Yes. I knew this no-goodnik would show his true colors in the church," Sister Courtney continued.

"My mama used to say, 'The devil is still the devil, even on Sunday,'" Brother Banks said.

Sister Patterson's jaw was clenched so tightly, it was a miracle she could speak. But she did. "The moment he set foot in this church, I knew he was trouble, but nobody asked me. They just—"

"Hold on a minute," Devin interrupted. "What did he steal?" He stepped back a bit and stared at the three, who reminded him of an old-time gospel choir that would be better off singing, "I Know I Been Changed," than accusing a young boy of stealing.

"A painting," Sister Patterson replied.

"And not one of the old ones," Brother Banks added.

"He stole one of the new ones," Sister Courtney finished.

Devin glanced at Malcolm, The boy shook his head.

"Man, what would I do with a painting like that? I don't even know any-body who *likes* art, especially that kind."

"See what I'm tellin' ya, Brother McKenna? Only a heathen would call it *that kind*."

"That's not what I meant!" Malcolm snapped.

"Would did you mean?" Devin asked, wanting to hear his explanation.

"I mean I just can't relate is all."

"The only thing you can relate to is a jail cell, young man," Brother Banks said, picking up the phone. "I'mmo see cain't I arrange one for you."

Sister Patterson worked her neck as she talked. "Look, Brother McKenna, the only reason we're here at the church, especially on a Saturday night, is that someone had to keep an eye on this boy. And for him to be given per-mission to clean up by himself so soon, well . . . something like this was bound to happen."

"Devin . . . Mr. McKenna . . . I told Miss Connor they were checkin' for me. Just not on the positive at all. But the only reason they left me alone so soon is because I do a good job! I'd like to see one of y'all do as good a job as I do! Heck, none of y'all want to empty no damn trash and clean up after yourselves!"

"Malcolm! That's enough!" Devin shouted.

The boy's eyes widened like saucers. So did everyone else's in the room. Realizing that he must have raised his voice just a little too loudly, Devin measured his volume this time. "Malcolm, please wait for me outside."

"What about One Time?" he asked, referring to the police.

"No one's going to call the cops. Just wait for me. Okay?"

"Yeah," he said, but not before getting off one last round of lethal stares.

"All right," Devin said, taking a seat on the edge of the desk. "Which one of you saw him take the painting?"

"Brother Banks noticed that the painting was missing," Sister Patterson said.

"Brother Banks, does Malcolm know you saw him take it?"

"Well . . . ," Stuart Banks said, getting that look he always had when it was his turn to bring refreshments to the entrepreneurial ministry meeting and he'd forgotten to do it.

"I didn't *see* him take it. I just noticed that since we been 'on watch' tonight, that the painting had disappeared."

The words 'on watch' stuck in Devin's mind. He would ask about that later.

"Sister Courtney, did you see him take it?"

"No, but . . ."

"Sister Patterson?"

"You know what, Devin McKenna, I don't have to see the devil to know that he exists. Now, when we got here this evenin', that painting was on the wall. Now it's not, and the only people in the church—"

"Stop," Devin said, holding up his hand. He couldn't stand to hear another word. He had to get out of there. Renata was having an adverse effect on him, because just then a profane retort came to his mind. Something about Jesus and the Pharisees. But he'd been taught to respect his elders, so he didn't say it. Instead, he said, "Look, don't call the police. I'll contact Pastor Avery. Let him know what's going on. In the meantime, I'll do what I can to get to the bottom of this and, with any luck, get the painting back."

"We'll give you a week, Brother McKenna. After that, I'm going to speak with Brother Ewing," Sister Patterson said.

Devin took a deep breath. Brother Ewing was also Lieutenant Ewing of the Red Oaks Police Department. The last thing Devin wanted was a scandal in the church. And that's just what would happen if these three had their way.

"That's fair," he said, hoping he meant it, and walked out of the study. He wondered if Malcolm had the guts to stick around or if the boy had done what he himself would have done in his youth, bolted as fast as he could.

Devin didn't know if he was shocked or just plain grateful to see Malcolm sulking next to his SUV. Feelings he'd had the moment he'd considered entering into a relationship with Success Unlimited surfaced again with fury. Some folks just couldn't be rehabbed. And maybe this kid was one of them.

"Okay, kid," he said, walking up to the young man, who looked as though his best friend had just been shot. "Your story, now."

"I didn't take it. Finito. End of story."

"Then why are there three members of Red Oaks Church mad as hornets and ready to turn you over to the law?"

"I told you. They preach all men are brothers and Jesus is love. But when it comes down to it, they're hypocrites, just like Ms. Connor says."

A flame of anger ignited inside Devin. What had Renata been telling the boy? No wonder he was resentful.

Devin would not allow her to usurp even the smallest chance Malcolm had of becoming a decent human being.

But that was neither here nor there right now. What mattered now was whether Devin could determine Malcolm's guilt or innocence. He resisted the urge to question him about Renata's comment. Instead, he opened his passenger door and said, "Get in."

Malcolm did as he was told and the two were off from the church and headed to The Bottoms.

"Are you taking me to One Time?"

"No, I'm taking you home."

"So are they gonna meet us there?"

"No. I persuaded the parishioners not to press charges . . . yet."

～

The Smiths lived in a really nice house . . . really. It was kind of a sad pink with white gray shutters and a chain-link fence. It was shaped like a rectangle turned sideways. The grass was cut, the siding was clean, and a pair of lace curtains flapped in an open window. The problem wasn't the house at all.

It was the neighborhood.

Where this little, one-level house had cut green grass, other houses on the block had dirt, toys, and some even had trash in the yard. Where the pink siding was clean and recently washed on the Smith house, other homes had peeling paint and chipped wood.

And where the Smith's house looked like a place you would want to come home to, others, sadly, looked to Devin like places to run away from.

Malcolm reached for the door handle on the Chevy Tahoe. Devin couldn't let him leave, not without seeing his eyes as he asked him once again.

"Look, Malcolm. I'm sorry about all that back there."

"No, you're not," he said, sounding more tired and older than he had ever sounded. The typical easy-flowing hip-hop assurance and bravado had gotten lost somewhere in the church between accusations. No, the person sitting next to him, the soon-to-be-man, looked depleted and ready to retire.

"You're just like every other adult I've met in my life. You're all the same. Judgmental. Unfair, and too preoccupied with yourself to care about anyone or anything else." He stepped out of the car, but left door open. "It's too bad, too. You could have been different."

He closed the door then and headed toward the nicest little house on the block. He left Devin, who thought, *Darn. That's the same thing I was beginning to think about you.*

By the time he drove home, Renata was already in front of his apartment waiting for him. Obviously, the boy had called her, told her what had happened, and she had come right over. He expected her to be her regular excitable, hyper-vigilant self. She wasn't, though. Instead, she was calm, cool, and casual, and when they went inside, she discussed the issue of Malcolm with a level head and a practical heart.

"Malcolm said you don't believe him."

Devin scratched his head and sat down in on the loveseat in his living room. He was almost disappointed that she hadn't bristled, hadn't gotten her back up and given him a fight. He admitted he would have enjoyed sparring with her. She seemed perfectly capable of holding her own, and, more importantly, he would have gotten to see those beautiful eyes of hers flash like cinnamon fire. He could warm his whole body in that fire. He was sure of it.

"It's a strange coincidence that suddenly—while Malcolm just happens to be cleaning up the building by himself—a painting turns up missing."

"He wasn't by himself. Those nosy, uh—there were several members of the congregation there with him."

"Yes, but—"

"But nothing. How do you know one of them didn't take the painting? How do you know he isn't being set up?"

"Set up? By some silly church folk? You've been watching too much *Law & Order*."

"Me? You're the one who thinks that one innocent teenager, trying to turn his life around, went up in a church and stole a painting. A painting! What would someone like Malcolm want with a painting?"

"Maybe not him, but I'll bet one of his homies would sell a painting like that to the highest bidder."

"Please!"

That's it, Devin thought. There's some of the fire I've come to look forward to.

And he wasn't lying. Since he'd spent so much time with Renata, he'd grown used to her spark of life. Her flicker of no nonsense. She was so unlike many of the women he knew. They could be so tame and accepting. They didn't challenge or push back much.

The more he thought about it, the more he realized that those were the kind of women he'd been drawn to. Well-mannered, well-behaved, easy-going women.

But this woman across from him was a handful. He hoped he wasn't dazed and dazzled by what could quite possibly be the devil putting a temptress in his vision. Because lately, all he could see was Renata.

"Truce," he said, finally. He was allowing himself to get too caught up. He could feel his judgment already clouding over, becoming fuzzy. The more he stared at her and looked her over, the more he wanted to believe anything she said. If she said Malcolm didn't do it, then by God, he didn't do it. And that was that. End of story, turn the lights out when you leave!

"What's so funny?" she asked.

Not realizing he was smiling, Devin chuckled at his involuntary betrayal. "Me . . . you . . . us maybe."

"What about me, you . . . us?"

"Well, he said thoughtfully. "Maybe it is just *you* that I find funny. Or rather, your effect on me."

Her eyebrows rose. "What's that got to do with anything?" she asked, leaning forward slightly in the seat she taken across from him. "My effect on you."

"Even though I'm almost one hundred percent sure that that boy—"

"Malcolm."

"*Young man* took the painting, just because you believe that he didn't makes me want to believe it, too."

"Why?" she asked, concern turning the pretty features of her face into deep lines and angles.

"Because you don't strike me as the type of person who would believe, or not believe, in anything frivolously."

She nodded. "I guess you're right about that."

"My reaction to that surprises me. Makes me laugh sometimes."

"What's funny is you're just now figuring that out. I've known it since the moment we met."

He laughed heartily. She was right of course. And he had pushed away his growing feelings, believing that it was ten kinds of wrong for him to fall for a woman out of the church, and that the last thing he needed was someone to change his mind about his plans to leave Red Oaks. But he was finally admitting to himself that having Renata in his life felt good. Felt right. Puffed out his chest, blew up his ego, and woke up his libido.

She was a force. A force that turned his monochrome existence into Intel Inside color. She was a brilliant light shining in a cave which had been pitch dark for far too long.

He dared not think what his life would be like after the outreach ministry agreement was over.

"Now, what are you thinking?"

"I'm thinking I want to kiss you so bad, angels in heaven can hear my thoughts."

She smiled, just when he thought she couldn't light up any brighter. "Man, those are the words I've been waiting weeks to hear, but right now I'm too concerned about Malcolm to do anything about it."

Devin's disappointment was as hard as the loveseat he sat on.

"I've got to prove that Malcolm is innocent. Will you help me?" she asked.

The fire in her eyes rose again. Warmed and melted him again.

"Yes," he said, knowing he could deny her nothing. "I'll help you."

"Thank you," she said, and stood.

When Devin stood with her, she walked over to deliver what was obviously a grateful peck on the cheek. Only he wasn't satisfied with that. Instead, he made sure that their lips touched for a long, long time.

"How big is your bed, Devin?" Renata asked, breaking their kiss.

Ten

He had to grit his teeth before answering. The sweet taste of Renata's mouth had haunted him since their first kiss.

Desire roared through his veins, an inferno, unchecked and blazing like a California wildfire. From the moment they'd met, Renata had captivated him in every way possible, her eyes, her smile, the move of her hand, an extra bounce in her behind. Now all he wanted to do was captivate her the way she had him. Take his time looking her luscious body over. Strut around to get her attention, touch her neck, her arm, her backside.

If he had been Catholic, he would have said at least a thousand "Hail Marys" by now. As it stood, he'd been on his knees more times than he could count, asking God to take away the image of Renata's shapely figure that kept his mind active these days.

So, when she stood in the middle of his apartment and asked him about his bed, his need to be near her, closer than they'd been, to feel her heat through the night, fought with everything inside him that knew better, and won.

He pulled her to him, tilted her head up, took her mouth.

His imagination hadn't done justice to his memory. Kissing Renata was unlike any kiss he could ever remember. So overwhelming, it made him crazy for more. Before he could get carried away, he pulled back gently.

"De-vin!" Renata protested. "Why does one of us always pull away?"

"So we don't get carried away."

Renata sighed heavily. Her disappointment pained him. He couldn't stand to see her unhappy.

He kissed her forehead. *God, if I'm about to do wrong, please forgive me, but I think I love this woman.* "Stay with me tonight." The words came out in a whisper. He hadn't meant them to. He could tell Renata liked the sound of the idea.

Her eyes darkened dangerously with passion. She drew her arms around his neck, stepped in closer.

He could smell her skin and feel the warmth of it. She pressed against him boldly, and oh so familiarly. He took a deep breath; she caught it with her lips, and he surrendered when her mouth possessed his.

He could not get her close enough. He wrapped his arms around her, pulling, pulling. He let his wonder of her, his fascination, take over his hands and roam over her, touching every inch.

His free will faded away and he struggled to recover it, but the moan escaping Renata's lips became his undoing. He picked her up, swiftly, urgently, and carried her to his bedroom.

He didn't turn on a light. Instead, he let the light from the living room be their only illumination and lay her on his bed. Her face was a beautiful combination of love, lust, and unrequited need. He meant to quench all three.

He undressed her first. Selfish, he knew, but he couldn't wait another second to see what he'd been imagining for days and weeks.

When he removed the last article of clothing, he was not disappointed. He was surprised that his mind had not been effective at all in conjuring images of her magnificence. He'd been off, way off. There were no words to describe the brilliance of beauty that nearly blinded him.

He murmured a prayer of thanks to the Almighty for creating a woman so spectacular. Then he kissed her again.

Before she could pull him on top of her, he undressed and flung his clothes far into the corner of the room, as if they offended his flesh, as if he never wanted to see them again. He needed to rid himself of the last barrier between them.

Her eyes widened in anticipation, darkened even more with need and he knew exactly what he wanted to do with her, to her, for her.

"I'll be right back," he whispered and walked out of the room.

"Devin," Renata said huskily, but it was too late. He was already gone a second, maybe two, and she missed him. As if half of her body had just left the room.

Maybe he's gone to get condoms, she hoped.

When he returned, he had a pitcher of water and a cup in his hand.

"Devin, what—" she began and sat up.

"Lay back," he ordered, in a voice so full of sexual longing she could do nothing but obey. She breathed harder, wondering what he was doing, knowing she was so close to making love with him she could smell their need in the air. She couldn't contain herself any longer. She had waited too long.

"Devin, please . . . ," she said wanting his hands on her again, roaming, finding all the places she'd imagined him touching.

He stood over her with the pitcher and the cup. He was breathing hard, too, and she could see his excitement growing before her eyes.

"Renata, I'm not going to make love to you."

"What!" she said, not believing what she just heard.

"Relax. I want to tell you something. I want you to feel what I feel."

She did as he asked, but her disappointment was palpable. She wondered what had changed his mind. She stared into his eyes, but nothing had changed. The need on his face was as raw as it had been just a few seconds ago.

He began to pour water into the cup in a thin slow stream.

"I love you, Renata," he said. "I've fantasized about us being together, touching, kissing, making love, every day since we met."

His words fell over her like a gentle touch. She closed her eyes and let them sink in.

"I've imagined your body, Renata and all the places my lips would go. Tell me, Renata. Have you imagined mine?"

"Yes," she whispered. "Yes." The place between her thighs throbbed urgently. She squeezed her legs together to allay the feeling.

"You think I don't want you, haven't wanted you. That I don't think about you as you do me. But you're wrong. I want you to know how much I want you, need you . . . love you."

Renata gasped, and her eyes snapped open as a cool splash of liquid hit her belly.

The need in Devin's eyes had grown even more intense. He did want her. He continued to pour. The sensation of water falling slowly on her body drove the sensual current of her longing deeper into her. She gasped again and muttered his name.

"Just like this cup, my love for you is overflowing, Renata. Do you hear me? What I feel for you is overflowing."

Just then he placed the cup and pitcher on the nightstand and dropped to his knees. He lowered his head to her abdomen and his lips and tongue found all of the places on her body where the water had traveled.

The feeling was so exquisite she could only grab him, hold on, and whimper.

He followed the trail of wetness across her breasts, down to her navel, and down farther still, until she burst open and screamed his name.

She opened her eyes. Devin lay beside her smiling. He was still fully aroused and she resisted the deep urge to touch him where he was most sensitive.

He twirled a strand of her hair between his fingers. "I wanted you to see how much I want you."

He reached down and pulled a sheet over them. Then he reached out and held her hand and stared at her so intensely she thought he was looking straight into her soul. "Do you still want to make love?" he asked.

The mere question from his lips sent a hot chill vibrating through her. She could only nod. If she opened her mouth, no telling what part of Devin's body would end up kissed by it.

"Then let this connection bring us together tonight and we will." He squeezed her hand tighter. "Sweet dreams," he whispered.

Content to be near him in this way, Renata closed her eyes. In her sated state, she fell asleep quickly. Her dreams were filled with Devin. And in them they made love for . . . hours.

So as to not give an appearance of impropriety, Renata got up in the middle of the night and left Devin sleeping peacefully in his bed. She went home hoping that they'd shared a new beginning that would not end with the light of day.

∼

The next day brought Renata a great Sunday morning surprise. Devin was at her front door, bright and smiling.

"Good day!" he said more cheerfully than she could ever remember. "I was hoping you were home."

She opened the door wide. "Well, good day to you, too!"

He sounded good. He looked good. The blue suit he had on made him look professional and sexy at the same time. She decided to take a chance to find out whether he felt as good as he looked.

She stepped into his arms. Their embrace was magnetic—as though they'd been sealed together by an invisible force. And she was right.

He did feel good.

"This is serious, isn't it?" she murmured nuzzling in, snuggling closer.

"Yes. If we don't find out what really happened to that painting, my fellow parishioners are going to make sure that the police put Malcolm *under* the jail."

She sighed. It was true. Although, when she'd asked about being serious, she hadn't meant Malcolm.

Devin picked up on her meaning. He pulled away and bent down to look her in the eye.

"Yes, it is," he said, his voice deep and silken. "It's *very* serious."

His lips kissed her chest through her blouse. The heat from his breath flowed through the cotton fabric, warming her skin. She shuddered.

He kissed her again and again. Delicately. Deliberately. *Deliciously.*

Her shoulder. Her collar bone. The crook of her neck. The space behind her ear. The hollow of her cheek. Her eyelid.

By the time his lips touched hers, she was already melting into his body, already surrendering. This thing pulsing between them was no longer a harmless flirtation on her part. No longer a man retreating or a woman giving in to passion.

What they had together was a serious love affair. A serious dedication to each other.

A serious commitment.

She opened her eyes. He was already staring back. His dark topaz orbs were serious and playful at the same time.

His lips brushed warmly across hers. "Before I lose my mind, let's go for a ride and talk about Malcolm."

"I can't go like this," she said tugging at her casual clothes.

"Sure you can. Come on!"

He grabbed Renata's wrist and her hand disappeared in his. When she got into Devin's SUV, she was prepared to listen to any ideas he had about investigating the missing painting. Renata even had a couple of ideas of her own.

Devin spoke before she did. "Early this morning, I went back to the Smiths' house. I'm sure you don't want to hear why, but I'm going to say it anyway." He turned on the engine and pulled into the street. "God led me back there.

"As my good blessing would have it, I had breakfast with Malcolm and the Smiths. Remarkable people. They are obviously getting on in years, but they were the most gracious, energetic, sincere hosts whose home I've ever had the pleasure of dining in. First, we all talked, broke bread, shared a laugh. After a short while, the couple went to sit on their front porch leaving me alone with Malcolm.

"After I assured him that I wasn't there to turn him over to the police, we had a discussion—more like a meeting of the minds. And I realized something. Malcolm is not just like I was at that age. He's smarter, wiser. It became very clear that all the anger that I was projecting onto him was coming from the resentment I have of myself for behaving like a fool in my youth. When the truth of that settled in my mind, I began to see Malcolm for the young man that he is and not the scoundrel that *I* used to be.

"That's why, no matter what, I'm going to make sure that the painting is returned by whoever stole it."

She turned to Devin then. So sure of himself, so calm. His resolve inspired her. Gave her confidence.

And the courage to say something that had been on her mind since last night.

"I love you, Devin."

"Renata . . . I love you, too."

Eleven

They arrived at the church just before the service began. It only took a few moments to confirm their suspicions. There had been someone else in the sanctuary last night. The first guard on duty, Brother Kellog, told them that Sister Edna had showed up like she sometimes did and just wanted to have a prayer meeting—with herself. He'd indulged her, but after a while, he'd forgotten that she was there.

According to Brother Kellog, she was probably still inside when he left and the second guard, Brother Banks, came on duty.

Grateful for the information, Renata was hoping to skip out before the service began, but no such luck. She and Devin had been investigating the theft for a few minutes too long, which meant the only polite thing to do would be to stay for the message. Besides, it would take Devin too long to drive her to her place and then get back in time to attend the service.

She swallowed the lump forming in her throat and followed Devin as he led her though the crowd to seats toward the middle of the sanctuary.

Renata sat down and blew out a breath. Although Red Oaks had a "come as you are" dress code, Renata felt way under-dressed in her cotton blouse and soft capris. The words claustrophobic and *get out* played in her mind over and over like phrases spoken in an echo chamber. She fidgeted, first with her clothing, then with the hymnals in the pocket in front of her. When she started clicking a pen she found in her pocket, Devin placed a calming hand over hers.

"Relax," he whispered. "This is a house of worship and love. No one is out to get you."

But that was just the problem. Every time she'd set foot in Red Oaks Christian Fellowship Church, she'd felt as though something, or rather, *someone*, was out to get her. And that it absolutely would not stop until she was taken over.

Her hands shook with nervousness. To keep at least one of them busy, she grabbed a fan and fanned herself furiously.

"Is it hot in here?" she asked, feeling sweat pop through her pores in tiny beads.

Devin bent nearer. His manly scent danced into her nostrils, calming her a bit. "No. It's not." He took the fan from her and placed it back into the pocket. Then he stretched his long arm around her and squeezed her close. "Don't worry," he said. "I'm here. Pastor Avery will probably talk about the importance of living right, and we'll be out of here in no time. Since this kind of stuff doesn't really interest you, try not to fall asleep," he said, smiling.

Renata nodded, feeling suddenly that after today, she may find it hard to sleep for awhile. She glanced around the church and tried to order her thoughts. The sanctuary was packed with people wearing everything from fine rags to blue jeans. Some of the women had hairdos that must have taken days, not hours, to coif. These women were jeweled down and sparkling. The scene brought some of her more pleasant childhood church memories back to her, giving her a small measure of comfort.

True to Devin's prediction, the first part of the service flew by with lightning-quick speed. Praise and worship, offering, and announcements all in a matter of minutes. Then Reverend Avery took the pulpit and Renata started to feel that she should have walked home instead of staying for the service.

She gulped and slowly realized that no matter what she did, no matter how hard she resisted, no matter how many excuses she came up with, she somehow kept ending up in Red Oaks Church. From the moment Devin had come into her life, she'd seen the inside of a church more times in the past few weeks than in the past few years.

It was always something, and today, this morning, it was her being in the presence of the man she loved. She sighed with the thought.

Love.

And she knew exactly when it had happened. When her attraction for the handsome toffee cool of a man had turned to love. It was the night of the entrepreneurial ministry, when she'd seen Devin in purpose. It was the walk they'd taken afterwards, when he'd comforted her. It was the way he'd made her laugh time and again. It was the way he'd taken on the challenge of Malcolm.

It was the moment he'd walked into her office.

Her heart had turned over in her chest and started beating to the phrase, "I love you, Devin McKenna. I love you." And her body had thrummed that chant ever since.

Oh, she felt the same rush of anxiety being there. The same tingling sensation in the pit of her stomach. Her mouth had gone dry and every nerve ending in her body screamed for her to bolt out of there while she still had the chance.

Then like an answer to a prayer, Devin reached over, placed his hand on top of hers, and calmed her.

Reassurance flooded her body.

The skin beneath his large firm hand warmed. But there was nothing sensual about it. More like a life-affirming connectedness, and all the proof she needed to know that Devin's feelings for her were strong. She hoped that he would always be there for her. The bridge over her troubled, unsure, hedonistic waters. Her stabilizer. And from now on, she would never have to worry about being afraid again.

When Pastor Avery moved and stood behind the pulpit, a tremor in Renata's body made her swallow hard. Her palms became sweaty, and she rubbed them together hoping he would be quick.

He wasn't.

As a matter of fact, he stood there for over a minute before he actually spoke. When he did, his eyes scanned the row upon row of parishioners, but his words settled directly upon her.

"Beloved of His word, I tell you I had a *message* prepared this morning.

"I had a message prepared, and it was good, too! I worked all week on it. I tell you, I was preparin' some holy word gumbo for you to feast on up in here!"

"A-men!" someone shouted.

"I mean, I had gotten the divine roux just right! And the second I stepped behind the pulpit this morning, God tapped me on the shoulder and said, "I have something else for you, pastor."

"Oh, beloved, listen to what I'm saying this morning. God said, 'My plan is bigger than your plan. My plan is better than your plan.' Now, some of you *know* what I'm talking about, some of you are just *pretending* to know what I'm talking about, and some of you *wish* you knew what I was talking about."

Renata and Devin chuckled together.

Pastor Avery moved away from the pulpit and marched out into the congregation. His words propelled powerfully through the air, as if they leapt from his soul and were on their way to heaven.

"Oh y'all must excuse me today, but the *Lord* is talking. He's talking this morning and He wants you to know that there was nothing you could do. There's nothing anyone can do to change anything once God's mind is made up. He wants you to know that His plan may not always be your plan, but He says—and I'm going to break it down for ya—He says, trust that it's *all good all the time*."

The deep remorse Renata felt for the loss of her brother spilled out of her in a quiet stream of tears. Devin pulled her closer, the look of loving concern on his face.

From a voice that had risen like thunder, came Pastor Avery's calm admonishment. "Don't ever think that you are in charge. Because when you do, the devil will exploit your ignorance. There are so many temptations, diversions, and wrong paths to walk that no one lowly human can do it all or know it all."

"Yes," Renata whispered, as the truth of the reverend's words washed into her.

"Is there someone here today who has some unfinished business with the Lord? If you haven't been placed in Christ, I ask that you please, please, please come. Meet him at the altar," he coaxed. "He's been waiting for you."

Renata wiped her eyes and knew why she'd stayed away from church for so long. The truth had been waiting for her here. She glanced up at Devin, grateful that he'd been placed in her life to show her what she'd been missing.

She knew she would not join church today, but one day . . . maybe.

~

No one really knew much about Sister Edna. She walked to church every Sunday. She always came by herself. She had a tendency to talk to people that no one else could see.

She lived in a structure that just barely fit the definition of house. On the corner of Laughlin and Merit Streets, it appeared barely habitable and seemed to be held together by some invisible force. Devin walked up to the front porch, which was neat and tidy.

He crept up the weather-worn staircase praying that he didn't fall through. It would be terrible luck if the wood crumbled beneath him and he broke his skull just when he'd finally created a life worth living by finding love.

Taking his time, he gave a cautious knock at the door. There was a flurry of voices behind it. Funny thing, but all of the voices sounded like variations of Sister Edna—only in different octaves. Finally, the large wooden door creaked loudly open.

"Oh, Brother McKenna," she said, fussing with her hair. "Praise the Lord today."

"Praise him," Devin responded.

Her nervous fiddling traveled down the ties on her housedress. Sister Edna shook as though she might be suffering from palsy.

"Did you want something, Brother McKenna?"

"Yes," he said, wishing he'd taken the time to plan a script. But since he hadn't . . . "I was wondering if I could come in and speak with you about your, er, prayer service yesterday."

"Certainly," she responded swinging the door wider to let him enter.

As he stepped across the threshold, he rehearsed all the ways in which he could broach the subject of the painting. When he followed her out of the entryway and into the living room, he realized no rehearsal was necessary. The painting was propped up against the foot of a very old and overused couch.

His first thought about all of Sister Edna's furniture was that it was secondhand. But upon longer inspection, it appeared more like third- or fourthhand. And sprawled among the dilapidated and stained high-back chair, the crooked table, the fleabag couch and the painting, were stacks of Bibles, mounds of hymnals, and enough Red Oaks fans to wallpaper a room.

Chances were that Sister Edna had been appropriating items for years from every church she'd ever belonged to. By the looks of the painting and the stack of collection plates sitting on the floor next to it, Sister Edna had graduated to bigger and better things.

"May I use your bathroom?" he asked, partly concerned about what he would find there, but knowing he needed a place to use his cell phone in private.

"Certainly. This way."

He followed her down a short, narrow hallway cluttered with church bulletins and ministry newsletters. He slipped on one but recovered before slamming butt first onto a carpet that looked as though it hadn't been vacuumed in years.

Luckily, the bathroom was only a few steps away and surprisingly clean.

He went inside, shut the door, and dialed directory assistance. When they answered, he asked for the number to the Red Oaks Health & Human Services Department, then sent a prayer to the Lord to bless him that he was making the right decision.

Twelve

"**W**hat you know about *this*!" Malcolm shouted. He stood directly in front of Devin's face, taunting and ragging like a man about to go to war. He held his arms out to his sides and his head rocked back and forth like a bull. "Huh, huh? What you got to say now?"

Devin never blinked, flinched, or stepped back. Instead, he gave Malcolm a cool once-over and then spoke in measured tones. "I know you better step off before I break you off." Then a half grin replaced the stern expression on Devin's face.

"Give me that ball!" he said.

Renata chuckled. The Red Oaks church picnic had been in full swing all afternoon. While the older men from the congregation sweated over grills packed with hot dogs, hamburgers, ribs, and round steaks, the younger men split into teams and played football. The younger teens watched over the smaller children at the playground end of Metcalf Park, and the women—under the pretense of preparing side dishes—clustered together to talk about the men. Renata had a great time watching the guys Malcolm's age open up a can of beat down on the men Devin's age. Malcolm had just scored another touchdown, and was rubbing it in Devin's face like a pro.

Renata had volunteered to hide the small metal crosses for the kids' Faith Hunt which would take place that evening. Placing the crosses behind bushes and at the bases of trees, she took the opportunity to watch the men play their game—especially Devin and Malcolm. Renata was not used to seeing them getting along. Or rather, Devin having such a positive attitude toward Malcolm. The wall of dislike that Devin sometimes put between them had been intact until the painting incident. Renata placed a small cross in the petals of a tulip and wondered if Devin had recognized his own bias in the way the three members of the church had jumped to conclusions about Malcolm.

"Who's *baaaad* now!" Devin shouted. His chest was heaving from having just run several yards to score a touchdown.

"Man, slow your roll before you have a heart attack!" came Malcolm's response.

Funny how adversarial relationships have the opposite impact on men, Renata thought. The closest Devin and Malcolm had ever been was now, as they were trying to outscore each other on their imaginary gridiron.

They weren't even this close after the apology, Renata remembered. She placed a cross near a drinking fountain, thinking back to when she, Devin, and Malcolm had gone back to the church and met with Sister Patterson, Brother Banks, and Sister Courtney about the missing painting. Reverend Avery himself had facilitated the meeting, and the apologies from the three members of the congregation had been heartfelt and sincere. After that, Devin had taken Renata and Malcolm out for pizza and the three of them had gotten along fine. They talked about Sister Edna, who seemed to be getting the help she needed at the town hospital, and how Success Unlimited seemed to be getting the help it needed, thanks to Renata's reworking of the agency budget. Throughout dinner, Devin's attitude toward Malcolm had obviously shifted and, in his own way, Devin was apologizing also.

When Devin had invited Renata to attend church the following Sunday, she'd refused. She wasn't quite ready to become a regular church goer, but embracing that routine again was no longer out of the question and was something she was seriously considering.

When she was ready.

She was surprised to find that Malcolm had accompanied Devin to church on that Sunday, and although neither of them had provided her with any details, she could tell by the way they seemed more at ease in each other's company that it had been another concession—this time on both their parts.

But she'd never seen them like this. She stopped her cross hiding for a moment and watched as the two men in her life talked trash to each other as if they'd been doing it for years. *Another small victory,* she thought. Maybe one day, they would actually be friends.

A perfect spring had turned into a perfect summer in Red Oaks. Every flower, plant, and tree had been treated to just enough sun, rain, and favorable temperature to the point where they all looked pregnant with green. Renata could almost hear the trees growing. She inhaled as deeply as she could, taking in the smells of loose dirt, oak, peaches from nearby peach trees, and the impending rain from an overcast sky. She hoped that the picnic would be over before they all got a good soaking.

"Miss Connor!" Malcolm shouted, jogging over to her and unexpectedly giving her a hug. He could barely breathe, but his excitement spilled over onto her. She'd never seen him so happy. "We stomped on those old guys!"

"Don't gloat," Devin said, limping up behind Malcolm. "You just got lucky. Next time—"

"Next time, we will beat your geriatric butts again!"

Both men laughed, and Renata joined in. Without thinking, she walked over and hugged Devin. Without hesitation, he embraced her. He was hot, sweaty, and smelled so intoxicatingly manly she had to pull away before she did something embarrassing, like stick her tongue down his throat in front of Malcolm and the entire Red Oaks congregation.

"I know I need a shower," he said.

"And some strong safety lessons," Malcolm said.

"Okay, mister not-so-gracious winner," Renata said. "Ease up a bit, huh?"

Malcolm leaned against a tree, his T-shirt ripped on one side and soaked though with sweat on the other. "Do you think he would be easy on me if *his* team had won?"

Renata thought about that, gave Devin a quick peck on the cheek, and said, "You're right, Malcolm. One more shot, and then let's go get something to eat."

Devin glanced at her and smirked. "Next time, I'd like to see *you* get out there and play some ball, Ms. Renata."

Sadness closed coldly over her heart. "Next time," she murmured. While Devin and Malcolm chuckled, she thought about those two words. She knew that Red Oaks planned a picnic like this every year, but with the end of Malcolm's sponsorship only weeks away, she didn't know if there would be a next time . . . for her.

"Stop bein' antisocial, and come on over here with the rest of us!"

There was no mistaking Mother Maybelle's voice. She stood halfway between the open area where the men had played football and the wooded area where Devin and Malcolm stood trading pot shots.

Just the perfect diversion, Renata thought. Eating would take her mind off of the uncertain future she'd been wondering about the past few days.

"Malcolm, you go on ahead. Let Mother Maybelle know we'll be there directly," Devin said.

"Okay," he said, trotting off. "Twenty-eight to seven!" he shouted. "Remember that!"

Shrieks and squeals of glee ignited the air. The children scampered back from their time at the playground. Their happy sounds almost got through to Renata, but uncertainty siphoned off some of the happiness she'd felt only a few moments ago.

Devin breathed heavily, as if he was still tired from the game. "Let me talk to you for a minute," he said, and led her to a wrought iron bench. They sat down, and Renata bolstered herself for the "Look, I love you, but I can't get seriously involved with a woman unless she's *in church*" speech.

Paranoia had Renata in its cold grasp. Whenever she'd spent time with Devin lately, she'd expected him to break the news to her. Even though her rational mind believed that it was highly unlikely that Devin would shatter her heart during the church picnic, she couldn't stop her mind from going to that terrible place where all her fears lived. The agency contract with the outreach ministry was almost up. What glue would hold her and Devin together after that?

"Yes?" she said, forcing herself to look into his eyes.

"I wasn't going to do this now," he said.

Renata chewed the inside of her bottom lip. He *was* going to end their relationship here. She took a deep breath, raised her chin, squared her shoulders, prepared herself for the emotional blow.

"Look at you," he said, lifting a lock of her hair with his fingertip and smoothing it back into place. "From the moment I first saw you, I never had a chance."

"A chance for what?" Renata asked, searching for meaning.

"A chance to . . . look, Renata . . . ," he said, taking her hands. She tried to attribute the rise in her body temperature to the tiny sunrays peeking suddenly through the clouds, but it was more than that. It was the connection she felt with Devin McKenna spreading though her soul like a wildfire.

God, please, she prayed. *Don't let me lose him.*

Devin turned toward her. The intensity of his gaze made her shudder with nervousness. Her hands trembled in his.

"I know you don't feel comfortable being in a church just yet, but I'd like to ask you to go to church with me at least one more time."

Devin stared adoringly into Renata's eyes, and that's when she knew that the kind of church service he was talking about involved flower girls and ring bearers.

Suddenly, the sun was *inside* her, not just on her skin. "Devin—"

"I know this is fast. Heck, I don't even have a ring. You can think about it if you want. You can ask for a two-year engagement. You can even tell me I'm crazy. But please, whatever you do, don't say no."

"Brother McKenna, what's wrong with your knees?" Mother Maybelle asked. Renata glanced over and saw that Mother Maybelle and Malcolm hadn't joined everyone else. Instead, they'd come and stood next to the tree just near the bench.

"Nothing, Mother Maybelle. Nothing's wrong with my knees," Devin said without taking his eyes off of Renata.

Mother Maybelle put a hand to her hip. "Then you best get on one of them."

Devin smiled. It was a smile Renata wanted in her life, from the man she wanted in her life . . . forever. He got down on one knee.

Renata's hands stopped trembling. She took a deep breath and let loose a smile of her own.

"Well?" Malcolm said. His eyes were bright and his smile was bigger than hers and Devin's put together.

"Say somethin', sugar. Mother Maybelle is hungry," the eldest among them said.

"Yes," Renata said. "My answer is yes!"

In an instant, Devin was off of his knees and kissing her so passionately she let go of her earlier reservations and went where the sensation took her.

"It's about *time*," Mother Maybelle said.

"I'm sayin'," Malcolm echoed.

"Come with me, young man. If we wait for them, we may never eat, and I dipped my toes in my pound cake if I do say so myself."

"Yes, ma'am," Malcolm said.

Devin and Renata ended their kiss and pulled away from each other slowly, reluctantly. Devin motioned to where the Red Oaks Christian Fellowship Church members were settling into their dinner.

"You wanna go grab something to eat?"

Renata snuggled close and couldn't prevent herself from sounding like a love-struck teen. "I want to go anywhere you want to go."

Devin's eyebrow rose in a challenge.

Before he could open his mouth, Renata said, "Except to prayer meeting tonight. I think I've had enough *fellowship* for one day."

They both laughed and headed hand in hand toward the picnic area.

Renata could not believe how content she felt. After the death of her brother, it was as if a feeling like this no longer existed for her. But with Devin in her life, and Malcolm too, she had to admit, she'd been changed.

She'd stopped believing in love and happiness for awhile, but now, as sunlight broke though the clouds like a mighty beacon and shined on her, she knew anything was possible.

A Love Like That

Natalie Dunbar

Dedication

This novella is dedicated to my husband, with all my love.

Natalie Dunbar

Acknowledgments

I want to acknowledge and thank my wonderful family for all of their patience, support, and love while I spent time writing this novella. Love you all!

Natalie

One

Children laughed and played in the sun-painted background, while adults lounged on the green carpet of grass and the scattered white lawn chairs. Busy helping with the Red Oaks Christian Fellowship Men's Day picnic, Dominique Winston washed off the wooden picnic tables with an old dishrag.

Lately, she'd begun to think of moving to Atlanta, where the pace was faster, there was more to do, and there was none of the intense scrutiny that characterized a small town. Would she miss the close community and genuine caring the residents of the town enjoyed? She didn't know, but in Red Oaks, memories of the past and the need for peace in her life still held her back.

Dragging a clean towel from one of her bags, she carefully dried each table. She wet her lips and swallowed. She was thirsty. Glancing around, she saw that so far no one had thought to unload the rest of the bottled water and beverages from Reverend Avery's truck. The garbage cans were half full of empty cans and bottles.

Tablecloths first, then make the lemonade, she reminded herself. She found the red plastic tablecloths in a large pack near the bench of one of the picnic tables. Drawing one cotton-backed cover out, she placed it on top of a picnic table and pulled it smooth.

She was smoothing a tablecloth onto another picnic table, when an infectious, good-hearted belly laugh caught her attention.

Looking up at the unfamiliar sound, she saw a tall, handsome man in an expensive white shorts outfit laughing and talking with Deacon Jones. Long lashes curled over his sexy brown eyes, trumpeting nose, and wide mouth. Shiny black hair waved back from a face carved out of brown velvet. It stole Dominique's breath. That was one fine-looking man.

You've been bored for years. Here is a man to shake up your life and this town too! Dominique shook off the thought as she forced her gaze back to the tablecloth. There wasn't a wrinkle on it. She glanced around quickly to see if anyone had noticed her staring. Everyone's attention was otherwise engaged, except for Mother Maybelle, who winked at her.

No. Not again. Turning away, Dominique bent over to pull catsup, mustard, and pickle relish from the cardboard box at her feet and set them on the table. The brother looked like a player anyway, and she'd had more than her share of that kind of man five years ago, when she married Phil Crater, wealthy Red Oaks ladies man. The marriage had lasted less than a year.

She'd been crazy about Phil and thrilled when he proposed, picking her from the crowded field of women eager to please him any way they could. There'd been hints that he might have been keeping to some of his old habits, but Dominique had remained blissfully ignorant until she came home unexpectedly early one day and caught him in bed with Lainey Mikelson, a hussy who'd been an ex-girlfriend and after him from the very beginning.

Slamming the jar of pickles onto the table, Dominique caught herself. The past was the past and she'd learned her lesson real well. She wasn't about to repeat those mistakes.

Stacking the empty box with the others, she looked around for something else to do. Though several men had shown up to work the picnic, they weren't working very efficiently, and most of the women were lounging in lawn chairs.

Dominique prided herself on efficiency. She found a box of lemons and powdered lemonade mix, washed her hands, and went to work. Soon, she was immersed in the task and forgot all about Mister Tall, Dark, and Handsome.

Ten-year-old Carmen, one of Reverend Avery's kids, appeared at her elbow. "Ms. Winston, Mother Maybelle says she's dying for something to drink. Is the lemonade ready?"

Dominique paused to smile at her. "No, it isn't, Sugar. It'll be a few more minutes. Go check your daddy's van for some of that bottled water."

While the child trekked off to the van with her braids flopping, Dominique cut more lemons and pressed them into the juicer. She could hear Deacon Jones and his friend laughing and talking with Mother Maybelle. With a swift, casual glance, she saw Mother Maybelle getting a big hug and kiss from Mister Tall, Dark, and Handsome. They obviously knew each other.

Finishing with the lemons, she poured the juice into the big cooler of water the Men's Day committee had brought and added sugar and some of the powdered mix. Stirring the concoction until everything blended, she cut the lemon hulls into pieces and put them on top.

"Dominique."

She glanced up at the sound of Mother Maybelle's voice, nodded, and looked around for Carmen. The child was nowhere around. "I'll be right there." Dominique got a glass, added ice from a bucket, and filled it with lemonade.

"I can get that for you, Mrs. Carmichael," the stranger offered, his eyes brightening at the sight of Dominique.

"I've got it," Dominique said confidently, lifting the glass and heading for Mother Maybelle. Just the feel of the man's gaze on her had her insides buzzing like a nest of bees. She worked hard to appear unaffected.

"Thank you, honey." The older woman accepted the glass with a thin, delicate hand graced with an enormous emerald-cut diamond that flashed outrageously. "Now, honey, I want you to meet Blair Thomas. I've known his momma, daddy, and granddaddy for years and he's like a son to me. Blair, this is Dominique Winston, one of the brightest angels in our church. If something's going on, Dominique's right there in the middle of it."

Blair and Dominique stared at each other for a moment, and then responded to each other with friendly smiles. Dominique felt the warmth of Blair's smile clear down to her bones. She shifted her feet, attempting to hide her shaking knees.

Blair held her hand several moments longer than necessary. His big hands were warm. "I'm real pleased to meet you, Ms. Winston."

"It's good to meet you, too." She thought she would fall into those cocoa-brown eyes as her heart beat in her chest like a bass drum. The last time she'd been affected like this was when Phil Crater focused all his charm on her.

That thought freed her from the daze. Tugging her hand, she managed to free it. She smiled brightly to lessen the effect of what she'd done. "Well, I'm going to get back to work. Enjoy our picnic, Mr. Thomas."

"Please, call me Blair," he corrected in a mellow voice that caressed her ears.

"Blair," she repeated, letting her mouth shape the name. Then she remembered her manners and acknowledged Deacon Jones. He simply smiled and nodded.

Dominique felt hot as she walked back to the picnic table, the weight of Blair's gaze still on her. Hadn't she been wishing for a more exciting life? Somehow this was more than she'd hoped for. She forced air through her lungs. All these thrills and turmoil over a man were unnecessary.

~

Blair tried to keep his wandering gaze off Ms. Dominique Winston, but it strayed back time and again to the tall, slim beauty in the tailored blue shorts and top. He usually liked his women more voluptuous, but something about her had his hormones leaping. Was it the strength and grace in the way she carried herself and the ring of confidence in her smoky Southern drawl? Or the way her shoulder-length auburn hair framed the masterpiece of her face and her sherry-brown eyes seemed to size him up? She was someone he definitely wanted to talk to, and he sensed interest on her part, but he also sensed a problem. "What's up with Dominique?" he asked Scooter.

Known to the group as Deacon Jones, Scooter pulled him aside. "Man, she's single now, but she used to be married to the town player. She went through a lot with him. I'm not going into the dirty details. Let's just say that she's been super cautious every since. And who could blame her?"

"Hmmm." Blair stroked his chin with a thumb and forefinger. "Maybe you could help a brother out. Fill her in on me and tell her that I'm one of the good guys."

Scooter chuckled. "Brother, I know you're a man of your word, but you love the ladies, too. I've never heard you talk about settling down."

"Is that what Dominique is looking for?" Blair asked, watching her set the plastic cups on the picnic table.

"I can't speak for her," Scooter told him, "but I did detect a little energy when you two met and shook hands. If you're honest with her, she can make her own decision about whether she wants to see you or not. I'll see what I can do for you."

They shook hands on it.

Blair watched Scooter work the crowd as he helped with the picnic but grew impatient waiting for his friend to talk to Dominique. He saw that she'd left the lemonade table and was busy cutting the barbecued ribs into manageable pieces. Too anxious to wait, he decided to go and talk to her.

He usually knew what to say to women to get their attention, but his mouth was dry as he approached Dominique.

"Can I help you? Get you something?" she offered, an intense look in her eyes.

A spark of sensual awareness sizzled between them. Blair flashed her a warm, flattering smile. "Actually, I was hoping I could help you. I'd like to talk to you, get to know you."

She stiffened, the warmth in her smile cooling. "I don't really need any help."

He stood there awkwardly, her statement hanging in the air. Had he misinterpreted the vibes? She obviously didn't want to be bothered. He started thinking of graceful ways to walk away.

Blinking, she wet her soft, kissable lips. "Excuse me," she said, some of the warmth seeping back in her voice. "I didn't mean to sound so rude. What did you want to talk about?"

"I'd like to know more about you, but we can talk about me and what I do."

"Let's talk about you," she drawled softly. "How do you know Deacon Jones and Mother Maybelle?"

Blair relaxed as he began to describe how he knew his friends. "Deacon Jones was my roommate at Grambling State, and Mrs. Carmichael used to visit the people down the street from my parents all the time. I used to live in Rally, Georgia."

"Small world, huh?" She continued to cut the meat and place it in a large pan. Her glance met his for just a moment and sent a charge rushing through him. "What about you, Blair? What brings you to Red Oaks?"

"I'm taking a little break from work. I design and race cars. Sometimes I even win. I've been so deep into my work that I haven't had a vacation for some time. Scooter came to my last race and invited me down to spend some time with y'all."

Dominique's eyes widened. "Scooter?"

Blair grinned. "Deacon Jones."

She laughed, a light, musical sound that he could listen to all day. "I'm going to have to remember that one."

He laughed too, making the moment seem more intimate.

"So, Blair Thomas, champion race car driver and designer, how long are you going to be in Red Oaks?"

"I planned to stay about a month, but I don't have anywhere I really have to be until the exhibition race in Atlanta. That's in six weeks."

"That's long enough to get comfortable and get to know everyone," she said.

He nodded. "And I intend to spend time getting to know everyone. I'm flexible, and I believe in good friends and good times. That means that until the Atlanta race, I'm staying as long as I'm having fun."

Some of the intimacy and warmth left the connection between them. Blair scanned her face, wondering what he'd said wrong.

"Hey, aren't you Blair Thomas, the race car driver?"

Blair turned to see a pretty young woman in tight black shorts and a body-molding top. "Yes, I am."

She offered a sleek, long-fingered hand. "Well, I'm Cissy Slade and I'm absolutely thrilled to meet you."

"The pleasure's mine," he replied, shaking it.

"Is that gorgeous red Thunderbird out in the parking lot yours?" she asked, eyes wide with admiration. "Ooh," she said at his nod, "will you show it to me? I just love sports cars."

"Of course, but give me a few minutes. I was talking with Dominique." Blair saw that Dominique hadn't skipped a beat. She was still cutting meat and stacking it on the tray.

Cissy greeted Dominique and the women shared a polite interchange.

"So, Dominique, how long have you been in Red Oaks?" Blair asked, determined to continue his conversation with the very attractive woman standing before him.

"All my life, except when I went off to college."

"Dominique's parents own those Winston Banks," Cissy put in. "And I've lived here all my life, too."

Blair feasted his eyes on Dominique. Yeah, he could believe she was an heiress. She had beauty and class. "So where did you go to college?"

Her lips slowly curved upward. "Spelman."

"I didn't get to go," Cissy informed him breaking in on their conversation once more, "but I've been thinking of taking some classes at the community college. What do you think?"

"I think that any sort of higher-level learning is a good thing in this day and age." Blair wanted Cissy to go away. His sixth sense told him that the only way to get rid of her was to show her his car. "Dominique, I'm going to show Cissy my car, then, if you're not too busy, maybe we can sit in the shade or go for a walk."

"Maybe," she repeated.

Blair hurried off with Cissy, surprised when they picked up three other "car enthusiasts" along the way.

Watching them head into the parking lot, Dominique thought about what he'd said. Blair Thomas would be in town six weeks or as long as he was having fun. Hadn't she had enough of men who were only around as long as it was fun?

That's unfair, she admonished herself. She didn't know anything about the real Blair Thomas, even if there were now no less than four giggling and grinning women traipsing out to the parking lot with him.

Hmmmph! Dominique finished cutting the ribs. That was one man who probably had his pick of the women. She found the aluminum foil and covered the meat. Then she glanced around past Blair Thomas and those silly, giggling women to note that the Men's Day Picnic was remarkably short of men.

Mother Maybelle appeared at her elbow. "I want you to know that Blair is a fine, fun-loving young man."

Dominique let her glance stray to the parking lot where several of the women were piling into Blair's car. "I can see that," she said.

The older woman chuckled. Leaning closer, Mother Maybelle said, "Chile, you needs more joy in your life, and a man like that'll help you find it."

Dominique shook her head. "I've had enough of men who love to play so much that they can't stop."

Maybelle's eyebrows furrowed. "You needs a little playtime, girl. You ain't had no fun since you caught Phil dropping his drawers."

Dominique's hands formed fists. Her face felt hot, and she was sure steam was coming out of her ears. Would she ever live down all the crap her ex-husband had put her through?

Patting her shoulder gently, Maybelle said, "I wasn't trying to embarrass you or make you feel bad, chile, just trying to get yo attention. Ya need to set yo sights on something else besides work and being an old maid. You hear?"

Nodding, Dominique took a deep breath and tried to stop feeling sorry for herself.

Maybelle nudged her towards the other table. "Let's get some of that lemonade."

As Dominique poured the beverage, she glanced around again. "I wonder where Reverend Danforth, Deacon Wilson, and Deacon Taylor are? They always help out with the Men's Day activities."

"I dunno." Maybelle confided, "but Reverend Avery's been on the phone for a while and he looks a mite upset. Must be some kind of emergency."

At the opposite end of the clearing, Reverend Avery paced back and forth, his expression anxious as he spoke into his cell phone.

"Looks like you might be right," Dominique remarked, taking a sip of her lemonade.

Maybelle laughed softly. "Ain't I always?"

Dominique set her cup on a corner of the table. "I'm going to see if there's anything I can do."

"Hold on, chile. Look like he's got some help."

Dominique whirled around. Just that quick, Deacon Jones and Blair Thomas had approached Reverend Avery and the three men were deep in a serious conversation.

Dominique waited as long as she could. Then she went over to offer her help.

Two

Stepping across the thick grass in her low-heeled white sandals, Dominique approached the group of men. Blair saw her first and turned mesmerizing eyes on her. Reverend Avery and Deacon Jones stopped talking and waited for her to speak.

With Blair's gaze warming her, she addressed the men. "Excuse me, gentlemen. I know that some of the key members of the Men's Day committee haven't made it here yet. Is everything okay? Can I do anything to help?"

Reverend Avery nodded. "Bless you, Dominique. Reverend Danforth had a personal emergency, Deacon Taylor is stranded in Macon, and we haven't been able to contact Deacon Wilson. The good Lord prompted us to do a lot in advance, but a significant amount of work remains. We've been trying to divide up the work. More meat needs to be cooked. We have to start the organized games and get the prizes ready. Then, we don't have enough beverages. We're running out of supplies fast."

With another step forward, Dominique spoke up. "I'd be happy to go back to town and get whatever you need."

"Actually, I just offered to do just that," Blair cut in, giving her a meaningful smile.

Her heart leaped in response. Dominique wet her lips and swallowed.

"I'd really like to help," he added.

With a glint in his dark eyes, Reverend Avery looked from one to the other. "Why don't you both go? It'll makes things easier, and Dominique, you can tell Blair about our town and point out some of the landmarks along the way."

Dominique hesitated. This was something she hadn't planned on. She struggled with Blair's effect on her and tried to think of a polite excuse to go alone. After what she'd seen of Blair and the women in the parking lot, she was certain that she didn't want to act on her powerful attraction to him. With that handsome face and riveting charm, he had the same M.O. as Phil, no matter what Mother Maybelle said. Being alone with him for any length of time would just make things worse. "Well I—I . . ."

Reverend Avery's smile went up a notch and his dimples appeared. "Thank you, Dominique. I appreciate the way you're always ready to pitch in and help. The Lord is going to bless you for that."

Schooling her expression, she bit down hard on her tongue while the reverend made out a voucher for the store and gave it to her.

Giving in gracefully, she headed for the parking lot with Blair. "Here's my car," she said, stopping in front of her midnight blue Mercedes E320 sedan and pressing the remote button that released the locks.

Blair gave her car a quick uninterested glance and kept walking. "My car is over here."

"I've got more room to put the beverages in my car," Dominique called, sensing that she was losing control of the situation. She didn't want to ride in his female magnet of a car.

"I've got a big trunk," Blair shouted back.

In a matter of seconds he'd jumped into his vintage red Thunderbird convertible, pulled out of his spot, and stopped beside her. The passenger door opened and she saw Blair leaning towards her. "Get in," he ordered. "We don't want them to run out before we get back."

Grumbling to herself, Dominique climbed in, surprised at the plush black interior. Not only had he spiffed up the outside with new paint and a new top, but he'd had the original seats restored and covered with soft, smooth black leather. Dominique cinched the seatbelt and shut the door.

"Which way to town?" Blair asked as they made it to the entrance of the park.

"Left," she said, emphasizing with her thumb, "and a right when you get to Morgan Road."

"Thanks." Inclining his head, he followed her directions. The car engine roared as he zipped out of the park. He was silent until he made it to the interstate entrance on Morgan. "Are you an only child?"

The question startled her. Was he implying that she was a spoiled brat? She shot him a quick glance. His expression seemed innocent enough. "No, I have an eleven-year-old brother, Jon, who lives just outside of town with my parents."

With a quick glance, he registered mild surprise as he accelerated into traffic. "I have three older sisters and we're pretty close. They follow my racing career and even show up at some of the races."

She noticed the way he smiled when he mentioned his sisters. "I wish I had that sort of relationship with my brother. He's so young that he's still in the annoying little brother stage. I'm hoping we'll connect better when he's older."

"I'm sure you will," Blair said confidently. He sped up, matching and then passing several cars.

Dominique turned her head to check the area behind the car. There wasn't a cop in sight. Maybe Blair was just lucky. "I'd slow down if I were you. This area is notorious for its speed traps. The state troopers just love to catch tourists zipping through here."

"If I get caught speeding, then I deserve to pay a penalty." Blair sped past a red truck and changed lanes smoothly.

Dominique watched as the speedometer shot past ninety. The lush roadside greenery whizzed past. She wasn't afraid of Blair hitting anyone. In fact, she sensed exhilaration in his reckless dash up the freeway.

Just sitting next to him in the car sent sensual thrills radiating through her. Her mouth watered at the tantalizing patch of milk chocolate–colored skin revealed by the opening in his shirt. She focused on his strong, competent hands gripping the wheel and wondered how they would feel on her. Would he be a rushed and reckless lover? Or would he be slow and devastatingly sensual?

She forced her gaze to the scenery outside the window. After a few moments, she relaxed into the seat, against the smooth hum of his car's engine.

"You're getting off at the next exit," she announced when the one-mile warning came up for Red Oak Avenue.

He cut his speed smoothly and took the curving exit at forty-five miles per hour. "Where are we going?" he asked when they stopped at a red light.

"The Foodmax on the corner of Harper," she replied, noting that they were already drawing attention. The people in the next car were staring. "It has the best prices around here. Drive past the next light and it'll be on your left."

Blair drove into the spacious store lot and parked in the back. Getting out of the car and walking into the store, Dominique matched steps with him. Inside the store, they filled the shopping cart with bottled lemonade, soda, and water and then stood in the checkout line.

As luck would have it, Bobbi Lee Hankerson, Dominique's parents' neighbor was in the store getting fresh pork chops for dinner. Spotting Dominique with Blair, she made a point of speaking to them *and* being introduced to Blair. Watching Bobbi Lee's eyes light up when she spoke to the handsome visitor, and noting the way she smiled so hard her face must have hurt, Dominique knew that her parents would know about her being in Blair's company before she got home from the church picnic.

They filled the large trunk of Blair's car with the drinks. Then they climbed back into the car and headed back to the park. Along the way, Dominique showed him the Red Oaks Grand Hotel, a beautiful and historical lodge which had been in the town since before the Civil War.

Once they were back on the interstate, Blair flew through the traffic. The white-dashed blacktop on the road stretched before them, mirroring and dipping in the distance, reflecting the heat of the Georgia sun. In the air-conditioned cool of the car, Dominique pointed out the old water tower and the town zoo. They were close to Mt. Glacy, the local lover's lane, when the red and blue lights of a Georgia State Patrol car flashed in the rear.

"Pull over," a voice ordered over the loud speaker.

Blair cursed under his breath. "I guess might I be paying a fine after all," he muttered as he pulled over to the side of the road.

A little worried, Dominique sat quietly while Blair found his car registration and proof of insurance in the glove box, and drew his license from the wallet he'd stuffed in his shorts. Saying "I told you so" was the last thing on her mind.

The low hum of the engine and the swish of the air conditioning system were the only sounds in the car. She scanned the two beefy, blue and gray clad state troopers approaching the car on each side, hoping things wouldn't get ugly.

Blair rolled down his window. Steam billowed out where the cool air in the car met the sun-roasted air outside.

A badge with the name "Jones" was on the trooper's chest. He gazed down at Blair. "Good afternoon, sir. You in a hurry for something? You sped by us at ninety-five miles an hour."

Blair managed to look humble. "I'm sorry officer. We've been helping out at the Red Oaks Christian Fellowship picnic, and they're running out of drinks. We've been to the store in town and I was in a hurry to get back."

The trooper stared at him for a moment. "You've got Georgia plates, but you're not from around here are you?"

Nodding, Blair answered. "No, sir, I'm not."

"He looks familiar, though," the dark-skinned trooper with "Smith" on his name plate said from the other side of the car.

"I'll need your driver's license, registration, and proof of insurance," the sandy-haired trooper said.

Blair gave him the documents.

The trooper stared at the license for a moment. "Hey, I know you. You're that championship racer who nearly won the 2003 FedEx Championship Series race at Monterrey. Man, I was watching that one on television and rooting for you every bit of that last lap! Let me shake your hand."

Blair shook hands with Trooper Jones, while the other trooper walked around the car to join his partner at the driver's window. "Can I get your autograph for my son? He watches your races all the time."

"For sure." Blair smiled pleasantly. "Have you got some paper?"

Dominique found paper in her Coach organizer and handed it to Blair. Then she watched in amazement as Blair signed autographs and joked and chatted with the troopers. The man had turned a potential speeding ticket into a signing session. She listened to their conversation, realizing that Blair was well known on the racing circuit.

After a few minutes of talk about the races and Blair's car, Trooper Jones got back to the situation at hand. "Blair, we're going to let you go with a warning. You can't be speeding around these parts like that, man. Save it for the racetrack."

"Thank you, sir. I sure will," Blair said carefully.

"You know, for a minute there, I thought you were in a hurry to get to Mt. Glacy, the lover's lane around here," the other officer put in.

"I wouldn't have blamed you," Smith cracked, "cause you've got a beautiful lady with you." They all laughed then. "No offense, ma'am," Trooper Smith added.

"None taken," Dominique told them, trying to keep the heat out of her face. She glanced at her watch. They should have been back with the drinks by now.

Trooper Jones shifted his feet and patted the car. "Blair, we're going to escort you back to that picnic, and then we'll be on our way."

Inclining his head, Blair thanked him.

"Does this happen all the time?" she asked, as Blair started the car and eased back into traffic.

Blair gave her a look filled with regret. "No. Sorry I caused us to get pulled over."

She met his gaze, noting the sincerity there. "It's okay, I just hope we get back before they run out of drinks at the picnic."

"I'm not getting pulled over again. That's for sure," he cracked.

Seeing the state troopers close on their tail in the rearview mirror, Dominique had to agree. When they made it back to the park, Reverend Avery and some of the men met them at the car and began unloading the beverages.

The state troopers got out and spoke with the group for a few minutes. At first the situation was a little tense, then everyone relaxed.

"Did you run out of drinks?" Dominique asked the reverend.

He hefted a box from the trunk and gave it to a volunteer. "Yes, but it's only been about an hour," he answered carefully. A question he was too polite to voice glimmered in the depths of his eyes.

Trooper Jones took that moment to tell the reverend that that he'd encountered Blair heading enthusiastically up the interstate toward Mt. Glacy and had followed him to the park to make sure he arrived safely.

"Did I hear you say you stopped Mr. Thomas and Ms. Winston at Mt. Glacy?" Cissy Slade asked in a loud voice.

Trooper Smith nodded. "Technically, yes."

"Are you sure you didn't catch them making out at Mt. Glacy while we waited for them to get back with those drinks?" Jalisa Howard, Dominique's biggest critic, cracked.

"So what were they doing there?" someone else asked.

"What do you think people do up on Mt. Glacy? It's the lover's lane after all!" someone else put in huffily.

Dominique felt her temperature rising. She glared at the crowd in dismay, her attitude growing by the second. "Just one cotton-picking minute!" she said.

"You folks are drawing some wrong conclusions," Blair countered.

"People, this ain't no time to jump to conclusions," Mother Maybelle put in.

Reverend Avery threw up his hands. "Everyone, I need quiet here. Reputations are at stake and we're talking about people who volunteered their time to help us out. Now, Officer Jones, could you tell us how you came to be escorting Mr. Thomas back to our picnic?"

Jones went through the entire incident, mentioning that Blair was driving above the speed limit and that they'd cut him a break and decided to escort him back to the picnic to make sure he got there safely.

Stark silence reigned in the group for several moments. Then someone said loudly, "If you believe that, I've got a bridge to sell you."

A big part of the group laughed loudly. As Reverend Avery talked to the crowd about gossip and rumors, Dominique got her purse and sweater. Mother Maybelle followed her, trying to talk her into staying.

"Chile, don't slink off like you done something wrong," Mother Maybelle told Dominique.

Dominique slung her bag on one shoulder and her purse on the other. "I'm so mad that I'm liable to say something I'm going to regret. I can't believe the things they're saying."

She still remembered the things people said before her marriage to Phil. They'd whispered that he was just playing her, that he'd been paid to marry her, and that he still had a thing for Lainey Mikelson and RoAnn Tackett. Lainey had even gotten in her face and told her that if she married Phil, she'd be sorry because he was addicted to Lainey's love.

Dominique could still see the vengeful smirk on Lainey's face when she'd caught the hussy in her bed with Phil. Later she'd discovered that Phil's parents had opened his trust fund and added a bonus after his marriage to her. She didn't think she could ever listen to rumors and gossip again without reliving pain and heartache.

Maybelle put an arm around Dominique's shoulders. "Some of 'em are just kidding. Others like to gossip. Don't let them drive you away from folks who care about you."

Dominique's chest felt heavy. Her eyelids stung from her need to cry. Pure stubbornness kept her from it. "I've got to get out of here before I do something to embarrass myself," she declared.

Gently removing the older woman's arm, she started the walk to her car.

"Don't blame Blair," Mother Maybelle called after her, "It's not his fault."

Dominique's breath came out in a huff. *His fault indeed.* If Blair Thomas hadn't been speeding, this latest round of idle speculation wouldn't have happened. That thought stayed with Dominique as she got into her car and drove out of the park. Blair appeared near the lot entrance and held up a hand to stop her, but she just kept going.

Back on the interstate, she let the tears flow. More than ever, she was convinced that nothing would go right for her until left Red Oaks for good. Small-town life was like living in a fishbowl, and she needed at least a lake to live her life freely.

She would do everything she could to stay away from Blair during his visit. He'd landed her in a bad situation and brought a scrutiny she didn't need and put her name out there to be trashed. Again.

Three

Dominique got up early the next morning to jog through the park across the street from her apartment complex. The slightly cool breeze caressed her cheeks and played with her hair. By the time she got back home, she felt energized.

The phone was ringing when she let herself in and kicked off her shoes. She lifted the receiver and spoke into it. "Hello?"

"Good morning, Dominique. Is there something you want to tell me?" a voice inquired on the other end.

Dominique recognized her mother's soft Southern drawl. "Not really, Mama. What's up?"

"Something about you and some racing guy making out in lover's lane?"

Dominique's temper shot up and boiled over. The town gossip squad must have stayed up all night to get the word out. It was only eight o'clock in the morning, a record, even for them. "Don't those people have anything thing better to do?"

Her mother's voice was soothing. "Now honey, you've lived here most of your life, so you know how it is in a small town. The best thing to do is to avoid giving them anything to feed the fire."

"I can't help it if Blair Thomas decided to race back to the picnic and the state troopers caught him at it," Dominique snapped.

"But what were you two doing in lovers lane? I haven't seen you so much as look at a man in years! This man must be something special."

"Mama, we weren't in lover's lane. When the state troopers stopped him on the interstate, we were at Mt. Glacy."

"So technically speaking, you *were* in lover's lane."

Dominique was tired of hearing that particular phrase. She hit the laminated kitchen table with a fist. "Mama, I can't talk about this. Nothing happened, and if anyone says it did, they're making it up!"

Her mother's voice took on the gentle, controlling note which had worked well when Dominique had been a child. "Now Dominique, you need to calm yourself down. They aren't saying anything worth you getting so upset about."

"Mama, I was about to go for a run," she lied. "I'll call you later, okay?"

Her mother sighed. "Certainly, dear. Don't forget you're expected for supper tomorrow evening, six-thirty sharp."

Dominique said her good-bye and replaced the receiver. *This mess will blow over in a day or two*, she told herself as she fried bacon and eggs and made toast and raspberry tea. *It's not like the situation with Phil, where they saw him cheating and talked about it for years.*

With her favorite breakfast and the morning paper, Dominique settled down at the kitchen table to enjoy herself. She nearly choked on her tea when she saw the Busy Bee column in the Red Oaks *Monitor*.

Rumor has it that one of our own got busy up on Mt. Glacy with infamous race car driver, Blair Thomas. Romance was all but over when a couple of Georgia state troopers happened along, escorted the couple back to the picnic, and ensured that the parched citizens at the Red Oaks Christian Fellowship Men's Day picnic got something to drink.

Dominique's breath caught in her throat. She knew that the real reason she was upset was because she hadn't gotten over Phil's betrayal or the town's reaction to it. In her heart, she still couldn't forgive herself for being taken in by him. Quick tears pricked her eyelids and slipped down her face at the sheer unfairness of the entire situation. She'd seen Blair Thomas coming and kept her distance, and she'd still wound up on the short end of the stick.

She didn't like being in the limelight, and she hated being talked about. No longer hungry, she grabbed her sunglasses and went back to the park across the street.

~

Blair woke up at Scooter's house with an uneasy feeling. He'd spent a good part of the previous night trying to explain what had happened, but the more he talked, the less people believed him. He'd seen the vulnerable look in Dominique's eyes, despite her anger, and knew that she'd been hurt by what had happened. Although it was the town gossips who'd upset her, he accepted some of the blame for speeding in the first place.

After a hot shower and a fresh set of clothes, Blair made ham and cheese omelets and coffee for Scooter and himself. They ate breakfast in the cheery yellow kitchen with the ceramic tile floor before Scooter took off for his job at Southern Software.

With the sprawling house to himself, Blair settled in front of the television with the local newspaper. When he got to the Busy Bee column, he shook his head and reread the words in dismay. By now he knew that the only thing he and Dominique could do was hold their heads high and move forward. Things had gotten to the point where the more they denied the story, the more people believed it. Still, he wanted to talk to her and tell her how much he regretted everything that had happened.

Searching the cabinets in the bottom of the old china cabinet and the buffet in the dining room, he found the white pages and searched for "Winston." The single number listed had an address on Magnolia Road. Pondering it, he guessed that the number belonged to Dominique's parents. Deciding to try the number, he lifted the telephone receiver and started dialing.

The doorbell rang. Replacing the receiver, he went to answer it. The door wasn't locked, so he merely turned the knob and pulled it open.

With her frosted hair impeccably coiffed, Maybelle Carmichael stood on the doorstep in a lavender pantsuit and matching accessories, beaming at him. "Good morning, Blair. How ya doing, son?"

"Morning, Mrs. Carmichael. I'm okay. Come on in. Would you like some coffee? I could make you breakfast," he offered before realizing that he and Scooter had eaten everything he'd cooked.

"Why thank you, Blair, but I already ate. I was hoping ya'd want to go visiting with me. A woman needs a handsome young escort to drive her around town," she said, with a smile in her voice.

He knew she was teasing him, but the fact was that several men still scrambled to do her bidding. Blair grinned. "Sure, I'll tag along. Where are you going?"

"We can go to the Winston's first and then I have a few other places in mind. What'cha think?"

The thought pepped up his spirits. She knew where to go and getting in to talk to Dominique would be easy with Maybelle Carmichael. "Ma'am, that's a fine idea," he responded, "I'll get my keys."

"You don't need no keys cause we're taking my car," she informed him in a pleasant tone that brooked no argument. Her sharp eyes skimmed his jeans and T-shirt. She frowned and made a sucking sound with her teeth. "And you better change into some visiting clothes. We don't want them thinking you ain't got no manners."

He knew she was right. Blair headed toward Scooter's spare bedroom, then turned back, realizing that in his excitement to get to the Winstons, he'd left Mother Maybelle standing in the doorway. Maybelle Carmichael was stepping into the house and placing her lavender purse on the living room coffee table like it belonged there. "You go ahead. I'll have some of that coffee while I wait," she informed him absently.

Blair hurried to change. In the dresser mirror he checked his appearance, and, satisfied with the result, returned to the living room. At the back of the house, Mrs. Carmichael had already started the dishwasher, washed off the table, and was in the kitchen sipping coffee with the paper. She worked fast.

She glanced up to scan the tan pants and shirt he'd matched with a navy blazer. Then she scrutinized his Hugo Boss Italian leather shoes and nodded approvingly. "You clean up pretty good, son."

Acknowledging the compliment, he followed her out of the house. As instructed by Scooter, he slammed the door shut, but didn't lock it. Escorting Mrs. Carmichael down the steps to her gold Cadillac, he helped her into the posh tan interior and accepted the keys. Then he got in and started the car.

Under Mrs. Carmichael's direction, the drive to the Winston's took him back to the interstate and two exits south. The wind from his open window filled Blair's ears as he turned onto Magnolia Road. Beautifully landscaped trees, grass and flowers lined the road and flowed along the sides. At the end of the road stood a luxurious white mansion built in the Southern tradition of antebellum homes. A facade of floor-length windows and lavishly framed antique porches stood behind tall white columns.

The elaborate white picket fence opened as he approached, and two guards wearing blue uniforms appeared and asked him to identify himself. Then he was directed to a spot on the long circular drive that led to the mansion.

The front door opened as Blair mounted the wood steps with Mrs. Carmichael. A maid in blue and a tall, slender woman in a cream silk pantsuit stood in the doorway. The woman had Dominique's soft brown eyes and generous mouth, but instead of shoulder-length auburn hair, she sported a cap of golden brown curls.

The woman smiled at them as the maid opened the door. Then she stepped forward to greet and hug Maybelle Carmichael. She turned to Blair and spoke in a sweet and cultured voice. "Hello, how do you do? I'm Deborah Winston, and this is Lally Ryker."

He gave his name, noting that her eyes widened as she warmly shook his hand.

"I've known this young man since he was in diapers and I'm so proud of everything he's done," Mrs. Carmichael said proudly. "They done already started gossiping about him and Dominique, but I didn't want that to ruin their chances of getting together. I brought him along so you could get to know him and see what a fine young man he is."

"We're glad you did," Deborah Winston said. She gave Blair her attention. "Welcome to our home." Her smile widened. "Now ya'all come on in and get comfortable."

They stepped into the lavish white foyer, their feet sinking into the plush carpet.

"Is Dominique at home?" Blair asked as the front door closed.

"She's probably working, but she does visit us when she gets the chance," Deborah Winston answered. "Come join us out on the deck," she said pleasantly, leading the way down a long hall, past an opulently furnished living room and a formal dining room.

Blair followed with a supporting hand on Maybelle's elbow. His thoughts were on Dominique. So she had her own place. Considering that she had to be at least twenty-eight, it didn't really surprise him, but he imagined that her parents' home would be hard to beat in terms of comfort and class.

Deborah Winston drew open a screen door to reveal a canopy-covered wood porch that ran the length of the house.

A tall, beefy brown man with dark eyes and a touch of gray at his temples sat in a lounger with his feet up. He greeted Maybelle warmly, then nodded and scanned Blair quietly while his wife made introductions.

"So Mr. Thomas," the older man bit out testily once they'd finished introductions, "I've been hearing a lot about you and my daughter. What really happened last night?"

That was to the point. Blair didn't know what he'd been expecting, but this wasn't it. It wasn't as if Dominique was a teenager who needed to be protected by her parents. She was a grown woman with a place of her own. With a deep breath, he launched into a long explanation.

John and Deborah Winston and Mrs. Carmichael listened intently. When Blair had finished, Winston's eyes narrowed and he was silent for a few moments more. "I thought it might be something like that." A sudden smile transformed his face.

The women laughed.

Blair exhaled an involuntary sigh of relief.

Winston patted him on the shoulder and motioned him to a chair. "So Blair, how long are you going to be in town?"

Blair filled him in.

"I thought you two mens would have a lot in common," Maybelle added. "John, Blair is out there struggling to build his business like you did before you lucked up on that first bank."

"Do you have a plan?" Winston asked Blair.

Blair nodded. "Yes. I'm hoping to retire from racing by the time I'm forty. When I win, I pay my people and put the rest into the company. I'm incorporated, you know. The company isn't only about racing, we're constantly improving our high-performance engines and developing new ones. We have a few automotive manufacturers interested in some of the toned-down versions. We use endorsements to cut the costs of racing and maintaining the cars."

"John's been looking for ways to advertise the Winston Banks," Deborah interjected. "Do you have any bank sponsors?"

Surprised at the change in the conversation, Blair turned to met her gaze. "No, I don't." Sponsors were hard to get. He turned back to John, trying not to appear too eager. "I'm always looking for sponsors. Do you think you might be interested, sir?"

"Call me John," he corrected. "And yes, I've got some serious interest. I believe in supporting the African-American community, and I've been thinking about this ever since Deacon Jones told the congregation that you were coming to town. What would you think about an endorsement from the bank in exchange for a television commercial or two?"

Blair nearly fell over with shock. "I'd love it."

The older man nodded. "The publicity would be good for both of us. I'll talk to my lawyer and have him draw up something in the morning. Then we can discuss it after dinner tomorrow."

"You're invited to have dinner with us tomorrow, Blair," Deborah chimed in. "Please come. You're always welcome, Mother Maybelle, so you come, too. We'll all be here and so will Dominique. The chef will be whipping up something extra special."

An endorsement and dinner with Dominique? Blair was pleased with the turn of events. "Thank you for inviting me. I'd love to come. What time are you having dinner?"

Deborah flashed him a brilliant smile. "We start at six-thirty sharp and we dress for dinner."

Diamonds flashed as Maybelle touched Deborah's hand. "I'm won't make this one, honey, but thank you for inviting me."

John's voice took on a teasing note. "You got a hot date, Maybelle?"

Maybelle laughed playfully. "Other plans."

Just then, Lally Ryker appeared with a double-decker rolling cart which contained a large tray of appetizers, plates, utensils, and napkins. Conversation continued as they spent the next half hour snacking on wing dings, shrimp, carrot and celery sticks, and a fruit tray. Blair and John washed theirs down with beer, while the ladies drank wine and soda.

Blair got full and relaxed in the friendly atmosphere. The Winstons talked about their business, some of Deborah's teaching experiences, and life in Red Oaks. Blair countered with talk of the life he'd experienced in Rally, Georgia, which was a bigger city and one that had sheltered him until his late teens and his parents' divorce.

When it was time to go, John stood at the door with Blair and shook his hand. Unlike Blair's dad, who worked the racing circuit with him, Winston had parlayed a small, independent neighborhood bank into an empire. He was a shrewd and successful businessman whom Blair admired.

Looking forward to dinner the next day, Blair left the mansion with Mother Maybelle. Fleetingly, he wondered how Dominique would react to him showing up on her territory, but he couldn't imagine her making an issue out of it in front of her hospitable parents.

$\sim$

Back at Scooter's, Blair found his friend in the living room, already home from work.

"I came home early so we could go somewhere for dinner," Scooter said. "Where've you been?"

Blair plopped down into a padded chair. "Mother Maybelle came by and asked me to go visiting with her."

Scooter nodded. "Cool. So where'd you go?"

"The Winstons'."

"Sounds like Mother Maybelle's trying to match make," Scooter muttered.

"No, Dominique wasn't there," Blair said, defending his family friend. "She wasn't even mentioned, except in passing."

Scooter's glance sharpened. "But you got invited back, right?"

Blair inclined his head. "Yeah."

Scooter sighed. "The Winstons are good people, and they want what's best for their children. They messed up by trying to make sure Dominique got a husband from a well-to-do family last time, and that ended badly. Her ex's family had money, but he was a big problem."

Blair shot his friend a look of annoyance. "Why don't you just come out tell me everything?"

"Because that would be adding to all the nasty gossip that's been circling around Dominique for years. I swear she's been afraid to even look at another man. And don't think the town bachelors haven't been trying to get a date."

Blair's eyes narrowed. "Scooter, cut the bull and tell me. I'm not about to spread any rumors, and everyone around here but me knows all about it anyway!"

Considering those words silently, Scooter shrugged. "I guess that's true. Dominique was married to Phil Crater, the town player. The Winstons must have thought it would be good for her to have a husband who came from money, but that was a pipe dream. Phil was one of the big family problems. The man went all out to charm Dominique, and then when she finally agreed to marry him, he put the ring on her finger and slipped right back into his old habits. Rumor has it that she caught him in their bed with two women, but you already know how we exaggerate things around here. Anyway, she dumped him so fast his head spun. She ain't been the same since."

Blair considered what his friend had said. He knew that dealing with women who had been hurt or mistreated by other men was usually a balancing act, and sometimes more trouble than it was worth. But something about Dominique made it hard for him stay away from her. From what he'd seen of her, he thought he could handle anything that came up. Anything, that is, except the marriage issue. "I like what I've seen of Dominique, but I'm not ready to settle down. I don't even have a real place to sit on a regular basis that I could call my home."

Scooter just shook his head disparagingly. "I'm not getting any further into this one. Just know that you're dealing with a home girl and a real sweetheart," he warned.

Four

Dominique should have suspected something when her mother called as she was getting dressed and asked her to wear that apricot silk dress she'd worn to the Working Women Helping Others charity luncheon.

"Why?" she asked, noting that her mother rarely meddled in her clothing choices.

"To tell you the truth, your dad has invited one or two people to dinner. I hope you don't mind."

"So who did he invite?" Dominique asked, going back to her closet to find the requested dress.

"Uh—do you want me to ask him?" Perennially gracious, her mother suddenly sounded slightly put upon.

"No, that's okay," Dominique answered, not wanting to be unreasonable. As a businessman who was proud of his family, her father often brought friends and associates home to enjoy dinner at his home. "I'll see you at six, Ma," she said before hanging up the phone.

Dominique brushed and coaxed her auburn hair until it framed her face in shiny curls. She applied makeup to emphasize her brown eyes, and coated her full lips with a rum color. Then she stepped into a pair of delicate apricot sandals and added a little of her favorite fragrance, *Desire*, to her thighs.

Grabbing her purse, Dominique left the condo and hurried to her car. Her parents did not like late guests for dinner because they said it affected the quality of the food their chef painstakingly prepared.

Traffic was much lighter than she'd anticipated, so she arrived at her parents' home fifteen minutes early. Inside, she greeted and kissed her mother, noting that her mother had also taken more care than usual with her appearance.

When she entered the living room to greet her dad, she stopped short.

Impossibly handsome in a tan suit and cream shirt that brought out his sexy brown eyes, Blair Thomas sat on the sofa with her father discussing the basketball game.

Her stomach dropped and sucked the air from her lungs. The thin silk slip dress suddenly felt hot and constricting.

Blair stood at the sight of her. "Dominique."

"Blair," she choked out, managing to get the word past the sudden dryness in her throat. Her father brought guests to dinner from time to time, but having Blair in their fortress seemed more like an invasion. She'd been brought up to adhere to a strict code of behavior toward guests in their home. Despite her shock, she pasted on a smile. "W-what a surprise. Welcome."

Blair eyed her intensely, not sure of her sincerity. "It's good to see you. You look beautiful."

A hunger lurked in those eyes and strengthened the caress in his tone. No one had ever looked at her in quite the same way. Dominique's thoughts swam with images of hot bodies and twisted sheets. Blinking, she caught herself and thanked him for the compliment.

Drawing closer, Blair continued. "I was here visiting your parents with Mrs. Carmichael yesterday. One thing led to another, and they invited me to dinner."

"I hope you don't mind," her father said, extending a hand to her. "From all accounts, you two do know each other."

Escaping Blair's mesmerizing presence, she went to hug her dad and kiss his cheek. "Yes, we do know each other, and no Daddy, I don't mind," she lied, knowing that he saw right through it. "But I still think you're picking with me."

"Would I do that, princess?" he asked innocently.

Dominique shot him a wise glance. "Mm-hmmm."

"Actually Blair and I have business to discuss after dinner," he said.

"Good. I'll go see if Mama needs any help."

Dominique's father tossed her an impatient glance. "You know your mother's not in there doing any real work. That's why we have a full staff. Stay here and help me entertain Blair."

With a slight grin over being caught trying to get away, Dominique dropped down into the chair across from Blair. "Are you enjoying your visit to Red Oaks?" she asked pleasantly.

"I'm having a great time," Blair said, his brown eyes attentive. "This town has a lot to offer. Everyone has been helpful and friendly."

"You've got to come to church on Sunday," she said. It's beautiful and the reverend is a joy to listen to."

"I'll be there. Deacon Jones has already threatened to haul me out of bed if I'm not up and ready to go by ten-thirty," he chuckled.

"Don't feel bad, they threaten me, too," her father commiserated. "I've enjoyed the sermons, but every now and then I'd like to sleep in on a Sunday morning."

Dominique smiled. "What do you usually do on Sundays?"

"Race cars, fix them, take my sisters to lunch, and sometimes I go to church. Now that I'm here, I'd like to get in some fishing, swimming, horseback riding, and tennis."

"If you're looking for challenging company, Dominique is good at just about everything sports-related," her father said proudly.

She glanced at her father from beneath her lashes, wishing that it didn't sound like she was a horse he was trying to convince Blair Thomas to buy. The look on Blair's face melted her insides. He looked fascinated.

"Would you like to play some tennis or go horseback riding this week?" Blair asked.

Dominique choked. Maybe it was too soon. The prospect of a date with

Blair gave her the shivers. Blair seemed like the kind of man who went after whatever he wanted and usually got it. He was too close to what she dreamed of, too close to what she thought she'd found in her rotten ex-husband. "Actually, I—I've been pretty busy lately," she said, "I have my company, DWIS, to run, and I've been doing a lot in the church."

"Maybe you could take some time next week?" Blair asked. "Everyone needs a little time off."

Heat rushed her face. She didn't need to look up to see her father's gaze centered on her. She knew that he still felt guilty about the part he'd played in ensuring she married Phil. In the back of her mind, all the hurt and embarrassment she'd suffered replayed. Still, she couldn't bring herself to offer another lame excuse. "Why don't you call me?" she asked finally.

Just then her mother appeared and called them to dinner. Dominique wasn't surprised to discover that Blair was the only dinner guest who wasn't a family member. The Winston family took turns engaging him in conversation and keeping him entertained.

Blair's manners throughout dinner were impeccable. He seemed to be enjoying himself and the prime rib. But despite his interaction with her family, his gaze found and settled on Dominique over and over again.

"You said your company was called DWIS. What does it stand for and what type of company is it?" he asked over the crème brulée dessert.

She swallowed a mouthful of the light confection. "Dominique Winston Investment Services."

"I'm impressed. How long have you been in business?"

Dominique's lips curved upward. "Four years."

"I'd like to discuss your company's services sometime," Blair said, "Maybe we can do business together."

"Maybe so," she agreed.

Dominique's father cleared his throat. "Speaking of business, isn't it time we had our talk?" he asked Blair as he pushed his chair away from the table.

"I'm ready when you are, sir." After using his napkin, Blair eased his own chair back and stood.

"Let's go out on the porch and visit for a while," her mother suggested to Dominique.

They stepped out onto the spacious wood deck to the sound of crickets and the occasional hoot of an owl. A soft Southern breeze caressed their faces.

When they were both settled onto the flower-splashed pillows of the white oak glider, Dominique's mother turned to her and said, "You like Blair a lot, don't you?"

Dominique sighed. "I hardly know him, Mama."

"Exactly." Her mother started the glider. "You can't let the mistakes of the past destroy your future, honey. You've got to live your life."

"What are you saying, Mama? The man's in town for as long as he's having a good time. According to him, that's six weeks at the most."

"It can be six weeks of pure heaven if he's the right guy."

"If," Dominique echoed. "So what do I do if we really hit it off and he rides off into the sunset after six weeks?"

Her mother smiled. "You kiss him good-bye and you wish him the best. Life holds no guarantees for anyone, sugah. Your daddy and I were just lucky."

Dominique's fingers curved around the armrest. "What if he's just like Phil?"

Her mother shrugged. "What if he is? You already know how to handle that type of man."

Dominique nodded. "True." She wished she didn't feel like such a coward. Despite her fears about repeating the past, she was strongly attracted to Blair. She rode the glider with her mother in companionable silence.

After a while, they exchanged stories about their charity work at the church. By the time the men returned, they were both relaxing against the pillows.

"Dominique, I need a favor," her father said, motioning Blair to one of the gliding oak chairs before dropping himself into a matching recliner.

"Of course, Daddy," she said without thinking. "What do you need?"

"Blair already signed on the dotted line of my endorsement contract, but he's got his heart set on one thing more."

"What's that?" she asked, the heavy feeling growing in her stomach and lifting to her chest.

"A picnic with you," her father said, eying her carefully. "He promises to behave himself. If you would be uncomfortable, we can all picnic at the lake instead. What do you say, princess?"

Dominique's hands shook a little. She dropped them to her lap, conscious of the fact that, although she'd agreed before she knew what the favor was, her father had given her an out. She barely recognized her voice. "Sure, Daddy. I'll do it."

Both men beamed.

"I'll have the staff prepare the picnic basket and you can have the picnic up by the private lake," her mother suggested. "Would that be okay?"

Blair and Dominique nodded in unison. Dominique found herself smiling.

"Could we picnic sometime next week? How about next Saturday?" Blair asked.

"I'll call and confirm it tomorrow," Dominique said.

Blair leaned forward and grasped her hand. "Thank you. You're going to enjoy it. I promise."

"I'm certain I will," she returned pleasantly. She saw that her parents were working hard to conceal their joy at the turn of events.

~

On the day of the picnic, Dominique got up early to prepare. She showered and did her morning routine, then put on her bathing suit and a summery green capri pants set which made her slim figure look more curvaceous. Despite the way her date had come about, she was excited and looking forward to it. Blair Thomas could never be boring.

Slipping her feet into a matching pair of sandals, she headed for her parents' house, intent on arriving before Blair did.

She found her mother in the kitchen, helping Lally pack the picnic basket. "You look beautiful," she told Dominique and gave her a hug. "You're going to give that man a heart attack."

Thanking her, Dominique asked about the contents of the basket. She saw wine and champagne, shrimp, smoked salmon, ham, roast beef, pickles and olives, a fruit and cheese tray, chocolate-covered strawberries, and plates, cups, and utensils before her mother shooed her out of the kitchen.

Dominique was on the porch in the glider when Blair arrived in a white cotton shirt that was open for enough to reveal the smooth, milk chocolate skin on his chest. Navy Bermuda shorts reached his knees and left his muscular calves bare. Leather sandals encased his feet.

With a flattering show of welcome, he stopped to admire her. "Dominique, you've got to be the most beautiful woman in Red Oaks, and I'm definitely the luckiest man. Today I'll have you all to myself."

It sounded a little bit corny, but Dominique felt the heat rush her face. She hadn't blushed so much in years, but it felt good to be appreciated.

"Can I join you?" he asked coming closer.

"Of course." She stopped the glider's motion and shifted to the side so that Blair could fit his tall frame into the space beside her.

Their hips and arms touched. She could feel the heat radiating off his body as he started the glider's motion again, matching his leg movements to hers.

"Have you been here long?"

"I came early so I wouldn't have to rush," she confessed.

"I came early hoping I'd get to spend more time with you," he declared, his warm brown eyes shining in an open invitation.

"You are smooth," she said, determined to keep herself from falling under his spell.

"Would you like me to be a little more rough?" he asked, his voice going deeper.

A current of heat shimmered through her. She laughed it off. "I'd like you to be yourself," she managed in a normal voice.

"I could never be anything else." He chuckled. "What you see is what you get."

Dominique swallowed. What she saw appealed to her on several different levels.

"How are we getting to the lake? Can I drive there?" he asked.

"If you'd like. It's only about a mile to a mile and a half away." She peered out at the sun painted landscape and issued a challenge. "It's a nice day. We could walk if you're up to it."

His gaze was steady. "I want you to be happy. We can walk if that's what you'd like to do."

She glanced at her watch. "It is. Why don't we get started?"

"What about the picnic basket?"

She shrugged. "When we picnic at the lake, Daddy usually has it brought up." She stopped the glider and stood. "I'll tell Mama that we're going to walk up there."

In the kitchen, Lally and her mother were almost done with the picnic basket. Dominique saw Lally add nuts and assorted crackers to their meal. There was no way she and Blair would be able to eat all that food.

As Dominique had expected, her mother planned to send the basket down to the lake with one of the household staff members. Dominique told them about her plans to walk, then found her sun visor and sunglasses and an extra hat for Blair.

"Did you bring a hat?" she asked, when she returned to the porch. "And are you planning to swim?"

"I've got the swimsuit covered, but I left the hat in the car."

She proffered the navy cap she'd found. "What about this one?"

"Is it yours?" he asked, examining it with his eyes.

"Yes, but I've never worn it."

"Then I'd love to wear it," he said, accepting it and drawing it on over his neatly cut hair. "Give me minute. I still need to get my CD player from the car."

Minutes later he was back with the CD player in hand. Dominique took the steps, and they headed the for path through the pecan trees several feet away from the house and gardens. It was warm, but hours remained before the hottest part of the day arrived.

Blair matched her step for step in companionable silence as they mounted the trail and delved into the grove of trees. They kept a good pace that was somewhere between a walk and a jog. Twenty minutes later, they rounded a bend of red maple and oak trees to catch their first real glimpse of the blue waters of the lake.

Blair walked forward. "It's beautiful! I'm surprised that your house isn't right here on the lake."

"Daddy talks about a cozy little cottage here, away from the house, sometimes, but that's all. We like keeping the lake secluded."

Walking through some of the brush, he unearthed a canoe and its paddles. "Want to paddle around the lake?"

Dominique helped him turn the canoe over and drag it into the water. Then they both climbed in.

She was surprised that she was able to relax and enjoy the canoe ride up and down the lake. As they took turns paddling, Blair entertained her with stories of his exploits with his sisters, Thelma and Marie. Thelma was the strong and studious one, and Marie was a diva to her heart.

"I've heard a lot about your sisters. What about you? How do you describe yourself?" she asked Blair, after they chuckled over a story of how he and Thelma had ruined eighteen-year-old Marie's date with a much older man.

"I'm the man with a plan," Blair told her. "One day I'm going to be really big, and I'll have the grand house, and the land, and a garage full of cars."

"And a black book full of gorgeous women to share it with?" she prodded gently.

He shook his head. "No. By that time I'll be ready to settle down with one special woman. I'll be ready to quit the racing circuit and stay home."

He wasn't much different from her dad, Dominique thought, who'd pursued his dreams relentlessly until he'd made the bank happen. The most significant difference was that her father had accomplished most of his success with her mother at his side. Blair had just as good as told her that he wasn't ready to settle down yet. Was she? She felt the weight of his gaze on her. Suppressing her disappointment, she stared out over the deep blue water and listened to the buzz of insects in the breeze.

They both turned at the sound of a vehicle and saw the SUV the staff used to run errands. The chauffeur got out and carried a large picnic basket and a bright red comforter to the shade of a big oak tree. With a wave, he was back in the truck and gone before they were a quarter of the way from the shore.

"Lunch is ready," she said, suddenly aware that she was very hungry. "I'm hungry. Give me one of those paddles. I know how to use it."

Blair's soft cotton shirt brushed her arm while he adjusted his hands on the paddles. "Let me handle this, Dominique. I'll have us there in a minute." His strong arms flexed as he bent forward and pulled the paddles back in a smooth series of strokes that demonstrated his competence. This time he was all business. Catching a tantalizing whiff of his tangy aftershave as he leaned forward, Dominique admired his sculpted muscles and flawless technique. Where had he learned that? She asked him.

"Crew team in college," he answered with a confident grin.

In no time at all, they reached the other side of the lake and Blair was helping Dominique out of the boat.

He wasn't breathing hard, but she noted a faint sheet of moisture on his forehead. His big hand enveloped hers when they crossed the grass and headed for the picnic basket beneath the tree.

Five

Blair spread the red comforter on the grass while Dominique unpacked the basket. He switched on his portable CD player to fill the air with the sounds of classical music. Somehow it complimented the serene beauty of the lake and the surrounding land.

Together, they cleaned their hands with the moist wipes they found in a small plastic canister and went through the packages of food. Dominique ate carefully at first, conscious of Blair's attention and her own desire to make a good impression. Gradually, she relaxed enough to really enjoy the food. They stuffed themselves on the sumptuous feast.

As they worked their way through the rest of the basket, Dominique leaned against the tree trunk and let the bubbling champagne fizz on her tongue. Blair sat close with his flute of champagne and the container full of their dessert.

"Chocolate-covered strawberry?"

Blair grasped one of the treats by its green foliage and offered it close to her mouth. Dominique blinked. This was getting kind of intimate. She opened her mouth to sink her teeth into the firm fruit and closed her lips to relish the flavor of decadent chocolate.

"Good?" He held the last little chunk of strawberry for another bite.

Nodding, she took the last piece and let the sweet taste fill her mouth. She picked another strawberry from the container and was surprised when Blair leaned close expectantly.

She fed him, her fingertips tingling against the warm brush of his lips.

Their gazes met and held as he chewed and swallowed. Then he was leaning close to gently kiss her lips with a wet warmth that sent sinful currents of desire spreading through her. His mouth was soft and provocative. The man could kiss something fierce.

Her fingers gripped the soft cotton collar of his shirt and she inhaled his scent, an intoxicating blend of Blair, his cologne, soap, mint, and a hint of sweat. She felt his hand massaging up and down her arm, while the other caressed the nape of her neck.

Dominique sighed and let the moment end, but a part of her wanted to go up in the flames he'd generated.

"I could spend the day kissing you," Blair remarked.

"It was wonderful," she said, still feeling the afterglow. In a series of quick, efficient movements, she began closing the containers and repacking the basket. She was a little nervous and didn't want to get too caught up in what they had just shared.

A clump of bushes nearby erupted with rustling sounds. With a suspicious glance, Dominique turned to investigate. She relaxed at the sight of a squirrel scrambling up the tree.

Blair's fingers brushed her arm. "Feeling a little jumpy?"

At the contact, her stomach dropped and she realized just how vulnerable she was. "No, just making sure my little brother's not spying on us."

"Would he do that?" He snapped the lid on a couple of containers and handed them to her.

"Yes, he would." She fitted them back into the basket, her ears full of the sound of Mozart coming from the CD player and Blair's laughter.

With the basket repacked, they made themselves comfortable on the pillowy softness of the comforter.

The champagne had relaxed Dominique to the point that she actually felt a little drowsy. Beneath the shade of the tree, she lay on her stomach with her chin in one hand. Blair sat with his back against the tree.

She asked Blair what made his company's high-performance engines different from others and watched his eyes light up with enthusiasm. He talked about combustion chamber designs and the engine stroke. Though she was interested in what he was saying, she felt her lids grow heavy. As he waxed poetic about maximum torque, she drifted off to sleep.

~

The provocative beat and lyrics of an Usher song awakened her. Dominique lifted her lashes and looked around.

Blair was off the comforter and standing near the lake, dancing. As she watched, he executed a few of the steps she'd seen in the music video. Then he stopped to grab the hem of his shirt and pull it over his head. Ultra-smooth brown skin, the color of a creamy chocolate bar, rippled with the play of his muscles. Dominique's mouth watered.

She watched him fold the shirt and place it on the grass. Then the zipper of his pants came down. Staring hard, Dominique glimpsed black material in the opening. With his hips flexing, Blair bent over and removed his shorts. She stared, transfixed by the sight of prime male flesh clad only in mid-cut swimming trunks that hugged his shapely rear and athletic thighs like spandex. She swallowed hard.

The man possessed the perfect body. Nice chest, tight butt, flat abs, and toned thighs. Unaware of her scrutiny, he took the last couple of steps to the lake and slowly walked into the water.

Dominique sat up, blinking. Blair Thomas had a body to die for. Suddenly the water swallowing his form looked mighty inviting. She kicked off her sandals and stood.

Unbuttoning her blouse, she watched Blair swim across the lake. Sliding her arms out, she dropped the blouse on the comforter and undid the button and zipper on her capri pants. As she shimmied out of them, she saw that he'd stopped swimming to tread water.

He was watching her with simmering eyes that scorched her skin. "Oh, Dominique," he said a low, vibrating tone that tickled her ears, "on a scale of one to ten, you get a twelve."

"Thank you." A sensual thrill arced through her and almost made her lose her balance. She stepped out of the pants and placed them on the comforter.

In nothing but her caramel-colored bikini, she stretched in the sun.

"Come on in, the water feels good."

Striding towards the water, she locked gazes with him. Slowly wading in, she barely felt the cool water.

Blair met her halfway. He leaned close to touch his lips to hers. "You're so beautiful that I can't stop looking at you," he murmured. His hands smoothed up and down her arms. "And all I can think about is kissing and touching you."

"I'm enjoying you, too," she admitted. "And it sounds like you're having fun."

"Yes, I am." He bent towards her and their lips met again for several little kisses that culminated in a deep tongue lock with their bodies clinched tightly together.

Dominique moaned softly and was surprised to hear Blair's groan. They were still standing in the water, but she was virtually lying on his sexy body. Sensual heat filled her and flowed down her insides, melting her all the way. She gasped involuntarily at the glide of his hand on her bare waist, just above her hips. The other hand gently stroked her face and neck.

"Dominique," he whispered.

Lifting her hands, she cupped his face and brought it close for another searching kiss. His arms tightened around her. When the kiss ended, her fingers traced a path down his neck and glorious chest to his flat stomach. She felt his muscles harden. She was hot, hot, too hot to be standing in the lake with Blair like this, only a short distance from her family's home.

"We're going to boil this lake over," she laughed softly, stumbling back a half step.

"But we'd both go up in flames," he countered, catching her hand.

"Oh yeah." Her gaze locked with his and she trembled beneath the heat she saw there. It was too soon to be thinking of jumping his bones, she told herself, but the feeling persisted.

His grin released some of the tension. Still holding hands, they dropped down into the water. For the first time she realized how refreshingly cool it was.

"Can you swim with one hand?" he asked. "I want to keep this one."

"I'm a good swimmer, but I haven't learned that one yet," she said. "Maybe you could show me?"

"I'm kind of busy watching you right now." He countered. "You've broken new ground. I've never had a date fall asleep on me before."

"It was the champagne," she said, trying to justify her actions.

"Sure, tell me anything."

Her mouth curved upward. She stretched out on the surface of the water to float and look up at him.

Standing next to her, his hands supported her until she was floating. Then he turned, moved away, and dived down into the lake.

The motion shifted her body on the surface but didn't turn her over. The surface of the lake stilled and remained smooth for several minutes. Listening hard, Dominique watched and waited anxiously for him to surface. Hadn't he said he was a good swimmer? Just when she thought she'd have to mount a rescue, his head broke water. He swam towards her with a series of strong kicks.

"Want to race to the other side of the lake?"

"You're on," she said, accepting his challenge.

On the count of three they took off. Blair made it to the other side first, but Dominique caught up with him on the way back. Trying not to laugh as she swam as fast as she could, Dominique flew through the water.

With an eye on Blair and the shore where she was heading, she saw a small figure running on the land ahead. It was her brother, Jon. She saw him gather something green and something blue into his arms and run off.

Dominique swam even faster, pulling ahead of Blair. When she reached the shore, she ran across the thick grass, calling out to her brother, who'd already disappeared.

"You win," Blair called from the shore. "What's up?"

"I think my brother's playing tricks on us," she explained, filling him in. Briefly, she wondered how long her brother had been hiding and spying on them. She and Blair had done nothing but kiss and strip down to their suits. Even so, she didn't relish the idea of her parents hearing about every little detail.

Dominique and Blair searched the grass and bushes, only to confirm that Jon had taken their clothes. Luckily, they both found their shoes. Dominique shivered as she slipped into her sandals. Despite the sun, cold lake water still dripped down her legs. She squeezed some of the moisture from her hair. She knew she looked a mess.

"I'm going to strangle him," she fumed, remembering all the other little dirty tricks he'd played on her and her dates. There was the time she'd been living with her parents and he'd told her date that she was out with another man; then there was the time he'd told one boyfriend he was about to get dumped. And how could she forget the time that he'd torpedoed an egg into Phil's Mercedes?

"Let's walk back to the house," Blair suggested. "It's not as hot as it was earlier, and the house isn't that far."

"You didn't bring your cell phone?" she asked, taking one last look around the area, hoping they'd missed something.

"It's in my car. I didn't want any interruptions," Blair explained.

She expelled the breath from her lungs. "Mine is in my purse at the house. Right now walking is the number one choice. The only other option is to wait here until my parents miss us and who knows how long that would take?"

Blair lifted his CD player. "Let's leave the basket. We walked over here. We can walk back." As they stepped back through the clearing, he took her hand. "I really enjoyed myself, Dominique. I hope you'll go out with me again, without any prompting on your dad's part."

She squeezed his hand. "Sure. I had fun, too."

The late afternoon sun beat down on them as they trekked back to the house, but the walk was pleasant because they enjoyed each other. Dominique turned her enjoyment of Blair over in her thoughts. What did it mean for her and her life in Red Oaks? She didn't have an answer.

A green Chevy pulled up behind them as they made their way up the driveway.

Dominique cursed under her breath. She recognized it as town gossip, Willie May Ryker's, car. Dominique sped up. She and Blair were nearly at the front door when the car door slammed and the woman hurried to catch up with them on the steps.

"Yoo-hoo, Dominique! Have you guys been for a swim?"

Dominique eyed the older woman, who was sweating a little around the edges of her short, natural hair. Although she addressed Dominique, the woman's big eyes were all for Blair.

"Yes, we have been swimming," Dominique answered politely. "How are you Mrs. Ryker?"

"A little parched, but otherwise fine."

"Maybe Mama has something cool for you to drink," Dominique said, aware that she'd opened the door for a grilling session.

Willie May nodded. "I surely hope so. Why don't you introduce me to your young man?"

As Dominique made hasty introductions, the front door opened and Willie May's daughter, Lally, hustled them into the house. "There's no need to stand out there in this heat," she remarked.

Inside, Lally got Willie May a glass of lemonade. Willie May held on to it, sipping and grilling Blair shamelessly. Dominique heard that the absolute last day Blair would be in town was June twenty-ninth, and she also got to hear the names of Blair's other sponsors. She even recognized some of the names. Apparently Blair needed all the sponsors he could get to fund the work on his cars and his races.

The grilling session continued until Dominique's mother entered the kitchen. "Why Willie May, I didn't know you were here. Lally just got finished with her work. Are you picking her up or staying to visit with us?"

Willie May's dark brown coloring deepened. "I was here to pick up Lally and I felt a little parched," she began.

"Not a problem." Dominique's mother surveyed the entire group. "You're all welcome to stay to dinner."

Lally rolled her eyes at her mother. Willie May was known for the lengths she went to get an entire story.

Willie May cleared her throat. "Thank you, Deborah, but I believe we need to get on home. It was nice to see you, Dominique. Nice meeting and chatting with you, Blair."

With that, the woman turned and made her escape with her daughter.

When the door closed, Deborah Winston eyed Dominique and Blair. "You can thank me later."

Dominique ran a hand through her frizzy wet hair. She knew she was not looking her best. "Thanks, Mama. I didn't think she would ever leave."

Shifting his feet uncomfortably, Blair added his thanks.

Deborah's gaze took in their damp swimming suits. "You two do look mighty attractive in those swim suits, but aren't you a bit uncomfortable? Where are your clothes?"

Dominique straightened her shoulders. "You'll have to ask Jon that one. I saw him running from the lake with them."

Mrs. Winston gasped. "My Lord, what will that boy think of next? I'm so sorry." She went to the bottom of the stairs and gazed up expectantly. Then her voice rose in pitch and volume. "Jon . . ."

Deborah Winston talked to her son alone, so Blair and Dominique didn't know what she said, but when she was done, he apologized profusely and returned their clothing.

Afterward, Deborah talked Blair and Dominique into staying for dinner. The chef had selected a Chinese theme, so they dined on General Tso's chicken, vegetable chow mein, and egg rolls. They ate the delicious meal with lots of spirited conversation and laughter.

While the cook served almond cookies and ice cream for dessert, Dominique's brother Jon ruined everything for her. He turned to Blair and said, "I saw you two kissing at the lake. Are you Dominique's boyfriend now?"

Blair eyed him calmly. "Dominique and I are friends."

Dominique didn't know what the right response should be, but Blair's seemed flat after what they'd shared. She placed her water glass back on the table before she could embarrass herself by dropping it.

Jon didn't let things end there. "Are you two going to get married?"

"Jon!" Deborah said in a scandalized voice, "That will be enough. I want to see you display the good manners we've taught you, or you can go to your room right now."

In the following silence, Blair surprised everyone by answering the question. "I'm not planning to marry anyone for quite some time. I'm too busy trying to make my business the success I know it can be."

Dominique's hands twisted nervously in her lap under the table. Her face burned and she felt as if everyone was staring at her. When she dared look up, she saw it wasn't true.

"I know you have to do what you think is best," her father said. "But I made the most progress on my road to success with Deborah at my side. She's the best partner I've ever had."

"Thank you, John," Deborah said, her eyes moist. She clasped her husband's hand briefly. They looked as if they wanted to kiss.

Watching them, Dominique promised herself that when she married again, it would be a love like that. Meeting Blair's gaze, she smiled and got through the rest of dinner with all the grace she could muster.

As Blair and Dominique said their good-byes, Blair extracted a promise that Dominique would go out with him again soon.

Dominique drove home on a cloud of happiness. She'd enjoyed the outing with Blair and looked forward to seeing more of him. He'd brought new excitement to the dull routine of her life.

As she showered and washed and blow dried her hair, her brown eyes sparkled in the mirror. Preparing for bed and climbing between the sheets, she suppressed the niggling worries about falling in love with a man who was only going to be around for a limited time, and the fallout from the questions and innuendo that would follow when Willie May Ryker started talking about seeing Blair and Dominique in their bathing suits.

Dominique's head touched the pillows and she closed her eyes. Her lips curved into a smile as she relived Blair's kisses. She fell asleep with a sigh.

Six

The following Sunday, Dominique got up early and went to church to practice the hymns before the service. That day she had a solo, "Precious Lord," to perform.

When it was time for church to begin, she walked in with the rest of the choir. She still managed to catch a few giggles and whispered comments about her picnic with Blair. It seemed Willie May Ryker had been busy.

Holding her head high, she continued up the aisle and took her place in the choir stand. That day, she was determined that no small-town gossip would touch her. She was too happy.

Looking out on the congregation, she saw her parents in the third row and spotted Blair in a dark gray suit in the pew behind the deacons. Next to him was Mother Maybelle in a white lace suit and matching hat.

Mother Maybelle's face was serious as she spoke to Blair. He shook his head vigorously and gestured as if he were defending himself. Mother Maybelle's hand closed on his arm, and she leaned close to get in a few more words. Nodding carefully, he glanced up at Dominique. She guessed they were talking about her and wondered what Mother Maybelle might have told Blair. Continuing her perusal of the crowd, she greeted each person she knew with a nod.

When the time came for Dominique's solo, she stepped up to the microphone. Her voice rang out in the church as she put her heart and soul into the song. When she was finished, she knew she'd done her best rendition yet. Tears of emotion filled her eyes as several members of the congregation shouted "Amen!"

Later, Dominique stood at the microphone again as she breezed through the church announcements and the chair reports. Then she returned to the choir. The service ended with an inspiring hymn and benediction. Following the choir out of the stand, Dominique went to the room where she'd stowed her robe and retrieved her purse. When she came out, she went to greet Mother Maybelle.

"Dominique, you look happy," Mother Maybelle told her with a big hug. "Whatever you doing, keep on doing it."

"I will," she promised.

She greeted her parents and promised to come for the evening meal. Moving on, she stopped to chat with Reverend Avery for a few minutes.

Off to the side, Blair was waiting for her.

"I enjoyed your solo," he said when she'd finished. "You have a beautiful voice."

Thanking Blair, she let him walk her to her car.

"I had a lot of fun yesterday," he said as they strolled out the side door.

"Me too," she confessed, stepping down to the cement walkway. Dominique stopped at her car and used the remote to unlock it. She opened the door and sat in the driver's seat.

"Scooter made plans for this evening, but maybe we can do something to-morrow," he suggested.

Dominique smiled into his chocolate-brown eyes. "I'd like that."

She drove home and piddled around the house until it was time to go to dinner at her parents' house.

Dinner at the Winstons' home was a fancy Italian-themed meal, with chicken and eggplant parmesan served with spaghetti, garlic bread, and an antipasto salad. She drank chardonnay and enjoyed the food.

Afterward, the adults retired to the family room. Dominique's mother wasted no time in asking about Blair. Dominique admitted to liking him, and cited his brains, ambition, and upbeat personality.

"Honey, please," her mother said rolling her eyes. "He ain't bad to look at, either. I've seen the two of you together. You could do a lot worse for fun and excitement."

When her mother quizzed her on the picnic, Dominique they'd eaten, swam, and canoed, providing little information beyond the things her brother Jon had already said.

Her father had been watching her quietly. "Everything all right with this one, princess?"

"Yes, Daddy. Except for the fact that he's only here for a little while, I couldn't have done better."

"Don't worry about the time. When a man meets his soul mate he knows it. If he knows what good for him, he won't walk away."

Dominique pinned her father with a glance. "Daddy, I know you're trying to help me, and I love you for it, but I don't know if he's my soul mate, he's not interested in anything permanent, and he's already said that he'll be gone on the twenty-ninth of June."

In the ensuing silence, her father could only incline his head in agreement.

Dominique was glad when the conversation turned to the upcoming visit of her cousin Lucy. She was around Dominique's age and a diva who loved to party.

Noting the time, Dominique made her escape. It was nearly eight o'clock when she got home. The name "Jones" was on the caller ID more than once, but there was no message. Since Blair was staying with Deacon Jones, she guessed that he had called. However, the fact that he'd left no message was puzzling.

Dominique put on her pajamas and spent the rest of the evening in bed watching movies until she fell asleep.

The ringing telephone awakened her. Disoriented, she sat up in bed, noting that it was after nine a.m. She eyed the phone cautiously, then checked the caller ID. The name on the display was "Jones." It had to be Blair. Her pulse sped as she grabbed the receiver and lifted it to her ear. "Good morning."

"Good morning, Dominique." Blair's voice filled her ears, wrapping around her name in an aural caress. "After the good time we had Saturday, I couldn't wait to get back with you. Are you up? You said you were an early riser."

"I don't have any business appointments on Mondays, so I sometimes sleep a little later," she explained.

"I'm going to be in your area and thought you might like to go for a morning ride. Should I call back later?"

"No!" The word tumbled from her lips. Dominique collected her wits and managed a more ladylike response. "I can be ready in about half an hour."

"Good. Wear your jeans and some boots or walking shoes."

"Why?" she asked curiously. Why should he care what she wore for a ride in his car?

"We could be riding in a car, on a motorcycle, a horse, or a helicopter. It'll just make things easier. You'll see."

"Okay," she said, trying to be agreeable. Her anticipation grew at the thought of the rides he'd mentioned. She ended the call and leapt out of bed to sprint into her bathroom. Glad she'd washed her hair the night before, she got ready for her date.

She was pulling her hair into a ponytail and running the comb through it when the phone rang again. It was Blair.

"I'm waiting outside," he said.

Stuffing her wallet and cell phone into her jeans, she hurried to the door. Outside the condo, she saw Blair in jeans and boots sitting atop a handsome black stallion. As usual, the sight of him took her breath, but this time her pulse jumped. He looked like something out of one of her fantasies. Was he her knight in shining armor come to rescue her from her boring life? Dominique was used to saving herself.

A horse nickered softly and the familiar sound caught her attention. Tied to a tree nearby was a chestnut mare. It was Salsa, the horse she usually rode at the riding stable near her condo.

Dominique went over to Salsa and stroked her firmly on the neck. Salsa nickered again in welcome. Blair tossed Dominique an apple, which she gave to the horse. She remembered telling Blair that she liked to ride as they hiked to the lake yesterday. She was impressed at what he'd done with the information.

She untied the reins and climbed up into the worn leather saddle. "So, where are we going?"

He pulled out the riding stable's map of the area. "I thought we'd ride over to the national park and hit some of the trails, but if you have a favorite route."

"I do, but I go that way all the time," she said, turning the horse to face the path. "I'm ready for something new."

With that, they took off for the park at a trot. Dominique enjoyed being up high on the smooth-riding Salsa in the pleasant morning air. Having Blair at her side on the stallion made everything more exciting. He talked about his business, and, although she knew nothing of engines and racing, he made it sound interesting. Then he teased and cajoled her into having the time of her life.

They rode to the park and tried several trails. Dominique's favorite was a challenging one that ended on a ridge looking down at a small lake. They stopped to sit on the grass and talk, then made their way down to a trail Dominique often used.

Blair's stallion had been exercised, but he was anxious to run. Blair suggested that they race to the end of the trail before returning the horses. Knowing that Salsa was fast, she agreed. "What do I win?" she asked confidently.

Blair burst out laughing. "Mighty confident, aren't you?"

She shrugged. "Salsa's a fast horse."

"So is Black Thunder," he said, referring to his stallion. "The loser has to cook breakfast for the winner. Okay?"

She agreed, already planning to request waffles and bacon.

Blair took off on the stallion in a flash of speed, and Dominique shot after him. Salsa was fast, but the stallion was a powerhouse. Halfway through the trail, Dominique suspected that she would not be able to win this one. Still, she hung on to Salsa and urged the mare to go as fast as she could.

At the end of the trail, Blair waited for her while he fed Black Thunder a treat. "I'll make it easy for you," he quipped. "I'd like bacon, scrambled eggs with cheese, and grits."

"Congratulations." She shook his hand, working hard to cover her disappointment at the loss. She hated to lose anything. "We can go back to my place for breakfast."

"I'm looking forward to it," he answered. He held on to her hand and pulled her close for a deep, dizzying kiss.

Dominique arced against him, her body warming to his sensual heat. "Congratulations," she said again, her voice ringing with conviction.

On the way back from the stable, Dominique glanced at her watch and remembered the missionary society's fundraising meeting that was scheduled to begin in half an hour. Retrieving her cell phone, she called Nona, the group's secretary and made an excuse for her absence. When Nona promised to handle the meeting, Dominique breathed a sigh of relief and made a quick rundown of the important agenda items. When she ended the call, she felt the weight of Blair's gaze.

"I forgot," she confessed.

"It happens," he said in a light tone. "I would have understood if you wanted to postpone my victory breakfast."

She shot him a quick glance, certain he'd the word "victory" in the sentence just to tease her. "I can miss one missionary meeting."

Blair nodded and kept driving. Back at the condo, she washed her hands and began to prepare breakfast. Blair washed his hands, too, and used her juicer and coffee maker to make fresh beverages. They worked well together.

As they ate, Dominique found herself thinking that this was what it would be like to be married to a man like Blair. The pleasant conversation, smooth camaraderie, and the electricity between them were all things she craved.

Before he left, he lingered at the door with Dominique, holding her in his arms and showering her with hot kisses. Sighing, she tilted her face up and reveled in the moment. Desire shot through her when she felt the touch of his hands on her breasts. Her knees shook as they kissed for several minutes. Blair held her tight. Prying himself away regretfully, he finally said good bye. She felt the sensual effects of his kisses and caresses long after he'd gone, and comforted herself with the prospect of their next date.

Seven

The rest of the month was a blur of exciting dates with Blair. Dominique had so much fun that she nearly forgot she had ever been bored and lonely. They went motorcycle riding, fishing, dancing, bicycling, and hang-gliding. Sometimes they just hung out together, enjoying each other's company. Whatever they did, Dominique was happy to be with Blair. He was always courteous, considerate, and exciting. The attraction between them sizzled, but they never went past the sumptuous kisses and he never indicated he wanted more. Dominique said nothing, but it grew to be a sensitive point. Blair Thomas was haunting her dreams.

Dominique didn't know when it started, but her efficiency began to slip. The missed meetings and appointments here and there began to add up, and the reasons behind them varied from forgetfulness and stress to being ill. For so long, her efficiency had generated success and been the constant in her life. Now she couldn't count on anything.

She was having the time of her life on a personal level, but she'd begun to get worry headaches that incapacitated her. Blair had shaken up her ordered life and she wasn't sure it was a good thing. She was falling in love with him. The man was perfect for her, but she suspected that she was just a pleasant way for him to pass the time in Red Oaks.

Sitting with the choir in church one Sunday, she was called to the podium to give the chair reports. Somehow she muddled through. And when they asked for a chairman and volunteers for the Women's Day program, her temples pounded so hard that she couldn't even think of volunteering. Before she left church, she heard the whispers and rumors starting back up, and this time they hurt twice as much. She was making a fool out of herself again.

While in a ladies' bathroom stall, she heard Cissy Slade tell her sister that Blair was dating Dominique in return for the Winston Bank endorsement, and that Dominique's parents were worried that she was going to have a nervous breakdown when Blair left town. Both women laughed.

Dominique was so hurt and angry that she nearly threw the stall door open right then to confront the women. Instead, she finished her business and then exited the stall with her head high. The women had already left.

In the mirror, she saw her eyes were red and her nose had a pinkish tint. She was upset and it showed. What hurt most was the grain of truth that resonated in her thoughts. Though she hated to admit it, she did have some doubt about Blair's feelings for her. She splashed her face with cold water and patted it dry with a paper towel.

Always thoughtful and charming, Blair was waiting to walk her to her car, and he reminded her of their plans for the evening. She wanted to be with him, but physically she wasn't up to it. With her head pounding, Dominique could barely speak. Her stomach gurgled nervously. She slumped forward. "Blair," she managed, "I'm not feeling well. I'm going home to get in the bed."

Concerned for her, he insisted on driving her home. Once there, he took off her shoes and jacket and put her to bed. While she slept, he made chicken noodle soup from scratch.

Blair brought a tray with a bowl and crackers into her room and sat with her while she ate. The soup was delicious and full of chicken, carrots, onion, noodles, and a flavorful broth.

"You're spoiling me," she said, thanking him for taking care of her.

"You deserve to be spoiled," he said, caressing her cheek. "I'm worried about you. Maybe you should see a doctor."

"I'm okay," she insisted. "I've been a little stressed lately. I just need to get more rest."

"I'm going to do everything I can to make sure you do," he said. Then he sat and talked with her until she fell back asleep.

~

As soon as Dominique was asleep, Blair ate a bowl of the soup and put the rest in the refrigerator. He didn't like the heavy feeling he got in his chest when he saw Dominique lying around like a wilted flower. He knew he cared for her a lot and didn't want to think about how much. He wished he had been able to persuade Dominique to go to the doctor. Her symptoms closely resembled those of a friend who had sunk into depression.

Checking on Dominique one last time, he kissed her cheek. Then he went into the kitchen and called Scooter to pick him up.

When his friend's car pulled up, Blair closed Dominique's door and headed outside.

"I didn't know what to think when I saw your car still in the parking lot after church," Scooter said as Blair got in, shut the door, and fastened the seatbelt.

"Dominique wasn't feeling well, so I drove her home."

Scooter's gaze pierced him to the bone. "There's been a lot of gossip going around about you two. You're not from here, so it doesn't touch you, but she's been taking a lot of heat," he said, pulling off.

"I didn't know," Blair said honestly. "What can I do to help her?"

"That depends on you." Scooter looked at him, looked away, and did it again. "How do you really feel about Dominique? Do you love her?"

"It's too soon for that," Blair said quickly.

"Do you think you could love her?"

"Of course. That's why I like her so much, why I care about her."

Scooter entered the freeway and changed lanes. "Look Blair, those of us who love Dominique are beginning to worry. She hasn't been herself. I look at her and see her going down the same path she traveled with that creep she married. I know you like her, but I've seen you walk away from women that I could have sworn you loved. Are you going to walk away from Dominique?"

"Yeah." Blair's hands balled into fists. He'd had a similar conversation with Mother Maybelle before church started. "Dominique knows that I'm leaving."

"Does she? If I were Dominique, I'd find your behavior confusing. You see her almost every day."

Blair slammed his fist against the seat. "Why shouldn't I? We enjoy each other's company and we're both adults."

Scooter pulled over to the side of the road. "You're *not* sleeping with her?"

"No, not that's it's any of your business," Blair snapped.

Scooter's eyes sparked and stuck out. Blair hadn't seen this side of Scooter in years. The man was furious. "If you were, you'd have to go, and I'd kick your ass to kingdom come."

If it came to violence, Blair knew he could hold his own, but he didn't want to fight his friend, especially over Dominique. He felt frustrated. His hometown had been more liberal. He wasn't used to living in the small community of Red Oaks and having every move scrutinized. Hurting Dominique was the last thing on his mind. "Look man, chill. I've been holding back on purpose. I'm not at a place in my life where I can even consider marrying anyone."

"Tell Dominique that," Scooter said, working the car back into traffic.

～

After a difficult appointment where Dominique and her accountant audited the books of one of the town's oldest department stores, Dominique was elated when Blair called and asked her to lunch. She needed a pick-me-up, and seeing Blair always lifted her spirits.

He waited for her outside the department store and drove her to the restaurant. She was still so wrapped up in what had come out during the audit, that she initially failed to notice the change in Blair.

Sitting across from him in a booth at Paradiso, a Mexican restaurant, she didn't know what to think. Blair was so deep into himself that he wasn't really there with her. Minutes went by when nothing was said. Dominique had never seen him like this. She tried to draw him into the moment by asking questions, but his short answers required little thought.

She ordered taco salad and a glass of sangria, noting that he opted for nachos and coffee.

"Blair, what's the matter?" she asked finally. "You seem distracted. Is there a problem? You can tell me anything."

He studied her, his eyes telling her that he needed her statement to be true. "You know I've been worried about you," he began.

"I'll be fine," she said quickly. "I've had a few headaches, but I'm taking better care of myself."

"I know there's been a lot of gossip about us. The last thing I want is for you to get hurt by it."

She shrugged with a casualness she didn't really feel. She wondered if she was about to be dumped for her own good. "I'm a big girl. I can handle it. Is there something else?"

"Yes." He reached out to clasp her hand. "Dominique, I like you a lot. I think you know that."

"Yes, I do." She gave him a reassuring smile. "I like you a lot, too."

He didn't seem reassured. The warm affection she was used to seeing in his gaze was missing and so was the easy flow of his conversation. Dominique held her breath and waited.

"Remember the picnic?" he continued. "When I told you where I was in my life? How I'm not ready to settle down?"

Moistening her dry lips, she leaned forward. "I remember."

He rubbed the space between his brows and stumbled through his words. "Well I, um, wanted you to know that it's still true. I'm not ready to marry anyone, and I don't want to lead you on."

Removing her hand from his, Dominique set her back straight against the cushioned booth. Blair hadn't led her on, but until he'd actually repeated what he'd told her at the picnic, she'd been hoping deep inside that he'd fall in love with her and want to marry her. When had she become so naive?

Her gaze locked with his. He sat across from her, waiting uncomfortably for her response. She expelled the air from her lungs with a loud sigh. Then she laughed out loud. "You haven't led me on. I'm not expecting you to suddenly declare your undying love and marry me," she lied. "And for the record, I haven't asked you to marry me, either."

He ran a hand over his eyes and sighed. Then he chuckled, too.

"What brought this on?" she asked.

He shrugged. "This is a close-knit community. The people who love you are worried about you."

She shot him an incredulous look. "Did my parents—"

"No." He reached across the table to gently massage her hand. "Your parents had nothing to do with this."

"Then who?" She glanced up as the waitress placed her sangria and salad, and Blair's nachos, on the table.

"Does it matter who?" Blair asked when their server was gone.

"I guess not." Dominique sipped her sangria and suspected Mother Maybelle and Reverend Avery, maybe even Deacon Jones. Her initial anger dissipated. Someone had made sure she got a wake up call. They'd done her a favor because what she'd suspected all along was true. She was just something pleasant for Blair to do while he was in town.

Now that he'd cleared things up with her, Blair relaxed and put in an order for his usual beef and cheese enchiladas.

Dominique ate the food she usually loved without tasting it. Focusing on Blair's handsome face, she wondered what it took to really touch his heart, to earn his love. She managed to laugh and joke with him like always, but deep inside she knew that things would never be the same between them.

When Blair drove her to her car, she leaned across the seat and pressed her mouth to his in the deep, heartfelt kiss she'd been dreaming about. She threaded her fingers through his soft hair, caressed his face, and tangled her tongue with his. He groaned and his heart pounded beneath her fingers Behind her closed lids, she savored all that he was and told herself that the love, the warmth, and the happiness she felt with him were temporary. He wasn't really hers and would never be.

She turned to gather her purse and briefcase when the kiss ended. Blair came around and opened her door. He helped her out and stood there, suddenly reluctant to let go of her hand.

"I'll see you later," she said as she gently tugged her hand from his.

Blair hovered. "I'll call you."

"Okay," she agreed, certain that he wouldn't and not sure how she would react if he did. She opened her car door and climbed in. He stared as she closed the door, clicked the seatbelt, and started the engine.

Driving home, Dominique went over all her business appointments in her head and all the things that required some action on her part. She had a lot to do. Inside her condo she cleaned the kitchen and bathroom to keep her mind off Blair.

It wasn't until she sat at the table, alone with her glass of wine, that the first tear fell and hit her linen placemat. Dominique slumped forward on the table and cried.

She was angry with herself for being naïve enough to fall in love with Blair and hurt that he didn't have the good sense to love her back. She wasn't headed for the public humiliation she'd had with her ex-husband, but the pain in her heart overwhelmed her.

When the telephone rang, she checked the caller ID display and saw the name "Jones." Dominique's throat clogged up at the thought of talking to Blair. With her shoulders straight, she turned off the ringer and headed into her bedroom.

Eight

On Sunday, church started pretty much the way it always did. Dominique finished the announcements and took her seat as Blair made his way to the microphone.

Gathering himself, he looked at the congregation with sincere appreciation. His gaze even swept the choir stand, but Dominique did not react. "Good morning everyone. I want to thank each and every one of you for welcoming me to Red Oaks and making my stay here the best I've ever had," he began. "I'm especially grateful to Deacon Jones, Mother Maybelle, the Winston family, and several others, too numerous to mention. To show my sincere appreciation, I'd like to invite you to my race next Sunday in Atlanta. I've reserved and paid for enough tickets to cover everyone. You can pick them up at the arena box office. I hope you'll all come and be my guests."

Reverend Avery stood and approached Blair to pat him on the shoulder. "I love it when our young folks succeed and make us proud," the reverend said. "Mother Maybelle and Deacon Jones have been filling my ears with this young man's accomplishments for years. I'm proud to see him standing here, well on the road to big-time success. Now I don't know about the rest of you, but I intend to be at that race in Atlanta next Saturday."

In a pink silk suit and matching hat, Mother Maybelle stood. "Excuse me, Reverend Avery. I'm going to that race to show my support for Blair, too. I just wanted to announce that I rented a bus, and anyone who wants a ride to Atlanta is welcome to come along for free."

The congregation murmured in approval.

"Deborah and I will be there, too," Dominique's father called out.

Several of the choir members gave Dominique expectant glances. She ignored them. She thought it was nice of him to invite the church to his race, but it didn't mean that Dominique had to tag along to get a taste of what she was missing. Dominique already knew what she was missing—Blair's love—and she had no intention of airing her loss in public.

After leaving the choir stand at the end of service, Dominique stashed her robe while Blair talked to her parents. Then she slipped out of the church while most of the congregation was still socializing.

～

On Wednesday night, Dominique sat with her visiting cousin, Lucy, at a corner table in the Red Velvet Room. In the past she'd gone there several times with Blair to dance, but showing up for the ladies' night activities was new for her.

Tall and voluptuous, Lucy had the waiters running to get her drinks and several of the male patrons buying them. She'd already caused major drama when two men argued over her and were asked to leave.

Dressed in a red-fringed slip dress and matching heels, Dominique had danced several times with different partners and sipped wine in between. She'd forgotten how it felt to be single and available. Before Blair, she'd been too hung up on not repeating past mistakes and concerned about what other people thought. Now she was enjoying herself.

In the five days since she'd stopped dating Blair, a few of the town's eligible bachelors had made their interest known. She'd gone to high school with Deke Winters, the city attorney, who had spent time at her table earlier in the evening. He was also divorced, and all the wiser for his past mistakes. In addition, Rob Tolbert had caught her in one of his supermarkets and asked her out.

Dominique danced in her seat, certain that things would be fine as soon as she got over Blair Thomas.

As if she'd conjured him up, his handsome and exciting face appeared in the crowd. Butterflies rushed her stomach. Glad that Lucy was on the floor dancing, she watched as he made a path straight to her table.

"Dominique," he greeted, looking at her like he expected her to get up and run. "Mind if I sit down?"

She extended her hand to point at the chair across from her.

"Are you still avoiding me?"

"No. Would you like something to drink?"

He shook his head. "I didn't handle things right when we had lunch the other day, did I?"

This time Dominique shook her head. "I realize that you tried very hard, and I appreciate that. I got a wake-up call. I was getting much too attached and I didn't know."

His gaze covered her face with a hint of longing. "I'm sorry if I said anything that hurt you. I miss you. We were too good together to let things go down like this."

Her insides tightened, the butterflies shifting nervously.

"I miss you, too," she said honestly. "I knew you were only going to be here a short time. Aren't you leaving for good on Friday?"

"Yeah." He flashed the good-natured grin she'd seen him use to cover awkward situations. "You were in church on Sunday. You heard me issue the racing invitation to the congregation?"

Lifting her glass, she sipped, not quite willing to make things easy for him. "Yes, I was there. And?"

There was an unspoken plea in his brown eyes. "And I wanted to extend a personal invitation to you. You get your own room and a front row seat at the Four Star Championship Auto Racing Exhibition. I'll drive you down to Atlanta and provide your meals. And . . . we part as friends."

He extended his hand, palm up across the table.

She stared at it, evaluating her options and knowing that if she refused she would never see him again. Eyes moist, her hand inched across the table to clasp his.

"Thank you." He held it with both hands, massaging it. "We pull out at six on Friday morning."

The first few bars of Lionel Richie's "Three Times A Lady" began to play. Blair's hands gripped hers as he stood. "One dance and I'm gone. Will you dance with me?"

At her consent, he drew her to the dance floor and into his arms. Closing her eyes, she breathed in his woodsy scent and laid her head against his chest. He held her as if she were the most precious thing in the world.

After the dance, he took her back to her table and disappeared into the crowd.

∼

The next morning, Dominique called her parents and informed them that she was going to Blair's race in Atlanta. Her mother was overjoyed. Her father wished her a good trip and said he'd see her there. Her little brother was asleep.

Nervous excitement and anticipation ate at her as she packed an overnight bag with her toiletries, a nightgown, a champagne-colored dress and matching shoes for dinner, and a black and blue pants outfit to wear to the race.

She ignored the knowing glances when she got her hair done at her favorite shop. Then she checked her calendar and rearranged her appointments. For better or worse, the next two days with Blair marked the end of a time in her life that she would remember forever.

Blair came to pick her up at six a.m. sharp on Friday. When she opened the door, he simply hugged her tight. Then he put her bag in the trunk, helped her into the car, and they headed out.

The warm wind whipped at her scarf and caressed her skin as they drove. Dominique enjoyed the ride with Blair, laughing and talking. It was as if they'd never been apart. Knowing that it was their last time together made it even more special. The two-hour drive was over in no time.

Blair took her to Perkin's for waffles and bacon. They talked about the next day's race and his toughest competition. Dominique was sure he could win.

Later, he took her to the garage where his crew was preparing his car for the race. In the shop area, he introduced her to Seymour, Tim, and Holden, his mechanics, who also doubled as his pit crew. They greeted her warmly and explained the repairs and upgrades they were doing to his car.

Dominique touched the sides of Blair's car, the Blue Dream. A life-sized version of some of the toys she'd seen her brother playing with when he was little; it looked light and fast, and almost too fragile to hold Blair. On the back quarter panel she found the Winston Banks logo, along with other well-known sponsors.

In the back of the garage, she met his father, Jay Thomas, who was watching tapes of past races. Tall and handsome, with a touch of silver at his temples and a few strands threaded through his hair, he looked like a slightly older version of Blair. They could have been brothers.

Taking her hand, Jay welcomed her and told her that he'd heard a lot about her. He had Blair's chocolate-brown eyes, but his seemed to see clear through to her soul. She caught him noting the way she and Blair interacted and the way Blair held her hand.

After a while, Blair sent Dominique to the shopping mall while he worked with the crew. Dominique walked through Lennox Mall looking at the beautiful clothes in Saks and Bloomingdale's, but was too keyed up to buy anything. She found a bookstore and spent hours perusing the shelves. When Blair called on her cell phone, she was ready to go.

Dominique went to dinner with Blair and his dad at Fogo de Chao, a Brazilian steakhouse with a large salad bar and a nonstop parade of grilled meat. After getting their vegetables and salads at the food bar, they sat down at their table.

They were given little poker-sized chips with a green side and a red side. Blair explained that if she left green side of the chip facing up, the waitrer would serve platters of beef, pork, lamb, and chicken. When she'd had enough, she could turn the chip over to display the red side to indicate she was through.

Following dinner, Jay went back to the garage while Blair and Dominique spent some time at a dance club. They danced for hours, holding on to each other, touching, and talking. Finally, though, Blair had to go back to the hotel to rest.

Outside Dominique's room, sensual awareness sparked and flamed. He stepped forward and gathered her so close that her soft curves molded to the contours of his body. She tilted her face up. The simmering heat in his eyes burned through her clothes.

Blair bent down to kiss her. The touch of his lips on hers overwhelmed her with a shock of sensation. He deepened the kiss, his mouth covering hers hungrily as his tongue sent thrills of desire arcing through her. Sighing, she shook in his arms. His arms dropped.

On shaky legs, Dominique turned to open her door. Her fingers fumbled with key. It took two tries to open it. She stepped inside, her fingers hitting the light switch as she turned back to face Blair.

Their gazes locked. He leaned forward for one last sizzling kiss. Dominique felt dizzy. Before she could collect her wits, he was in her room with her and she was bending beneath the storm of his kisses. His hands, his lips, and his mouth were heated lightning against her sensitive skin, and they were everywhere.

"Blair," she moaned as she stretched out on the bed with her dress around her hips and her bra on the floor. This moment was everything she'd dreamed. Her fingers caressed the smooth skin on his chest through his open shirt.

His mouth was warm and wet on her breasts and stomach as he drew the dress off her hips and down her long legs. His hands slid up her waist and down to cup her lace-covered buttocks. "I've been dreaming of this for weeks," he grunted. "If you don't want this, send me away. Say no, Dominique."

She arched upward as he mouthed the tips of her breasts. "Yes," she sighed, trailing her fingers down his naked chest. "I want you, too."

The storm of passion returned with a vengeance, and they were rubbing, sliding, and undulating together in a searing heat that burned from the inside out. They tossed the last remnants of clothing aside and lay together on the sheets.

Blair drew a packet of protection from his pants on the floor, and Dominique smoothed the condom down the swollen length of him. Soon he was thrusting into her with a wild erotic rhythm which she punctuated with sighs and moans of pleasure. When she arched against him and melted, he held her tightly, trembling with the force of his release, his cry echoing her own.

He whispered her name in the darkness as they lay together on the damp sheets, still kissing. "We should have done this a long time ago."

"Mmm-hmm." She curled herself against his furnace-like warmth, not ready to end their time together. "Should we make up for lost time?"

His hands slid down her body to cup her intimately. "Just say the word. I'm down for anything you want."

She lowered her lips to his for a kiss. "Yes, yes, yes . . ."

The passion storm between them continued until they fell asleep in the tangled sheets.

Blair awakened Dominique in the twilight hours of the morning. He'd already showered and dressed, and was headed to the garage and then the racetrack. He made her promise that she'd get up in time to make the start of the race.

After getting herself ready, Dominique took a taxi to the racetrack and sat in the front row of the stands. She was early enough to give Blair a kiss and offer him her scarf for good luck.

The stands filled quickly with a lively crowd. Dominique saw several women sitting near her in the front row that she assumed were with the racers. All of them were beautiful and dressed to get attention. Behind them, families filled the stands.

The roar and the hum of powerful engines filled the air. Dominique turned back to face the racecars as the roar grew louder. The flag went down, and she saw them take off with Blair in the middle of the pack.

She watched his sky-blue car with the number seven until it was out of sight. Then she switched her attention to the monitors to watch the cars and listened to the announcer.

The race went on for hours. Dominique was on her feet for most of the time, anxious for Blair. She waved to him every time his car stopped for service in the nearby maintenance area that they called the pit. It was used for quick maintenance, tire changes, and gas refills.

Suddenly, two cars collided and one crashed into the wall and flipped over. The first driver got out of his wreck on his own. A team sprinted out and rescued the second man just before his car burst into flames.

Dominique watched, gripping the edges of the stand, and saying a prayer for the driver and his family. Then she said another for Blair. She knew he was skilled, but this was a dangerous sport.

On the last lap, she yelled and cheered so long and loud that her voice was hoarse. Blair was one of the three leaders.

The three cars flew around the bend and headed for the finish line with Blair in the lead. The yellow car edged closer, but Blair sped past the finish line, still in the lead. The crowd roared.

Dominique ran from the stands to the pit area, flashing the pass which Blair had given her to get by the security guards. Blair opened his arms and she flew into them.

"I knew you'd win," she said before their lips met in a congratulatory kiss.

He picked her up and swung her around. His heart was still beating fast as he held her tightly.

"Oh Blair, I'm so happy for you," she said, knowing that he would put the $300,000 in prize money to good use.

Reporters approached with cameras to interview Blair. He tried to hold on to Dominique, but they pulled him away and quickly surrounded him.

"Wait for me," he called.

Dominique sat and waited. Her heart was with Blair as he talked to the reporters and sponsors and answered questions. Still basking in the glow of the love they'd made, she wanted him to know that she loved him and wanted him to be happy.

He stood in the limelight and handled the press like a pro. She'd never loved any man as much. Her heart was so full that she couldn't think past what she would say.

As the stands emptied, she scanned them, knowing that her parents were somewhere out there. They were nowhere in sight. After an hour, the only people left were some of the women who were with the racers and the racers' families.

Center stage, the press was taking pictures of Blair and the second- and third-place winners with their cars. He waved to her, blew kisses, and signaled her to wait several times. Each time her pulse sped up.

An hour and a half passed before she saw her parents approaching. They were ready to drive back to Red Oaks, but she knew they would wait if she asked. In her thoughts, she tried to clarify why she was waiting for—and what she expected—from Blair. That's when she realized that it was time for her to go.

Her chest was heavy and her eyelids stung. She bit down on her bottom lip. Blair was doing something he loved. He was a success and where he wanted to be in his life. It did not include her. That was the reality of her situation with him.

She didn't want a public ending to what they'd shared. It would be difficult for both of them. Waiting for Blair could only involve an awkward moment and another good-bye.

She found the paper at the back of the planner she kept in her purse and used it to write him a note. Then she folded it and wrote his name on it.

"You're not going to stay?" Jay asked in a surprised tone when she asked him to give Blair the note.

She shook her head, her throat so clogged she could barely speak. "It wouldn't do any good. Blair's got his mind made up on where he is in his life and what he wants. He's not ready for anything permanent."

Jay pushed his cap back on his head. "Well, I enjoyed meeting you and going to dinner with you and Blair. You're the nicest young lady I've ever seen him with."

Thanking him, Dominique left with her parents. Her chest hurt. She sat in the back of her parents' car and mopped her tear-stained face with a wad of tissue. She felt as if she were leaving a part of herself behind, and no amount of logic could make the feeling go away.

Huddling in the corner of the seat, she closed her eyes. It was hard to believe that the drive back to Red Oaks was the same one she'd taken with Blair only yesterday.

Nine

Blair escaped the crowd of reporters, sponsors, and well-wishers to look for Dominique. "Where is she?" he asked his dad, who was perched on Blair's tool kit near the pit.

"She left," Jay said, giving him the folded sheet of paper. "She sat and waited until her parents came, then she wrote this note for you."

Blair pulled the sheet open hurriedly, and read:

Blair,

You're all that any woman could want. I enjoyed every minute we spent together. You made a lasting impression on me. I wish you happiness, love, and victory in everything you do. Have a nice life.

Love,
Dominique

Love? Blair reread the ending on the note. Dominique had signed the note with love. Did it mean she loved him? Better yet, did he love her?

Despite his elation at winning, he fought the blues as he collected the prize check and signed the paperwork. He liked this life, and it was the vehicle he'd chosen to make his dreams come true. But, right now, it seemed empty.

The crew packed up everything and got ready to get on the road for the next race. Blair gave each member of the team a share of the prize money, and they left Atlanta for the next town on the racing circuit.

Blair sat with his dad in the front seat of the truck and watched it eat up the road.

Jay gave his son a concerned glance. "You okay, son?"

"Fine." Blair closed his eyes and pretended to sleep. He could hear the guys in the back of the cab laughing and joking over the steady hum of the truck's engine. Usually, he joined in with choice comments and laughter, but he wasn't feeling sociable. He was tired from staying up late with Dominique and then racing for hours with the adrenaline raging. Gradually, he fell into slumber.

The sound of a woman's laughter awakened Blair. He sat up and looked around. The truck was stopped. They'd arrived at the hotel in Rally, Georgia, and a woman was passing through the hotel parking lot with her escort. Tomorrow the team would move on to a town closer to the next race and get the car ready.

It was Holden's turn to spend the night with the car, so he was busy pulling blankets and a mattress across the flattened seats. The rest of the crew checked into the hotel.

Blair got his room key and escaped. The room was huge. He lay on the king-sized bed and gazed at the ceiling. He kept hearing Dominique's voice and her laughter. Right then he knew she was his. She'd signed her note with love.

It was three in the morning by the time he realized what he had to do. He got up from the bed and freshened up. Then he went outside and retrieved the car from the tow bar behind the truck.

Jay was outside the hotel checking out the noise before Blair could get away. Sensing what was going on, he nodded and grinned at his son. "Go get her, boy," he said.

Turning the car around, Blair got back on the road and headed for Red Oaks.

~

Dominique had a rotten night. She fielded questions about Blair from her parents all the way home from Atlanta, and then returned gratefully to her condo.

For most of the night, she tossed and turned in her bed, too troubled to sleep. By seven, she was in her kitchen making coffee and preparing for her run. She stood on tiptoe to get a large cup from the top shelf of the cabinet.

When a tear ran down her cheek, she cursed loudly. She'd promised herself that there would be no more tears for Blair. Another tear fell. Dominique set the cup down and balled up her fists. She covered her eyes with her hands and cried.

It took a while for her notice the hammering noise outside. She stood and looked out the window. There was nothing going on outside. When the pounding continued, she went to the door and checked the peephole. She drew in a hard, pain-filled breath. The tears ran faster. Then she was flinging the door wide and letting Blair pull her into his arms.

"Baby, oh baby," Blair whispered holding her so tight she could barely breathe. "I thought about you all night I couldn't sleep because I kept thinking that I would never see you again, and my life would be an endless cycle of work and races."

Willing the tears to stop, she gazed at him with wet eyes. "You needed me to go away, so you could go on with the racing and the business without me hanging around," she said.

"I asked you to wait," he muttered, leaning down to kiss her.

Dominique pounded his shoulder playfully with her fist. "Yeah, so that you could say good-bye."

He framed her face with his hands and covered it with soft kisses. His eyes were sincere. "No. I don't think I would have been able to do it," he confessed. "I couldn't believe you'd just left me like that."

"I didn't think you cared," she told him. "And I didn't want to say good-bye."

"Dominique, I love you. I came back because I missed you. I'm not going to do without you. Understand?"

"You love me?" She stared at him incredulously. "You *love* me?"

"Yeah, I do." With a half grin that lacked his usual confidence, he wiped the moisture from her eyes with his fingertips and kissed her eyelids. "I didn't know because I've never felt like this before. Then there's the fact that I'm a stubborn guy who's used to having things his way. Love and marriage have been things that other people talk about and do, not me. Now I know that you're what I want. I'll go crazy if we're not going to be together. What do you say, Dominique? Will you marry me?"

She stared at him, her fingers digging into his shoulders to convince herself that this was real. He was saying all the things she'd longed to hear. Practical questions filled her mind. "Where would I live?"

He touched her hair and stroked her neck. "Here, and with me as much as possible. I want you to live your dreams, too."

She pulled his head down for a deep, drugging kiss.

He nibbled on her lips and grasped her hands. "Is that a yes?"

Dominique gazed into his eyes and answered straight from her heart. "Yes."

"Woo hoo!" Blair lifted her in the air and swung her around. Then he set her down on the kitchen table. "It's going to be good. Everything you ever dreamed of," he assured her.

"I'm going to make you happy, too," Dominique promised, bending forward to circle him with her arms and legs. Holding Blair and laughing as he slid his hands up her gown and joked about fantasies in the kitchen, she knew she'd finally found a love that would grow into one to rival the one her parents had.

Love Under New Management

Nathasha Brooks-Harris

This book is dedicated to the memory of my favorite aunt,
Bessie Mae Clark, August 26, 1925–April 21, 1965.

Your time was too short on earth, but you touched my life in a way you'll never know. After finding some of your fine poems which should've been published so many years ago, I realized where my passion for writing comes from. I know you're up in Heaven watching over me and guiding my hand as I write. This book is because of the blood and gifts which runs through our veins. I only hope that I did you proud. Rest on, sweet Auntie, I'll always love you.

Acknowledgments

First and foremost, I would like to thank God for laying this project on my heart. I don't know why He did; I just hope that the words contained in my novella are a word in season for someone. I'd like to say an extra special thank you to Demetria Lucas, my very patient editor. Thanks so much for bringing this book to life and for believing in it. Your enthusiasm sparked my creativity more than you'll ever know. Thanks also for hanging in there with me (and the group) when things got a little rough. To my agent, Sha-Shana Crichton, I cannot thank you enough for all you've done. Thank you, thank you, thank you. You're the absolute best! To my co-authors, Janice Sims, Natalie Dunbar, and Kim Louise, you ladies are wonderful! It was a pleasure working with each of you, and I hope that we can do it again real soon. I felt so blessed to work with such talented ladies who are not only great authors, but also dear friends.

One

Valerie Freeman drummed her professionally manicured nails on the side of her drafting table as she designed an ad for Delta Airlines' newest promotional campaign. "It's as quiet as a mausoleum in here," she muttered to herself, strolling across the floor of her small home studio to turn on the stereo. "A little background noise is exactly what I need while I work."

Switching on the FM radio, she skipped past classic soul, traditional jazz, and hip-hop, in favor of some down-home Sunday morning gospel music. Satisfied with her choice, she went back to her desk and picked up where she'd left off. As she penciled in the colors that would best attract consumers' eyes when they saw the nationwide advertisement, Valerie began humming along with the melodious sounds of the music she heard. At that moment, her mind burned with the memory of how much she enjoyed singing in the choir at the White Rock Baptist Church in Atlanta, where she was a member while she attended college. But singing was a thing of her past and she didn't dare do it anymore—at least not professionally, as she'd had hoped to do when she was younger.

These days, she was content with her job as a graphic artist. The pay was great, the benefits were even better, and there was little chance of someone taking advantage of her again. Just put her at a drafting table, give her an assignment, a computer, the right desktop publishing programs, and art supplies, and she'd crank out the tightest designs in Red Oaks, Georgia.

As quickly as Valerie's mind reminisced about her days as a lead soloist, her thoughts drifted back to the contemporary rendition of "The Battle Hymn of the Republic," sung by the choir on the radio. Although she didn't realize it, her feet began tapping the floor, and her head bobbed in time with the rhythm of the song.

Sipping a cup of coffee, she tried her hardest to concentrate on her work, but she couldn't because she was enjoying the music much more than she expected or wanted to. Soon, she was so caught up that she stopped creating and listened to the soul-stirring songs that seemed to beckon her, call out to her. The beginnings of a smile tipped the corners of Valerie's full, bow-shaped lips, as she listened to the announcer end the show.

"This has been Everlasting Praise, the best of contemporary praise and gospel music as sung by Witness, the award-winning choir from Red Oaks Christian Fellowship," the deejay said in a smooth voice. "For more of this wonderful music and a heaping helping of the word of God, Reverend Terrance Avery and his staff invite you to come to the 11:00 a.m. morning worship service at the church, located on South Green Fork Road." It was as if he were extending Valerie a personal invitation.

She added some lettering to the advertisement she was working on, but she kept crossing and uncrossing her cinnamon-brown legs, unable to sit still. There was a tugging in her spirit. Some unanswered fire was shut up in her bones and it had to be let out. Within minutes, Valerie was in the shower, gelling herself down with juniper berry body scrub. Afterward, she dried herself off and lotioned her well-endowed body, then chose an outfit from her overflowing walk-in closet. She got dressed, applied a light coating of makeup, styled her bronze shoulder-length hair, and spritzed on her signature Sung cologne. Finally, she declared herself ready.

Checking her watch on the way to the car, she grabbed her purse. "It's eleven-fifteen now," she said to her curious cat, Girlfriend. "If I take the expressway across town, I'll be late, but I should still be able to catch some of the service and, hopefully, hear that bad choir sing a few songs." Valerie put

on a winter-white wool and cashmere blend wrap and began the trip she
never—not even in her wildest dreams—expected to make.

~

The few minutes of singing and praising preceding the morning worship
service were ending as Valerie arrived at the medium-sized church. She
quickly scanned the beautifully designed sanctuary and its stadium seating.
She noticed the rich green, brown, russet, and sky-blue color scheme, as well
as the afrocentric fabrics that accentuated the church's comfortable décor.
Her eyes were drawn to the pulpit where several floral arrangements and an
array of green plants sat on both sides of a crystal podium. On an otherwise
chilly winter day, a warm feeling washed over Valerie as she saw that every
seat was filled with people of all ages. Dressed in their Sunday finery, they
were a gorgeous kaleidoscope of colors.

The sound of a woman's voice stirred Valerie out of her musings. "Mornin',
ma'am. Follow me, please," an usher clad in a white uniform greeted. Valerie
looked at the nametag pinned to a handkerchief on the woman's ample
bosom and smiled at her before following her to a seat in a back section that
was reserved for latecomers. The usher handed Valerie a weekly bulletin,
pointed to a hymnal in the back of the pew, then gave her an information
card for visitors and asked her to fill it out. She did and handed it back to the
woman, who smiled and walked away to seat others who were lined up at
the door.

Valerie watched as Witness, the one hundred and seventy-five–voice mass
choir, assembled and made themselves comfortable in preparation to minister in song. The church applauded, then there was a moment of absolute silence. Suddenly, the beautiful sound from the acoustic piano filled the
church, then the Red Oaks Christian Fellowship band joined in with its
Hammond organ, percussion, horns, and strings. The melody wrapped
around Valerie like water around a rock in a river. The choir warmed the

congregation up with "Majesty," a slow song, and worked their way up to "I Stand On The Rock," an old mid-tempo gospel favorite. The members danced and got their praise on in the aisles to "I'll Be Satisfied," a syncopated tune which filled several members with the Holy Spirit.

Valerie had no idea how it happened, but she stood, clapping her hands, tapping her feet, and rocking her body from side to side to the melody of one of her favorite songs. It was one of the songs she'd sung with her choir back at White Rock Baptist. That old feeling welled up inside of her soul and she threw her head back, closed her eyes, and let it rip. Before long, she was in the zone—that place of perfect peace where she went whenever she sang. That which she had kept silent for so long could no longer contain itself, and Valerie let her five-octave soprano voice ring out in all of its splendor.

When she sang, a shiver of vivid recollection shot up her spine as her failed attempt to break into the music business ran through her mind. Tears glistened on her oval face.

A nurse arrived and put her arm around Valerie, handing her tissues to dry her eyes. Valerie managed a tiny smile for her, knowing that the kind woman assumed that she was "happy," caught up in the spirit, and praising the Lord. *If only she knew*, Valerie thought as she wiped her face, determined not to let her past steal her joy. She closed her eyes and meditated for a few minutes, then continued singing along with the choir as they healed troubled spirits through song.

The worshippers in Valerie's immediate vicinity heard a honeyed voice the first time Valerie sang, but they weren't sure if it belonged to the visitor. But they were sure when she began to sing again. They quieted to listen to Valerie, enjoying the loveliest voice they'd heard in quite a while. She thought she overheard a few of them whispering to each other that they'd try to recruit her for the music ministry. A tumble of confused feelings assailed Valerie then, but she didn't give into them. She would worry about what she *thought* she'd heard later. It had been too long since she'd found comfort and solace in music and she wanted to enjoy the moment.

Valerie closed her eyes as she sang and danced to the extended version of the song, getting back into her special zone. She managed to tune out everyone and everything around her, losing herself in the message the choir crooned.

When she finally opened her lids, she caught a glimpse of the choir's spirited director. Valerie watched as the strinkingly handsome man with flowing dreadlocks winked at a beautiful elderly woman who held court in the second row. She could've put any of the top super models to shame, with her mink-trimmed salmon-colored suit and well-styled salt-and-pepper hairdo, which peeked out from a matching hat which was tilted just right on her head.

The director forced his beloved choir to modulate and follow his lead as the Holy Spirit led him. With a single directive, the choir broke the song down into its vocal parts: first, the bass section; then the baritones; tenors; altos; ending with the sopranos. There was vigorous applause when the man signaled for them to sing together, blending their voices in a perfect four-part harmony. His arms flailed wildly as he jumped up and down, screaming directions over the music. He looked over at the musicians, pumping his right arm in the air—his way of telling them to play with even more fervor than they already were. He danced from side to side as his arms pointed left or right, indicating the direction in which the choir should rock. For Valerie, watching him was a sight to behold.

Fascinated by his knowledge of music and his obvious passion for it, she studied his techniques. She recognized a professional when she saw one and knew that he was more than a choir director. Almost in a flash, he turned around to face the church members, beginning to testify about being satisfied, having the Lord Jesus Christ as his personal Lord and Savior; then he asked them if they felt the same. In call and response style, there was a conversation between him, the members, and the choir, who added their answer through the lyrics they sang.

It was when he walked all the way to the back of the church and began to testify to the people in her row that Valerie became undone. His voice was velvet-edged and strong. Huskiness lingered in its tone, causing the pit of her stomach to tingle. Her heartbeat skyrocketed to double-time. Fully aware of his manly appeal, and unable to stop herself, she studied the handsome, six-foot-two, amber-colored cutie from head to toe. Even under his turquoise and gold choir robe, she saw that he was powerfully built—muscular, thick, and chiseled.

Valerie tried her best to throttle the dizzying current racing through her body. She placed her hand on her chest to still the wild pounding of her heart, but it didn't do any good. Although the temperature was forty-two degrees and dropping outside, it felt to her as if were ninety-five degrees. Her knees buckled, and she felt her cheeks warm and flush as she looked at the sumptuous choir director who stood a mere few feet away from her. It should have been a sin for a man to be that sexy. He was the finest man she'd seen in a long time, and, although she'd tried to force herself to put men, relationships, and love on the back burner, those feelings weren't dead. *They are very much alive*, Valerie thought.

She plucked a funeral-home fan from the back of the pew and began to fan herself, hoping the heat that overtook her would go away. The women in her row shot her a curious look, and Valerie figured that they thought she was crazy, since she was too young for hot flashes. But she ignored them. All she cared about was chasing away the heat wave in which she was engulfed and getting another look at that finer-than-fine man.

He must have been thinking the same thing, because in the midst of her fanning, their gazes caught and held. Peering intently into his light brown eyes, the prolonged staring was almost unbearable for Valerie. She felt as if he saw straight into her soul as she studied the long, neatly-coiffed dreadlocks that framed his broad shoulders. His gaze was fastened on Valerie as if he were photographing her with his eyes.

Her pulse pounded, and a sense of tingling delight flowed through her, heating up her womanly depths. She was flattered by his interest, as his eyes traveled over her face, moved slowly over her body, then returned to search her eyes. This time, her heart turned over in response as his passion-filled orbs spoke to her. Valerie's heart was in perfect harmony with what they were saying.

Two

Norman Grant scanned Valerie critically and beamed his approval, telling himself that she was a beauty if ever he saw one. His gaze dropped from her eyes, to her shoulders, to her perky breasts, then back to the buttery expanse of her cinnamon-colored neck. Unaware that he was running his tongue slowly over his lips, or that his pupils had dilated, he stared into her eyes in silent expectation of what he wanted—once he got to know her, of course. His hands still directed the choir, but his eyes were on her.

He noticed her curvy brick-house shape, accentuated by a pair of shapely, pretty legs. She also had the most gorgeous lips he'd seen on any woman in all of his thirty years. Everything was in its rightful place and perfectly proportioned to her body. To his way of thinking, Valerie was a sister made for loving, and Lord help him, he wanted to love her!

Casting his eyes downward, he studied the plush forest-green carpet under his feet and began to pray silently. *Lord Jesus, You know this woman's making me so weak. I'm a man first—and I have needs. Help me, Father God; please help your child.*

His eyes caught Valerie's and their gazes held. Instantly, he knew that she was a woman of class and distinction, judging from her choice of a stylish burgundy and white tweed suit with a fitted jacket and leather-trimmed sleeves. His blood was set aflame as he watched her whip her shoulder-length blunt-cut bronze hair out of her face as the choir moved her more and more. With a shiver of recollection, he realized that looking at Valerie rekindled memories of his deceased biological mother, Belle, a classy, together woman who died when he was ten years old.

And that voice. That harmonious sound seemed to speak to his spirit. He took notice of the way it had mesmerized everyone around her. He craned his neck and inched a little closer to her pew in order to hear her better.

Although he continued to direct the choir and they kept singing a medley of great gospel favorites, his mind and eyes wouldn't stay off the unnamed visitor, who was beautiful—and talented, too. The more he looked at her, the more he was determined to find a way to get to know her. But it wasn't until she hit a high C over E—an extremely difficult note to sing—that he had his answer. He knew, without a doubt, *how* he'd make it happen.

Coming out of his reverie, he thought about the task which needed his expertise at the moment. He balled up his fists and moved them in a winding motion, signaling the choir to keep singing the refrain until he told them to stop. He kept his mind on his directing duties, and indeed, the saints shouted like crazy. The choir's voice fell under a special anointing, and their songs, filled with Biblical principles, moved the congregation until the church became a flurry of activity. The saved danced, shouted, and paced the aisles, proclaiming their love and devotion to Jesus Christ for all to hear. Others trembled and cried out, "Mercy," "Hallelujah," and "Thank you, Jesus." Their spiritual joy was like a wildfire that ignited the saved and unsaved alike.

When the church quieted from the near-deafening roar of praising and shouting, the church pastor, Reverend Terrance Avery, took his place at the podium. A feeling of contentment filled his soul as he rubbed his bald caramel-colored pate. "That's right church, if you know that you know that you *know* God is good, praise Him! Give God His due whenever you feel it deep down in your soul. Can I get an amen?" he wailed, winding up his congregation even more. He clutched the gold satin stole around his neck, pulling on it for emphasis. Cries of "Well," "Fix it," and "That's all right," were heard over the organist playing a series of chords to punctuate the fluctuation in Reverend Avery's voice. Valerie became caught up in the spirit and called out, too.

"Church, if you desire prayer this morning, come to the altar and let's talk to God. Tell Him what you need and believe that you will receive it in Jesus' name. He knows the groaning of *every* heart and knows your needs before you even ask Him."

Although Reverend Avery was standing many rows down from Valerie, it seemed as if he were looking straight at her, into the depths of her soul. Her eyes widened to the size of half dollars, and her toes curled in her shoes. A sheepish grin played over her face as she was overtaken by the deepening hue of shame. No matter what she did, Valerie couldn't shake the feverish warmth that consumed her body like a fast-spreading cancer. *He knows . . . the pastor knows that I'm sinning right here in his church—looking at that fine man like I've lost my ever-loving mind. I need prayer like yesterday*, she thought.

Valerie tore out of her seat, making her way to the altar. She excused herself so she could get as close as she could to the pastor, elders, and prayer staff to get a double dose of whatever anointing power they had in their healing hands. She wanted—no needed—to be on the receiving end of whatever would make her right again.

As the elders and the prayer staff snaked through the throngs of people congregated at the altar, Valerie couldn't quell the spasms in her face or the twitching of her lips. As Reverend Avery placed his hand on her forehead and prayed for her, she felt as though the world was spinning and careening off its axis. She became dizzy and thought she was going to faint. A male elder noticed her unsteadiness and stood over her in case she needed help.

Suddenly, a presence of warmth surrounded Valerie. Not knowing what it was or why it was happening, she surrendered to it and whispered a silent prayer. When the feeling left her, Valerie felt renewed, energetic—as if the hand of God had touched her. There was peacefulness in her spirit that she'd never known before. No longer did thoughts of the handsome choir director invade her mind.

Still feeling a bit lightheaded, she made it through the rest of the service. A sense of calmness surrounded her, and when the benediction was said two hours later, Valerie was ready to go downstairs to the Fellowship Hall for Social Hour. The promise of a cup of coffee and a slice of cake before her drive home sounded good to her.

On her way to the basement, she couldn't count the number of people who stopped to compliment her voice, to tell her that she had a calling to sing His praises, and she should use her gift to bring the unsaved to God. All she could do was nod, mostly because she couldn't get a word in edgewise as men and women, young and old, invited her to return to the church real soon. They begged her to join Red Oaks Christian Fellowship so she could become a member of the choir and begin her ministry in song.

～

Norman kept his eye on Valerie until the crowd of well-wishers dissipated. Then, he took off his robe, hung it over his arm, and straightened out his brown wool suit, making sure that it didn't appear wrinkled. He remembered hearing the church matriarch, Mother Maybelle, telling him that first impressions were lasting. Impressing Valerie was the only thing on his mind right then. Remembering a tiny bottle of Kouros cologne in his suit pocket, he discreetly sprayed some on the sides of his neck and decided he was ready to meet the visitor with the heavenly voice.

He sauntered to the back of the church, where Valerie stood, and waited until an overzealous member who wouldn't stop talking finally ran out of things to say and left. Then Norman seized the opportunity to approach Valerie before someone else beat him to it. His mouth curved into an unconscious smile, setting the tone of his introduction.

"Good afternoon, ma'am," he said, unable to stop smiling. "I couldn't help admiring your lovely voice."

His smile was unlike anything Valerie had ever seen before. It transformed his face into pure sunlight—an intimate smile, beautiful with brightness—warming her insides. "Thank you, sir. I've been getting a lot of that today," she replied with a laugh.

Regarding her with a provocative look in his eye, Norman enjoyed the sound of her gentle laughter rippling through the air. It pervaded his entire body like a bolt of electricity—strong, powerful, magnetic. "Every word of what they said is true. I've never heard such a beautiful voice. Please excuse my manners. My name is Norman Grant, and yours?" he asked, extending his hand.

"Valerie Freeman," she told him, placing her palm against his. She felt the electricity of his touch, and an unwelcome surge of excitement hit her in places that she didn't want to feel it. He'd struck a vibrant chord within her, and quivers of desire surged through her veins. "I'm happy to meet you."

"Oh no, the pleasure is *all* mine." It was easy for Norman to get lost in the way he looked at Valerie. He was totally entranced by her compelling presence and felt as if he wanted to wrap himself around her like a warm blanket on a cold winter's night.

Valerie enjoyed the touch of his hand—warm, strong, and firm—much like the man she imagined him to be. The scent of his cologne wafted through the air, assaulting her senses. A wonderful shiver of wanting ran through her again and made her knees buckle. Her heart hammered in her ears, and her pulse skittered at an alarming rate.

Norman released her hand and embraced her, catching her as she swooned. "What's wrong, Valerie? Are you all right?"

You can't fix what's wrong with me here in church, Valerie thought. She was so busy checking out how handsome he was in his suit that her breath caught in her throat. "I—I'm . . . a little lightheaded . . . from not eating this morning, I guess."

He took her hand, and saw this as a chance to show her how chivalrous he could be. He wanted to protect her in every possible way, and here was a heaven-sent opportunity. "Well, we'll just have to do something about that, won't we, Valerie?"

His touch upset her balance, and she stumbled on the way to wherever he was taking her. Her body tingled at the way he said her name. "Where are we going?" she quizzed.

Without warning, he wrapped his strong arm around her waist to steady her. "Just trust me, okay?" His expression stilled, letting her know that he took taking care of her very seriously.

The mystery in his eyes beckoned to her irresistibly, and she didn't want to dull the sparkle she saw in them. "That sounds good to me," she said, enjoying the safety and security of her protector's arms.

At that moment, Valerie didn't want to be anywhere else.

Three

Norman's strong hands continued to circle Valerie's waist as he led her downstairs to the Fellowship Hall. He helped her to a table, pulled her seat out, and she sat down, thanking him for his kindness. After making sure she felt better, he hung his robe over the back of a chair, excused himself, and went to the kitchen to see what he could find for her to eat before lunch was officially served.

Finding Sister Lawson, the head of the food ministry, he explained Valerie's situation. She stopped loading food platters and fixed an emergency meal to hold Valerie over so she couldn't say she'd visited Red Oaks Christian Fellowship and no one fed her after she'd nearly passed out.

"Sister Lawson, have you seen Mother Maybelle?" Norman asked. Surely, if the feisty church elder had seen him with Valerie, she would've been right by their sides, interrogating the poor woman with dozens of questions. Norman bristled at the thought. Very little happened in that church that Mother Maybelle didn't know about, but Norman didn't want to share Valerie with her or anyone else—at least, not that day.

Sister Lawson retrieved a steaming pan of cornbread from the oven and smeared several pats of butter on top of it before she responded. "Yes, baby, I saw Mother Maybelle a little while ago. She cornered Reverend Avery and had him hemmed up in his office about something that needed her 'immediate attention.' There's no need to look for her, because she's going to be there for a while."

Breathing a sigh of relief, Norman kissed Sister Lawson on the cheek, much to her surprise, then grabbed the tray she'd made and took it to Valerie.

Taking charge with quiet assurance, Norman set a plate with a fried chicken sandwich and a generous helping of macaroni salad before her. He put a cup of coffee and a slice of sweet potato pie next to that.

"You need sustenance," he advised Valerie, as if he had the cure for whatever ailed her. The satisfaction of being able to give her what she needed showed in his eyes. "I hope you enjoy this snack. The food ministry is one of our church's most successful outreach programs. The ladies who run the kitchen are excellent cooks, and they love what they do."

Valerie bowed her head and blessed her food. "You really shouldn't have gone to all this trouble, Norman," she said when her prayer was complete. "It's my fault that I didn't eat breakfast this morning." She looked up at him and realized that an air of calm and self-confidence surrounded the man by her side. She liked that. His arresting good looks totally captured her attention. "Thank you for your hospitality. If I had known that you were bringing me down here to feed me, I wouldn't have let you do it. I could've waited until I got home to fix myself a salad or something."

He answered her with a deep chuckle. "I figured that, so that's why I didn't tell you. It was no trouble to get you something. You don't usually eat in the morning?"

The scent of his cologne tantalized her again, and she felt the power that emanated from him as he sat closer to her. He had a certain air of command that matched his polished veneer. There was no doubt in Valerie's mind that Norman Grant was *all* man because he exuded masculinity in every possible way. She knew that he could have his choice of women if he wanted, but she convinced herself not to worry about things over which she had no control. *She* was in his company at this time, and she'd leave it at that.

"I got up early today to work on a project that's due tomorrow. I hadn't planned on coming to church, but when I heard your choir on the radio, the next thing I knew, I was at the morning service."

Norman nodded with understanding, his eyes remaining steady on Valerie's face. "You don't usually go to church?"

She thought she'd dissolve under his gaze—so warm, so gentle, but so intense. "I used to go regularly but haven't since I moved from Atlanta after my job transferred me here six months ago." Valerie nervously used her fork to move her macaroni salad around on her plate.

"That's a shame," Norman said. He was disappointed that Valerie was not a faithful churchgoer, but a small part of him was pleased that she didn't already belong to a choir. If he could convince this beautiful woman with the magnificent voice to join Red Oaks *and* his choir, he would be more than happy to see that she was made to feel welcome in the congregation, and he would even provide one-on-one rehearsals to bring her up to date on their music. "Did you sing in the choir there?"

Valerie sprinkled hot sauce on her sandwich and took a bite. The memory of singing at White Rock Baptist brought a twisted smile to her face. Singing at church had been one of the things that made her feel whole, but the thought of using her voice again—even for the Lord—was too painful for her to do just yet. "Actually, I did. I even sang solos, sometimes."

His smile widened with approval. Thoughts of Valerie standing front and center at Red Oaks, belting out the church's favorite gospel songs, ran rampant in his head. If she joined his choir, he would get a chance to enjoy her precious voice and her curvaceous figure every Sunday morning. Now that was something for him to look forward to.

"You should consider joining Red Oaks, Valerie. I'm looking for a new lead soloist, and I could certainly use a strong, trained voice like yours, especially for the choir's annual concert later this year." Valerie was looking down at her plate, but he saw the look of apprehension that crossed her face. Norman cleared his throat to make sure he had her undivided attention. When she looked up at him, he caught and held her gaze as he continued. "Of course, I'd be happy to teach you any songs you don't already know. I can make time, if you're interested in learning."

A shudder of sexual awareness shook Valerie's body, as spurts of hungry desire spiraled through her. Was Norman trying to recruit a singer for his choir or a mate for his bedroom? It didn't matter to her. As good as he looked and as well as he was built, she was finding it mighty difficult to think of anything other than being crushed underneath him while he was buried deep inside her.

Valerie cleared her throat and fixed her gaze on the small, gold, hoop earring in his left ear; she was too afraid to look directly at Norman for fear that he'd know she was imagining what was under his clothes. She wished she could find a way to see him again that wouldn't involve her singing. "I—I can't make a decision about that now. I'll think about it, though," she promised, gracing him with the smile he'd come to love, although he'd known her for less than an hour.

Norman studied her as she spoke and was unable to ignore the attraction building between them. He enjoyed watching the cute thing her nose did when she talked and the way she licked her lips after each bite without having a clue how much she was turning him on.

To Norman's way of thinking, Valerie was a woman worth getting to know—a diamond in the rough. With her, he'd have to give all or nothing. She was the kind of woman with whom he'd have to take his time and cultivate something real. Just from the way she carried herself, he could tell that she was a woman of class and substance. There was no doubt in his mind that he could bring Valerie home to Mama and be proud doing it.

Momentarily lost in his own reveries, Norman recalled the many women he'd dated and dumped. He'd bedded many women before he joined Red Oaks and cleaned up his act, but none of them had meant anything to him. Looking for Miss Right, he still dated his fair share, but he hadn't met a woman who made him want to settle down yet. But although he'd just met Valerie, so far she seemed like the type of woman who had what it took.

"That's fair enough. In the meantime, if you make a decision before you come back to visit the church, please give me a call. I'd love to hear from you again." Norman reached in his pocket and produced a business card to hand to Valerie.

It was something about the way he said he'd love to hear from her again that made Valerie's senses spin. Her breasts tingled under the fabric of her suit jacket, and the wild fluttering of her heart was the only movement she felt in that large room. When Norman looked at her, it was as if his eyes burned right through her body. It was how close he seemed to stand to her that made her realize just how very compelling and potent a man he was. There was some tangible bond between them that she couldn't deny—even if it was unwelcome and she didn't want it.

Quickly, every sinew in her body heated up and she broke out in a cold sweat. "Ooh, excuse me. I—I think I need . . . some air," she stuttered, shooting up from her chair, grabbing her coat and purse. In a whirlwind, Valerie ran out of the room, leaving Norman stunned.

Not thinking twice, he decided to run after her. His footsteps thundered down the huge room. He'd turned on his heel and was almost to the door when he bumped into someone.

"Hey, pay attention to where you're going!" an attractive youthful-sounding senior citizen chastised. "You could've knocked me down!" She looked up at the tall stranger who'd nearly knocked her over and was immediately apologetic for her harsh tone. "Norman, I'm sorry, baby," she told him, feeling a shudder of embarrassment over having snapped at him.

He kissed the feisty church matriarch on the cheek, indicating his forgiveness, then attempted to resume his getaway.

"Oh, no you don't! Not so fast," Mother Maybelle said, noticing the frantic look in his eyes. She grabbed his lower arm to slow him down.

Norman stopped in place.

Mother Maybelle couldn't help but see that his brain and whole being were in turmoil. She stared at him for a moment, baffled. If she didn't know better, she'd think her foster son was in love. "Well, what do you have to say for yourself, Norman? What has you looking so confused? What's her name?"

A war of emotions raged within Norman. He'd just met Valerie, but already he cared what happened to her. His mind refused to register the significance of Mother Maybelle's words. All Norman knew was that he had to get to Valerie—and quick!

"I'm listening, Norman, but I'm not hearing anything," Mother Maybelle pressed. She couldn't have cared less if he thought she was dipping in his business. "I know that your mind is on one of these fast-tailed gals in here. I don't know which one, though, but you can't fool me. Whatever you do, don't let them get into something you might regret."

Norman felt frozen in limbo, where all thoughts, decisions, and actions were impossible—except one—getting to Valerie. "Mother Maybelle, I don't mean to cut you short, but can we talk later? There's something I *really* need to do."

She drew in a breath and shrugged in mock resignation. "You might as well, because I can't get any sense out of you. You're surely not paying me a bit of attention. Go on to your gal—whoever she is!" she replied, looking at Norman as if she were looking through him.

Without any words of thanks, Norman took long, purposeful strides to the door. Then, he took the steps—two at a time. He was determined to find out what had spooked Valerie into running away.

～

Valerie stood outside the church getting some much-needed fresh air. There was no way that she could stay around Norman for any length of time. It was the second time in one day that he'd raised her body temperature. For sure, the fine Norman Grant was a hazard to her health! If she stayed around him any longer, she was sure to short circuit, have a stroke or a heart attack—and she couldn't risk that.

She looked around the beautifully landscaped seventy-five acres that made up the church grounds. As far as she could see there were hedges, trees, and an assortment of greenery which hadn't given way to the detritus of winter. She knew that the property would be lush and colorful when all the flowers and other plants were in full bloom. Valerie sucked in a breath, and the smell of magnolia trees, bougainvillea, silk oaks, and lemon eucalyptus infiltrated her nostrils. As refreshing as those smells were, they still didn't take her mind off Norman. All she could think about was the intoxicating smell of his cologne.

"Okay, Valerie, chill, girl. It's time to go home and repent," she told herself, looking around to make sure no one heard her. Valerie's runaway thoughts played in counterpoint to her admonition.

What Valerie felt at that moment was far from ladylike. Instinctively, she knew that Norman Grant was the kind of man who'd make her forget every bit of the home training her mama had taught her. The heat which permeated Valerie's body in all the wrong places reminded her that she wouldn't act like a lady if Norman were near her. The only thing that she could do was to pray for strength and ask the Lord to have mercy on her sinful soul. At the rate she was going, she thought, she'd end up in hell for sure, especially since she'd just lusted for Norman in a church.

As she walked to her car, Valerie conveniently rationalized her wicked musings. After all, she didn't tell him to be so drop-dead fine that he looked as though he should've been a model on the cover of GQ magazine instead of directing a small-town church choir, did she?

"Valerie, wait," Norman called out. "Don't go . . . " He spoke with quiet, but desperate, firmness.

Before she could go any further, the sound of his footsteps padding behind her made her halt. Norman caught up to Valerie and gently turned her around to face him.

Valerie kept her head down, avoiding looking at him. She knew that being in Norman's presence would be her undoing. Valerie was sure that

Norman could tell how handsome she thought he was, how wonderful he looked in his Armani suit, and how manly his cologne smelled. No one could tell her that he didn't know about the lust-filled thoughts running through her mind at that moment. He just had to know what she wanted to do to him, she thought.

Valerie had better things to do—like get on with her life without any man holding her back or turning her very existence upside down. The further away she stayed from Norman, the better. Although he seemed like a decent man and a good catch, she had no intention of permitting herself to fall under his spell.

"Ah . . . nothing's wrong, Norman," she said, creating the words on the spot. "I just thought of something I have to do at home—and it needs my immediate attention."

He didn't quite buy that excuse. It seemed too easy, too convenient. He decided to play along, knowing that doing otherwise would make her bolt. "Well, I guess you'd better get to it then."

"That's right, Norman," she agreed. "I'll see you next Sunday. "With that, she added a certain springy bounce to her step and headed toward her car. She got in, started the ignition, and was about to pull off when she saw Norman standing by her window.

"By the way, here's my cell phone number should you ever want or need to talk." Norman handed her another University of Georgia at Red Oaks business card—the school where he worked as a music professor—with the number written on the back of it. He flashed a knowing smile at her, hoping to get a number from Valerie in return.

She remained stoic. "Thanks, Norman, I'll keep that in mind."

Valerie drove off before Norman could think of anything else to say. Inside, her heart thumped erratically and she did some deep breathing to help. But it didn't. The only thing that would help Valerie was to stay out of Norman's presence, because he was man enough to make her do unspeakable things—and then some.

As soon as Valerie got home, she changed into a Spelman College sweat suit and got comfortable. Hearing Girlfriend meow more than usual, she checked on her to see if she needed food or water, and, sure enough, her tray was empty. Refilling it, Valerie listened to her voice-mail messages and determined that none of them was urgent. She decided to return the calls later. Then she did something she hadn't done in a *long* time—prayed.

Finding a comfortable spot at the side of her bed, Valerie knelt and began her monologue to God.

"Heavenly Father, I know it's been a long, long time since You heard from me," she avowed, clasping her hands tightly together. "It seems that You're trying to tell me something, but I don't know exactly what it is. I have a feeling that it has to do with my singing. But Lord, *I* don't want to sing again—especially after what happened back in Atlanta. I know that I've been backsliding since I've moved to Red Oaks, and I'm not going to make excuses for it. I know that I was wrong, but I'm going to be obedient and am willing to do whatever you have in mind for me.

"Lord, please show me what I need to know—in Your time. Give me a word in season. Reveal Your plan for me so I will be clear about it, and I promise to do my best to follow whatever path You've prepared for me . . . and Lord, one more thing, please forgive me for fornicating in my mind with Norman Grant. Please give me the strength, the self-control that I don't have now, so that I will behave myself whenever I'm around him. In Your precious name I pray, asking these and all things, amen."

The nervous fluttering that had pricked her chest earlier disappeared. Valerie didn't have an answer as to whether God was directing her to sing again, or if being a member of Witness was her chosen ministry. She'd made the request, and she knew that God wouldn't let her down about giving her an answer.

Four

A creeping uneasiness gnawed at Norman's heart. He'd been rude to Mother Maybelle and that bothered him. Right was right, and he, most assuredly, had been wrong. Picking up the receiver, he pressed the button on the phone to speed-dial her number.

"Good evening, Norman," she answered, glancing at the caller ID. "What can I do for you?"

Norman heard a chilliness in her voice that wasn't usually there. "I'm calling to apologize for running out so abruptly earlier. I thought someone needed my help, and I wanted to get there in time. I didn't mean to be short with you."

Mother Maybelle laughed. "That's okay, baby, but I'll let you off the hook on one condition . . . tell me the name of the gal you're so sweet on."

"I never mentioned anything like that to you," he replied, hoping she wouldn't question him further. Norman knew that he'd have to tell her what she wanted to know eventually, because Mother Maybelle was like a dog with a bone when she was on to something. Especially when someone was trying to hide things from her.

"Don't get new on me, Norman. Remember, I've been married five times, so I think that gives me enough life experience to know a lovesick man when I see one!" she reminded him.

Norman knew she had a good point, so he told Mother Maybelle what she'd been waiting to hear. "Her name is Valerie Freeman, and I think that she's the woman for me. She's the *one*."

For the next hour, Norman bent his foster mother's ear about Valerie, and about how much he wanted to get to know her better. Mother Maybelle wanted to see Norman happy with a good woman who was worthy of him, but she knew nothing about Valerie or the Freeman clan. She wasn't going to rest until she sized Valerie up for herself.

Although Mother Maybelle knew Norman was his own man and able to take care of himself, she still worried. She wanted the best for him in every aspect of his life. No way was she going to stand idly by while her foster son got involved with just any girl. His choice had to be a classy top-shelf lady, because no one less would do. After she spoke with Valerie, Mother Maybelle would decide if Norman needed her "help" to land his Ms. Right.

After ending the call with Norman, it took just a few minutes for her to get Valerie's phone number. The deaconess who took her information during Sunday service had put it in the church's files. She dialed, hoping the call would prove to be successful.

"Yes, I'd like to speak to Valerie Freeman, please," Mother Maybelle said in her most professional-sounding voice when a young woman answered the call.

Valerie hesitated for a minute, not knowing if it was a bill collector calling her illegally on a Sunday night or a long-lost relative in trouble.

Not known for her patience, Mother Maybelle hurried Valerie along. "Still there? Valerie, this is Mother Maybelle Carmichael from Red Oaks Christian Fellowship."

Valerie blew out a sigh, relieved that it wasn't a caller with bad news. "Oh, how are you, Mrs. Carmichael? I didn't realize—"

"Of course, you didn't," she said, cutting Valerie off. "Just call me Mother Maybelle. Everyone does."

Judging by her clipped tone, Valerie gathered that Mother Maybelle was a woman on a mission that she intended to fulfill.

"I'd like to invite you to my house for dinner tomorrow night," she said. "Are you available?"

"I'll have to decline, Mother Maybelle. I'm working on a special project and I'm tied up this week. I'd love to do it another time, though." Valerie found the invitation odd because she didn't know this woman. But then she remembered how friendly the church members were and decided not to think too much of it.

"Do you have any idea *when* you'll be free, then?" Mother Maybelle pressed. She wanted to pick Valerie's brain in the worst way. The best way to make that happen was to break bread with her.

Valerie picked up her Palm Pilot from the kitchen counter and scrolled through her schedule. "It'll be quite a while, but I'll take a rain check—if that's okay?"

At least the child sounds like she had some home training, Mother Maybelle noted as she agreed to that. By the time the conversation was over, Valerie had committed to having lunch with Mother Maybelle after church one Sunday, and for some reason, she looked forward to it.

~

Two Sundays later, Valerie found herself at Red Oaks Christian Fellowship once again. Full of anticipatory adrenalin, she arrived early to ensure herself a seat in the front—the best and only way she could enjoy Witness *and* take in as much of Norman as she wanted. Fidgeting in her seat, she felt sweat rising at her brow.

Barely able to contain his excitement, Norman gave Valerie a wide, warm smile that reached straight to her heart when their eyes met. Disappointed that she hadn't attended church the previous Sunday, he wanted her to know how happy he was to see her again. And he showed her in the way he directed the choir that morning—a precise military-like style in which every member knew his or her place. They sang to the rafters as if someone's life depended on the glory of their musical gospel.

Mesmerized by the choir's close harmony and Norman's impeccable directorial skills, Valerie remembered what her mother used to say about the choir at the church where she'd grown up in Macon—and how it applied to what she was watching at that moment. Witness was indeed "showing out." They went through an arsenal of vocal runs and phrasings which easily explained why they had recorded professionally and had won two Grammys. The choir's message had members under such a powerful anointing that after they finished ministering, Reverend Avery opened the doors of church and made an altar call. At least a dozen new souls were won for the Lord that morning, and twelve more recommitted themselves to Him. By the end of the singing, nearly thirty new members joined Red Oaks Christian Fellowship—but Valerie wasn't one of them.

Although tears streamed down her face and her feet praised the Lord with a heartfelt holy dance, she still hadn't received a word in season, so she knew that meant to be patient. Between the joy inside her soul and the thrill of seeing Norman, which made great exultation shoot through her senses, Valerie was quite content.

Reverend Avery took his seat, and another minister with a café-au-lait face that was drawn and pinched replaced him at the podium. Slight lines furrowed his brows as he tugged on the Kente cloth stole that accentuated his black robe. Before he spoke, he held his arms high above his head, spreading them out in an action that looked like Moses parting the Red Sea. "Saints," he said, his resonant baritone voice booming. "I want all movement to stop, *now*. Please be still—wherever you are. The Lord is speaking to my heart. Musicians, choir, all, please close your eyes, bow your heads, and wait on what thus saith the Lord."

The entire church, which was a whirlwind of praise and worship a few moments earlier, stood stark still. No one dared move. They knew that when their assistant minister, Reverend O'Dell Hunter Danforth, was on the hotline with God, they would be chastised like errant children if they were bold enough to interrupt that important communication.

Valerie gulped and dug her nails into her palms, not knowing why she was so uneasy. She started to crack her knuckles, but hesitated when one of the church sisters a few seats down gave her "the eye." Both women shut their eyes and waited until Reverend Danforth received the revelation. They, and the rest of the flock, had no other choice but to sit—even if it took all morning.

"We're grateful for *each* and *every* soul that we win for the Lord," Reverend Danforth intoned. He attached a cordless mike to his robe and paced the pulpit. "And you know we don't turn any souls away. We encourage you to come to God as you are, and *He* will deal with you. Today was indeed a good day for souls being saved, but the Lord told me there's one more here—and you know who you are—who has been on bended knee asking for some direction. He said that He gave you something special, and if you don't use it for His glory, you will lose it. Now I don't know who that's meant for or what it means, but it's a word in season for someone. Please, if that's you, or you," he said, pointing a well-groomed finger toward various members of the congregation, "God demands his sheep to be obedient. Choir, see if you can help that person to get here this morning."

Reverend Danforth looked at Norman, and immediately he knew what was needed. He took his place at the shiny white grand piano and began to play. Witness began singing "I Surrender All," a church favorite that was always sure to flush out the soul God wanted. He played so sweetly, with notes so pure and round, that the piano seemed to have a voice all its own.

Valerie blushed, an insipid grin creasing her face. Her eyes widened and became round. She was sure that she had the answer she'd prayed for. No one had to tell her twice that the word which Reverend Danforth had gotten from the Lord was meant for her. Her face warmed, and tears trickled freely down her cheeks. She bawled, giving in to the uncontrollable sobs that shook her body. The woman sitting next to Valerie attempted to rub her back.

"Leave her alone, sister," a brawny usher ordered, scaring the woman into placing her hand back in her lap. "God's dealing with her. Let Him do His work. She'll be fine."

Valerie began humming the melody of the song, then softly singing it. It was one of the old-time favorites that she used to sing as a little girl in church with her grandmother, Hattie Mae Cox. She was a popular local gospel singer who was known all over Macon for her silky voice. Memories of holding her Nana's hand as they belted out that song flashed through Valerie's mind as she stood in the pew.

Her feet, which felt heavier than two blocks of solid concrete, had the hardest time walking to the altar. Although she'd sat in the coveted front section, the walk felt like at least a mile. When she got to the second row, Mother Maybelle, resplendent in a tailored, deep aqua suit, her signature double strand of pearls and a fox fur adorning her neck, waited for her in the aisle. The first member to officially greet Valerie, she wore a friendly smile on her walnut-brown face, which looked decades younger than her seventy-five or more years.

"That's right, sugar, go on up there and get you some Jesus!" Mother Maybelle encouraged, grabbing Valerie around the waist. "I heard about you and that pretty voice of yours. You can't run from God if He got something for you to do," she whispered to Valerie as if it were a secret between two old friends.

Valerie nodded her head in agreement and replied, "Yes, ma'am," deferring to the elegantly dressed woman who had a shape that could rival that of women half her age. The scent of the Violets candy in Mother Maybelle's mouth calmed Valerie. It was the same candy her now-deceased grandmother had used to bribe Valerie to behave during Sunday service.

By then, the choir was really cranked up, rocking the church with their updated interpretation of "Just Like Fire Shut Up In My Bones."

Mother Maybelle loosened her hug from around Valerie's midsection and put her back on her way to the altar. Valerie glanced over at Norman at the piano, acknowledging him with a nod of her head, and he replied with an infectious grin that was as bright as the midday sun steaming through the crystal clear windows.

The church broke out into shouts of "hallelujah" and "thank you, Jesus" as she took her place at the altar. The applause was deafening when many of the members saw who she was and remembered hearing her songbird voice.

Suddenly, an indescribable serenity befell Valerie. She glanced out of the window, taking in the sight of the tall trees and the billowy clouds etching the sky. All she thought about was how beautiful they looked, how majestic. The only thing she could do was to say thank you in the way her Grandma Hattie had taught her best.

"Oh Lord, my God, when I in awesome wonder . . . ," Valerie sang, lifting her head and hands reverently. She delivered the words so purely, so round, and with great passion. It was clear from the way she sang that she meant every word.

So as not to disturb Valerie, Norman quietly placed a microphone near her so everyone could enjoy her singing as much as he was. He returned to the piano and accompanied her, beaming with a pride he'd never known before as he played.

"Consider all the works Thy hands hath made . . . ," she continued. Valerie closed her eyes, exhaled, then drew in a breath. She began modulating and doing an awesome vocal run. "Then sings my soul, my Savior God to Thee. How great Thou art, how great Thou art!"

Calm and quiet filled the sanctuary, and the members looked at Valerie with total incredulity. It was as if an angel had sung to them. They hoped that she'd grace them with her songbird voice again—for any reason—real soon. Even the ministers stood in awe of what they'd heard. It had been a while since anyone had moved them as Valerie had with a song.

Glorious happiness sprang up in Norman's heart. Still smiling, he began to play a standard that was perfect for that moment. Soon, everyone joined in, not knowing they'd confirmed his choice was correct.

"Praise Him, Praise Him, Praise Him in the morning, Praise Him in the noontime . . . ," Reverend Avery led his flock, the choir adding its full voice. "The Spirit is moving in here this day!" he proclaimed.

"Praise God, saints, now that's what I call having church," Reverend Danforth declared, shaking Valerie's hand when she walked back to the altar. "Our sister was obedient and answered God's call. The angels in heaven are rejoicing right now. Young lady, what's your name and where are you from?"

Valerie, no longer nervous, thought about Mother Maybelle and how her presence had calmed her. There was something peaceful about the older woman that centered Valerie. "My name is Valerie Cherrelle Freeman, Reverend, and I'm originally from Macon, but I now live in Red Oaks," she asserted in a loud and clear voice that rang with command.

"Praise Him, Valerie, that's all right. Welcome to Red Oaks Christian Fellowship, and please know that we're so happy to have you." Reverend Danforth's slight Georgia accent was heard as he spoke. "Are you a candidate for water baptism?"

"No, Reverend. I received water baptism years ago," she told him, looking at the sea of smiling faces around her.

"Amen, Valerie. There's nothing like being baptized in the water, becoming a new creature in Christ. No doubt about it, you've already been baptized in the Holy Spirit." An expression of satisfaction showed in his eyes. His chest filled with pride that he was the conduit through which this saint could come to Him and begin her spiritual journey.

"Can I get an amen, church?" Reverend Avery shouted. "Don't you know that God will find you *wherever* you are? You might run, but you can't hide. If He got some work for you to do, He's going to find you and make sure that you do it! There's something special in the works for our dear sister, Valerie Freeman—I feel it all in my soul. Stand on your feet and praise Him, church. God is *so* good and he's worthy to be praised! Amen?"

After the deacons, deaconesses, elders and ministerial staff gave her the Right Hand of Fellowship, a deaconess led Valerie into an area outside of the sanctuary that was reserved for the intake of new members. There, she filled out a short application for the church's membership rolls, and she received a packet of information about Red Oaks Christian Fellowship. Then, the intake staff sent Valerie back to the sanctuary so she wouldn't miss the day's lesson. She got back to her seat just in time for the sermon.

~

As soon as the benediction was said, Norman laid his robe on the piano bench and made his way to Valerie. Wildfire wouldn't have kept him away from her. Scanning her from head to toe, he enjoyed the contrast of her skin against her magenta, alpaca knit sweater-dress. "Good afternoon, Valerie," he said, excitement dancing in his eyes. "You really know how to give someone an answer, huh?" His smile melted into full-hearted laughter.

Valerie didn't miss his examination of her or his obvious approval. Her insides came alive, and she felt a vibrancy like never before. Being around Norman made her feel like a giddy schoolgirl again. "Hey there, Norman," she crooned, unable to hide the smile that came out in full force. "It's so nice to see you. Now, what was that wisecrack you made?" They both broke out in hearty laughter.

"Remember you said you'd think about whether or not you'd join the church and Witness, and you'd get back to me with an answer?"

The memory of the conversation ruffled her mind like wind on water. "Oh yes, I sure did, and I would have, except that I didn't expect my answer to come like it did here today."

Norman squared his shoulders. "Well, my dear, the Lord called you, and you gave Him quite an answer."

Valerie noticed how dapper Norman looked in his black double-breasted Ralph Lauren suit. She saw him as a powerful, muscular man who moved with easy grace as he got closer to her. "I guess I did at that."

"So what do you say about joining Witness? You can't keep that gorgeous voice bottled up inside of you; it has to be shared with others." He put his hands together as if he were begging. "Please? We *need* you."

She paused, pondering her uncertainty. Singing was the last thing Valerie wanted to do, but there *was* a powerful tugging in her spirit to join the choir. There was a reason she was sent to that church, she thought. Perhaps God wanted her there—to sing. Despite that, she knew she'd have to stay away from Norman because being around him could prove to be dangerous to her state of self-imposed celibacy. On the other hand, there was also the part of her that wouldn't mind seeing more of him, but Valerie promised herself she'd fight that part. But she wasn't a fool. She knew that would be real hard because Norman was as fine as he could be, and he always smelled so darned good. "Okay, Norman. I'll join the choir."

Wrapped in a cocoon of euphoria, an infinite peace came over Norman. "That's wonderful, Valerie, thank you. You won't be sorry. But now, there's something we must do." Taking Valerie by the hand, he led her to Reverend Avery's office.

After a short meeting with Reverends Avery and Danforth, Valerie was granted special permission to join Witness before she completed the mandatory six-week new member's orientation program. Norman explained that the choir needed a new lead soloist, because the current one was so embroiled in her own personal drama that she couldn't be depended upon anymore. He went on to tell them that he needed time to teach Valerie the solos for the songs he'd chosen for the choir's big annual concert that fall. Citing the names of the popular gospel artists who'd confirmed their participation, Norman did his best to make them understand that Witness had to be in top form that evening.

The two ministers questioned Valerie about her church background, consulted with each other, and discussed what had happened to her during the morning worship service. Then, they gave their answer.

"Valerie, welcome to Witness," Reverend Avery announced, shuffling through some documents on his desk. Reverend Danforth nodded his head in agreement. "The Lord has placed a call on your life, young lady. And from all the talk we've been hearing about the woman with the golden voice, it's pretty clear where you're supposed to be. As your spiritual leaders, we would be remiss to let a mere formality stand in the way of you doing God's work. We're sure that Norman will help you any way he can, and give you everything you need to make your music ministry meaningful." The last statement was Reverend Avery's way of letting Norman know that he wasn't unaware of his feelings for Valerie.

Both ministers shook her hand and gave her a warm, friendly hug. They also noticed how Norman looked at Valerie as if he could sop her up with a biscuit.

"Umph, umph, umph," Reverend Avery said to Reverend Danforth, shaking his head after Norman and Valerie left the office. "That boy got it bad."

Reverend Danforth chuckled, thinking that he wished he could be so lucky as to find a beautiful, classy woman to turn *his* head. "Well, at least he has good taste!"

~

Valerie kept her promise to Norman and joined Witness the following Thursday. No one was happier than Norman when he saw her strutting down the aisle en route to the choir stand. She saw how brightly his face lit up when she arrived, but what she didn't know was that he was more than pleased that her timing had been so impeccable.

He'd run into the choir's unreliable soloist, Sister Carolyn Washington at the convenience store in town, and she had another excuse about why she couldn't make it to rehearsal. She hadn't made it to church on consecutive Sundays for months, and he'd already been forced to think about getting a replacement lead soprano singer. Although Norman had the patience of Job, he had to do what was in the best interest of the choir. Valerie joining Witness right then was the answer to his prayer.

Valerie spent the rest of the evening meeting many of the choir members, rehearsing the songs they'd sing on Sunday, and learning some new ones they'd sing in the future. Because there was a little time left at the end of rehearsal, they went over two of what Norman called "standards." These were hymns that either of the ministers could request at a moment's notice and were known to add a good log when the church was on fire.

Valerie caught on well to everything except the standards.

"May I see you for a moment, Sister Freeman?" Norman asked, calling her to the piano.

Valerie went to him, a familiar tremor of awareness coursing through her body as she stood by his side. Norman's closeness was so masculine, so bracing—so much so that she barely knew how to play it off. "Yes, Norman?"

"Those standards seem to be giving you some difficulty," he said in a tone that was more a question than a statement. The faint scent of her perfume wafted past his nose, making him fully aware of her femininity. Glimpses of her womanly well-stacked body made his heart thud in his chest.

"Yes, they are. They're rather new to me."

"Really, how so?"

His nearness kindled feelings of fire inside of Valerie. Her arms quivered, and her knees were starting to go weak. *Oh Lord, what is wrong with me? Help me, Father*! she thought. "We had devotions to start off our services—a little singing, praying, and testifying," she explained. "Sometimes, the old moanin' kinds of songs where there weren't any words were sung, but folks knew the melodies and just hummed along as the Spirit moved them."

"Oh, okay, that explains it," he chuckled. "I tell you what, could you meet me here next Thursday night a half hour before rehearsal starts? I'll teach you the songs you need to know."

Without thinking or consulting her Palm Pilot, she agreed. "Sure, I would like that, Norman." *In more ways than one.*

Over the next few weeks, Valerie began to meet Norman at the piano a half hour before choir rehearsal began. Their private tutoring sessions paid off. Before long, Valerie knew all of the church standards and was able to sing them as if she'd done it all of her life. She breezed through rehearsals, but felt a little off balance because she noticed Norman's eyes found hers at every turn. At the close of one rehearsal, after the prayer for each member to get home safe and return to church on Sunday, Valerie and Norman became engaged in conversation about one thing, then another. They didn't realize they were the last ones in the church until the sanctuary became dim.

"Don't you young folks know how to go home? You want to stay here all night or something?"fussed Deacon Farley Brown, the longtime janitor. "I'd suggest y'all to get to getting. If you don't, you will be locked up in here until tomorrow!" They knew he meant business when he shut all of the lights off before they could get halfway up the aisle to the door.

"What's his problem?" Valerie complained.

"He's eccentric, but he means no harm. He's really a nice man."

"Humph, when he's asleep?" Valerie stumbled as she walked up the aisle, but Norman reached for her hand and held it, leading her slowly outside.

"Most of the time, he's nice. You'll see that when you get to know him. He just has a certain funny way about him."

"If you say so," she laughed.

"I've had such a pleasant conversation with you that I'm not ready to go home quite yet," Norman admitted, hoping Valerie felt the same way. "I have an idea. Let's have coffee at the all-night bookstore and café in town."

There was nowhere else she wanted to be than with him. "Sure, why not?" she agreed.

Taking separate cars, they followed each other to the café, where they sipped chocolate lattes and Norman brought Valerie up to speed about being a member of Red Oaks Christian Fellowship. Truth be told, Valerie had looked forward to seeing Norman outside church—especially sitting close to him on the sofa and feeling his thigh "accidentally" rub against her own. Over the next couple of hours, Valerie and Norman enjoyed getting to know each other and sharing each other's company. She told him about how much she liked living in Red Oaks. She loved being part of a *real* community that felt like home. "I feel as if I'm doing all the talking, Norman," she pointed out after a while. "What about you? Tell me about growing up here and what it was like."

Norman looked into her eyes, losing himself in their depths, and recounted his childhood. "Red Oaks was always a nice, quiet town, but not unlike any other. It stayed that way until I was about ten and the gang I ran with started to terrorize the people here."

Valerie's eyes became as round as a fifty-cent piece. "Not you, Norman?"

Her gentle naiveté was precious to him. "Yes, I kind of lost my mind after my mother was killed and my father ran out on me and my two brothers. I was hurting badly, but I didn't know how to tell anyone. Eventually, I was jumped into the gang."

Without realizing it, Valerie took his hand in hers and began to stroke it, hoping he'd feel the care and concern she felt for him. "I'm so sorry, Norman, I had no idea."

"There's no need to be sorry. I had to go through some things in order to grow," he elaborated, relishing her obvious concern and warmth. "I can't turn back time as much as I wish I could."

"So what happened to you—I mean after your father left you?"

He lowered his head, opening the door on the unpleasant memories he tried to forget. "My brothers were placed in an orphanage. I was young and cute, so they placed me in foster care, and I went from home to home until I wound up in a reform school because of my behavior."

"That's terrible, Norman." Sensing that he needed a little TLC, Valerie reached over and hugged him to her breast. "You stayed in foster care until college?"

Norman smiled. He felt as if he didn't have a care in the world. He was in the best place any man could be right then. She was so soft and smelled so womanly. "No, Mother Maybelle appointed herself the leader of the church's prison ministry and used to come over to the reform school. We hit it off really well, and before long, she bullied the judge into allowing her to be my foster mother. She raised me and put me through college. She's the only mother I *really* know."

"You don't mean that fly old lady who sits in the second row aisle seat?"

They both laughed. "Yes, the very same. She's a handful, but she's good people. She's my Mama for all intents and purposes."

"I knew there was something special about that woman that Sunday I got saved and joined the church."

"Mother Maybelle is in a class all by herself," Norman chuckled. "She's an enigma, and she has fun being that way. But as a mother, she was the best. I wanted for nothing, and she straightened my hard-headed behind out with a big helping of Jesus, tough love, and a whole lot of hickory switches."

They doubled over with laughter, and Norman realized that he really enjoyed spending time with Valerie. "Sounds like you love Mother Maybelle, Norman."

"I do—very much. "

In turn, Valerie told Norman all about her parents her big sister, and her two darling twin nephews. She kept thinking that if he kept on being so sweet to her and so kind, he'd probably meet them all one day.

By the end of their café experience, Norman had mustered up enough nerve to ask Valerie to be his date at the concert and reception that his students at the University of Georgia at Red Oaks were giving. She accepted, thinking that the event sounded innocent enough that she could go out with him but not feel pressured into committing herself to anything more.

~

Valerie's week was spent pulling together the right ensemble for her first official date with Norman. After he told her that the dress code was semi-formal, she went to a new boutique in town and found the perfect outfit for the occasion.

As she dressed for the concert, Valerie felt as if she were all thumbs. She couldn't get herself together if her life depended on it; couldn't decide on whether or not to wear jewelry with her outfit, or what kind of coat to wear over it. Then, when she got dressed, she put her skirt on backwards and couldn't find the opening for her top. She knew exactly what was bothering her; the thought of going out with Norman on a social basis both thrilled and frightened her. *What if something goes wrong? What if he expects more than just having fun tonight, and I'm not willing, ready, or able to give it?* she wondered, second-guessing herself.

Valerie didn't know how she'd done it, but she was finally dressed. She had just finished preparing a tiny bowl of milk for Girlfriend when the doorbell rang. Giving herself a final once-over in the full-length mirror, she looked out the peephole and opened the door.

Resplendent in a two-piece black Pierre Cardin suit and a gold-banded collar shirt, Norman stood tall and straight, looking so devilishly handsome. An air of confidence and self-assurance emanated from him.

"Good evening, Valerie, I'm so glad you could come with me, tonight." He beamed, handing her a bouquet of unusual roses. "These are for you."

Her eyes froze on his long, muscular form, acutely conscious of how good he looked. "Come in, Norman. Thank you." She accepted the roses and sniffed their strong fragrance. "These are absolutely gorgeous. I've never seen this kind of rose before. What are they?"

He accepted the seat she offered him in the living room while she put the flowers in a vase. "They're called Black Baccara roses because they're black before the bloom begins, then they turn that deep, rich blackberry-maroon color they are now."

"Thanks again," Valerie said, giving the roses another sniff. "These flowers are beyond beautiful."

"Not as beautiful as you, Valerie," he said, delighting in her gentle and overwhelming presence. Her regal movements took Norman's breath away as he enjoyed the look of her African two-piece brick-red and gold quad set. It was accented by an aubergine dress with a dazzling swirl of gold, belled sleeves, an asymmetrical hem, a matching gold turban, and triple-fan gold earrings. Queen Nefertiti couldn't have looked any better than Valerie in that outfit.

"We'd better be going, so I can get my students ready for their big performance," Norman said, checking his watch.

~

Soon they arrived at the college's auditorium. After checking Valerie's coat and getting her settled in the third row, Norman excused himself and went backstage to prepare his students for their big night.

The concert, titled "Jazz Through the Ages," began and was a resounding success. The students performed a number of songs, highlighting different styles and forms through the twentieth century, and Norman's directorial skills were even finer than those he demonstrated at church.

Valerie glowed with pride as she watched him lead his talented students from one style to the next, right into two rousing standing ovations. They performed two encores as the music-loving audience couldn't get enough of their sound and didn't want to let them off the stage.

After the performance was over, Norman was the man of the hour. Valerie stood back until the crowd thinned because she couldn't get anywhere near him. Between the students who *just had* to have photos with him, the local music critics covering the event, and the students' parents who'd wanted to meet the ever-popular Mr. Grant, Valerie had to wait her turn. And she did, noting how it was clear that music was Norman's calling, his passion—the thing he loved most after God.

Finally, she made her way through the crowd and congratulated him on a job well done. Having Valerie's support of his work made Norman feel more special than he remembered feeling in a long time. He led her upstairs to the Crystal Atrium, where the music department had set up an elegant reception.

By candlelight, they ate canapés, sipped wine, and talked about Norman's job. He introduced her to some of his students, and colleagues, and they posed for photos at his students' requests. They also listened to a speech given by the music department's chairperson, who touted Norman's love of music and how well he was loved by his school and his students.

They ended their evening wrapped tight in the circle of each other's arms, dancing to a lovely rendition of the jazz classic, "As Time Goes By," sung by a popular local vocalist. Valerie didn't have to wonder what Norman was thinking because she felt his male length strong and firm against her as they danced. Spellbound by the provocative smell of his cologne, she enjoyed every naughty inch of what she felt.

When their eyes met and held, before Valerie could stop him, Norman's lips brushed hers. It was a tantalizing invitation for more. His mouth moved over hers, possessing Valerie's lips in a soft, warm kiss. It was a light kiss, but a tender one that sent swirls of delight through her love-starved body. Like a morning glory, her lips opened fully, receiving Norman's tongue. Seeking each other's out, they sampled their tastes and flavors, thoroughly enjoying what they were given. Whimpers of desire escaped from Valerie's throat, causing Norman to kiss her even more urgently. Breathless, and reeling from the sensations, Valerie listened to her heart for the first time in a very long time. Although getting involved romantically was the last thing on her mind, for some reason Valerie hoped that Norman would ask her out again.

And he did, again and again. Over the next few weeks, they went out for dinner at various restaurants, to plays, art galleries, for walks in the park on unseasonably warm days, and they even drove to Athens, Georgia, for ice cream sodas at an old-fashioned soda shop in the town's drugstore. They lived for the nightly phone calls they shared before they went to sleep.

Finally, Valerie became the aggressor and asked Norman out. At work, her department was responsible for designing a television commercial which had won their company a prestigious Clio Award, and Delta Airlines honored them with a dinner dance at the Red Oaks Country Club. Without hesitation, Norman accepted and teased her about all the time they had begun to spend together and about how much he enjoyed it. Her mouth throbbed as she told him that the feeling was mutual.

Five

"*My baby deserves my help and that's what he's going to get*," Mother Maybelle thought, staring at Valerie talking with Norman outside the church before morning worship began.

Mother Maybelle had gotten the scoop that Norman and Valerie had been going out after choir rehearsals. That was a step in the right direction, but she didn't think he'd actually told Valerie how he really felt about her. The world would end before he did, Mother Maybelle thought. She put her hand on her hip and thought some more. It was plain to anyone who was around them that there were enough sparks between Norman and Valerie to set the towering inferno ablaze again. She had no idea who they were trying to fool. Surely not her, because she'd seen plenty of couples in love in her day. An idea sprang to mind, and Mother Maybelle knew what she was going to do.

She approached Valerie and Norman, each stride fluid. Valerie looked at Mother Maybelle and smiled in earnest. Norman kissed Mother Maybelle on the cheek and she brightened, her face radiant with good cheer.

"Good morning, Mother Maybelle," Valerie stated. "It feels like spring is in the air today, doesn't it?" She noted that a few birds flew overhead, although none of the flowers were yet in bloom.

"Yes, it is, sugar. Everyone's talking about how pretty the day turned out," she said, gently touching Valerie's shoulder. "As a matter of fact, I was hoping to see you today."

"Really, Mother Maybelle, about what?"

"I want you to come and have Sunday lunch with me after church today."

Valerie looked at Norman, searching his face for an answer to the invitation, since they'd already planned to do something. Just then, Valerie remembered that she had tentatively accepted a lunch invitation from Mother Maybelle several weeks prior. Norman nodded.

Valerie *still* had reservations—especially about doing it that day. She'd already promised to go out with Norman. "Are you sure that you want to have lunch with *me?*" she asked Mother Maybelle.

"Yes, very sure. And obviously, you don't know who I am," Mother Maybelle boasted with great pride, squaring her shoulders. "*No one* refuses Mother Maybelle!"

"In that case, I'd be happy to have lunch with you," Valerie informed her, not knowing how much she'd made the older woman's day.

"Now you're talking," Mother Maybelle quipped. "Norman baby, you'll come, too."

The prospect of having lunch with Mother Maybelle was nerve-racking for Valerie. Throughout the service, her heart thudded in her chest every time she thought about how she would have to play off how she *really* felt about Norman so that Mother Maybelle wouldn't find out. Part of her didn't mind any excuse to spend time with Norman. Another part of her didn't want to be that close to him because she knew that something in her actions would betray the fact that she was becoming more attracted to him by the day.

After church, Valerie and Norman waited for Mother Maybelle outside of the building. It took her a while to meet them because she had to talk with various people about their problems along the way. Others stopped her to say "Hey," and to compliment her on her ensemble with the matching hat and accessories.

Valerie received equal compliments on how well she wore her peach linen coatdress, accented by a brown silk scarf. Together, she and Mother Maybelle represented some of the finest fashions worn by the ladies of Red Oaks Christian Fellowship.

When Mother Maybelle finally made her way to Valerie and Norman, she insisted that they ride to her house in her gleaming gold Cadillac.

A short ride later, Valerie oohed and aahed at the sight of the sprawling traditional-style ranch house that Mother Maybelle called home. Stepping inside, she saw that it looked like one which could have been featured in *Better Homes & Gardens* or *Architectural Digest*. Mother Maybelle gave her the grand tour, showing off her spacious dressing area, master bedroom suite, and the beautiful artwork that hung on the walls. The place was a mini-mansion, accentuated by beautiful objets d'art which she'd collected during her travels around the world. Silently, Valerie hoped she'd grow up and live that well.

"I hope you've enjoyed the tour, y'all, because it's time to eat," Mother Maybelle announced, leading Valerie and Norman toward the front of the house. "Y'all go on in the living room and make yourselves comfy."

"May I help you with something?" Valerie asked, headed into the fully-equipped modern kitchen.

"No, sugar. I got this. You're my guest, so you sit down and relax. I'll call y'all when lunch is ready." Mother Maybelle washed her hands and tied a frilly apron around her waist. What she *didn't* say was that all she wanted Valerie to do was take care of her darling foster son and make him happy. In the meantime, she was going to put smiles on their faces with some of the best down home country cooking they'd ever eaten.

It was difficult for Valerie and Norman to choose a video to watch because Mother Maybelle's selection was vast. Norman took the initiative and made the decision for them. He grabbed the remote and began flipping through the channels. Finally, he stopped when he got to the movie, *Mission Impossible*. During a commercial break, he flipped channels again and found an Atlanta Braves game. They alternated between watching the movie and the game.

Valerie and Norman sat close together on the large, plush sofa, their bodies rubbing each other's. The game was at a high point, with the Braves stealing bases and winning, when Mother Maybelle called them to lunch. Norman switched off the set before they went into the dining room.

Valerie gawked at the spread on the table and wondered where she'd put it all. "You didn't have to go to all this trouble, Mother Maybelle," Valerie said, her stomach growling from the aroma and sight of the food. The table looked like it had been prepared by a world-class chef. "A sandwich would have been fine."

Mother Maybelle harrumphed. "Sugar, please. That's why y'all young folks are so sickly today—always hurting and under the doctor—because you don't know how to eat. You have to feed your body well in order for it to stay healthy. Please, don't get me started. Now, sit down and let's bless this food before it gets cold!"

They all sat down, grace was said, and Mother Maybelle began to pass the steaming platters of food around the table. There was golden brown fried chicken, chopped barbeque sandwiches, macaroni salad, potato salad, pre-buttered sweet corn on the cob, string beans with new potatoes and ham, and a pitcher of sweet tea with fresh spearmint.

"Don't nary one of y'all get up from this table until you're full, you hear me?" Mother Maybelle laughed. "If this ain't enough, there's more on the stove. And please, save a corner for dessert!"

"Yes, ma'am," they replied, filling their plates with a little of everything.

Valerie bit into a plump chicken leg and ate a forkful of potato salad. "Mother Maybelle, this food is so good it'll make you want to slap somebody, as my daddy always says."

"Thank you, Valerie." A powerful sense of relief filled her because she loved to cook and wanted her guests to enjoy themselves and eat as if they were at home.

Norman was so busy enjoying the chopped barbecue sandwich topped with the family's spicy sauce, that it took him a little while to add his comments. "Mother Maybelle, you outdid yourself. You put your foot in this food," he finally said.

"Thank you baby. You know I had to make your favorite, but enough about the food." She gaped at the pair pop-eyed, not blinking once. "Let's talk about what's up with the two of y'all."

Valerie and Norman looked at each other, both covering their mouths so their food wouldn't show. "What's up with *us*? What do you mean?" Valerie asked. Her eyebrows shot up in surprise and she felt a sudden spurt of adrenaline coursing through her veins.

Mother Maybelle looked over the glasses perched on the tip of her nose, and rolled her eyes. "Norman, you better tell this gal about my cooking spoon. Don't play all shy and innocent with me," she advised them. She dished up some macaroni salad and put a chicken wing on her plate, sprinkling some hot sauce on it. "A blind man could see how much y'all are feeling each other."

They laughed, and Valerie blinked with surprise. "She knows the young folks' slang, Valerie, and uses it pretty well, I might add," Norman told her. "I never said anything—"

"No, you didn't, in words, but it's obvious from the way you look at Valerie. I mean, she's a lovely young lady, and talented, too. She's a strong Christian, so what's your malfunction? Why aren't you two together?"

"Mother Maybelle—" Valerie attempted to say in her defense.

"Don't Mother Maybelle *me*," she warned, wagging her finger at her.

Norman felt a lecture coming on.

"Y'all listen to me and don't say *one* word until I'm through. It's clear that y'all are in love with each other, and you're both single. I know that because I already checked you out, Valerie."

Valerie's mouth hung agape.

"Close your mouth, sugar, before something gets in it," Mother Maybelle scolded. "That's right, *nothing* goes on at Red Oaks Christian Fellowship that I don't know about. What I don't know, I'll find out. Pardon me for being biased, but in terms of good men, Norman's as fine as they come, she told Valerie.

"Thank you for your vote of confidence in me, Mother Maybelle," he responded. "I'd prefer to speak up for myself—in my own time—if you don't mind."

Mother Maybelle continued her brand of kitchen wisdom after taking a few bites of corn and a swig of tea. "Men and women were put on this earth to be together, to marry, not to be alone. I know the way y'all are feeling that it's probably hard to keep your hands off each other. I was young once, too, and I can tell you all about having an itch that needed scratching—but I won't. I'm going to let you read all about that subject for yourselves in the word and make your own decisions."

Heat stole into Valerie's face and she grew hot with embarrassment. Her face flushed with shame. "We're just friends."

Mother Maybelle gawked at Valerie in disbelief. "You're trying to convince yourself? I'm not buying one bit of that mess you're telling me! I know what I see. You two are as in love as any couple can be. Besides, how many weddings have I gone to where the couples were 'just friends'?" she mocked, putting her hands on her hips. Seeing that everyone was finished eating, she cleared the table, loaded the dishwasher, and brought out the dessert: lemon butter pound cake and homemade vanilla ice cream.

"You're playing dirty, Mother Maybelle!" Norman exclaimed. "You know how much I love your pound cake and ice cream. When did you have time to do all this?"

She shot him a furtive glance, knowing what he was trying to do. "Don't think I'm through with y'all yet, because I'm not!"

Mother Maybelle sat down with a piece of cake and scoop of ice cream. "If God sends true love your way, you better grab it. It doesn't usually happen twice in a lifetime. Y'all don't want to grow old alone. I'm old and alone now, and I wouldn't wish this loneliness on anyone." Her features fell, her face darkening with pain. A look of melancholy came over her countenance.

In all the years Norman had known Mother Maybelle, she'd never shown any vulnerability until that moment. "You have a lot of friends, and everyone loves you. Don't you know that?" he asked, taking her hand in his and kissing it.

"Yes, baby, but it's not the same as having someone warm laying next to you on a cold night, or having someone who can warm your feet up or just cut the fool with whenever you want to. You want someone who's going to love you and think you're nine feet tall—whether you are dressed up in a tuxedo or looking busted with sleep in your eyes and morning breath. *Those are the things that are important in life.* Don't blow your chance of having that, okay? Valerie is the woman who can make you happy. Look at her—she's built right nice and is a sturdy enough woman to bear you some babies. You need to stop being so slow and handle your business. If you study long, you study wrong. Remember that."

Valerie sat speechless, watching them talk about her as if she weren't there and as Norman promised that he'd do the right thing—whatever that meant. Mother Maybelle continued lecturing them about love, marriage, and the importance of having a mate, while she plied them with scrumptious food to ensure they wouldn't go anywhere.

Norman's heart filled with love as he looked at Mother Maybelle. No one but she could invite him and a beautiful woman for lunch, feed them royally, then get all in their business. Thoughts of her putting up with his shenanigans and pranks throughout his childhood until her endless nights of prayer straightened him out, flashed before him. He *couldn't* be mad at her. She'd proven time and again that she loved him. After all he'd put her through, she was still there for him—unconditionally—and he knew that everything she did now was out of love.

Mother Maybelle was best known for dipping in everybody's business, but she was also known for her big heart filled with nothing but love. When she loved, she loved hard, and Norman could attest to that. No matter how unconventional her methods were, she had the wisdom of the elders, and she was right about one thing: he was head over heels about Valerie. *Nothing* would stop him from winning her love and making her his.

Valerie's eyes widened innocently. Inappropriately serene, she sniffed with haughty denial at what Mother Maybelle had said. She knew the wise old sage was right, and she felt as if the guilt she harbored inside would eat her alive. She also knew that she couldn't open up her heart to any man or she'd get hurt again. Lucas had made her believe he'd marry her, then left without one word. As far as she knew, Norman could do the same—or worse—and she wasn't taking that kind of risk.

Six

"Church, before we dismiss and have the benediction, I want to say something." Reverend Avery adjusted the mike he wore on his collar, making his way to the podium. He rubbed his bald head, deep in thought. The Hammond organ, piano, and band stopped playing, in deference to him. "I want to remind each and every one of you to buy your tickets for the church picnic coming up in two weeks." He chuckled before infusing a little levity into the morning's service. "Fellas, this is the right kind of date to ask that lady you've had your eye on for some time to attend with you. Ladies, if you like him, make his day and accept. I'm not performing nearly enough weddings. The weatherman promises a beautiful, unseasonably warm March day. Tickets are only $50 for adults, $15 for children, and are available in the Faith Circle office area in the lobby. Amen?"

Cries of amen filled the air.

"Put it on your calendar or in your Palm Pilot, and come on out and fellowship with each other. Meet someone you don't know and start a new friendship. I promise there will be something fun for everyone—from Junior to Big Mama. There'll be lots of mouth-watering food, games, prizes, fishing, music, entertainment, and more. I want each one to bring one, and let's all have a good time in the Lord. Amen! Stand on your feet, church, and let's go home." He bowed his head and began his closing prayer.

Witness sang a soulful seven-bar chorus of "Amen," and the organist sent the members dancing up the aisles with his hip medley of standard recessionals.

~

As soon as church let out, Mother Maybelle sauntered down the aisle to the choir loft to watch Norman as he asked Valerie to be his date for the church picnic. She knew her foster son and figured that he'd ask her before anyone else did. She also knew that he could handle himself when it came to women. Mother Maybelle was very aware that Norman would've had a fit if she helped him out anymore, but she was prepared—if he wanted it. She didn't care that she was being nosy, because that's just what she did.

Mother Maybelle's ebony eyes sparkled when she witnessed Norman and Valerie engrossed in conversation. She liked Valerie and thought she was a perfect match for Norman. Her thoughts raced far beyond the couple dating. Her mind was already on their wedding. She placed herself in the best position to see and hear everything clearly. Mother Maybelle knew that what she was about to overhear would be good. She didn't intend to miss a word and fixed her face so that anyone coming near her would know not to disturb her right then.

Valerie unzipped her robe and folded it over her arm as Norman stared at her with adoration. She smiled under his scrutiny, when his eyes stopped long enough to enjoy the curve of her ample hips and the swell of her soft, shapely bosom, accentuated by the tailored rose-colored pantsuit she wore so well. "You know, Reverend Avery made a good point about what he said about asking the woman you like to the picnic, Valerie," Norman said.

Her heart skipped at least two beats upon hearing Norman's revelation, of sorts. "Yes, he did. He has a really nice sense of humor," she added, not playing along with Norman.

He moved a little closer to Valerie and stroked a stray curl from her face. She inhaled a sharp breath at the familiar awareness between them. She tried to forget a pulsing knot that had formed in her stomach.

"Valerie, would you be my date at the church picnic?" Norman breathed.

Her head told her to resist, but her heart wouldn't let her. "Yes, Norman, I'll be your date. Thanks for asking."

Mother Maybelle, who would've turned blue if she had held her breath a minute longer, exhaled. *Well, I can see that my help's not needed here.* She strolled back up the aisle, en route to the next case she had to help out.

~

The Red Oaks Christian Fellowship's Annual Spring Church Picnic was turning out to be everything that Reverend Avery had promised his flock. There were games to test the agility and endurance of fairgoers young and old, routines performed by the church's praise dancers, and the Praise Steppers stepped in the name of the Lord. The food ministry outdid itself, providing lavish buffet items for breakfast, lunch, and dinner under a large tent on the verdant campgrounds. Where recreation and food were concerned, there was a flavor for every taste.

On that unseasonably warm seventy-nine degree day, the only flavor Valerie desired was Norman, and he, Valerie. He couldn't get enough of the sight of her and the way her womanly physique filled out her jeans, the clinging cotton shirt that cinched at her waist, or the kimono sleeve knit sweater that hugged her neck. Her hair was neatly tucked under a crocheted baseball cap, although a few errant curls framed her face. She looked so young, so sexy, so vivacious, and ripe for kissing. Norman's face burned with the memory of the searing kiss they'd shared, and he wanted more.

Throughout the day, they played horseshoes, climbed a greasy pole, participated in the one-legged potato sack race, and Valerie won a Double Dutch contest that Mother Maybelle had practically forced her to sign up for. But it was the tug-of-war that turned out to be extra special for her.

There were too many men on the team Norman was on, and that gave them an unfair advantage. The organizers chose Valerie, at random, and told her to join the other team. Norman grunted in protest, mumbling a cussword under his breath. He took matters into his own hands.

He took Valerie's arm, gently nudging her over to his team—right next to him—while several of the ladies from her former team grumbled and said they wished that some fine man would bring them to his team. They had hoped to be the lucky one chosen to stand next to Norman, so he could look at them the way he looked at Valerie. But they knew that would *never* happen because even Stevie Wonder would see that Norman only had eyes for the woman with the heavenly voice.

The game got underway, and Norman grabbed her around her waist in a possessive gesture, then placed his hands on hers. He implored Valerie to pull harder. Leaning back into the firm expanse of his chest, she had all the motivation she needed, and she pulled with all her might.

She couldn't quell the magnetism that crept up her thighs when she remained that close to Norman a moment too long. Her skin tingled under his touch, and she had no intention of backing away from it. Still, Valerie felt that Norman Grant was dangerous. He was the type of man who could make her think about things other than church or the picnic they were on. If he could ignite the kind of heat she was feeling in her body at that moment, she knew that she'd better concentrate on helping her team win the competition, and that would keep her mind off the gorgeous man whose loose dreadlocks swayed in the gentle breeze. She grimaced and gave the rope a huge tug, and it was just the amount of strength needed to overpower the other team.

What Valerie didn't anticipate was that when the other team fell over, it would cause a chain reaction of events that would end with Norman falling right on top of her. What she also didn't expect was how good his hard body would feel on top of hers, or how kissable his lips looked so close to hers. His breath was warm and moist against her face, causing her heart to race. Goose bumps developed on her whole body from their contact, as each of them shared an intense physical awareness of the other. Their gazes locked; they were the only two people in the world at that point in time.

Norman and Valerie's spell was broken by the booming sound of Reverend Danforth's voice calling everyone to attention.

The crowd gathered around at the bandstand area which served as the central meeting place for the church's entertainment and announcements. After a performance of Christian spoken word poetry by the drama ministry, Reverend Danforth came onstage again, garnering applause from the young people, who talked about how hip he looked in his Red Oaks Annual Spring Church Picnic 2004 T-shirt, jeans, and baseball hat worn backwards.

"Um hum, so you didn't think I could rock some jeans and a T-shirt, huh?" he teased them, chuckling. "I won't take long because I know y'all have been waiting for this *all* day. So let's get to it. He gave a stack of papers to several young people to pass out. "Please take a list of the seven items that are indigenous to Georgia which you'll have to find and bring back in order to win the scavenger hunt. The first five people to find and bring all of the items listed will receive a shopping spree at Jordan Marsh and a day at the Peachtree Villa, the hot new spa that opened up in town last month. The only rules are to play fair, no fighting, and remember that this is a Christian event. Please bring your findings to Mother Maybelle or me, and we will log in your number and let you know how you've placed. Godspeed."

Valerie took Norman's hand and led him away from the bandstand so they'd be out of earshot. "I have an idea," she whispered. In that moment, what she felt for Norman had nothing to do with reason or good sense.

Norman's heart raced. He was elated that Valerie wanted to share her thoughts with him. That was good, and it could only get better, he thought.

"I really want to win that shopping spree, so let's do something so we'll get the most out of this," she said in her sexiest voice, moving closer to Norman. She peered intently into his eyes. "If either of us wins, we can buy something for the other, so we'll both be winners, okay?"

Valerie didn't know how precious she was to him, because Norman knew that he couldn't have loved her anymore than he did then. He couldn't think of anything he *wouldn't* do for her. "Yes, baby. We can do that," he said pulling her to him, holding her for a moment. "We'd better go back because we don't want to miss the hunt."

Neither of them wanted to be out of each other's embrace, but they had to part if they intended to win anything.

Soon the participants dispersed in all directions in their hunt for the seven items. Valerie and Norman loved Jordan Marsh, the popular Southern department store chain, so any excuse to shop there—and especially on the church's dime—was good enough for them.

They started their search, double-checking behind each other, hoping to increase their odds. In approximately an hour, Valerie found the Laurel and Hardy video, the jar of red eye gravy, and the bottle of R.C. Cola. They still needed the other four items, and she could have sworn that they'd walked around that campground at least twice.

Weariness enveloped Valerie as she tried to concentrate on where they should go next. She couldn't walk another step. Her back ached between her shoulder blades. Every bone, muscle, and sinew in her body throbbed.

Valerie spied a stately oak tree in the distance, and she shuffled to it, propping herself against its trunk. Closing her eyes, she lost track of time and didn't feel anyone else's presence until a pair of soft arms encircled her. With one hand in the small of her back, and the other hand on her waist, Norman drew her body to him, and in one forward motion, she was in his arms.

Valerie's body came alive everywhere he touched. She hadn't noticed the scent of the cherry blossoms that were in bloom or the dogwood flowers that were opening up before Norman embraced her. Their scents mixed, with his intoxicating Eternity cologne overpowering and rendering her senseless. *Oh Lord, help me*, she silently prayed. "Norman, I . . . I—"

Tipping her face upward, he planted taunting little kisses along her cheek. He then kissed her in the moist hollow of her throat, continuing the torture of bypassing her lips.

Valerie's nipples hardened and ached underneath the fabric of her blouse.

Norman's warm lips smothered Valerie's mouth, holding it captive with his sweet kiss. They extended her an invitation that demanded an answer.

Valerie's lips opened to up to his, but nothing could have prepared her for the explosions she felt in her loins from his kiss.

Unhurriedly, his tongue entwined with Valerie's, sweeping inside to caress the walls of her mouth. Teasing, taunting, tasting, he sampled every drop of her brown sugar and searched for more. Norman's thrusting tongue pushed her over the edge, and electric sensations ignited from her mouth to her feminine core. Their tongues danced together in a silent melody to a tune of their own making.

While Norman explored her mouth, Valerie tasted him with a new hunger—the likes of which she'd never known before.

She moaned, relishing the feel of his velvet lips as his tongue explored everything she had to give.

His tongue moved inside her mouth, making love to it with strong, deep, impelling strokes. Valerie gave him as much of her sugar as he could stand, wishing their kiss would go on forever. Then, Norman tightened his arms around her, their bodies molding perfectly to each other's.

Valerie felt his steely manhood against her, and that was all she needed to get her feminine juices flowing. A shudder ran up the length of her body, fanning the sparks of arousal that would lead to a leaping flame. Soon, her body temperature hit the boiling point, and she broke out in a sweat. She unlocked her lips from his, knowing that if she didn't, she'd wind up on the grass with him doing only God knows what—not that she didn't want to. "Norman, I didn't mean—"

"I know you didn't, Valerie, but we can't deny what we feel for each other, or what is happening between us," he purred, his mouth closing over hers once again as he ignored the dull ache in his throbbing muscle.

"I—I—I—this shouldn't be—it's not—" Valerie stammered, reduced to a babbling idiot by Norman's kisses. But she didn't have to worry about speaking because he guided her into his arms, and they made out like two lovesick kids on prom night.

They finally broke away from each other when their lips became numb and swollen. Raising her chin with his finger, Norman was getting ready to press his mouth to Valerie's once more when the sound of a whistle startled him. He swore, pulling away from her.

She sighed as she saw the look on his face change from elation to exasperation.

Footsteps approached, coming closer to them. "The scavenger hunt is now over," the young woman announced through a bullhorn as she paced the area. "Please bring your finds back to the bandstand."

All Valerie and Norman could do at that point was to gather the items they'd found and place them in the canvas bag on her shoulder. Norman passed her the can of boiled peanuts and the Vidalia onion that he'd recently spotted. She took them and put them in the bag, her body still on fire from their make-out session.

"Baby, we don't have all seven items. We're still missing the Alice Walker book and the Georgia peach," Norman commented, frowning. "We don' t even have enough to put them together so you can win the shopping spree and the day at the spa."

Valerie nodded her head to acknowledge him, unable to quell the heat from Norman's touch which continued to radiate throughout her body.

Hand in hand, they walked back to the area where the picnic activities were—only to be seen by Mother Maybelle—who gave them a huge Kool-Aid grin. Although they'd looked everywhere they could along the way, they didn't find the other two items.

Disappointed, they listened as the winner was announced. But Valerie could barely hear it over the revelation haunting her mind. After having been hurled to a romantic paradise filled with tender kisses, she was unable to deny the truth that had been in her heart for some time. Knowing that there was something extra special about Norman, a startling realization washed over her: *I'm in love with Norman Grant.*

Seven

Norman paced the perimeter of his townhouse's large sunken living room like a caged panther. He didn't know why he felt so tense and out-of-sorts. The names and faces of the many women he'd dated slipped through his thoughts. Grimacing, he remembered how his older brothers, Cleotis and Leon, had taught him everything he needed to know about women. When he became a man, little had changed. He'd become quite a ladies' man, dating one woman or another, or several, taking them out, and then, after an evening of hot sex, on to the next one—never meaning any of them any good. Commitment and marriage were not options.

Norman found the remote and flipped on the television, finding a news program. He listened to a report about how terrorists blew up a train in Spain, and how Haiti had gotten a new president. Deciding that was too se rious for him at that time, he flipped to a movie on the Sci-Fi Channel. When he walked into the kitchen, the coffeemaker caught his eye. He prepared the pot with some Jamaican Blue Mountain coffee beans and turned the power on. He needed to be fully awake because he had some thinking to do.

Norman didn't realize it before he met Valerie, but there was something missing from his life: the love of a good woman. Sure, he'd dated one woman, then the next, but that was becoming old to him. At thirty, he felt he needed to stop the drama, find a woman to settle down with, and make some babies.

He ambled over to the countertop and fixed himself a cup of the steaming hot brew. He blew on it and sipped. No one had to knock him upside his head about how and where to find a good woman. Norman already knew one—Valerie!

He realized that she was perfect for him in every way. His brain seemed to be in overdrive as he thought about how Valerie was beautiful, intelligent, classy, talented, and she had grit to complete the package. To his way of thinking, Valerie was just right for him but was more than he deserved.

After all, Norman couldn't forget his checkered past with the numerous women he'd bedded but had meant no good. Would bad karma come back to bite him? Would he land Valerie, only to lose her to some fast-talking slickster who'd want nothing more than a cheap fling? Norman couldn't let that worry him just then. He had things to do. He had to somehow put his past in perspective, step to Valerie, and let her know exactly how he felt about her. Norman Grant had good sense—and plenty of it. It told him that he'd better grab her and do so in a hurry. *I'm positive that Valerie's the one*, he thought, walking into his spacious bedroom. *I'd better scoop her up before someone else does.*

~

Valerie came to rehearsal the following Thursday night exactly on time. Although her bearing was stiff and proud, her spirit was in chaos. She didn't arrive early to practice praise songs, since she'd learned them all, or to spend extra time rehearsing her solo parts.

Norman called her over and spoke to her away from the other choir members, who were looking over some new sheet music. "What happened to you, tonight, Valerie? You didn't call me to say you weren't coming in early like we've always done," he quizzed, hoping for a plausible explanation even though he hadn't talked to her since the picnic.

Being so near Norman both excited and disturbed her. She felt as if she were frozen in limbo, to the point where she couldn't make decisions or take any action where he was concerned. "I had something else to do," she snapped, turning her face away from him. Tormented by confusing emotions, Valerie swam through a haze of thoughts and desires.

He stared at her, baffled as to why she was so cold and terse toward him after what they'd shared in the park. *Didn't she feel the chemistry between us?* he wondered. Norman didn't have an inkling what could have spooked her, but he would find out—or he would die trying. But at that moment, he had a restless choir to attend to. "We'll pick this up later, Valerie," he informed her, taking his seat at the piano.

She went back to her seat, cradling her head in her trembling hands until it was time to go over her new solo.

Valerie kept up her silent treatment for nearly three weeks, ignoring Norman's around-the-clock phone calls. She didn't return any of them, but she continued to go to choir rehearsal. She left right after it was over and turned down his offers to have coffee or latte at the café in town. Tossing her hair across her shoulders in an act of defiance when Norman asked her out, she felt nauseous from the struggle that brewed within her. All of her loneliness, confusion, and the love she felt for him welded together in an upsurge of devouring yearning. *I love you, but I can't be with you,* she thought, wondering if she should confess what was really bothering her.

~

Valerie went about her life as if Norman didn't exist. He crossed her mind every now and then, but she ignored those thoughts and immersed herself in working lots of overtime. When she didn't do that, she worked on extra projects from home.

As she was working on a project one night, Valerie felt a trapdoor open on the floor of her stomach as she heard the song, "All About You," playing on the "Loving After Dark" program on her favorite radio station. Bile rose in her throat when the deejay announced that the singer's name was Trina Tucker, but Valerie knew better.

She didn't realize that her fists were balled up, but they were—and they convulsed with rage. In a clean sweep, she knocked all of the supplies and materials she'd been working with off her drafting table. Adrenaline pulsed through her arteries, inflaming her body. Valerie broke down and cried as the memories came flooding back in her mind.

She remembered hearing other singers croon her songs on the radio, and a few of them made the top ten lists on the *Billboard* magazine R&B charts. Had Lucas Williams been an honest producer, Valerie would have been a very wealthy woman because of all of the royalties she would have received.

Valerie pounded her fists on the table, still crying uncontrollably. "Why did Lucas steal my songs and give them to other singers?" she wailed into the air. No one was there to give her the answers she so badly needed. Girlfriend looked at her with a blank expression on her tiny face. "Why did he steal the thing that mattered so much to me? All I wanted to do was sing!"

After having such awful things happen at the hands of a man who claimed to love her, how could she possibly allow herself to give in to her love for Norman? How could Valerie trust him after she'd vowed that, after Lucas, she'd never trust another man ever again? Or fall in love?

Valerie felt as if she had a monopoly on being hurt. She'd been there, done that, and she wasn't ready to revisit that place just yet. Deep in her soul, she loved Norman, but she knew he'd only take her back there. Valerie Cherrelle Freeman wasn't having it!

～

The next night, Valerie brought home a project to finish up. Her boss had reminded her that the billboard design for the new travel destination promotion was overdue, and she wanted it yesterday. Since two of the senior artists had resigned and one was out on maternity leave, Valerie had been swamped with their workload. Because she was cool with her boss, Valerie asked for an extra day, assuring her that she'd finish the design at home. She promised her superior that it would be on her desk the next day.

Strictly old school when it came to designing anything, Valerie always worked manually so she'd have a back-up copy if the computer malfunctioned. She'd just finished the design and was duplicating it on the computer's desktop publishing program when she began tapping the keys in synch to the rhythm of the drippy bathroom sink faucet. Valerie didn't notice she was doing it until the dripping stopped, then she stopped. When it resumed pounding out its beat, so did Valerie.

As the evening wore on and the pressure mounted for her to finish the project, Valerie's nerves became frayed. The faucet's leaking certainly didn't help matters. Her right eye twitched, and she constantly ran her hands through her hair. "Okay, enough! I've had it!" she blurted out, padding across the floor to the bathroom to examine the leak. "This drip-drip-drip is driving me mad."

Valerie didn't know what she needed to make it stop, but she was determined to find out. A half hour later, she found herself at the Red Oaks shopping area on Main Street.

Valerie entered the Red Oaks True Value Hardware Store and waited in line for the clerk, an older, settled man, to assist her. After waiting on two customers, he finally got to her.

"Good evening, ma'am, lovely breeze we're having," he smiled. "What may I help you with, today?"

"My bathroom sink's faucet's leaking, and I need to fix it."

He exuded a quiet air of authority and warmth. "Is your hot water or cold water faucet leaking, ma'am?"

Valerie looked at him with a puzzled expression on her face, not knowing it made any difference. "Hot water."

"Okay, that's an easy do." He excused himself and went around the store collecting several items, then placed them on the counter for her. "Here's everything you need to fix that sink. Here are some pliers, an adjustable wrench, a screwdriver, and a repair kit with various size washers and screens. I'm also including some written instructions from our website and some duct tape to hold things in place if you don't have an extra pair of hands available."

Valerie thanked him, knowing that he had given her exceptional service. She'd never fixed a leaky faucet before, but she was determined to do it herself. She didn't have the time or the patience to sit and wait for a repairman to do it. She paid the salesman and was on her way out of the store. Not paying attention to where she was going, Valerie accidentally bumped into someone.

"I'm so sorry, I—" She stopped mid-sentence when she looked up at a handsome man she knew very well.

"Valerie, what a nice surprise to run into you, here," Norman chuckled, smiling as he remembered the pleasure of their kisses under the oak tree.

She felt the surging power of his presence, and noticed that he eyed her with scorching intent. She couldn't help but feel turned on, despite her attempts not to. "Yes, it's good to see *you*, too, Norman. What are you doing here?" That was all she could think to say.

"I came to pick up some picture hangers. I bought several paintings from an art show last week, and I want to hang them up."

She perused his tall well-toned body. The man was exquisite: there was no other word to describe someone so powerfully built. "I see."

"Valerie, I know something's wrong, and I won't get into that right now. I noticed what you bought a few minutes ago, and I know you have a leaky faucet. Please, let me fix it for you. I'm very handy that way."

"Thanks, but that's okay. I'll do it myself."

His insides warmed because he found her even more desirable because she was so unreachable. He knew that her pride stood in the way of accepting his help or asking for it. He admired that. "Really Valerie, I insist. You'd probably do a great job yourself, but please let me help you. I enjoy tinkering and fixing things around the house."

They continued bantering back and forth about his fixing her sink. What Valerie *really* wanted to do was tell him to go away, but she didn't because a crowd of nosy townspeople—who were also members she recognized from Red Oaks Christian Fellowship—had a ringside stance, enjoying their little floorshow. They seemed to be latching on to every word, and she knew that Red Oaks was like any other small town. Everyone knew everyone else and was prone to gossip about everything they heard or saw. Not wanting to be grist for the Red Oaks gossip mill, she agreed to let Norman help her. If these folks were going to have something to talk about, her business wouldn't be one of the topics.

Thinking ahead, Valerie told Norman to follow her in his car. That way, when he was finished with her sink, he could leave.

Soon, they arrived at her house, and, after taking off his jacket, Norman rolled up his sleeves and got right to work.

There was still the matter of a question that hung between them, unasked and not discussed. "Valerie, you've been so cold toward me, lately. Did I do something that I might not realize?" he asked, fiddling with the sink.

She wasn't sure if now was the time to tell Norman what was going on in her head. But if she wasn't anything else, she was fair. As things stood, it wasn't right of her to treat him so horribly when he'd done nothing wrong. The tension Valerie felt rose. She felt the palms of her hands get clammy, and she wrung them together. Swallowing the lump in her throat, she began. "When I was in college, I made a bad mistake, Norman. I met a music producer, Lucas Williams, who told me that he could help me get a record deal with a major New York label—and I believed him." She handed a wrench to Norman.

"Why shouldn't you have believed him if he presented himself as a professional?" he asked. "Did you have any reason to doubt him?"

"No, that's just it," she reminisced. "In the beginning, he was nothing but professional. He worked with me on my voice, wrote songs with me, then recorded those songs, as well as some I wrote. We even completed a master demo tape."

"Wow, a demo tape? You should've been on your way. Pass the pliers, please."

She passed them and continued her story. "Yes and no. Yes, that demo was to be shopped to the major record companies in New York, and we even discussed going through some of the labels in Nashville to tap into the country market. But no, nothing he promised ever happened."

His chest became heavy with pity because he had a bad feeling about what she was going to say. "Why not, Valerie?"

A bleak, wintry feeling engulfed her. "He made me fall in love with him, took my virginity, and led me to believe he loved me and that we'd get married. But when I got to the restaurant he had chosen for our engagement, where he was to give me the ring . . . He stood me up."

Norman's heart broke for her. He was beginning to understand why she was so afraid, and why she pulled away from him so suddenly after their relationship had reached a new plateau. "That's awful, Valerie. That's one of the lowest things a man can do to a woman."

She passed him a small washer and watched him change the worn-out device that was making her sink leak. "You think so, huh? Well, it gets worse. I went to the studio where we had recorded, which happened to be in the same complex where he lived. I thought that I'd lost my mind, because the studio was empty. Everything was gone—equipment, our tapes, the master reel, and all my songs! I found the housing manager, and he told me that Lucas had moved away, and he hadn't given management or anyone else advance notice."

"Valerie, don't beat up on yourself. You did nothing wrong; the guy was a liar from the get-go."

Stress lines formed on her brow and her eyes were haunted with anxiety. "That's not all. I cried so much and so hard that I made myself sick and almost flunked out of school. That happened in my junior year, but my parents and big sister helped pull me through with their prayers and TLC. That was bad enough, but what nearly killed me was hearing the songs that I had written and worked so hard on being sung by someone else! I *knew* they were mine and that I was owed some money. Well, I took everything I had to prove it to a lawyer. When he looked into the case, he told me that Lucas had the rights to them in perpetuity because I had signed some papers to that effect that *his* lawyer had drawn up. My attorney said that although that type of contract was unethical, it wasn't illegal. So there wasn't anything I could do."

Norman sucked in a breath. "Ouch, that must've hurt, Valerie."

"It did, and for a long time, I wouldn't and couldn't listen to the radio, because they played several of my songs. They'd hit the top of the charts, and I knew that Lucas was living large off my money and my lyrics. I also couldn't get involved with another man and give him my heart. I won't let any man hurt me ever again, Norman, not ever!" Tears cascaded down her cheeks, cleansing her of what she'd kept hidden away inside of her for so long.

So badly did Norman want to take her hurt away. If he could have borne it for her, he would have. He swept her into his loving arms, molding her body to his to keep her safe and secure. "I'm here, and I'll never hurt you, and I won't let anyone else hurt you. I will protect you, Valerie."

She kept her head on his hard chest until there weren't any tears left. She felt lighter having gotten that heavy burden out of her system, but she knew she wasn't quite ready to pursue a relationship with Norman yet. Her heart just wasn't ready. "Thanks, Norman, but I can take care of myself. I don't need you to protect me."

Looking into her eyes, cupping her chin and tilting it up so her eyes would meet his, he declared, "I love you, Valerie Freeman."

Although his words made her heart thud and her pulse race like never before, she couldn't and wouldn't process it—not right now—that would only complicate things for her. So she took the high road. "Thanks for fixing my sink, Norman. I really appreciate your help." With that, she gave him his jacket and pressed a twenty-dollar bill in his hand. Then, she opened the door and wished him a safe journey home.

Eight

Valerie signed up for every bit of overtime that her boss would give her. She did the same for volunteer projects—anything to keep her idle mind off Norman. To her way of thinking, between putting in her day hours, overtime hours, and volunteering to work on special projects, she'd be so tired that she'd pass right out and wouldn't have time to remember or realize how much she missed Norman, or how much she loved him—despite herself.

Like that old song about washing that man right out of one's hair, she was going to work him right out of her mind. And she did—for a time, but eventually love caught up to her, and every time she closed her eyes, she saw visions of Norman's handsome face kissing her, holding her hand, or saying sweet things to her that made her feel like a woman. Every time she fell asleep—exhausted though she was—Valerie dreamed of Norman, and all of the dreams were the same.

In that recurring dream, she sang her heart out in church, making the saints shout, dance, and praise like never before, but the only difference was that Norman wasn't there. Worried about him, her singing took on a melancholy tone because she wondered where he was. She poured every ounce of love she felt for him into the song, hoping that the synergy between them was strong enough for him to feel it—wherever he was. Obviously, it *was*, because he came charging down the aisle to where she stood, stopped the service, and proclaimed his love for her in front of the congregation, who said that was the best example of true agape love—sent from God—that they'd seen in a long time. Together, Valerie and Norman strutted off into the sunset.

Feeling that even her sleep was cruel in not allowing her to forget her beloved Norman, she pulled her listless body out of bed and prayed. She asked God to either take her mind off Norman or help them to get back together—if that was His will. She proposed in her mind that she would give that matter over to God and leave it with Him, because she sure wasn't handling it very well on her own. Then, after weeks of restlessness, she slept like an infant—soundly, and through the night.

Valerie went on about her life, dropping the volunteer work. It was too much, and she felt herself burning out. She still did overtime, but not to the extent she had a few weeks ago. Her apartment resembled a gift shop because of all the flowers, chocolates, and stuffed animals Norman sent her. She had read all of the cards enclosed with them, but she didn't call him to thank him, or accept any of his calls, because where Norman was concerned, she knew she was susceptible to his charms. If she was going to stay whole, strong, and unhurt, she had to ignore him—no matter how much her heart was breaking. The heaviness in her chest felt like a millstone. It was as if a rock had fallen through her heart, shattering it into little pieces. She took her head in her hands and cried tears that made the loneliness she felt for Norman even more chilling. *I love you, Norman, but this is for the best. If I give in, you'll wind up hurting me like Lucas, and I'd die before I let that happen*, she thought, the emptiness she felt wrapping around her like a cocoon of gloom.

～

Norman felt as if he were in a twilight world, half alive without Valerie. He missed their drinking vanilla chai together after rehearsal, their quiet dinners, and phone conversations right before bedtime. Every part of his body ached for her. But at this point, he was beyond pain, and was merely hanging on to survival.

"Lord, I love her so much, what should I do? How do I make her know that I'm the real deal and would never do her wrong?" he wailed, half in prayer, half in misery. A vein in Norman's neck pulsed. He kicked over a chair, and he punched the wall in frustration.

Not knowing why, he picked up his Bible and read various verses about manhood and a man's role in marriage. After reading them, he knew that the task of convincing Valerie she should marry him was on him.

~

As always, Mother Maybelle wasn't but a phone call away whenever Norman needed her. She had called him to come over to fix some loose tile in her shower, but decided not to when she heard the sullen tone in his voice. She had a sixth sense that told her whenever Norman was in trouble. She'd made several attempts to get him to talk about what was wrong, but he refused.

The feeling that Norman needed help was especially strong, so Mother Maybelle had an idea. She told him that she had something urgent to do and that she'd call him later.

Mother Maybelle spent the whole day preparing a delicious meal that was sure to keep him still so she could instill some more of her kitchen wisdom in him, as well as get inside of his head. If her home cooking wouldn't loosen his lips, nothing would. As she'd promised, she called Norman and invited him over that evening.

"Come on over here and love my neck, son," she quipped, setting two plates at her table when he arrived. "Give me some sugar."

Norman gave his foster mother a big hug and a kiss on her cheek.

Her heart soaring with good cheer, she loaded his plate with baked ham, red-eye gravy, collard greens, candied yams, and two cloverleaf rolls filled with sweet creamy butter. Then, she fixed her plate and blessed their bounty.

"This feels like bribery, having a Sunday or holiday meal during the week," he said, sprinkling hot sauce on his greens. "What gives?"

"Now, you just stay out of grown folk's business and listen to me," she ordered, not cracking a smile. She sounded as fierce and protective of him as he knew her to be. "I'm not blind, Norman. I see how Valerie's been chilly toward you, lately. What, you're in the doghouse with her, already?"

"No, ma'am," he answered, his mouth full of her tasty meal.

She cut her eyes at Norman and gave him "the look." "Looka here, Valerie Freeman is a class act. She's one heck of a woman, and the Lord has laid it on my heart to tell you that she is your *wife*. Y'all love each other so much that everyone's taking bets about your wedding date—except you both need to own up to it and do something about it. Any woman worth having is worth fighting for. Now, go fight for that gal. And don't stop there when you marry her, give her as much loving as she can stand and make it so good that she *won't ever* think about anyone or anything else except getting home for more!" She scooped more yams onto her plate.

Norman reeled with astonishment, his eyebrows shooting up. "Mother Maybelle!"

"You better do something about those eyes, boy, before they pop out of your head. Don't Mother Maybelle me! Remember, I've been married before and been around the block a few times! I know what time is, okay? Now, I've helped you all I can; the *rest* is on *you!*" she reminded him.

Over a second helping, he got an earful from Mother Maybelle about what a good husband should do to please his wife and about the virtues of marriage. Then, she put him to work as she'd originally planned.

～

After dinner, Norman raced home from Mother Maybelle's, his mind whirling with all of her advice and admonishments. In fact, he couldn't get there fast enough, moving in haste with hurried purpose. He was determined to get Valerie back, and now he had a plan.

He shook, as fearful images of her rejecting him built up in his mind. But that was a chance he was willing to take. Dialing the phone, he trusted in that knowledge, as well as in his love for Valerie. "Good evening, Valerie, it's

Norman," he intoned, feeling sure of himself. "This standoff between us has gone on *long* enough, and it's time to put some things on the table."

Expecting a return call from her boss with an answer to an important question, Valerie had answered the phone, not thinking that the caller could be Norman. There was no way that she could wiggle out of talking to him, now. "There's really nothing to talk about. Say whatever you have to while you have me on the line," she said with a coldness she didn't really feel.

He spoke firmly. "Have dinner with me tomorrow night—and I won't take no for an answer. By the way, the attire is after five."

Norman told her what time he'd pick her up and ended the call—not wanting to say anything that would cause her to change her mind. If he had his way, tomorrow's dinner date would change both of their lives.

~

Valerie was clueless about where Norman was taking her when they got to Macon and boarded the pontoon to cross the Ocmulgee River. A short while later, they walked into Armando's, the swankest supper club in that city. She gasped in stunned silence as she scanned the large room. Candlelight was reflected in the beveled mirrors and in the sparkling crystal. Candles flickered in several solid gold wall sconces around the room. The tables were elegantly dressed with crisp damask tablecloths—maroon on the bottom, deep maize on the top—accentuated by matching napkins. Her feet sank into the plush carpet. Taking in the small but functional stage at the front of the establishment, she noticed that the dance floor was made of perfectly polished parquet. "Norman, this place is breathtaking," she purred.

"Not as breathtaking as you, Valerie." His eyes were dark and smoldering, and he couldn't help but smile roguishly at how stunning she looked in her black sequined cocktail dress with the plunging neckline. Their evening would cost him a paycheck and a half, but it would be worth it—*if* he pulled his plan off.

Over a dinner of grilled Canadian salmon, sautéed sea scallops, risotto with slivers of almonds, and creamed spinach, they made small talk about the weather, sports, current events, and the restaurant—everything except what was going on between them. Norman was biding his time, trying to earn her trust and friendship once again—confident that the rest would play out naturally.

By this time, Frankie Sutton, a well-known local singer, was being introduced as the evening's entertainment. She began her set with "I Can't Make You Love Me," to thunderous applause.

"I love this song, Norman!" Valerie exclaimed, as if running on all eight cylinders.

Seizing the opportunity, Norman asked her to dance. The touch of his hand on hers sent a warming shiver through her. Stepping forward, he clasped her body tightly to his, her soft curves meshing with the contours of his firm form. Norman wrapped his arms around her midriff, and Valerie fastened her arms around his neck. Moving ever so slowly as one body to the sensuous melody of the ballad, Valerie's defenses began to subside. She buried her face against the corded muscles of his chest, drinking in the smell of the Quorum cologne on his charcoal gray suit jacket. She locked herself in his embrace, peering deeply into Norman's eyes and exchanging scorching glances with him.

With a pulse-pounding certainty, she couldn't deny that she was in love with him—and there was no turning back! She had been miserable without him, heartsick and heartbroken. The past few weeks had shown her that she was very much in love and that she shouldn't judge Norman for Lucas's wrongdoings. Very much a realist, Valerie knew in her soul that the only way she'd be *truly* happy was being with Norman—whatever that meant. She wanted him and was ready to give in to what her heart felt.

As the singer crooned "Teach Me, Tonight," Valerie sank into Norman's protective embrace and thought about certain lessons she was fully ready to teach him. Their dance was more than two people moving to the music; it became a private declaration of their feelings, expressing things only they understood. Their hearts, minds, bodies, and souls were in perfect harmony, and in that moment, Norman felt so full, so in love.

Knowing it was time to move on to the next part of his plan, Norman walked Valerie back to the table and signaled the waiter to bring the bill. After his credit card was returned, they walked downstairs and found that a shiny white and gold hansom carriage with two white horses awaited them on the other side of the river. Warm air blew through the trees, making the air fragrant with the scent of the pink cherry blossoms, camellias, azaleas, and Golden Lady Banksia roses. Clouds scudded playfully across the face of the moon. It was a perfect spring night.

In the carriage, Norman drew Valerie close to him, draping his arm around her shoulder as they rode around Macon, taking in fresh air and the sights and sounds along the way. She steeled herself against the immense pleasure that threatened to carry her away; her body conscious of his nearness, his touch, his lips.

Norman's mouth captured Valerie's, partaking of everything she had. His kiss was urgent, passionate, devouring every drop of her sweet nectar. It was a kiss for her needy soul to melt into, and was every bit as hot as the smoldering heat that joins metals. When he took her mouth with an intensity like none other, Valerie was shocked at her wanton response as she kissed him back with every ounce of love she felt for him. The fire within consumed Valerie, making her response instant, shameless, and total. She longed for Norman to love her like a *real* woman.

Divine ecstasy overtook Norman, and his breathing became harsh and uneven. As he stirred her passion, his grew stronger, and he didn't know if it was the scent of the cherry blossoms or the love he felt for Valerie that drove him so wild. "I love you, Valerie Freeman. I want to protect you and take away all your hurts. No other woman has made me feel the way you do. Will you marry me?" he proposed, pulling a two-carat marquise-cut diamond ring out of a blue velvet box.

Valerie drew in a deep breath and forced herself not to cry. Finally letting go of her hesitation and reservations, she gave him an answer. "Yes, Norman, I'll marry you!" She was dizzy with glee and she felt whole. The thought of being jilted at the altar, or Lucas running out on her, never crossed her mind. Her eyes danced, knowing she had all the man she'd ever need.

Norman slipped the ring on her finger, reassuring her that he'd never hurt her and would love her unconditionally for the rest of their days. He told her that she was a mighty special woman to take away his fear of commitment and make him want to settle down.

Through tears of joy, Valerie, too, confessed her undying love for Norman.

"Congratulations," the driver said, tipping his top hat to them, taking great pride in the fact that many couples had become engaged in his Hansom cab.

Their final stop was the St. Regis Hotel, the finest of its kind in Macon. Located just past the downtown area, Norman chose it to ensure that they didn't run into anyone from Red Oaks Christian Fellowship. Feverish with desire and downright horny, he swept Valerie in his arms and carried her to the room—which he'd reserved for them earlier that day.

Kissing her with an abandon that belied his outward calm, Norman felt her breasts thrust toward him: firm, round, and full. His tongue demanded her full surrender and she molded herself against Norman, wanting more. His hands roamed over her body, burning a path down her chest and stomach, discovering and unleashing the passionate woman within.

"Norman, baby, that feels so good," she whispered. Gentle moans of passion escaped her lips as he suckled on first one ripened bud, then the other.

In a matter of a few seconds, he stripped off her clothes with master speed and precision, laying her on the bed. He drank in every inch of her body with his eyes, marveling at her beauty. "You're so hot, honey, so beautiful. I'm going to love you right and give you as much of me as you can stand," he promised, knowing he'd soon extinguish the powerful ache pulsating in his loins.

Valerie's stomach twisted with the hard knot of need, and she gave herself freely to Norman, enjoying the warmth of his fingertips against her tingling skin. No longer could she stand the torture he was inflicting upon her, so she undressed him, flinging his clothes every which way.

They feathered their fingers over each other's bodies, teasing, probing, and exploring everything.

Feeling his throbbing hardness, she caressed it first with her hands, then with her mouth, setting fire to Norman's already burning flame.

"I love you, Valerie . . . don't stop," he begged.

She continued her path to ecstasy, lapping, laving, and loving him with her warm, wet tongue.

Norman reciprocated and seared his own path of ecstasy from her neck to her feet, stopping only long enough to find and taste the throbbing, engorged bud between her thighs. Sampling her love juices, he tested her readiness with three fleshy fingers, determining that she was ripe for what he had for her. Retrieving a foil packet from the nightstand next to the bed, he opened it and sheathed himself.

Valerie gasped as Norman eased himself into her boiling depths, and she welcomed him into her body. Understanding his rhythm, she caressed his enormous manhood with her pelvic muscles, engaging in the instinctive movements of a woman who longed to please her man.

"Ooh, yes, baby, work it. You're so good," Norman groaned, increasing his movements to a hungry, furious intensity.

With each deepening thrust, Valerie trembled. "Yes, Norman, give it to me. Please don't stop."

And he didn't. He mated her with piston-driving strength, his body possessing hers. Valerie locked her legs around his neck, rewarding herself with every inch he had to give until warm streamers of light enveloped her from the top of her head to the tips of her toes. Suddenly, her world exploded in a dazzling kaleidoscope of colors. Surrendering in a starburst of ecstasy, Valerie orgasmed as she never had before, screaming out Norman's name.

Involuntary tremors of arousal shook Norman's body, and his love for Valerie flowed out of him like warm honey. At long last, their bodies were in exquisite harmony with one another's—the hunger they had for each other finally satisfied.

"I love you, now, and for always, Valerie," Norman cried out, their lovemaking the only reality in his world.

Filled with a sense of completeness, she joined Norman in that place of rapture, totally fulfilled.

Afterward, they cuddled in silence, their bodies still wet from their lovemaking. Boring into each other's eyes, no words were said; none were necessary. What they felt in their hearts said it all. Soon, they fell into the sated sleep of lovers. Awaking revitalized, they made love again and again and again until dawn.

Nine

There was a buzz around Red Oaks Christian Fellowship that following Sunday after Valerie sang two solos. Her soprano voice, although velvet-edged and strong as always, seemed to possess a certain sweetness it didn't have before. Her voice brimmed with joy. Every member who paid attention to her body language and the words she sang felt the sunny feeling that came deep from her soul. Notes were passed from member to member, up and down the pews, gossiping about how Valerie and Norman kept beaming at each other with open fondness—and it didn't have *anything* to do with her watching him for musical cues.

Sister Brown saw them winking at each other, and Sister Terrell whispered to Sister Jackson that every time Valerie looked at Norman, she'd blush, and he'd smile like the proverbial Cheshire cat. None of the members were stuck on stupid or parked on crazy; they *knew* something was up, but they didn't know what.

Right after the choir sang, Mother Maybelle sashayed down the long aisle to the pulpit, moving with feline grace and charm. No one else had that kind of carte blanche to interrupt the morning worship service, so when she did, everyone braced themselves because they knew whatever she had to say would be good.

Adjusting the mike at the podium to her height, she ran her hand along her periwinkle silk dress studded with tiny pearls. "Pardon the interruption, church, but I couldn't hold this in a minute longer," she began. "Y'all know I'm like an old refrigerator: I can't keep nothing."

The congregation laughed, because if they didn't know much else, they knew *that* was certainly true.

"First, giving honor to God who is the head of my life, and my pastor, Reverend Terrance Avery, I'd like to say that I am glad to be in the house of the Lord one mo' time 'cause He brought me from a mighty long way." She waited for the chorus of amens and hallelujahs to wane, then she continued. "My dear son, Norman, and our soloist, Valerie, were engaged on Friday night. I know y'all probably noticed that something was different about her today. Well, she's a woman in love who's promised to one of the last good men left in Red Oaks. I want them to stand up, and y'all show them some love."

The congregation stood and applauded, except for a few jealous young women who'd failed to land Norman; they sucked their teeth in disgust. The organist broke out with a few bars of the "Wedding March."

When Norman and Valerie told Mother Maybelle about the engagement and swore her to secrecy, they hoped she wouldn't say anything. They wanted to be the first to reveal their happy news. Despite the fact that she was a busybody, they loved her dearly, so all Valerie and Norman could do was smile openly. They weren't at all surprised that Mother Maybelle had outed them and put their business on Front Street.

"The wedding date hasn't been set, but y'all can bet that they're going to have the best wedding that Red Oaks has ever seen!" she bragged like any proud parent of the bride or groom. "I'll have the details printed in the bulletin as soon as everything is set, because I know they'll want the whole church to share in their joy. Ain't that right?" She looked over at the happy couple, who shook their heads in agreement, knowing that they were obligated to invite their church family since Mother Maybelle put them on the spot.

Grinning, she said, "Please be sure to check out that rock Valerie's wearing after the service. Like our young folks love to say, 'it's the bomb!' "

～

The next few months were an endless round of parties, dress fittings, and pre-nuptial social events. First, there was their engagement party; then the bridesmaids' luncheon, two bridal showers, the rehearsal dinner, as well as the various trips to Jordan Marsh and other stores to shop for Valerie's trousseau, china, silver, and crystal settings. Between those appointments and activities, Valerie also had to attend mandatory pre-marital counseling with Reverend Avery at the church.

Valerie wanted to marry Norman more than anything in the world, but she never dreamed that there would be so much planning before the wedding. She was so tired her nerves throbbed. She felt drained, achy, and exhausted. The night before her wedding, Valerie slept for twelve hours, waking up feeling fresh and exhilarated, and knowing that she would've been a basket case without her parents and Mother Maybelle's coordination of her big day. She drew in a sigh and prepared to marry the man she loved.

～

The sun shone warm over the colorful array of country flowers and shrubs surrounding Red Oaks Christian Fellowship. The fragrance of tea, roses, daphne, pine trees, and, morning glories hung in the air. The cloudless sky reached out and over into the land. The August day couldn't have been more perfect for a wedding. The only thing to match its beauty was that of the bride and the wedding party.

The sanctuary was nearly full with friends and family of the bride and groom, church members, and local press. The sound of several carefully selected inspirational love songs filled the air. The guests couldn't stop talking about how pretty the church looked, decorated with white lilies and calla lily arrangements, pew corsages, and white taper candles burning by the altar. White tulle and satin ribbons adorned all of the doors and entryways.

The female audience members' hearts skipped a beat as Norman and his best man took their places at the altar. Each of them was resplendent in his black tuxedo and tails—especially Norman, who was about to jump the broom in a matter of minutes.

The wait was finally over when the organist played "Jesu, Joy of Man's Desiring" as Valerie's sister and two cousins marched down the aisle. Accompanied by Norman's brothers and a cousin, the women were lovely in their midi-length pastel pink bustier dresses. Everyone stood on the first bar of Wagner's "Wedding March," and their jaws dropped when they saw Valerie. Blushing with a glow that only a bride truly in love could have, she was graceful and opulent in her ivory Oleg Cassini gown with a cathedral train.

At the sight of his gorgeous bride, Norman looked at her with reverence. His pupils dilated. He shot a flitting glance up and down her body, drinking in every inch of her, basking in the knowledge that Valerie would soon be his wife.

Witness sang a musical tribute to Valerie and Norman, and a touching praise dance was performed in their honor. Reverend Danforth prayed for the couple, wished them well, then turned the wedding over to Reverend Avery.

"Marriage is not an easy thing; it's a life-long commitment between two people who vow to become one heart, one soul, one flesh," he said. "The best foundation from which to start a marriage is friendship. If you work on maintaining the friendship, the marriage will fall into place."

Valerie stared adoringly at Norman as Reverend Avery spoke to them. She heard nothing he said, as she was too busy thinking about what she wanted to do to Norman on their honeymoon. Hot waves swept her belly at the fact that she was marrying the most wonderful man she'd ever known, and it wasn't a dream. She loved Norman with everything inside of her, and Valerie knew that there wasn't a better man anywhere. She was grateful that she'd decided to give in to love and not let Norman get away.

Reverend Avery cleared his throat, and Valerie focused on the ceremony. She gave Norman a knowing wink. Then, they both nodded in agreement with Reverend Avery's charge and sage advice. After, they said their vows, exchanged rings, took Holy Communion, sealing their vows, and lit the unity candle, marking their two souls becoming one.

"By the power vested in me by the state of Georgia, I now pronounce Norman and Valerie, man and wife," Reverend Avery concluded, smiling with pride. "Norman, you may now salute your bride."

Nearly exploding with anticipation, Norman picked Valerie up a few inches from the ground, his mouth closing over hers. Their tongues dueled in a fiery melody that put the final seal on the vows they'd made to the Lord and to each other. Valerie returned his kiss with one full of passion, hunger, and need.

Reverend Avery laughed. "It's a good thing y'all are married. Ladies and gentleman, I'd like to present Mr. and Mrs. Norman Lawrence Grant."

The church clapped and cheered for the happy couple—especially Mother Maybelle, who let everyone know that Norman was her son, and that she now had a beautiful, God-fearing daughter-in-law that she loved as her own.

～

The reception was in full swing in the foyer at the Red Oaks Museum of Art. The usually plain, but large, space was transformed into something almost magical with the help of a well-dressed bridal table, fine linens, china, silverware, crystal, the best soul food in Red Oaks, a champagne fountain, old school R&B music, and a Viennese dessert table.

The tears that Valerie hadn't shed at the wedding flowed freely at the reception. She looked in Norman's eyes and saw only love in them. Even the air seemed to hold its breath. She couldn't believe that everything she ever wanted was wrapped up in one man. Norman held her close to his firm, muscular body for support. Everything in his life was perfect.

As the reception progressed and the cake was cut, Valerie tossed her bouquet of hydrangeas, eucalyptus, dogwood blossoms, and berries to the single women. The room burst out in a cacophony of laughter when Mother Maybelle caught it.

"This here bouquet has nothing to do with me," she quipped. "I've had enough husbands."

Right then, she had more important things to do. She went up to the makeshift podium area and took the microphone. "Norman and Valerie, you need to say your good-byes and get ready to go to the airport. Your luggage is packed and in the limo. My wedding gift to you is a ten-day honeymoon on the French Rivera. It's the best place I know to get a marriage started right. Now y'all go and handle your business and start working on making me a grandbaby." She hugged and kissed them, the three of them sobbing with happiness. She walked away, smiling as bright as the Georgia summer sun, knowing her work was done.

"Are you ready to start your new life with me, Mrs. Grant?" Norman teased, raining gentle kisses on Valerie's face and neck.

"Now and forever." She looked up at heaven and thanked God for blessing her with her soul mate. She reassured Norman that she was his in every possible way, and that she was deliriously happy that he believed in second chances.

About the Authors

Janice Sims is the author of eleven novels. She has had stories included in five anthologies. During her career, her work has been critically acclaimed, and she is deemed a favorite among readers.

She is the recipient of the 2004 Emma Award for Favorite Heroine in her novel, *Desert Heat*. She has also received an Award of Excellence from Romance in Color for her 1999 novel, *For Keeps*. In 2000, she won the novella of the Year Award from Romance in Color for "The Keys to My Heart," her contribution to the Arabesque Mother's Day anthology, "*A Very Special Love*."

Romantic Times Book Club nominated her for their Career Achievement Award in 2000. She was nominated again in 2002.

She lives in central Florida with her husband and daughter.

Kim Louise resides in Omaha, Nebraska. She's been writing since grade school and has always dreamed of penning the great American novel. She has an undergraduate degree in journalism and a graduate degree in adult learning. She has one son, Steve, and one grandson, Zayvier. In her spare time, she enjoys reading, making cards, and has recently become addicted to scrapbooking.

Natalie Dunbar has been writing for the joy of it for as long as she can remember. Eventually she joined her local RWA chapter, GDRWA, and learned how to hone her craft. Her first novel, the critically acclaimed *Best of Friends*, was published by Genesis Press, Inc., and followed by *The Love We Had* and *Everything but Love*. Her action/adventure novel, *Private Agenda*, was an October 2004 Silhouette Bombshell which was followed by the Genesis Press novel, *Falling*. The novella, "A Love Like That," is her first effort for BET Books.

Natalie lives and works in the Detroit area, where she lives with her husband and two children. She loves to hear from her readers, and can be contacted by e-mail at *Natalie@nataliedunbar.com*. Her website is located at *www.nataliedunbar.com*

Nathasha Brooks-Harris lives in New York, where she successfully juggles a career as the Associate Editor of *True Confessions* magazine, freelance journalism, copyediting, and teaching writing with the demands of being a romance author. Her first romance novel, *Panache*, was released by Domhan Books in August 2001 and earned her the prestigious Emma Award for Best New Author in 2002.